Lyn Andrews was born and brought up on Merseyside, the daughter of a policeman. Now married to a policeman, she is the mother of grown-up triplets, and the author of *The White Empress*, *The Sisters O'Donnell*, *Liverpool Lou*, *Ellan Vannin*, *The Leaving of Liverpool*, *Maggie May*, *Mist Over the Mersey* and *Mersey Blues*, all published by Corgi.

THE LEAVING
OF LIVERPOOL

Lyn Andrews

CORGI BOOKS

THE LEAVING OF LIVERPOOL
A CORGI BOOK : 0 552 13933 5

First publication in Great Britain

PRINTING HISTORY
Corgi edition published 1992

5 7 9 10 8 6 4

Set in 10½/12pt Monotype Plantin by
Kestrel Data, Exeter

Corgi Books are published by Transworld Publishers Ltd,
61-63 Uxbridge Road, London W5 5SA,
in Australia by Transworld Publishers,
c/o Random House Australia Pty Ltd,
20 Alfred Street, Milsons Point, NSW 2061,
in New Zealand by Transworld Publishers,
c/o Random House New Zealand,
18 Poland Road, Glenfield, Auckland
and in South Africa by Transworld Publishers,
c/o Random House (Pty) Ltd,
Endulini, 5a Jubilee Road, Parktown 2193.

Reproduced, printed and bound in Great Britain by
Cox & Wyman Ltd, Reading, Berkshire.

Author's Note

The author is indebted to John Maxtone-Grahame for use of material from his book *The Only Way to Cross*, published by Macmillan, New York, 1972, and to Humfrey Jordan for his book *Mauretania*, published by Hodder and Stoughton, 1936. For their kind assistance with factual accounts and experiences of working life and conditions on board the liners of the 1920s, I would like to thank Mr J. Longrigg, Mr Wilfred P. Johnson and Mr Charles Best. I would also like to thank Derek Whale of the *Liverpool Daily Post and Echo*, for his co-operation and enthusiasm. My thanks go to all those Liverpudlians who have written to me from all over the UK and places as far apart as Canada and Australia, expressing their enjoyment of my books which makes my work very gratifying. Also, last but not least, my thanks to Mrs Mabel Fisher of Fisher's Books, Ormskirk, who has given me tremendous support and some very pleasant signing days.

Lyn Andrews
1991

PART I

1919

Chapter One

'Why's she going to marry that old misery? She can't love him! She just can't!'

'Of course she doesn't!' The door was slammed shut, throwing the tiny scullery into semi-gloom. Emily Parkinson glared at her younger sister. At eighteen years of age Phoebe-Ann had as much tact and understanding as a five year old. Phoebe-Ann had the beauty all right, with her fresh, clear skin, wide hazel eyes and the fine tresses of ash blonde hair that were her pride and joy, but she'd been a long way back in the queue when the brains were given out. Emily's features softened. That was unfair. It wasn't Phoebe-Ann's fault if she was a bit slow on the uptake.

'Oh, I'm sorry! I didn't mean to shout.' Emily lifted the heavy, soot-blackened kettle and poured the hot water into the small earthenware sink. 'I'll wash. You can dry.'

Mollified a little by the apology, Phoebe-Ann nodded and took the tea towel from its nail on the wall. She watched mutinously as Emily attacked the greasy dishes. Emily always understood things without having to have them explained in great detail. She supposed it was some kind of talent she had. Mam said it was to balance things out, for poor Emily certainly couldn't be called a beauty. Not with that straight, mousy-brown hair and those pale blue eyes that always looked sort of washed out.

'Well, are you going to tell me how you know that Mam doesn't love him?' she asked resentfully.

Emily sighed, scraping away with a knife at the remains of the potatoes stuck to the bottom of the pan. 'I just know, that's all!'

Phoebe-Ann banged the basin she'd been drying down hard on the wooden draining board. 'Oh, you're a fine help! What kind of an answer is that? Am I supposed to be a mind reader?'

'For God's sake, Fee, keep your voice down! Half the street can hear you. And stop banging stuff around, you'll break something and it all costs money!'

Phoebe-Ann gritted her teeth. She hated being called by her childhood nickname. When they had all been very young, neither her brothers nor Emily had been able to pronounce 'Phoebe-Ann' without difficulty, so she'd been called Fifi, an approximation of Phoebe, which had then been shortened to Fee. But she was grown up now. Something Emily seemed to forget these days. Emily was a year older but you'd think she was twenty-nine instead of nineteen the way she acted sometimes.

Suddenly she saw her mother's startling announcement in a bright flash of clarity. 'It's money, isn't it?'

Emily wiped away a strand of hair from her forehead with her damp forearm. 'Oh, the penny's finally dropped!'

'You never miss a chance to have a dig at me, do you?'

'That's not true and you know it! Don't I always stand up for you when there's an argument?'

'So, it is money?' Phoebe-Ann persisted.

'That and security and you can't blame her. She's had precious little of either for years.'

10

'She might have told us before she told our Jack and Jimmy.'

Emily was exasperated. 'They had to go to work, remember, and I think she wanted to get it off her chest.'

'She could have done that last night when we were all here.'

'Oh, shut up, Fee! He only asked her last night.'

'So *she* said but she must have known for ages that he was going to. She must have had some idea, she's been going around with a face as long as a fortnight for days! If you ask me it's not right and it's not fair!'

Emily threw the wet dish mop into the greasy water. It made a dull plop and then sank. 'Why isn't it right? He's not divorced or anything, she's a widow, and as for it not being fair, who isn't it fair to? Mam or you?'

Phoebe-Ann glared at her. What with one thing and another life was far from satisfactory at the moment. 'It's not just me I'm thinking about. It's going to affect us all. Where's he going to live? Here? You can't swing a cat in this house as it is. Our Jimmy and Jack are in the back bedroom. Mam, you and me have the other one, so that leaves the sofa.' Seeing the warning flash of anger in Emily's eyes and the sharp jut of her sister's chin she hastily added, 'I'm only being practical!'

Emily knew she was right. There was barely room for the five of them in the tiny terraced house. Two bedrooms, a kitchen and a tiny front room was all it consisted of and a minuscule yard at the back that led on to the entry, or jigger as it was called.

When Lonsdale Street had been built not much thought had been given to the size of the houses or the comfort of their occupants. It had been worse when Harry and Rob had also had to share the back bedroom but the war had taken its toll on number twenty-four, as it had on every house in the street. Except that of Albert Davies. The man her Mam had just announced she was going to marry.

Her thoughts automatically turned to her dead brothers. Harry, the oldest, with his shock of unruly brown hair and a grin that seemed to split his face in two. Her big brother but always referred to as 'our kid'. He'd looked so smart in his uniform. Much smarter than he'd ever looked before and she'd always remember him like that. Tall and straight and proud. And Rob. She glanced at Phoebe-Ann from under her lashes, remembering how she'd rocked her in her arms all that terrible night. Trying to comfort her and assuage her own grief. Mam had been too devastated to utter a single word for two days.

Rob and Phoebe-Ann were twins and she knew her sister felt the loss of her brother more deeply than any of them. They'd been inseparable when young, although they'd often fought and squabbled. Phoebe-Ann always tagged along behind the small gang of boys who made the narrow streets their playground. And when his mates got tired of her or teased or tormented her, Rob had always defended her. Poor Phoebe-Ann. Even now she sometimes heard her stifled sobs in the night. Bedrooms brought her back to the present with a jolt and she realized her sister had been speaking to her. 'What?'

'I said he could sleep in the parlour.'

'She'd never let him do that. You know how she cherishes that room. And they'll want to be together.'

'It's like a shrine in there. A shrine for me Da.'

Emily nodded her agreement. The tiny room was Mam's pride and joy. The few pieces of furniture, the oilcloth on the floor and the two photographs of Da were all lovingly polished every day and no-one was ever allowed in there. No, she couldn't see the sombre Mr Davies sleeping there with the smiling face of his predecessor looking down at him. She wrung out the dish mop and hung it on its peg next to the window that was so small it was little better than useless. 'I suppose she'll tell us the arrangements in her own good time.'

Phoebe-Ann raised her eyes to the ceiling and pursed her lips. Life was getting complicated and she hated complications. She liked things to be clear and simple. Black and white. She still couldn't take it in. Mam! Her Mam and old Mr Davies, the neighbourhood skinflint. She'd never once seen him smile let alone laugh. 'That fella's gorra face that'd stop de Liver clock!' she'd heard Mrs Harper next door say about him. And Mam was going to marry him, live with him and share the same bed. She shuddered at the latter realization. How could she? With him! It was too awful to think about and too complicated. You fell in love when you were young, then got married and had children. Mam had done all that. But she supposed that the older you got you just didn't do 'that' any more. She shuddered again. It was hard enough to imagine Mam and Dad doing 'it', but Mam and Albert Davies!

She stacked the dishes on the single narrow shelf and spread the tea towel to dry across the draining board that Emily had scrubbed down. 'When do you think her own good time will be then?'

Emily shrugged. 'Maybe tonight. Maybe tomorrow. Get your coat. You can come down to the bag-wash with me. I don't want you harping on at Mam while I'm out. And not another word about it. Anything you've got to say can be said later when you've had

13

time to calm down. When we've both had time to take it in properly.'

Phoebe-Ann assented. She didn't want to stay in with Mam, knowing her imagination would run riot and she was bound to say something that would upset Mam. The way she felt it was as certain as night follows day. Then Emily would get mad and there would be a slanging match. Besides, it was Saturday afternoon and very likely the last one she'd have to herself. When the washing was done she would persuade one of the neighbours to keep an eye on it and she and Emily could go into town. Then there was another matter she wanted to discuss with her sister. One that had been pushed to the back of her mind by her Mam's news.

She gave her sister a thin smile and Emily grinned back. Phoebe-Ann's ill humour never lasted long. Neither could she keep her mind on one subject for more than an hour or two. 'A head full of butterflies' was how Mam put it.

When the scullery door had slammed shut Lily Parkinson had dropped her head on her hands. She had dreaded telling them all, but telling the girls had worried her most. Especially Phoebe-Ann. She'd been prepared for the look of stunned disbelief that had crept over both their faces. It was only what she'd expected. She hadn't been foolish enough to believe that they would be over the moon with delight. Then she'd seen the softening of Emily's expression and understanding dawning in her pale eyes.

In her heart she'd known that Emily wouldn't get too upset but Phoebe-Ann was another matter. She'd opened and closed her mouth like a codfish and she knew the questions and protests were forming. Before they could be uttered, Emily had dragged her sister into the scullery and slammed the door. She could still hear the buzz of voices.

Was what she was doing really so terrible? That was a question she'd asked herself time and again over the past week. The final answer had been no. Oh, she knew people called him names but they didn't know him as well as she did.

He'd moved into Lonsdale Street two years after Joe had died and he'd kept himself to himself which hadn't suited some of the neighbours. What's more he had his own business, in a small way. More self-employed really. He had a wagon and two horses and hired himself out as an independent carter. It had been rumoured that he'd owned the house for the last couple of years but she'd refused to be drawn into speculation about that.

Being on the corner of Lonsdale Street and Bloom Street it was a bigger house than all the others with a larger yard with a wooden lean-to where he kept the cart. The horses were stabled up behind St Nathaniel's church. Yes, he was careful with his money, but she saw that as a virtue and one she approved of. At least he wasn't in the pub every night wasting it, or down a back jigger playing pitch and toss or in debt to the bookie. She began to smooth out imaginary creases in the faded and threadbare chenille cloth. It was a virtue she, too, had cultivated. Born of necessity. There hadn't been much choice about it. Circumstances had forced her to watch every farthing.

She got up slowly, placing her hands in the small of her back and grimacing. She caught sight of herself in the mirror that stood on the shelf above the range. She wasn't a bad-looking woman, she thought, her hand patting her tidily pinned-up hair. There was more silver than gold in it now though but what could she expect at fifty-two and after a lifetime of hard work?

She poured herself a cup of strong tea from the pot that sat on the hob beside the range and sat down in the battered old chair from which the horsehair was leaking. 'Oh, Joe. Am I doing the right thing?' she said softly. Twelve years was a long time to be alone. A young widow with a family of six to bring up by herself and God knows that hadn't been easy. She'd never been afraid of hard work but after that terrible day when they'd come to tell her that he'd fallen from a hatch cover into an empty hold and had broken his neck, she'd known she would have to work even harder. The neighbours had all rallied round and somehow she'd muddled through until the day came when she had finally faced the fact that only by her efforts alone could the family be kept together. She'd sworn she'd work until she dropped before she'd let them take the children and put them into a home.

She'd had four cleaning jobs. All in India Buildings. Two early in the morning, the other two in the evenings when the office staff had gone home. In between she had cleaned, washed, shopped and cooked, then once a week she had joined the army of cleaners who converged on the Cunard liners and worked like furies so the ship would be ready to sail again the following day. Twelve or fourteen hours at a stretch they worked and she often wondered how she'd found the energy to crawl home, but the money was good and she desperately needed it.

A smile hovered around her lips. Even from an early age Emily had been a great help. She always had the kettle on, the table set, the kitchen tidy. Lily sipped her tea and glanced towards the still tightly shut door from behind which voices still rose and fell and pots rattled.

It had been back-breaking work and she'd been weighed down with worries. Trying to make her meagre wages stretch to often impossible lengths. Fighting to keep poverty and destitution at bay and to keep up some standards. To make sure her home was clean, her step whitened, her children neat even though the clothes they wore were second and even third hand and their boots often had pieces of cardboard pushed inside to cover the holes until she could afford to have them patched.

For twelve long years she'd struggled on. Oh, things were not so grim now. Money wasn't so tight. These days she didn't have to beg bones from the butcher or 'fades' from the greengrocer to make a thin stew – often the only meal of the day. But she was desperately tired of battling with fate. She'd had to be strong and she'd managed to be so but the deaths of first Harry and then Rob at just seventeen had fatally sapped that strength. She was drained and empty. All the fight had gone out of her in the days that followed the arrival of those telegrams. Two in two days. Oh, they'd been dark days but she hadn't been alone in her grief. There wasn't a woman in the entire street who hadn't lost someone. Their sons, husbands and fathers had been in the same regiment, the 'Liverpool Pals' and street after street had been plunged into mourning.

The scullery door opened and Emily smiled at her.

'We're going down the bag-wash, Mam.'

'And we might go into town for an hour,' Phoebe-Ann added, ignoring the look her sister shot at her.

17

'Get my purse, Em, it's on the mantel.' Lily felt too tired to even get up and her head had begun to ache.

Emily took down the battered old purse and handed it to her mother. 'You look worn out.'

'No more than usual. Here, take this and get yourselves something. Have a bit of a treat to celebrate.' She handed out two silver shillings.

Emily shook her head. 'No, Mam, you might need it and I've got a few bob left from my wages.'

Lily felt annoyed. Was this Emily's way of showing her disapproval? 'Take it, girl. I've never been able to hand out coppers for treats since . . . well, not for a long time anyway.'

Emily took the coin. She'd buy Mam something. She looked so drawn and tired. Phoebe-Ann would spend hers on bits of finery; she thought of little else but her appearance. Mam never had anything for herself. She looked closely at her mother and then looked away for there were tears on Lily's lashes.

Lily followed them into the lobby, kissed them both and then went into the parlour to watch them from the window. They were good girls, she thought. The room smelled musty. The grate hadn't seen a fire in it for years. She shivered and the pain behind her eyes increased in severity. She sighed deeply. Albert Davies was a good man but who'd have thought that when he'd gone down with the influenza and she'd gone in to make up his fire, clean up a bit and get some food down him that it would lead to this? When he'd recovered she'd gone in a couple of times a week to clean, ignoring the avid curiosity and barbed remarks of her neighbours and she'd got to know him better. He was a quiet, reserved man, simple in his tastes and she'd come to like and respect him.

She'd realized in a short time that he was lonely.

He had no close family, just a cousin who still lived in the pit village in a green, Welsh valley, as he'd described it when she'd asked. Gradually, he had told her more about himself and she'd divulged her background. She had found it easy to talk to him, to confide in him, to make him laugh at the antics and escapades of her family and her daily life. And then a week ago he'd said, 'It's not been much of a life, Lil, has it – for us both?'

She'd just smiled thinking how comforting it was to have someone who listened, someone who cared.

'I know this will come as a shock, it's shocked me, the realization that . . . Well, would you consider marrying me, Lily? You'd have no more worries. No need for you to work yourself to death and we do . . . get on well, like?'

She'd been too stunned to utter a word.

'No need to rush. Take your time, like I said "consider".' He'd looked bashful and suddenly very vulnerable and tears had sprung to her eyes.

'I'll take good care of you, Lil! I promise!'

'I'll . . . I'll consider it, Albert,' she'd managed to stammer.

In the days and nights that had followed she'd thought of it to the exclusion of everything else. She'd been distant and preoccupied when people spoke to her. She'd weighed all the 'pros' and 'cons'. She was fond of him but would it be enough? Could she give herself to a man after all these years? Would he be happy with her and her family. And what about the family? In the end she'd become so confused that she felt she couldn't go on in such a state. They had discussed a few things and then she'd given him her answer. Yes. When she'd said it she felt so relieved.

The fog of confusion had lifted. She'd felt almost elated.

She turned from the window and reached out for the framed photo of Joe that stood on the mantel. Her hand hovered hesitantly for a second before she picked it up. 'I don't want to have to slave for ever, Joe. I'm middle-aged and the kids are grown up.'

The smiling features of the young man stared silently back.

'I'm worn out. You understand, Joe, don't you? I'm fond of him. I don't love him the way I loved you, but he's offering me peace of mind, company, and I don't want to be left on my own. The kids have got their own lives to lead. You do understand, don't you, Joe?'

She raised the photograph to her lips and kissed the image, then she replaced it. An army of small men with hammers was pounding away inside her head. She'd go and lie down for an hour to see if it would lift. The lines in her forehead eased and she smiled ruefully. Never in her entire life had she taken to her bed with a headache, no matter how bad it had been. That was what marrying Albert Davies meant. She could take the time. Time for herself.

It was Emily who broached the subject at tea time. Jack and Jimmy Parkinson had had their own discussion about Lily's news on their way to work that morning. Indeed they'd discussed it all the way down Upper Parliament Street, on the tram to the Pierhead, and on the overhead railway to the Bramley Moor Dock. Back and forth it had been tossed. Opinions had been expressed, arguments for and against presented and finally they had decided that if it was what Lily wanted they wouldn't put up any objections.

As Emily placed the teapot with its knitted cosy on

the circle of cork, she looked around at the assembled family. She wondered what her brothers were thinking and hoped that what she was about to say wouldn't start off an almighty row. She'd bought a big bunch of flowers from the flower ladies in Clayton Square and they reposed in two jam jars on the dresser, their colours brightening up the dingy room. Phoebe-Ann had refused to be drawn on the subject. In fact she seemed to have forgotten her outburst and had spent hours at the counters in Woolworth's in Church Street. But Emily was suspicious of her sister and hoped she wasn't going to start acting up again. 'Mam . . .' she began.

Lily looked at her apprehensively. 'Well, spit it out, Emily?'

'Where will we . . . ? I mean he . . . Mr Davies. Where will . . . ?

Lily put her out of her misery. 'Where will he sleep?'

Emily nodded.

Phoebe-Ann fidgeted with a spoon. She didn't want to think about this at all.

Jack and Jimmy looked down at their hands.

'I had thought I would move in with him. On my own.'

'Oh, Mam, you can't do that!' Phoebe-Ann cried, dropping the spoon which fell into her cup and splashed tea on the table.

Lily was contrite. 'I'm sorry. I shouldn't tease.'

Emily and Jack exchanged glances of relief.

'I discussed it all with Albert, before I gave him my answer. I wanted it sorted out I told him, just in case I did accept.'

Jimmy stirred his tea slowly. He'd agreed with Jack in the end that Mam deserved something better out of life, but he didn't really approve.

21

'He has a much bigger house than this one,' Lily went on.

'Nearly everyone has a bigger house than this one,' Phoebe-Ann muttered to herself.

Lily ignored her. 'There are three bedrooms, a parlour, a kitchen, a back kitchen and a scullery. There's more room in the yard and a wash-house, so it makes sense all round for us all to move in there.' She stopped and held her breath, wondering how this decision would be received.

'Makes no difference to us, Mam. Does it Jim? One house is much like another.'

Jimmy nodded slowly and Lily let out her breath in a sigh of relief. The girls she could manage but she'd wondered about the lads.

Emily smiled, then glanced at Phoebe-Ann.

Phoebe-Ann could see she was outnumbered but she didn't care. She'd made a decision of her own. 'Well, I'm not going to live with him even if there are three bedrooms! I'm not going to have everyone pointing and nudging each other and jangling!'

'That'll do you!' Jack's voice was dangerously quiet for he feared a desertion of unity from Jimmy.

Emily saw that her mother was tightly twisting the hem of her apron. She could kill Phoebe-Ann. 'And just what are you going to do?'

'I'm going to live in at the Mercers'. If I have to go back into service I might as well go the whole hog and live in as well!' She sprang up from the table and turned and ran quickly up the stairs.

Lily made to rise and go after her but Emily laid a restraining hand on her arm.

'Leave her, Mam! She'll come round and if she doesn't . . . well, it might be better her living in instead of moving under protest and throwing tantrums if anyone looks sideways at her.' She smiled at her mother but she was wondering how it would work out. She knew fingers would be pointed, tongues would wag but it would also be a five minute wonder. But would they all get on? They were all noisy. She and Phoebe-Ann were always bickering. Jack and Jimmy often argued, especially about football, and Mr Davies was such a quiet man. She realized Lily was speaking.

'Of course it will be a quiet affair. I know it's usual for it to be in church, but I wanted it to be unusual, something different to what your Da and I had. So, it's to be at the Registry Office and no expensive "do" afterwards.' She looked a little embarrassed. 'After all, neither of us are spring chickens.'

'When?' Emily asked.

'Next Friday afternoon. The stuff I decide to take with me can go on Thursday night. Then after the ceremony we all go back . . . there.'

Emily raised her teacup. 'Here's to you and Mr Davies.'

Lily smiled at her. 'Albert. You'll have to learn to call him Albert.'

'To you and . . . Albert and a new life.' It wasn't exactly what she had wanted to say but the right words just wouldn't come, so it would have to do.

Chapter Two

'I mean it! I really mean it, so don't try and talk me out of it!' Phoebe-Ann cried when Emily pushed open the bedroom door.

'I know you do,' Emily said laconically, as she lit the gas jet and the room became bathed in its soft light, the warm glow muting the shabbiness of the furniture, hiding the faded colours of the patchwork quilt on the bed and the curtain on the window. It softened the harshness of the bare floorboards and picked out the colours of the peg rug by the side of the bed.

The quilt was creased and the bolster rumpled where Phoebe-Ann had tossed and turned. Emily sat at the foot of the bed.

'You can change your mind, if you wanted to.'

Phoebe-Ann shot upright. 'No! You might not care that everyone will be talking about us, but I do! We'll be the laughing stock of Toxteth! It was bad enough when Mam started going in a couple of times a week after he was ill. Her next door said "See your Mam's gettin' 'er feet under the table, like!" I was so mortified I could have died!'

'Oh, come off it, Fee! You don't mean to tell me you take any notice of her? She's all mouth! She can eat a banana sideways that one!'

Phoebe-Ann walked over to the window and stared out at the bulk of St Nathaniel's church, outlined against the indigo sky of the midsummer's night.

Seeing she was getting nowhere, Emily decided to change the subject. 'What was the other important event you were harping on about before all . . . this?'

'Going back into service, although now I'm glad I am!'

Emily sighed. She just couldn't win. Phoebe-Ann seemed determined to be contrary. 'I thought you said you would hate working for the Mercers again?'

'What else can I do now the munitions have closed down and Mam won't hear of me working in any other factory, and now . . . this mess?'

Emily did not share her sister's enthusiasm for factory work. From the day they'd patriotically joined the thousands of girls and women in munitions she'd hated it. It was boring, dirty work and often dangerous. She tried not to think of Annie Moran's face, or what had been left of it, when a detonator had exploded. Phoebe-Ann had enjoyed the companionship of the other girls. The lighter atmosphere. The less autocratic supervision, but most of all she liked the money in her pocket. Far more than she was paid as a lady's maid.

She herself would be glad to go back to the large house in Upper Huskisson Street owned by Richard Mercer, a director of the Cunard Shipping Company. She liked the usually tranquil atmosphere, the well-ordered routine, the expensive furniture, fine carpets and beautiful furnishings.

Phoebe-Ann was rubbing away her tears with the back of her hand. 'At least Miss Olivia will be glad to have me back. I'll have my self-respect and be able to hold my head up when I come home to see Mam and . . . him!'

'I don't know why you're so dead set against Mr

25

Davies. Albert,' she corrected herself and studiously ignored the look Phoebe-Ann shot at her. 'You don't know him so how can you judge him?'

'That's just it! We *don't* know him, and I don't want to!'

Emily was getting tired of the whole matter. 'Oh, suit yourself but don't come moaning to me when Cook gets on to you or Miss Olivia is in one of those moods when even the Angel Gabriel himself couldn't please her.' She took out the pins that held up her thick, straight hair and began to brush it.

'I've always got on well with Miss Olivia,' Phoebe-Ann said defensively.

'That's because you're both scatty and spoiled. She having no mam and you being the youngest.'

'I'm not spoiled!'

'You're certainly giving a good impression of it at the moment!'

Phoebe-Ann pulled a face. Now that a solution was in sight, although not the one she would readily admit was perfect, she felt better. If she lived in she'd have that small room at the top of the house to which she could escape at night, should she want to, with a bed of her own. No sharing. And she did get on well with Olivia Mercer who was indeed spoiled.

Olivia was the same age as herself and could be a Tartar when she chose to be. At other times she treated her just like a friend or a sister and they had often giggled together for hours until Madge Webster, the housekeeper, had admonished her and delivered long lectures on 'knowing your place'. 'So, when is it to be then?'

Emily put down the hairbrush. 'Next Friday afternoon and don't think you are going to get out of going! It's only going to be a quiet "do" at Brougham

26

Terrace and you'll go if I have to drag you every foot of the way!'

Phoebe-Ann pouted and then tried to look nonchalant. 'That won't be necessary!'

'Good!' Emily slipped her clean but darned nightdress over her head. Her clothes were folded neatly on top of the tiny chest.

Phoebe-Ann started to get undressed. 'Em, do you think we could get something new, to wear? Do you think if Mam asked . . .'

'You've got a flamin' nerve, Phoebe-Ann Parkinson! Don't be two-faced! And don't be mithering Mam about new clothes. If you want something, you pay for it!'

Next morning, as had become her habit, Lily slipped quietly in through the back door of the house on the corner. She smiled to herself as she looked around the kitchen. The furniture was plain but of good quality. The range glimmered from recent blackleading and the kettle sang on the hob.

For months now she'd made his Sunday dinner. He was an early riser, even on Sunday. He usually checked on the horses then went for a long walk, bought a newspaper and returned home, midmorning. She looked at the clock on the mantel. He must have cut short his morning constitutional she surmised. He wouldn't leave the kettle to boil dry.

She busied herself with the piece of brisket, thinking it would be the last time she would cook him a solitary meal and that from now on there would always be meat for Sunday lunch. Something that was a rarity in her house.

She didn't hear him come down the stairs or open the door. Nor did she see him standing watching her.

He was a stocky man of no great height. His face was weatherbeaten from the years spent working in the open. His hair had once been black but now it was grizzled. His dark eyes beneath thick, straight eyebrows were kind.

She turned around. 'Oh! Good grief! You gave me a turn!'

'I'm sorry, Lil, I didn't mean to.' His quiet tones still retained the sing-song lilt of the small Welsh village he'd left so many years ago. 'How did it go, then? Come and sit down and tell me.'

She smiled, wiping her hands on her apron and sitting in the wooden rocker opposite him. 'They were surprised to say the least.'

'Did they kick up?'

'No. Not really.'

Albert Davies looked at her and for the hundredth time wondered how he had ever managed to pluck up the courage to ask her to marry him. She was an attractive woman and a kind one, too. He'd experienced many instances of her thoughtfulness and generosity. Not that she'd had much to give in the way of material things. It was the little things that had touched him. The mugs of homemade soup she'd brought him when he'd been ill; the kettle holders and oven mitts that Emily or Phoebe-Ann had made that suddenly 'appeared' in the kitchen. Things like that. And her time and patience given so gladly and without thought of payment. She'd brought a warmth to his home and a brightness into a life that had been increasingly lonely. She, too, had confessed to loneliness, despite the fact that she was always surrounded by people. There were times when she felt a great emptiness in her life, she'd told him. That was something he understood only too well.

'And did you decide about the . . . arrangements?'

'Yes. We'll come and live here, if that's still all right?'

'Didn't I say it would be, Lil?' It was so long since he'd had any kind of family life that he welcomed it, although there had been moments when he'd wondered if he'd regret it. He'd been so used to solitude, so used to his own routine. Would a family of five with their bickering and laughter and noise annoy him? He'd pushed the doubts to the back of his mind. They were good, hardworking lads were Jack and Jimmy; no falling in blind drunk on pay day or any other day; no gambling or hanging around with loose women. She'd done well. It wasn't easy to bring up lads without a man behind you and the two girls were well turned out and seemed pleasant enough. He noticed a shadow cross her face. 'What's wrong?'

Lily sighed then shrugged. 'It's Phoebe-Ann. She's decided to live in with the Mercers. They always wanted her to – wanted both of them to live in – but they never would agree to. Until now.'

'Rather than come and live here?' He felt a little hurt but then shrugged it off. He'd prepared himself for this kind of rejection. He'd have been even more disturbed had either Jack or Jimmy refused.

'I'm sorry. She can be very stubborn at times. You know the performance I had to get her to go back there at all. She got used to the money and the companionship in munitions and was hellbent on going to work at Bibby's or Tate's until I put my foot down. They'd both promised Mr Mercer that when the war was over they'd go back.'

'And a promise is a promise,' he added.

'Aye, it is. Emily thinks her "living in" might be for the best.'

29

'She's got a lot of common sense has Emily.'

Lily smiled as she rose. 'She takes after me. Down to earth and practical. Phoebe-Ann takes after her dad.' She hadn't meant to bring the conversation around to Joe. 'You don't mind me talking about Joe, do you?'

'No. You were married to him. That's a fact. No getting away from it. No use getting jealous either.'

She crossed to his side and laid a hand on his arm. 'You're a good, kind man Albert Davies and I'm lucky to have you.'

'Get away with you, Lil! It's me who's the lucky one. Now, before you start tearing around the kitchen like a dervish, there's something else we should discuss.'

'What?'

'Work. I don't want you to go on going out to work. It's not necessary any more.'

'But I've always worked. Ever since I was a girl.'

'I know and I think it's time you stopped. You'll have enough to do here. No more half killing yourself to help get the *Aquitania* or the *Berengaria* or anything else ready for sea again. From now on you'll be getting me, Jack and Jimmy ready for work and that's enough.' He didn't say that she was getting too old for such work. He did have some tact and sensitivity. He was also a proud man in his own way. If she continued to work it would reflect badly on him. It would be viewed as his inability to provide for her.

She directed a smile brimfull of gratitude at him. 'It will be a joy to be able to do everything properly. Time to enjoy preparing meals, baking,' she laughed. 'Even to do my own washing in my own wash-house, instead of having to take it down to the public wash-house. Does that sound strange to you?'

'No. I can remember my old mam on washdays. She fair wore herself out with rubbing and scrubbing, dollypegging and mangling, but when it was all blowing on the line, white as driven snow, she'd have such a look of pride and satisfaction on her face. It was a ritual, see, and God help anyone who dared to interrupt it!'

'At least she didn't have to contend with the soot and smuts! I've cursed many a time when the wash has been covered in it; black as the hobs of hell sometimes and the windows and doorsteps too.'

'That's city life, Lil. One day I'll take you to the valley. Bit of a holiday like.' A thought suddenly occurred to him 'Would we go there soon? A honeymoon, like?'

She felt the colour rise in her cheeks. It was as though she was a tongue-tied, embarrassed girl. She shook her head.

'Maybe it was a daft idea. I've plenty of work at the moment and can't afford to lose it. Not the way things are. Maybe later on?'

'I'm a lucky woman, Albert.' She smiled.

Early on Monday morning, before dawn and before the streets were aired, as Lily put it, Emily and Phoebe-Ann walked up Lonsdale Street and around the corner into Bloom Street and then into Upper Huskisson Street which was a wide thoroughfare, lined with trees and flanked on either side by large, elegant Georgian houses; some with Corinthian porticoes and elaborately ornate facades; some with first floor balconies, bounded by delicate wrought-iron; all with gardens and drives. These were the residences of the rich: the shipowners, bankers, cotton merchants. Not so many of them now, Emily mused.

Many had moved out to West Derby and even Crosby and Blundel, sands. She didn't think it extraordinary that wide roads and avenues like Princes Avenue and Upper Parliament Street and the quiet squares with their own parks and gardens were surrounded by rows of narrow streets like Lonsdale, Almond and Pine Streets. Some of them very rundown; some with no windows at the back of the house at all. Splendour, ostentation and wealth side by side with poverty and squalor.

Phoebe-Ann carried a small, battered suitcase tied up with string and a brown paper parcel tucked under one arm. This contained her uniform, the case her few personal belongings. There had been no further arguments or attempts to persuade her to change her mind. They had all agreed to let sleeping dogs lie.

'I like this time of the day. It's so still and quiet and everything smells . . . fresh.' Emily breathed deeply, savouring the newness of the day.

Phoebe-Ann wrinkled her nose. 'I don't. It's miserable and it doesn't smell fresh to me. It smells of soot and unemptied middens. At least I won't have to get up two hours earlier in future.'

Emily raised her eyes to the now pink-streaked sky. At least she would be spared having to listen to Phoebe-Ann's carping and moaning each morning.

They walked the rest of the way in silence and ran lightly down the cellar steps that led to the kitchen and servants' hall. Although the main part of the house was in darkness, the curtains still tightly closed, below stairs lights burned, their brightness diffused by the ever-strengthening rays of the morning sun. As Emily pushed open the door, three heads were turned in their direction. She grinned. 'Mornin' all! We're back!'

Mrs Ransom, the cook, hauled her ample frame from the chair at the side of the table. A broad smile spreading across her face. 'You're a sight for sore eyes, Emily, and you Phoebe-Ann! Come on in the pair of you!'

Young Kitty, who had only been with the family a month, stifled a yawn and peered at them with eyes still heavy with sleep.

'Who got you ready?' Edwin Leeson, the only manservant, grinned at Phoebe-Ann, pointing to the parcel and suitcase.

'Miss Olivia's been on at me for ages to live in, so I decided to do just that. There's no objection is there?'

'None that I can think of,' Cook replied, indicating that Phoebe-Ann put down her case. 'You'd better see Madge first though.'

Phoebe-Ann slipped off her jacket. She'd always been able to get round Mrs Webster, although she'd never dared to address her as anything other than 'Mrs Webster'. The 'Mrs' was a courtesy title. Madge was a spinster, a tall, thin woman who looked constantly harassed, an expression that belied the calm efficiency with which she'd always run the house. The war years with the shortages both in staff and provisions had etched the worry lines more deeply. 'Where is she?'

'In the pantry, putting the last touches to the week's expenses. You'd best go and see her.'

Phoebe-Ann nodded as she smoothed down the collar and apron and donned the white starched cap.

Emily, who had also taken off her jacket and was clipping on her cap, smiled at Edwin who was polishing the cutlery. A baize apron covered his morning livery. He was still the same cheerful Edwin, despite

33

four years in the trenches from which he had miraculously returned unscathed. No sign on his face of the horrors he had witnessed and endured. She'd always liked him. He always had a quip and a smile that brightened the dullest hour and lightened the darkest moments. He had open, honest features and blue eyes that could shine with merriment or become cold and piercing when he was angry, which wasn't often. His dark brown curly hair was plastered down each morning but refused to remain obedient to the brush or comb by early afternoon, much to his chagrin and everyone else's amusement, except Madge Webster's.

'The Master told me a few days ago we were going to have the pleasure of your company again. How long for, though, I asked myself? I thought you'd both have been swept off your feet and married by now.'

'Chance would be a fine thing! Besides, there's not many princes or knights on white chargers come calling at munitions factories and, if they did, those awful caps and overalls and the stink of chemicals would soon have them "charging" in the opposite direction,' Emily laughed.

Edwin grinned as he laid the last knife down on the tray and took off the apron. They were so different, he thought. Some would call Emily plain but he didn't think so and she was far more intelligent and lively than Phoebe-Ann who he had to admit was a real beauty. 'It's great to see you. Both of you.'

Phoebe-Ann had returned, a smile on her face.

'You might be changing your mind about that after she's been back a few days,' Emily laughed and nodded towards her sister.

'Don't you start, our Emily! Mrs Webster said she was pleased to see me and she'd hoped I would live in. So much more convenient. So sensible.'

'Must be the first time you've ever done anything sensible!' Edwin laughed.

'And that's enough from you as well!' Phoebe-Ann tossed her head.

'If Miss Olivia's tray is ready, Cook, I'll take it up to her.'

Cook indicated the breakfast tray. 'Needs the toast making. You're keen to get going, it's only seven and she won't thank you for waking her up at this hour, no matter how glad she'll be to see you back.'

Phoebe-Ann hesitated. She wanted to appear eager, yet Cook was right. Olivia Mercer wouldn't be overly delighted to be woken up quite so soon. 'I expect you're right. Maybe I should make up the bed and put this stuff away.'

'Get the linen out of the cupboard, and I'd put a hot water bottle in that bed. It won't be aired. It hasn't been slept in for years.'

Phoebe-Ann nodded her agreement and, picking up her things, went upstairs by the narrow back staircase.

'Kitty, pour Emily a cup of tea. There's time for one before we have to get going.'

The girl did as she was bid and Emily sat down at the table.

'She didn't want to come back really. Mam said she had to because she'd promised.'

'Oh, aye! What did the bold rossi want to do instead?'

'Wanted to go on working in a factory, that's if she could have got a job. The pay is better and she liked the company of the other girls.'

'So, what *really* changed her mind then?' Edwin asked. He'd been glad to get his old job back. So many of his mates hadn't been so lucky, but then Mr

35

Mercer was an honourable man. He didn't make empty promises and good staff were getting harder to find. Higher wages could be earned in the factories and shops, when work was available.

Emily finished her tea. She'd have to tell them and it was better that they heard it from her and not strangers. 'Mam's getting married again and Phoebe-Ann's being awkward. She won't come with us to live with Mr Davies.'

'By, that's a turn up for the book!' Cook didn't try to disguise her surprise. In her position she felt she didn't have to.

Emily was instantly on the defensive. 'Why shouldn't she? He's a good man, he has his own cart and horses and he owns the house!'

'Oh, get down off your high horse, girl! I didn't mean anything. I'm just a bit taken aback that's all. But if anyone deserves a bit of comfort in her life, it's your mam. Each time I've seen her she's looked worn to a frazzle.'

Emily was placated and she smiled at Edwin who tapped the side of his nose with his forefinger. She knew what he meant. Cook was a nosey woman who liked nothing better than a bit of gossip.

'So, that madam has got all uppity, has she?'

'She just said she was going to live in, so we thought it best to let her get on with it.'

'Must be bad if she's all set to lodge here. She always swore she'd have to be desperate.'

'Don't you start teasing her Edwin Leeson or she might decide to move back home and we can do without her hysterics, thank you!' Although her words were sharp her smile softened them. 'I'll go and start in the dining room.'

'The fire's laid but there's no need to light it, it's

warm enough. Just put the screen in front of the grate,' he called as she moved to the door.

'Thanks. I'll set the table.'

'You'll need these then.'

Emily picked up the tray on which the cutlery had been laid and Cook stirred herself with a heavy sigh.

'You, Kitty, move yourself! Tidy this lot up while I make a start on the kedgeree. Shake yourself, girl! You always look half asleep, what time do you get to bed?'

'Never later than ten, ma'am, an' that's the God's own truth! I'm worn out, gettin' up at four an' all.'

'Don't take the Lord's name in vain! I'll not have it in my kitchen and especially from a chit like you! When I was a young skivvy I was up at four and not in me bed until midnight most nights. Soft, that's what life is for you now!'

Kitty pursed her lips. Soft. She called this soft! She must be joking. As soon as she was old enough she intended to get a job at Ogden's like their Annie. The hours were shorter and the money nearly three times what she got here.

Emily had begun to lay out the fine china and heavy silver cutlery. She smoothed the crisp, white damask tablecloth. It was good to be back, to be surrounded by good things and good friends. She was contemplating the future, idly polishing a knife on her apron, when Edwin came in carrying a huge tray on which were half a dozen covered dishes.

'I've already done that! Here, give me a hand with these, seeing as you've nothing better to do than stand day-dreaming!'

'I wasn't!'

'You can't kid me, I know you too well. Standing

37

there looking all gormless and polishing a knife that's already been polished to death and, what's more, you watched me doing it! I thought we'd seen the last of you.'

'I hated that damned factory! It was filthy work, some of the stuff turned your hair green and rotted your fingernails. I'm glad you came through it all, I really am,' she said, sincerely.

His face clouded and he nodded curtly. He had no wish to look back over the last four years. 'Poor Master James wasn't so lucky.'

'What's the matter with him? He wasn't wounded, was he?'

He moved the dishes around and pretended to study their layout more closely. 'No, he wasn't, but he's not the same. He's changed. A lot of men have.'

She sensed his reluctance to discuss it further. 'And what about Miss Olivia and the Master?'

The old grin was back. 'Oh, aye, they're still the same. The Master's getting older and a bit more portly and as for Miss Olivia . . .'

'Still spoiled rotten.' It was a statement not a question.

'I don't envy the man that gets her. He'll have a dog's life unless he can control her. Any of those feeble-looking blokes she calls her "friends" just couldn't cope. She'd have ground them down in no time.'

'Is there anyone special then?'

'No. You know her. Flighty. Can't think of anything other than what's she's going to wear and who she's going to meet and will she have any fun!'

Emily gave the knife a last polish and placed it down. 'That makes two of them then,' she muttered, thinking it was an apt description of Phoebe-Ann.

38

Phoebe-Ann had made up the bed and had arranged her brush, comb and hair pins neatly on the wash-stand, next to her soap and toothbrush and towel. Her few clothes she had hung up in the oddly-shaped cupboard under the sloping eaves. She'd stood on tiptoe and peered out of the tiny window that gave a wonderful view right over the city and the river. Then she'd readjusted her cap and peered at herself in the tiny, speckled mirror on the wall, the only con-cession to adornment in the room. She rubbed an imaginary smut from her cheek. Maybe she'd buy a picture or one of those fancy calendars with paper lace threaded with ribbon she'd seen the street pedlars selling for a penny. That would look nice. She sat down on the bed and looked around. It wasn't the height of luxury but then it was *hers* and she'd never had a room to herself in her entire life. The thought pleased her. Perhaps she'd get a small vase and put some flowers in it and change the curtains for something prettier and the bedspread. Then she shrugged. What was the point? She wouldn't spend much time in here. She was getting carried away with herself. Any money she got would be spent on clothes.

The realization that she wouldn't have much time to spend in her room dampened her spirits. Up at five in summer, six in winter, working all day and most of the evening, she knew from past experience that she'd fall gratefully into bed at night without even noticing chintzy curtains or vases of flowers. She could earn twice as much and have more free time if only Mam had let her try for one of the factories. And she'd have had lots of other girls and women to chat to, laugh with, confide in. Maybe Mam would change her mind later on. She wished now she hadn't been so hasty about deciding to live in. She'd waited for one of them to say something, to try to coax her to change her mind and last night it really wouldn't have taken much effort, but the subject hadn't even been mentioned. All Mam had said was 'Make sure you ask for the time off to come to the Registry Office'. And that had been that. Oh, blast them all! It must be time to take Miss Olivia's tray now. She brightened up and went down to the kitchen.

With expertise born of practice, she manoeuvred the door open and closed it gently with her foot. She placed the tray on the chest of drawers and looked around. Nothing in the room seemed to have changed and she grinned as she caught sight of the figure curled up in the bed. With a deft flick of both wrists she drew back the curtains and the bright rays of sunlight dispelled the gloom.

'Mornin', Miss Olivia. It's nearly eight and I've brought your tray.'

A head appeared from beneath the pink silk eiderdown. A riot of copper curls spilled down over pale shoulders. Large grey-green eyes opened wide. 'Phoebe-Ann, is that you?'

'Yes, miss. I'm back.'

Olivia Mercer sat up in bed, wide awake now. 'Oh! It is!'

Phoebe-Ann brought the tray to the bed.

'I've had no-one to chat to! All I've had is an endless stream of useless girls! No-one who could do my hair or see to my clothes like you do! The last one was utterly, utterly useless! I know we all had to make sacrifices and Papa got to be so boring about that, but it was a terrible nuisance!'

Phoebe-Ann glowed at the intended praise. 'And

what will you be needing today, miss? It's going to be warm.'

Olivia sipped the tea. 'I don't know. Life is very tedious just now and James is as dull as ditchwater. He lives in a world of his own. He's no fun at all. Papa doesn't really care what I do. He's more interested in his damned ships and what sort of state they're in now that the Government has finished with them!'

'Oh, I'm sure he is interested.' Phoebe-Ann plumped up the lace-edged pillows.

'What shall I do today?' Olivia mused. 'I think I'll go into town and do some shopping, maybe I'll meet Dora or Katie and have lunch.'

Phoebe-Ann opened the doors of the ornately carved wardrobe and flicked expertly through the many garments. 'You always look very nice in green, Miss. And it looks so cool and fresh I always think.'

'Um.' Olivia chewed thoughtfully on a piece of toast. Maybe she would go and call on Marjorie. She was rather bold and could be extremely outrageous at times and life was so boring at present. 'The green voile dress with the cream lace collar.'

'I'll take it down and give it a bit of a press after I've run your bath.' Phoebe-Ann stroked the cream lace collar lovingly. She'd forgotten what beautiful clothes Miss Olivia had.

Olivia swung long, shapely legs over the side of the bed. 'Oh, it really is good to have you back Phoebe-Ann!'

Phoebe-Ann remembered her mother's instructions. 'I hate to have to ask miss. But could I have a couple of hours off on Friday afternoon, please?'

Olivia's brow furrowed in a frown. 'What on earth

for? You have your Wednesday afternoon off and every second Sunday?'

'Could I change my Wednesday to Friday? It's my mam. She's getting married – again.'

Olivia's eyes widened. 'Who is she marrying?'

'A Mr Davies. He lives at the corner of our street and has a sort of business.' She didn't want Olivia Mercer to think her mam would just up and marry anyone.

Olivia pulled on her wrap and tossed back her mane of hair. 'What sort of business?'

'He's a carter. So, is that all right, miss?'

'I suppose so. What are you going to wear?'

'My Sunday dress and hat.' Phoebe-Ann wished she had something as fine as the dress folded over her arm.

'I suppose you haven't had time to shop.'

Phoebe-Ann felt annoyed. She'd had neither the time nor the money to shop. At least if she'd gone to work at Tate's she would have had the money. Sometimes Miss Olivia was so stupid. 'I'll run your bath, miss.'

Olivia smiled as Phoebe-Ann forgot her irritation and, smiling, left the room. She was quite a pretty girl, Olivia mused. Of course she didn't have the clothes or the style to carry them off, but she had beautiful skin and hair. She ran her fingers impatiently through her own hair. Why did it have to curl so tightly? She hated it. Still, Phoebe-Ann could work wonders with it and, if she was to impress everyone at the theatre and then at the party her papa was giving later in the month to celebrate the Treaty of Versailles, she would need Phoebe-Ann's help. She'd already chosen the materials and styles, for she was having two gowns made, and she'd had the fittings.

42

But she needed gloves and shoes and hair ornaments. Maybe she'd get them today. She glanced at herself in the mirror of the dressing table and searched her memory for the quaint description Phoebe-Ann had once used when untangling her unruly locks. She'd thought it extremely droll at the time. Oh, yes. 'Like a mop hanging over the banister.' Phoebe-Ann did use some quite comic expressions, that was part of her charm. She was so down to earth, so . . . so common.

Richard Mercer glanced up from his paper as Emily brought in a pot of freshly made tea. His dark eyes watched the girl thoughtfully. At least that was one of his problems solved. The growing shortage of good domestic staff was causing much concern in many households. Most young girls now went into the shops and factories and those of Emily's age were usually married with children. He looked perturbed. Widowed with young children would be a more apt description.

'Good morning, sir.'

'Good morning, Emily. Nice to see you.'

She dipped a curtsey. 'We're both glad to be back. Phoebe-Ann is up with Miss Olivia. Will Master James be down or should I make another pot for him?'

At the mention of his son, Richard Mercer's heavy eyebrows rushed together. 'He won't be down just yet, Emily. He has to rest a good deal these days. Doctor's orders.'

'I see.'

She didn't. Couldn't, he thought. He didn't see it very clearly himself. Oh, he'd heard how bad things had been. The whole horror had unfolded day by day, month by month in the newspapers, but didn't James

43

realize how lucky – no that was too mild a word – how miraculous had been his deliverance to come through with not so much as a scratch. He didn't realize it and he had such mood changes; days and nights filled with dark depression, but he'd get over it. He must not be rushed, old Coleman advised. He wouldn't even let himself think that there was anything mentally wrong with his son. Just a bit of shell shock, that's what it was. A few more weeks and he'd be his old self again. Bright, confident and with a sharp mind and wit. 'Is your mother well, Emily?' he asked politely as she poured his tea.

'Yes, thank you. She's getting married again on Friday.'

She'd gained his full attention. 'Indeed. Then you must convey my felicitations to her.' He smiled. 'I take it she won't be amongst my army of willing workers who help to expedite the speedy turnarounds we at Cunard are so famous for?'

'No, sir. Albert . . . Mr Davies, says she has to give up work.'

'Quite right too. Woman's place is in the home. If it's at all possible,' he added, not wishing to sound critical.

'Is there anything else, sir?'

'No, Emily. You get on.'

She dipped another bow and left and he sighed. She was a nice girl; quiet, willing, a good worker. He only wished Olivia had the same qualities, but then he shouldn't blame her. After poor Adele had died he had indulged her shamelessly. He couldn't now complain. He was reaping what he had sown.

He folded the paper and, taking his watch from his waistcoat pocket, checked the time against the black marble clock on the mantel. Time to go. Important

44

decisions to make today. How much could the Company afford to spend on refitting the ships now being decommissioned? Would it be worth the expense to convert the twelve-year-old *Mauretania* from coal to oil? Speed was the all important thing. Speed and safety. She'd held the Blue Riband now for a dozen years but for how much longer? They had to move with the times.

Chapter Three

The afternoon of the wedding was sultry. Even at six o'clock in the morning it had been warm, Emily had thought as she'd walked to work. 'Headachey weather' Mam called it. She and Phoebe-Ann had left Upper Huskisson Street just after twelve and were home by fifteen minutes past. The house looked oddly bare, Phoebe-Ann thought, glancing around. Emily had told her that most of the things they wanted to take had been loaded on to a borrowed handcart and moved four doors up. What had been left would benefit the new tenants who would move in that evening. They'd be glad of the stuff.

'Mam's upstairs,' Jimmy stated as they walked in. 'It's too damned hot for this collar!' he muttered, stretching his neck and running a finger around the stiffly starched collar.

'It's just too hot!' Phoebe-Ann complained.

'At least you don't have to dress up like the organ grinder's monkey!' Jimmy mopped his face with his handkerchief.

'Stop complaining. You'll probably lead the stampede into the nearest pub once it's all over,' Emily chided, laughingly.

'Fat chance of that! Mam would have a blue fit!'

'He's got beer in. I saw it last night,' Emily confided.

'Thank God for that, then! I was expecting it to be a "dry" house. Him bein' Welsh, like. I ain't never seen him in the pub. We'll all be spittin' feathers by the time we get back. You look nice, our Phoebe-Ann. Got a new frock then?'

Phoebe-Ann was leaning against the window ledge in the absence of any chairs. 'Miss Olivia gave it to me. She said it's not every day you get asked to your mam's wedding. She thought that was dead funny. I don't know why.'

Emily grimaced. 'You explain it to her, Jimmy. I'm off up to see Mam.'

Jimmy, who was in no mood to explain away Olivia Mercer's sarcasm, jerked his head at Emily's departing back. 'I'd get up the "dancers" with our Em. Mam's gettin' a bit airyated!'

Phoebe-Ann smoothed down the skirt of the blue and white print dress that Miss Olivia had told her was called an afternoon dress and patted the cream straw hat with the blue ribbon and decided to follow her sister. She had the distinct feeling that both Emily and Jimmy were poking fun at her.

'Oh! Mam!' Emily couldn't hide the emotion in her voice as she caught sight of Lily. 'Oh, Mam! You look lovely, you really do!'

'You don't think it's . . . well, a bit too dressy?' Lily stood up and turned around slowly.

'If you can't wear something dressy today then it's a poor do!'

'I got it at Sturla's in Great Homer Street this morning. Albert gave me the money to treat myself. I felt so extravagant. I've never spent so much on a dress!'

'It's about time you thought more of your-self and less of everyone else. Here, let me fix your hat.' Emily picked up the small grey hat and placed it on her mother's head. It had a bow of

47

plum-coloured ribbon that matched the plainly cut cotton dress.

Phoebe-Ann felt she was being left out and she was a little ashamed that she had caused such a fuss about the wedding. 'Oh, give it here, Em! Let me do it. It looks like a pimple on a mount stuck on like that! You've no idea! No style!'

Emily and Lily exchanged glances and Lily smiled. 'You always did have a way with hair and clothes.' She could read both her daughters like a book and she'd seen the contrition in Phoebe-Ann's face. And, even though she was nervous and getting more so by the minute, she had noted the new dress. 'Did Miss Olivia give you that?'

Emily prayed that Phoebe-Ann wouldn't tactlessly repeat Olivia's remarks but her sister was too engrossed in finding the right angle for the hat and only muttered 'Um.'

At last she stood back and admired her handiwork. 'There. Her next door will have eyes like hat pegs when she sees you!'

'Well, she's about as happy as an open grave anyway,' Emily added.

'Mam! Are you ready? Our Jack's going to lose 'is rag if he has to wait much longer! Says 'e's goin' down to the tram stop now! And this collar will 'ave wilted with the heat soon an all!'

Emily and Phoebe-Ann grinned. Jack wasn't noted for his patience.

Lily glanced around the room for the last time and felt a wave of sadness engulf her. She'd come here as a new bride. It held so many memories. All her children had been born in this room. It had been in here that she'd cried brokenly when Joe had died, and when Harry and then Rob had been killed. She felt a hand on her arm and saw Emily looking at her with concern.

'You're not going to start crying are you, Mam?'

'No, luv. I'm just being a bit daft, that's all.' She tilted her chin upwards. 'Let's get going or those two will have started without us and I wouldn't put it past them to tell Albert I'm not coming!'

Albert was standing on the steps of Brougham Terrace as they alighted from the tram in West Derby Road and crossed over to the Registry Office. He had no relatives and no friend close enough to ask to be best man so Jack had agreed to stand for him. Emily would be the other witness.

'We're not late, are we?' Lily asked, patting the side of her hat and feeling her stomach muscles contract.

'Not at all. You look very . . . nice.' He gave a little cough of embarrassment. He wasn't used to paying compliments. In fact he wasn't used to being the centre of attention. That was something he avoided like the plague. But she was smiling and, when he looked around, he realized everyone was and he felt more at ease.

'Best get inside then instead of standing here like refugees from Lewis's window!' Jack grinned, opening the door.

Phoebe-Ann didn't take much notice of the actual ceremony. It was very dour and official. The room was dour too, she thought. Unadorned walls painted chocolate brown, the woodwork bottle green. Just a bare table with a large book on it, a few chairs and no carpet or rug on the floor. She sniffed. You'd think they would brighten the place up a bit. It looked like a funeral parlour or the Labour Exchange and the registrar looked positively grim. Poor Mam. At least they could have put a vase of flowers somewhere. It wasn't like getting married. Not the way she'd envisaged a wedding. She'd have a proper wedding in a church full of flowers. A choir and bells. She'd have a gorgeous long, white satin dress and veil and arrive in a motor car. Everyone would comment on how beautiful she was, how grand an affair it was. She'd have a huge bouquet of roses and she'd throw it for Emily to catch . . .

'Move yourself, Fee!'

Emily's voice interrupted her dreams. 'What?'

'It's all over. Can't you keep your mind on one thing for more than five minutes! Go and give Mam a kiss!'

'I don't have to kiss *him* as well do I, Em?' she hissed.

'Not if you don't want to. Just shake his hand like our Jimmy's doing.' Emily gave her sister a little push and watched as Phoebe-Ann hugged her mother and then held out her hand to Albert who was now officially their stepfather.

When it was her turn she kissed Lily on the cheek and hugged her, then, smiling, she surprised herself and Albert by giving him a quick hug before stepping back, her cheeks flushed.

'I regret that I must interrupt the congratulations, but could you vacate the room, Mr Davies . . . Mrs Davies.' The registrar tried to sound apologetic.

'Doesn't that sound strange? Mrs Davies,' Phoebe-Ann said as they filed out and back into the bright sunshine.

'Shall we go home then, Mrs Davies?' Albert also found it a little strange but Lily smiled up at him.

'I think we will.' She slipped her arm through his.

'There's plenty of ale in lads, and some sherry for you . . . ladies.'

'And ham sandwiches, pies and a cake,' Lily added.

'We've got to get back, Mam. I'm sorry. I promised Miss Olivia I'd spend longer on her hair as she's going to the theatre tonight.'

'Never mind, luv.' Lily was a little disappointed.

'Save me some. I'll be home just after eight. They're going at eight sharp. I heard the Master telling Edwin,' Emily said.

'I'll come for a couple of hours too. If you want me to?' Phoebe-Ann asked, beginning to regret that she had decided to live in. She had the feeling that she'd cut off her nose to spite her face, as the saying went. The evenings were dreary with only Cook and Kitty for company. Edwin had so many chores to do that he didn't seem to have time to stop and chat and, when he did, she always felt he was laughing at her in a kind sort of way. Mrs Webster never sat with them. She had her own little parlour and liked to read.

'Of course we want you to, Phoebe-Ann. It is your home, too. Should you ever feel you want to move,' Albert offered, expansively.

She rewarded him with a bright smile but already her thoughts were on the dress Olivia was to wear and she began to ponder on what style she would dress her hair.

They parted company on the corner of Upper Canning Street after promising to return as soon as they could.

'That wasn't too bad now was it?' Emily remarked.

'I never said it would be bad!'

'You weren't exactly overjoyed! I thought that was the reason why you wouldn't move in with us?'

'I didn't know him then, did I?'

'None of us did. We still don't. Not really. But you took umbrage and got all airyated.'

'Oh, don't start on that, Em.'

They walked on in silence. The sun was losing some of its burning heat but the pavements were dusty and little clouds of flies hovered around the horse droppings on the cobbles and the litter in the gutter. Phoebe-Ann wrinkled her nose with distaste.

'We need a good heavy shower of rain to clear the air and that lot.' She nodded towards the manure.

'It would help to clear that lot, too!' Emily remarked acidly.

'What?'

'Don't look now but the Mona Street Mobsters are staggering along on the other side of the road! No need to get the *Echo* to find out when the *Mauretania*'s in dock, just wait for the brothers Malone to come staggering out of the nearest pub!'

Phoebe-Ann automatically turned her head and saw the three figures weaving their way from lamp-post to lamp-post. Another two were bringing up the rear, one holding the other up. Despite the fact that Emily had half whispered, half hissed her observations, Phoebe-Ann giggled, thinking how ridiculous they looked.

Everyone knew the brothers Malone or the Mona Street Mob as they were usually referred to. They lived in Mona Street with their ma, a ferocious old shawlie who wore long, black skirts covered by the voluminous black knitted shawl, a clay pipe always in her mouth. Ma Malone's hairstyles were awesome; the fashions of fifty years ago with numerous braids and plaits and tortuously intricate curls. She was a real harridan who was known to beat her sons with a broom handle when the mood took her, big as they were. And they were all big. They were all stokers and trimmers on the *Mauretania*, part of the notoriously hard-working, hard-drinking, often unruly 'black squads' who sweated down in the engine room, shovelling tons of coal into the huge furnaces for hours at a time. They terrorized the entire street, not to say the neighbourhood, when they were home. There were many who heartily wished the *Mauretania* would go off on a world cruise, taking the brothers Malone with her and not come back for at least five years.

'How they manage to stay out of Walton Jail I'll never know! For God's sake, Fee, don't encourage them!' Emily hissed for she'd seen one of them detach himself from a lamp-post and look towards them.

'I'm not!'

'Oh, God! He's trying to cross over! Walk faster!'

'I'm trying to! What's he shouting?'

Emily grabbed her sister's arm. 'I don't know and I don't want to know!'

'Stuck up pair of judies!' The words were so slurred they were hardly distinguishable. ' 'Ere, girl! I'm talkin' to yer!'

Phoebe-Ann glanced quickly across the road and deduced that he was too far gone with drink to move quickly, if at all, or negotiate his way safely across the road. 'Who're you gawpin' at? On yer bike!' she called.

Emily froze. Had Phoebe-Ann gone stark raving mad!

'Who're yer yellin' at? I'll put yer bleedin' eye in a sling!'

'Now see what you've done!'

Phoebe-Ann tossed her head defiantly. 'I'm not frightened of the likes of him! Dead common the lot of them!'

'You're mad!' Emily was aghast.

Phoebe-Ann laughed. 'He's so paralytic he can't get across the road.'

'Don't bank on it!' But Emily was relieved to see that Phoebe-Ann was right. One of the others was pulling his arm and they seemed to be arguing. She quickened her steps until they had safely turned the corner.

'Don't ever do that to me again! You'll have my hair turning grey!'

Phoebe-Ann laughed again. 'I bet he's just a big, soft dope when he's sober and he was quite good looking – for a Malone.'

'He's about as soft as a lump of pig iron! You don't help to shift one thousand tons of coal a day and stay soft! Any decent tendencies he had, Ma Malone beat out of him years ago I shouldn't wonder. You don't give the likes of him a second glance, do you hear me?'

Emily related the events of the afternoon in detail to Cook and Kitty but Phoebe-Ann went straight upstairs. As she entered the bedroom she looked around in total disbelief. Olivia was sitting on the bed, her hair loose, a pale blue silk robe around her shoulders and the entire contents of the wardrobe, the tallboy and the chests of drawers was scattered heedlessly on the bed and the floor.

'What's the matter, miss?'

'This is what's the matter! I've nothing to wear!' Olivia flung out both her arms.

'But I thought you were going to wear one of your new dresses? The ones Miss Drinkwater had sent around this morning?'

Olivia pointed to a crumpled heap of apple green

silk on the floor by the window. 'That's too tight! They must have measured me wrong! I couldn't even bear to try that one!' A trembling finger indicated another discarded garment. This one of lilac and white chiffon and satin.

'But you had them fitted!'

'And they still managed to get it all wrong! I've told Papa not to pay for them and to cancel our account! I knew I should have gone to Cripps! I can't go! I just can't go! Papa will have to go without me!' Her voice had risen an octave and tears had sprung into her eyes.

Phoebe-Ann rushed to comfort her. 'Of course you can! You've plenty of other dresses!'

'I've worn them all before! Everyone who is important will be there. I can't wear any of those old things, you stupid, stupid girl!'

Phoebe-Ann felt like smacking her face. Instead she composed her features in what she hoped was a look of tranquil authority. 'I'm sure you've only worn that lovely ice-turquoise once and you know you look stunning in it! I'll put your hair up and fasten the diamond clip in it and if you wear your mam's necklace, you'll outshine every woman there! You'll just sparkle!'

Olivia sniffed. 'Do you really think so?'

'Of course! Just wait until I've finished with you, everyone will be green with envy!'

'It is a lovely colour, isn't it?'

Phoebe-Ann sighed. The battle was nearly won. 'I'll hang it in the bathroom while I draw your bath. The steam will soon have those few creases out.' She picked up the dress. 'Just look how well it drapes. You'll look as though you're floating, not walking.'

Olivia, good humour restored, smiled. 'How did I ever manage without you for so long, Phoebe-Ann?'

Phoebe-Ann smiled back. 'Everyone admired the afternoon dress, miss,' she said, drawing Olivia's attention away from the subject of evening gowns. Olivia Mercer could change her mind and her temper in a flash. She knew that from experience.

'It always looked a mess on me. I don't know why I bought it. It's much too . . . ordinary.'

Phoebe-Ann didn't answer. Her mind was already on the amount of time it would take her to hang up, fold and put away the clothes that Olivia had so carelessly discarded and all that after getting her ready, reassuring her, flattering her. She'd be lucky to get home tonight. Home. It was strange that suddenly she thought of Albert Davies' house as home, but that's where her family was now and where they were, that was home. She'd try to get back for a bit, even if it was just half an hour. Even if she had to let Emily go on ahead of her. Then she remembered the Malones and felt apprehensive. 'Oh, don't be so daft!' she scolded herself. 'They'll all have passed out somewhere by now.' Mona Street was across the other side of Faulkner Street, she didn't need to go anywhere near it.

As she began to pick up the discarded finery, her thoughts turned back to the little altercation. The one who had shouted at them had been quite good looking in a dark, well-muscled sort of way and she wondered whether it was Jake Malone or his younger brother Seamus. Then she shrugged and turned her attention to the devastated room. Her mam would have given her a good hiding if she'd thrown everything she owned on the floor. But that was the difference between them. She had her mam. Olivia didn't. And then there was the little matter of Mr Mercer's wealth.

She sighed again as she began to pick up discarded clothes.

In the time she'd been back, she'd only seen James Mercer a few times and each time he'd stared at her morosely. He'd remained silent when she'd spoken, as though he hadn't heard her polite greetings. Emily sighed, thinking of how cheerful he'd been before the war.

There had been such a to-do over the proposed visit to the theatre, with Mr Mercer getting more and more annoyed as the minutes ticked by. Each one checked against his watch. He'd paced up and down the hall, looking very distinguished in his evening clothes, but redder in the face as Olivia failed to appear. The motor car had been brought to the front of the house and Edwin sat patiently waiting in the driving seat.

She'd been sent upstairs with a message. If Olivia wasn't down in exactly three minutes he was going alone and that was final! She'd taken one look at Phoebe-Ann's harassed expression and grimaced at her sister before announcing the ultimatum. It had worked, for Olivia knew her father meant what he said. Such utterances were usually preceded by, 'You, miss, have gone your ninety nine and three quarters – you'll not make the hundred!' It was an odd saying, one of his idiosyncrasies, but she knew she'd pushed him to the limit of his patience.

As the door had slammed shut behind them, Phoebe-Ann had sunk down on the bottom stair, exhausted.

'I'm worn out!'

'Thank God she's gone! I've just got to take Master James his coffee, then I'll get my coat.'

'I can't see me getting home tonight! You should see what a mess she's left up there! Every bloody dress she owns is on the floor and all the stockings and shoes and wraps! I'll swing for her yet, so help me!'

Emily felt sorry for her. 'Tell you what, you take the coffee and I'll go and make a start upstairs.'

'Oh, Em, would you?'

'I said I would. Besides, I don't feel up to making polite conversation with Master James. He ignores me. Just looks at me with that blank expression. Gives me the creeps!'

Phoebe-Ann got up and straightened her cap. 'It's such a shame, but the last twice when I've spoken to him he's smiled.'

Emily shrugged. 'Must be something I said then.'

The twilight was deepening as Phoebe-Ann entered the drawing room carrying the small gallery tray. 'I've brought your coffee, Master James. Your Pa and Miss Olivia have gone. I thought there would be ructions she was so late and your Pa was getting madder and madder! Shall I switch on the lights and draw the curtains? It's getting dark,' she prattled on as she moved towards the light switch.

'No! I like to sit in the dark!'

She stopped and stared at him. It was such a shame to see him like this and he was so handsome. 'But why?'

He didn't answer but she moved closer, sensing his desolation and feeling drawn to him, though she didn't know why.

'I have to see things clearly in the light. I hate it! I hate the sunlight and I hate the harshness of electricity. Can you understand that, Phoebe-Ann?'

She tried. 'Is it like waking up with the sun shining

58

right into your eyes . . . a bit of a shock after the darkness?'

'A bit like that. In the darkness, images are blurred, sounds muffled. I don't see their faces, hear their cries . . .'

He looked so tormented that she was stricken with pity for him and she knelt down beside his chair. He was looking past her without really seeing her. 'Who, sir? Who don't you want to see?'

'All those men . . . boys . . . all my friends. My father and Doctor Coleman say I must forget. Banish them from my memory. I must not talk about them, but I can't! I can't! Don't the fools understand? I can never forget their screams, their pleading to die as they hung trapped by the wire . . . the bloody wire!' His voice was shaking and his hands trembled and the tears poured down his cheeks, unheeded.

Phoebe-Ann was mesmerized by his words. His tears caused a mist to blur her own vision. She forgot who he was and her own position. She reached out and touched his cheek and then he was in her arms, clinging to her.

'Tell me about it? You can tell me. I'll listen and it will help. I know it will. I'll listen.'

She didn't comprehend half of what he said. His words were jumbled. Names and places, some she'd heard of, others she hadn't. She only knew that he needed comforting the way she had. The way Emily had comforted her, held her and soothed her the night she heard that Rob had been killed.

At length he became quiet and drew away from her. He was more in control of himself she thought as she got to her feet, although he still held her hand.

'I'm sorry, Phoebe-Ann.' His voice was low.

59

'What for? There's no need to be sorry. I understand.'

He looked up at her. 'Do you? How can you?'

'I lost two brothers. One . . . one was my twin. He was part of me was our Rob.' She pressed her free hand to her breast, wishing she could find the right words to explain the bond that had been between them.

'Then you do understand. You're a sweet, kind girl, Phoebe-Ann.'

'Thank you.' Gently she withdrew her hand, feeling a little awkward now that reality seemed to have overtaken him. She bit her lip as she remembered Emily. She'd be mad at being left to clear up alone. She turned to go.

'Will you come and talk to me again? Sit with me and tell me about . . . Rob?'

'If you want me to. I . . . I've never really spoken about him to anyone except our Emily.'

'Then it will help us both. Will you promise, Phoebe-Ann?'

'I promise, sir.' She smiled and was rewarded with a ghost of his former smile and she knew a bond had been forged between them.

Chapter Four

Although the war had been over for nearly a year, it wasn't until the end of July that the street parties, or victory parties as they were called, were held, and Lonsdale Street prepared along with all the others.

For weeks, women had been gathering together the makings for sandwiches and cakes and sewing scraps of material for bunting. The men had all clubbed together to buy the beer. The old, one-legged organ grinder had been persuaded to 'come and cheer us all up', while Albert, who was the only one in the street who owned a piano and a house big enough to hold it, was cajoled by Lily into allowing it to be man-handled into the street and into playing it. His protestations that 'I can only play hymns, luv!' were laughingly ignored and, while Lily busied herself with sandwiches, he began to try to play the more popular songs by ear.

'I'm off to the *Grecian* for a bit of peace and quiet. It's like Fred Karno's circus in here!' Jack grumbled, wincing at Albert's attempt at 'It's a Long Way to Tipperary'.

'You'll be out of luck – they're closed!' Lily announced with a note of triumph in her voice.

'They can't be! They never close!'

'Well, they are today! This dinner time anyway. Open again later on, Dolly told me. "I can't be expected to get a party tea ready with half of Toxteth traipsing in and wanting serving!" were her exact words.'

'Some victory party if a bloke can't get a drink in peace!'

'You're lucky, lad. I've got to keep them all entertained on the piano and I don't think "Abide With Me" will go down too well. Not when they want "Pack Up Your Troubles".'

'I've got a good idea! Later on . . .' Jimmy got no further.

'Don't you dare think you're going to go sloping off, either of you nor our Jack either! You're going to enjoy yourselves here, in Lonsdale Street! Now get out of my way while I get a bit of muslin over this lot before the flies get at them!'

'Yes, Mam,' Jimmy answered glumly while Albert grinned and winked.

Hearing the door, Lily turned and shouted, 'Is that you, Emily?'

'No. It's me, Mam.' Phoebe-Ann looked pretty in her dark pink skirt and fresh white blouse and with her hair tied up with a pink ribbon.

'Where is she? She promised to give me a hand?'

'She'll be here soon. Can I have one of these? It's ages since I had my breakfast.'

Lily playfully slapped the outstretched hand. 'Hold your horses miss! You can have one, no more, or these two will start complaining.'

The plate was consigned to the dresser and Lily attacked another large loaf with the carving knife. 'Go and help Mrs Harper with the flags if you want to make yourself useful.'

Phoebe-Ann pulled a face. 'Do I have to?'

'No, you don't *have* to! You can sit here being Lady

Muck if you like, but don't expect anything to eat!' came the tart reply.

Phoebe-Ann raised her eyes, shrugged and went out into the street.

'Imagines herself to be like Miss Olivia Mercer she does. Oh, there's no harm in her, she just needs taking down a peg or two at times,' Lily said.

'Here's our Emily and she's got someone with her,' Jimmy remarked, peering out of the window.

Lily hastily wiped her hands on her apron. 'Who? Dear God, she hasn't gone and brought Miss Olivia with her has she?'

'Give over, Mam! The likes of that one wouldn't be seen dead in this street,' Jimmy scoffed.

'I hope you don't mind, but I brought Edwin along,' Emily announced as she entered, followed by a grinning Edwin.

Lily looked relieved. 'It's a while since I've seen you, lad. How's your aunty? I used to see her down Great Homer Street every Saturday but it's been months since I set eyes on her.'

'She doesn't get out as much now. Her rheumatics . . .' He'd lived with his Aunt Sarah for as long as he could remember. She was his mother's only sister and she'd never married. Something she didn't regret at all, she now said. His mam and dad had both died in an epidemic of fever when he'd been four.

'Poor soul. My old mam was a martyr to it.' Albert got up and offered his hand to the tall, dark-haired lad. 'You're welcome.'

'Emily Parkinson where's your manners? You should have introduced Edwin and Albert properly!'

'Sorry. Edwin, this is Albert, my stepfather. Albert, this is . . .'

'Oh, stop that! You're making a mockery of it all!' Lily cried and they all laughed.

'Will you have a glass of something?' Albert asked, not forgetting his position as host.

'Bit early in the day for me, yet, but thanks just the same.'

Emily had gone into the back kitchen followed by Lily and the two men stared at each other.

'Left it a bit late for victory parties to my mind. Should have had them months ago. Were you in the army or the navy?' Albert asked.

'Army. King's Own Liverpool Regiment, same as Jimmy here.'

Albert nodded. It was a regiment that had suffered as much as, if not more than, most.

'Never did understand what it was all about. Thought I did at first. King and country . . . all that.' Edwin faltered. He hated talking about it.

'We all did,' Jimmy muttered.

'You're not alone in that. I couldn't grasp all the ins and outs. Seemed such a bloody waste and all for a few miles of mud. Don't really understand all this treaty business either,' Albert continued.

'Maybe it's best we don't.'

'Aye. Let's just hope they've all learned their lessons this time. I was too old to go myself but I heard the stories and I've heard you and your brother yelling in your sleep.' Albert nodded towards Jimmy who looked down at his boots. No-one wanted to talk about their experiences.

'No need to think I think any the less of you, Jim, and I know how much your mam still grieves for Harry and young Rob.'

'There'll be thousands of women who have little to celebrate today.'

64

They all turned to see Lily standing in the doorway. Albert looked abashed. 'I'm sorry, luv.'

'You all look as though you've lost half a crown and found sixpence. It's supposed to be a party,' Emily reminded them, coming in behind her mother.

'You're right. Let's go and see how Phoebe-Ann's doing.'

'And I'm off to see if the *Grecian* really is closed.'

Lily began to protest but Albert silenced her with a quick shake of his head. When they'd gone he put his arm around her. 'Let them go, Lil. Let them look forward, not back. Let them enjoy themselves. God knows those lads went through enough!'

'We all did,' she sighed.

By the time the sun had become a huge ball of fire and had dipped below the spire of St Nathaniel's church and the streetlights were lit, everyone was in a high good humour. Every scrap of food had been eaten and most of the beer had gone too. Children, their faces sticky, their clothes dusty, dodged between the tables that had been placed end to end in the middle of the street. The younger ones sat on doorsteps, thumbs in their mouths, eyelids drooping, leaning contentedly against their older brothers and sisters.

They'd started the day off with 'The National Anthem', then 'Rule Britannia', followed by 'Land of Hope and Glory' and on to the popular songs until Albert declared that if he didn't have a bit of a rest his arms would drop off and his stomach felt that his throat had been cut.

He was instantly deluged with offers of food and drink. Lily leaned against her doorpost and smiled at him. She'd never known him to be so chatty and she'd caught the nudges and raised eyebrows of some of the other women and knew they were thinking the same thing. But he was enjoying himself, she knew that, and she was glad, for he had transformed her life and, although she didn't have a deep and burning passion for him, she was fond of him and she was grateful. Her smile faded as she caught sight of Phoebe-Ann flirting with the eldest of the Ashton brood from number sixteen. She worried about Phoebe-Ann. She wished she had Emily's quick, perceptive mind and common sense. Her one dread was that Phoebe-Ann would fall hopelessly in love with some 'no mark' who would treat her badly. Still, she comforted herself with the fact that she had little time for gallivanting now she was back with the Mercers.

Lily's smile returned as she caught sight of Emily and Edwin Leeson leaning on the top of the piano and laughing together. That was a sight that pleased her. He was a good lad and she liked him. She knew the sort of family he came from. His Aunt Sarah was much respected. He was a hard worker, honest and loyal and he had his old job back. She'd raise no objections to that match if it ever came about.

Emily was unaware of her mother's speculative gaze. She hadn't enjoyed herself so much for years. All the scraping and making do was over, as was the worrying and waiting. The future looked rosy and she'd found Edwin far more entertaining and interesting than she'd done before the war. But she'd been barely out of school then, she reasoned.

'I told you you'd enjoy it.'

'A right little Miss Knowall, aren't you?' he teased.

'Not always, but I thought you needed cheering up.'

66

'Oh, did you? Have I been going around with my chin on the floor or something?'

She laughed. 'No, but you just seemed a bit down and you're not the only one. What *is* the matter with Master James? Not a single word can I get out of him, although our Phoebe-Ann seems to find plenty to talk to him about and she swears he talks to her for hours, but then she always did exaggerate.'

Edwin's smile vanished. 'He just needs time to get over it. I saw a lot of men like that. He'll be all right.'

'Well, whatever it is they talk about must have some effect on him. I've seen him. He follows her with his eyes. Watches her every movement, sort of intent yet . . . hopefully, if you know what I mean? Oh, I'm useless at putting into the right words what I mean!'

'I can always understand you, Em.'

She let her gaze drop. Was she imagining it or was there a different tone in his voice and why did she suddenly feel confused and silly? She raised her hand to her cheek then snatched it away. She was blushing! Thank God it was dark and the bonfire at the top of the street had been lit and was blazing cheerfully, throwing out an orange glow that would disguise her flushed cheeks. But she was wrong.

'You're blushing, Emily Parkinson!'

'I'm not!' she retorted.

He reached and took her hand and squeezed it. 'You should be. All nice girls do when men pay this much attention to them.'

She tried to snatch her hand away but he held it tightly. 'Do you like me, Emily?'

'Of course I like you! I always have!'

'You know what I mean. Stop acting as though you don't. I like you. I'd go so far as to say I'm fond of you, Em.'

67

Things were going too fast and she should have some polite reply ready but she could think of nothing and her heart was beginning to thump wildly against her ribs. 'I . . . I . . . do like you, Edwin.'

'Enough to come out with me on our next day off?'

She nodded. Unable to trust herself to speak.

He squeezed her hand again but, as Albert returned to resume his expertise on the piano, urged on by half a dozen very merry men and women, she just smiled at him and was content to watch the merriment, her hand still in his, until the moment was shattered by the clanging of bells and the shout of 'Eh, up! It's the fire bobby come to put the damper on things! Stoke up the fire, kids! Give 'em something to work at!' and they both laughed.

The flames of the numerous bonfires and the sounds of the celebrations could be seen and heard in Upper Huskisson Street. James Mercer sat in his darkened room facing the half-open window and, as the festivities progressed, his depression increased. His mind was tormented by the horrific images and sounds that invaded it until he felt that his head would explode. It was all happening again: the thundering of the guns, the flashes of exploding shells, the cries, the screams and it was his fault. They had been his orders, he'd sent them all over the top, he'd sent them to their agonizing deaths while he'd come through unscathed. He could hear himself shouting to them now but it was too late! Too late!

A slow, gut-churning anger began to take hold of him. It hadn't been all his fault. Someone else had given those orders. Nameless, faceless men who sat in safe, warm, comfortable places. Well, he'd take no more of their orders! He'd send no more men or boys to die in the mud! Obstacles seemed to bar his way. Obstacles he really couldn't distinguish, but they were there, and they were stopping them all from leaving. The anger increased to fury and he lashed out, hurling the objects out of his path. He was getting out, they were getting out and nothing or no-one was going to stop them this time.

Richard Mercer and Olivia had just finished dinner when the first crash shattered the silence of the house. It was followed by another and the sound of breaking glass and china.

'Oh, Papa! Papa, what was that?' Olivia screamed.

'Sit down, Olivia! I'll see what's happened. You stay here.'

As he hastened up the stairs the splintering of furniture continued, accompanied by curses and shouts. His face paled as he thought, 'He's lost control! He's lost control of himself!'

Total devastation met his eyes as he flung open the door and switched on the light. Furniture lay broken and splintered and overturned. The long mirror had been shattered and the ornaments and clock lay amongst the debris. The curtains were torn and the window had been smashed, its glass carpeting the floor, its wooden lathes and spars hanging brokenly. But his horrified gaze rested on his son who was sitting on the bed, shaking, fighting for breath, his features haggard, his eyes wild with terror. Richard Mercer was shocked to the core.

'James! James! For God's sake what happened?' He laid a hand on his son's shoulder.

'I was trapped! We were all trapped! We couldn't get out!' He gazed up at his father, the terror receding, to be replaced by confusion. 'I didn't . . . I couldn't have done . . . this?'

Richard Mercer pulled himself together. 'It's all right, James! It was just a sort of nightmare. These things happen, so I'm told, after . . . after terrible experiences. There's no need to be alarmed or afraid. None of this matters.' He gestured with his hand towards the wrecked bedroom.

'I . . . I did all that? I can't remember. There were flames and shouting . . .' He was calmer.

'Just the victory parties in the streets around the corner. Nothing to worry about at all. Nothing. We'll move your things into one of the guest rooms for tonight.' He continued to pat his son's shoulder. 'Nothing but a nightmare. I'll get you a drink and then you'll be able to sleep peacefully.'

Olivia was standing at the bottom of the stairs, clutching the carved newel post. 'What's the matter, Papa?'

'Nothing to worry about. James had a rather bad nightmare, some things got broken. I'm going to put him in one of the guest rooms and get him a stiff drink.'

'But Edwin's not here. He's at the victory party, they all are!'

'That's not important. I'll help him . . . move. Now, off you go to where ever it was you said you were going. Abigail's, was it?' He managed a smile. 'And enjoy yourself, your brother's fine.'

As he watched her go up the stairs he sighed with relief. He was thankful that Edwin, Emily and Phoebe-Ann were not in the house. The least everyone knew the better. He'd clear up the mess himself and think up a suitable explanation. It *was* just a nightmare. Nothing more sinister than that, he told himself.

70

Chapter Five

Olivia was bored. The soirée was the only thing she had to look forward to and even the preparations for that had begun to pall. Twice her father had impressed upon her the fact that she should now try to perform the duties of hostess with the same calm dignity her mother had always radiated on such occasions. She'd been horrified. She was only eighteen and he wanted her to behave like a matron of twenty-eight! She was young. She wanted to have fun. She didn't want to be dignified, for that word she had in her mind substituted 'dull'. The more she thought about it, the less interested and excited she felt. The way things were going it would be a dreadful evening. And James would be no help either.

He was no fun at all these days, not the way he'd been before the war. Then he'd always been ready for a joke or some kind of a lark, and his recent violent outburst had frightened her. What had made him act like that? She supposed he had some kind of illness but everyone was very vague on the subject. She stared morosely out of the window. It was hot and sticky. There wasn't a breath of wind. Not a leaf rustled on the trees that lined the road. It was going to be a very boring weekend and a longer one than usual for Monday was a bank holiday. Everyone would be taking advantage of the good weather to go somewhere or do something.

She turned away and sat down at the dressing table

studying her reflection in the mirror with distaste. She hated her hair even more than usual today. When the weather was so hot it was heavy and even more inclined to curl up. She brightened as an idea took hold of her and she smiled. She'd have it cut in the new short style. Yes, that's what she'd do! Papa wouldn't like it but she wasn't going to let that stop her. She gathered up the copper ringlets and tried to arrange them in an approximation of the short bob. She was certain she would suit it and perhaps she would start a trend. She'd read that lots of girls in London had had their long locks shorn, but she'd not seen a single girl in Liverpool who'd dared to follow the new fashion. But she would and she might even get her picture in the paper, in the society column of course.

The sounds of the street came floating in through the open window and some of her excitement faded. It was Saturday lunch time so who could she ask to accompany her on her excursion? There was Abigail but she'd just go on and on about her forthcoming wedding and she was sick of hearing about how wonderful life would become when she was married. And Abbie was such a stick in the mud that she'd probably be horrified by her plan. She could ask Marjorie but then she remembered that she was playing tennis with Freddie and he was so sickeningly stupid.

'It's another scorcher, miss.'

Olivia turned at the sound of Phoebe-Ann's voice. 'I hate the heat and it gives me a headache!' she replied, peevishly.

Phoebe-Ann sighed. Olivia was obviously in one of her moods. It would take all her powers of persuasion and flattery to coax her into a better humour.

'Shall I get you an aspirin?'

'No, they make me feel sick!'

'Shall I draw you a bath? It may cool you a little as long as it's not too hot.'

Olivia glared at her. 'I've already had one bath today!' She paused and tilted her head to one side. 'Phoebe-Ann, do you think I'd suit my hair short?'

Phoebe-Ann's eyebrows shot up. 'Short!'

'Yes. I saw a new style in a magazine and it looked so . . . modern.'

'Oh, miss! Don't have your beautiful hair cut off!'

'Why not? It's so old fashioned and so impossible to manage and it gives me a headache! I honestly think that's why I get so many headaches! There is so much of it and it's so heavy! So, you see it will be for . . . medical reasons as well!'

Phoebe-Ann looked at her as though she had lost her senses. She often wished her own hair would curl, instead of being dead straight, but to cut it . . . !

'Don't look at me like that! As though I've suggested I walk stark naked down Bold Street! Look. It's so . . . chic!' Olivia picked up the magazine and leafed through the pages until she found what she was looking for, then she shoved it towards Phoebe-Ann.

'Well, it does look . . . different,' Phoebe-Ann conceded doubtfully.

'That's settled then! Has Papa gone out?'

'Yes. About fifteen minutes ago.'

Olivia's eyes were shining. 'I'll get dressed and we'll go to town.' A plan was forming in her mind and it made her eyes sparkle with mischief.

'We?'

'You can come with me.'

'Me?'

'Yes, you! I've got this wonderful idea! It will be such fun!'

73

Phoebe-Ann caught some of Olivia's excitement. It was a great treat to be allowed to accompany Olivia, to see all the beautiful things she bought and they were treated with such deference in the shops. At least Miss Olivia was. She just carried the parcels.

'I'll wear the cream linen two-piece with the blue blouse,' Olivia decided.

By the time they got to Bold Street it was crowded with shoppers and the sun's heat was fiery. A young lad, clad in trousers too big for him and a patched shirt, was standing outside the entrance to Central Station selling the *Daily Post*. 'Police strike! Police to go on strike! Read all about it!' he bawled.

Phoebe-Ann bought a copy. 'Oh, miss! Do you think it will come to a strike? What will we do if it does?'

Olivia looked at her as though she were speaking a foreign language. 'What does it matter if they do have their silly strike?'

'What will people do without them?'

'I'm sure I don't know, nor do I care! Throw it away and stop fussing!'

Phoebe-Ann did as she was told and followed her mistress into the Salon Augustine with trepidation and foreboding. Feelings that soon gave way to fascination as she watched Olivia's long, shining curls fall to the floor accompanied by cries of admiration from the whole staff. The small Frenchman deftly snipped and cut until at last he stood back and admired his handiwork with a cry of pure delight.

There was a communal sigh of approval from everyone.

Olivia clapped her hands. 'Oh, it feels so . . . so light! I feel light-headed! It's . . . it's gorgeous!

Everyone will come rushing to follow my lead, I know they will!'

Phoebe-Ann had to admit that it did suit Olivia's pert features and she herself had always been a devotee of fashion, in such minor ways as she could afford. For a second she envied Olivia her wealth and the freedom it brought. 'It does suit you, miss. It really does!'

Olivia's eyes sparkled as she jumped up. She smiled archly at the small, wiry hairdresser and winked. 'Now it's your turn.'

'Me!' Phoebe-Ann gasped.

'Yes! Today I'm going to transform you! It's my . . . my project for today! You're to have a completely new image and I will supervise it and pay for it! You should be delighted and very grateful that I take such an interest in you! Don't sit there with your mouth hanging open like a codfish! Monsieur is waiting!'

Phoebe-Ann's hands went instinctively to her long hair, neatly pinned up beneath her hat, her eyes wide with horror. Miss Olivia must be joking! She must be! 'My mam would kill me, miss! She really would! I mean it's . . . it's fine er . . . right that someone like you should . . . but me . . . ! She'll kill me!' she stammered.

Olivia was annoyed and impatient. 'Phoebe-Ann Parkinson you are the most ungrateful . . . stubborn . . . unimaginative person I've ever met! Do you want to look drab and dull all your life? You always used to say you'd give anything to look like me and now you're refusing the chance! How insulting! I know you would look wonderful with the right clothes and the right hairstyle! You could even find yourself a young man to sweep you off your feet and take you away from all that!' Olivia threw out a hand to indicate

Phoebe-Ann's plain clothes and demure hat. 'You could you know and don't tell me you would pass that up!' Olivia didn't really believe her own statement but she was annoyed that Phoebe-Ann would ruin her plans and besides, maybe Papa wouldn't be quite so difficult to handle if Phoebe-Ann's hair had been cut too.

Phoebe-Ann was finding that her alarm and trepidation were fading as she caught some of Olivia's excitement. She couldn't refuse such generosity. She'd be mad to pass up this opportunity and maybe she really could find a nice young man who wasn't short of money. Not dressed like this she couldn't, but in an outfit like Miss Olivia's . . . 'Well, if you really do think . . .'

Before she had time to protest further she was steered towards the chair. A fluffy white towel was draped around her shoulders, her hat removed, the hair pins withdrawn and her hair brushed out.

When the first blonde tress fell to the floor, her heart sank and she tried not to think about what her mam would say, but as Olivia darted from side to side exclaiming with little cries of delight, she forgot all about Lily.

When Monsieur had finished she couldn't believe it was really herself staring back at her from the mirror, for a shining cap of bouncy blonde hair framed her face. 'It doesn't look like me! I feel . . . new!'

'You will be "new" when I've finished with you! Next stop Cripps and then De Jong et Cie!' Olivia was in her element. She was wondering if she could pass Phoebe-Ann off as a new friend? Wouldn't that be fun! Maybe to Abbie; she was a bit dense.

Phoebe-Ann followed Olivia out into the street as the entire staff of the salon waved them goodbye. Her head felt curiously light and she looked around to see if anyone was looking at her. Quite a few heads turned in their direction.

Olivia sank down in the velvet covered chair the deferential assistant in Cripps set out for her. 'We want to try everything, please! And hats and shoes and gloves as well!' she demanded imperiously.

Two hours later they emerged carrying numerous parcels and Phoebe-Ann felt as though she was walking on air. A pert straw cloche hat with a large satin bow on the side, covered her hair and matched the coral-coloured dress with the dropped waist which made her look taller and even more slender. It had a handkerchief hemline that was shorter than she'd ever worn before. Her legs were encased in silk stockings and she wore cream kid shoes with an hour-glass heel and a strap over the instep. Her uniform had been packed in a box.

When the doorman held open the door and murmured 'Good afternoon, madam' she nearly giggled. He hadn't even given her a second look when they'd gone in. 'Do I really look . . . like a lady?' she whispered.

'Oh, every inch! Now, let's have some tea. I'm quite worn out.' Olivia feigned exhaustion.

As she followed Olivia into the tea rooms, Phoebe-Ann began to feel apprehensive. What if she did something wrong and made a terrible gaffe and embarrassed Miss Olivia and made a complete show of herself? 'Can I just sit here and not have any tea?' she whispered as Olivia smiled up at the waitress who was enquiring what 'modom' would like.

'Don't be silly! A pot of tea for two and . . . I think some scones?'

'Cream and jam, madam?'

Olivia nodded. The waitress scribbled on her pad and walked away. Olivia glanced around to see if there was anyone she knew to whom she could show off her handiwork. There wasn't. She sighed irritably. How disappointing.

Phoebe-Ann ate very slowly, praying the cream wouldn't ooze out nor the jam slide off and on to her dress. Olivia drank her tea quickly and then started to tap her fingers on the table impatiently. 'What shall we do now? It's far too early to go back.'

'We could go down to the Pierhead and perhaps go for a sail on the ferry?' Phoebe-Ann suggested. She, too, was loath to return to Upper Huskisson Street. She wanted to be admired and stared at.

Olivia looked disdainful. 'With all those common people! It's such a crush!' Then she smiled. 'Yes, we will go to the Pierhead! There's bound to be one of Papa's ships in. We could ask someone to take us on a tour.'

'The *Mauretania*'s in. I do know that,' Phoebe-Ann supplied, thinking of the Malones.

'She'll do. Finish your tea and collect your things! We'll take a taxi.'

Phoebe-Ann did as she was told for she'd never been in a taxi before. Olivia was offering another treat.

The Pierhead was crowded but, as she followed Olivia to the Princes Landing Stage and craned her neck to see the towering black hull and four red and black funnels of the *Mauretania*, she felt her spirits soar. 'Oh, miss, wouldn't it be wonderful to be sailing on her?'

'That's what we'll do! We'll pretend we're just starting off on a cruise. It could be fun! I don't know why I never thought of that before. A cruise! Yes, I think I'd like to go on a cruise.'

'She doesn't do that, miss. She only goes to America.'

Olivia cast her a withering look. 'I know that! I was just pretending! Use your imagination!' She looked thoughtful. 'I could go on another ship. One that does cruise. I might even take you with me.'

When they reached the bottom of the gangway, Olivia tapped the arm of the young officer. 'My name is Olivia Mercer.' She paused waiting for his reaction.

Instead he scanned the long list of names he was holding. 'Sorry, miss. I can't find you on here.'

'Don't be impertinent! I'm not a passenger! My father is Richard Mercer, he owns this ship!'

He stared at her hard.

'Well, he is a director of the Company! I . . . we would like to "look around". Do a tour of inspection, so to speak.'

He was sceptical and became flustered for other passengers were milling around and starting to complain. 'I'd better get the Chief, miss.'

Olivia was annoyed. 'Get whoever you wish but don't take all day about it!'

The confusion at the bottom of the gangway had been spotted and another officer appeared. 'What's the hold up?'

'Er, this lady says she is Mr Richard Mercer's daughter and she and her friend would like to look around before we sail.'

George Moore, the Chief Electrical Officer, gritted his teeth and was sorry he'd intervened. God Almighty! Wasn't there enough confusion and enough work to do before they sailed without having to escort two spoiled brats around a ship already crowded with passengers and their families and friends who had come to see them off! But if she complained to her father, and by the look on her face she would do just that, he shrugged. 'Would you follow me, ladies?' He even managed a smile. Spoiled bitch!

Phoebe-Ann was more excited than she'd ever been in her entire life. He had called her a 'lady'! She just wished the brothers Malone could see her now. Their eyes would be like doorstops but they'd be down in the engine room.

Along the miles of crowded corridors they went. Through the second and third class smoking rooms and dining rooms. Up the magnificent sweeping staircase and on through the first class lounge with its ornate glass ceiling, wood panelled walls, brocade covered chairs and sofas. Its long windows were draped with velvet hangings while rich carpet covered the entire floor. She'd never seen such magnificence and splendour and glancing at Olivia she could see even she was impressed.

Each room was more sumptuous than the last, she thought, and it was so big. In fact it wasn't like being on a ship at all. She was mesmerized by the beauty and the activity as stewards and stewardesses and bellboys and passengers rushed past them.

When they reached the promenade deck and she looked down over the side she felt dizzy. They were so high up!

With the end of the tour now in sight, George Moore hastily pointed out the landmarks of the Liverpool waterfront and those on the opposite bank of the Mersey. Olivia didn't seem interested but Phoebe-Ann hung on his every word.

They both jumped as the ship's whistle blasted out.

A great bellow of sound that obliterated all other noises. They'd seen the bellboys beating their gongs and shouting 'All ashore that's going ashore!' but like everyone else they'd ignored them.

'Time to leave,' the chief 'sparks' announced. 'We sail in a few minutes. Better get ashore or you might find yourselves passengers,' he joked.

Phoebe-Ann thought how wonderful that would be but already he was walking briskly ahead of them and they joined the crowd of people assembling at the top of the gangway.

She would have liked to have watched the ship leave but Olivia hustled her towards the taxi rank as it was dusk. She'd been so engrossed that she'd lost track of the time. As she leaned back against the seat in the taxi she felt as though the whole day had been a wonderful dream. It had been glorious. 'I can never thank you enough, miss, for today. It's been . . . Oh, I wish I could find the right words!'

Olivia smiled. Phoebe-Ann's naive enthusiasm was becoming tiresome and she was now absorbed in a new plan. She would see Papa about it this very evening. A trip to America, that's what she wanted him to sanction. To New York, Boston. Why had she never thought of it before? She had been very impressed with the *Mauretania*. Of course she knew the Cunard ships were the best, the fastest, the safest, but she'd never really realized just how luxurious they were. She had also been attracted by the number of young men she'd seen in the palatial public rooms; men who had looked at her with open admiration. She'd been under the impression that only old men and wealthy spinsters or dowagers went cruising. There were, of course, all those second and third class passengers, but she would never even contemplate having anything to do with them. She fell silent, engrossed in her thoughts and schemes.

As they reached the bottom of Brownlow Hill the cab stopped.

Olivia leaned forward. 'Why have we stopped?'

'Don't like the look of this crowd, miss.'

'Don't be stupid! Drive on!' she demanded.

The cabby ignored her.

Phoebe-Ann looked out of the window and gasped. Ahead of them there was a mob of about a hundred people, shouting and jeering. She could hear the sound of breaking glass and then she remembered the newspaper. 'Oh, miss! The police are on strike! Don't you remember the newspaper?'

'What has that to do with us for heaven's sake!' Olivia snapped.

'Sorry, ladies! I ain't goin' any further and if you take my advice you'll get out and run back to Church Street.'

'I am not running anywhere and neither are you! Drive on!' Olivia shouted.

To their consternation he got out and opened the passenger door.

Olivia lost her temper. 'Oh, go away! Run away if you want to! I'm not frightened of those . . . those common people!'

'You should be! They're drunk and capable of anything! Give me your parcels and we'll all scarper! Hurry up!'

'I'll do no such thing! You get back in the driving seat and do what you're paid to do – drive!'

'Don't be bloody stupid! This cab is my living but if I try to drive through them I'll have no bloody cab and no bloody life either! Now get a move on! I'm not waiting for much longer!'

Phoebe-Ann was afraid and she tugged at Olivia's arm. 'He's right! I mean if he's willing to leave his taxi he must be right!'

'He's a fool, that's what he is! And a coward to boot! I'll drive the damned thing myself!'

'Well, I'm off! You've had your chance!' The driver turned and began to run.

Panic began to grip Phoebe-Ann. 'If we hurry we can catch him up!'

'Oh, let him go! We'll manage!'

'Do you know how to drive, miss?' Phoebe-Ann was near to tears.

'Of course I do! James used to let me drive his car, it's easy!'

Olivia climbed into the front seat and started to push and pull the gear lever. At least the engine was still running, she didn't have to crank it with the heavy handle. Not that there would have been time for that. They jerked forward, stopped and jerked forward again and Phoebe-Ann uttered a scream.

'Shut up, Phoebe-Ann! I'm doing my best!' Olivia's frown disappeared as they moved forward again, slowly but evenly this time and she became more confident as they picked up speed.

Phoebe-Ann stuck her head out of the window. The crowd was getting nearer and she could clearly hear the cries and curses. Soon they would be in the thick of it. She began to shake and gnawed nervously on her bottom lip. She was terrified.

Olivia's confidence was waning as she suddenly realized the consequences of her actions. She hadn't thought there were so many of them and they did appear to be drunk and some of the curses brought a flush to her cheeks. She had to get away from them! She looked around for an avenue of escape. There was none. In her fright she pushed her foot down hard on the accelerator and the car shot forward, taking them into the front ranks of the mob.

'This is all your fault!' she screamed at Phoebe-Ann as the crowd surged around them.

Phoebe-Ann didn't hear her. She had sunk back against the seat as far away from the rough, villainous faces that were pressing against the windows as possible. She wanted to go home. She wanted to be plain Phoebe-Ann Parkinson again in her dull clothes and with her long hair pinned up under her hat. She wanted her mam and Emily and Jack and Jimmy. She uttered a terrified scream as she felt the cab rock. She heard the sound of breaking glass as the head-lights were smashed and a tattoo of blows rained upon the roof. She was rigid with terror.

Then the crowd seemed to be moving on and thinning out and she started to cry in earnest and with relief as she caught sight of the men in dark blue uniforms who charged past, truncheons drawn and flailing, their faces grim.

Olivia screamed at her. 'You said they were on strike! You stupid little liar!'

Phoebe-Ann sobbed harder. She didn't care if she was stupid or a liar or anything else. She just wanted to go home.

The door was opened by a burly, bewhiskered policeman. His uniform was torn and dusty, his face streaked with sweat and dust and blood. 'Are you two all right?'

Olivia swallowed hard and nodded.

'Then I'd get out of here and as quickly as you can! There's only a handful of us to protect the whole city and things look like getting worse before the night is over.'

Olivia found her voice. 'Can . . . can you drive us home, please?'

'Sorry, luv. There's not enough of us. I can't go chasing off and leave the lads. How far are you going?'

'Upper Huskisson Street.'

'You'll be all right. I've not heard of any trouble up that way. Just keep driving, don't stop for anyone and keep to the main roads!'

Olivia stared at his retreating back. Phoebe-Ann's sobs grated on nerves that were already shredded. 'For God's sake! Shut up whingeing! Haven't I got enough to think about without you having hysterics?' she yelled. 'You don't deserve a penny of the money I spent on you! In fact when we get home you can take all those things off and throw them out! You shan't have them!'

Phoebe-Ann didn't answer. She was past caring and in fact had begun to hate the coral dress and the shoes that were pinching her feet.

It was dark when they finally arrived home but both their hearts plummeted when they saw Richard Mercer standing on the front step with Lily, Albert and Emily.

Chapter Six

Olivia summed up both the situation and her predicament in a second. Shaken though she was by the experience, she recognized the stern jut of her father's chin and the tightly compressed lips as signs of anger that would be vented on her head. She threw her arms around him. 'Oh, Papa! I'm so glad to get home! I was so scared. I was terrified out of my wits. It was horrible. Horrible!' Tears of genuine remorse and relief welled up in her eyes.

Richard Mercer patted her. His anger had been mixed with concern and not only for Olivia. In fact it had been the arrival of Lily and Albert with news of the growing unrest that had caused his anxiety. Anxiety that had increased when he heard from Emily that they had gone into town hours ago. 'You're safely home now and that's all that matters.'

Olivia dabbed at her eyes. Now that it was all over she found she was shaking.

'Where did you get the taxi from and where's the driver?' her father questioned.

'He left us. He ran away and left us at the mercy of those . . . people. I drove home.' She clung to her father's arm.

'We heard there were mobs on the streets. That's why Mr and Mrs Davies came to see me. You should have come home much earlier . . . We've all been worried to death.' He turned apologetically to Lily and Albert. 'I'm sorry you've been subjected to all this anxiety. I'll get Edwin to drive you home. It's safer that way and Phoebe-Ann's had a nasty experience.' He was once more in charge of the situation, ushering Olivia inside and into the ministrations of Mrs Webster.

Edwin had heard the whole conversation from where he stood at Emily's side just inside the hall. He had worked in this house for so many years that he knew that, although shaken, Olivia was manipulating her father, seeking his pity to draw his attention away from the fact that she had been jaunting around town, putting herself and Phoebe-Ann in danger. No-one other than Mr Mercer had spoken so he turned and made for the back of the house to bring the car around.

Emily, too, had been relieved when the car had pulled up and they'd both got out safe and sound. She'd made up her mind to tell Phoebe-Ann just what she thought of her, worrying Mam, but all those thoughts had disappeared when she'd caught sight of her sister. In that split second in the dim light filtering from the hallway, she hadn't recognized Phoebe-Ann. Then she had gasped. What had Phoebe-Ann done to herself? Where had she got that outfit from? She looked like a socialite and her hair! She'd glanced at her mother's face but Lily was still overcome with the initial relief that Phoebe-Ann was safe. Emily bit her lip. There was trouble ahead, she was sure of it.

No-one spoke on the short journey to Lonsdale Street. Edwin sensed the tension and asked no questions nor made any cryptic or comical remarks. When they drew up outside the house, Albert helped Lily out and thanked Edwin, commenting that it was a waste of time, effort and petrol to get the car out for such a short journey.

'Next door's curtains are twitching,' Edwin whispered to Emily.

'I know and there's a dozen more doing the same thing up the whole street. We could have walked.'

'Did you see her hair?'

'I saw what's left of it. I've a feeling Mam will snatch her bald before the night's out.'

Edwin rolled his eyes and put the car into gear. 'Sooner you than me! See you tomorrow, Em.'

She watched the car turn the corner, then after studiedly glancing up the street she turned and went indoors.

Jack had taken refuge behind the *Echo* and Jimmy was conspicuous by his absence.

'Put the kettle on, Em, I think we all need a cup,' Albert instructed with a knowing look that silenced Emily's intended questions.

'Right, madam! Now explain all this away – if you can!' Lily's pent-up feelings of anger, relief and outrage burst out as she pushed Phoebe-Ann into the centre of the room and under the full glare of the light.

Phoebe-Ann was near to tears. She wanted comforting, as Miss Olivia had been. She had been through a terrible ordeal and wanted sympathy, soothing words and pats, declarations that nothing mattered except her safety. She shied away from her mother. 'It was Miss Olivia! It was all her idea, Mam. It was. I swear to God it was. What could I say?'

Lily snatched off the smart little hat and threw it in the general direction of the table. 'In the name of heaven, look at her! Look at her, Albert.' Lily caught hold of her daughter's face and jerked it upwards. 'You've got face powder on and rouge! You little trollop!'

Phoebe-Ann's tears were making tracks down her cheeks, accentuated by the white powder.

Emily hadn't noticed the make-up, only the shorn locks. 'Oh, your hair! Your beautiful hair!' she cried.

'I didn't want it cut! She made me!' Phoebe-Ann sobbed.

'Haven't you a tongue in your head, miss? It wouldn't have been out of place for you to refuse.' Lily shook her daughter. 'You're not a doll to be dressed and prinked and shown off by Miss Olivia Mercer. She doesn't own you. She's made you look cheap, like a floosie. And you let her do it! You bloody little fool!'

Everyone's eyes were on Lily. She hardly ever swore. It was a measure of the depth of her anger that she did so now.

'I tried, mam! I did! I said you'd kill me.'

Lily shook her again. 'Traipsing around town trying to pass yourself off as something you'll never be . . . a lady. You bold rossi! And where were you until this hour and with the streets crammed with all the riff-raff of the city?'

Phoebe-Ann was sobbing in earnest now. 'We . . . we went to see over the *Mauretania*. We had a tour.'

Her sobs had no effect on Lily who was consumed with fury that Phoebe-Ann had allowed herself to be patronized by that spoiled Olivia who had no doubt viewed it all as a joke. She had striven hard to bring up both her girls to be modest but here was Phoebe-Ann decked out like a high-class hussy, her face powdered and painted, the calves of her legs on display for all to leer at, prancing around the decks of the *Mauretania* and, no doubt, leaving herself open to more ogling. She raised her hand to slap her youngest daughter but Albert caught it.

89

'I know it's not my place, but she's just been foolish. Led astray if you like by someone who should know better.'

'It's the back of my hand she should be feeling, making a show of herself – of us all.'

Emily felt sorry for her sister and tried to intercede. 'Mam, she's awfully upset and you know what Miss Olivia's like.'

'You keep out of this, Emily. She wouldn't have needed much encouragement, if I know her. She probably thought she'd have dozens of men falling at her feet. Let me tell you this, miss, you can't make a silk purse out of a sow's ear. Now get up those stairs and get those things off. Our Emily will take them back in the morning and I suppose your hair will grow again. In the name of heaven, girl, what possessed you?'

'I'm sorry, Mam. I really am. I don't want these things. She chose them and paid for them.'

'She has far too much money and far too much freedom. It's a good hiding that little madam needs. And tomorrow you can collect your things, you're coming home to live where I can keep my eye on you. You can share with Emily. I'm not having you staying there and getting up to God knows what else!'

Emily pushed her sister towards the stairs then turned. 'Have a nice cup of tea, Mam.'

'You go on up with your sister. I'll make the tea,' Albert offered, gently pushing Lily down on the sofa.

Lily closed her eyes. 'She'll have me in my grave before my time, will that one. She just doesn't think. She just goes along with whatever she thinks can offer a bit of fun and excitement without a thought for the consequences.'

'She wasn't to know there would be riots. She is pretty shaken up.'

'Then I hope it's all done her some good. Oh, Albert, what does she look like with her beautiful hair shorn off like that? Where have I gone wrong?'

He placed a cup in her hand and smiled. 'I think she looks rather fetching.' Seeing the widening of Lily's eyes he went on hurriedly, 'She's just a bit of a girl, love. You know how they love to dress themselves up in the latest fashions.'

'Our Emily doesn't.'

'Emily's different. Now don't be taking on, we should be thankful she came to no harm.'

Lily emptied her cup. 'Oh, I suppose you're right.'

'Let's just look on the dressing up as a storm in a teacup. And, talking of tea, will I get us another cup?'

Lily smiled gratefully. What had she done before she married him? She'd have fretted and worried for hours on end, that's what she would have done. Compared with the trouble that was facing the city now it did all seem like a storm in a teacup.

As the city seethed with unrest that very quickly turned into open riots and wholesale looting there was another 'storm in a teacup' going on in the stokehold of the *Mauretania*.

It took eighteen hours to get up steam and warm up the engines and, as the stokers, trimmers and firemen gradually reported back, many still the worse for drink, tempers were short.

Jake Malone had been woken at six that morning by a deluge of icy cold water that jerked him upright from his inert position on the kitchen floor. His head thudded as though all the fiends of hell were hammering inside it and his tongue felt too large for his mouth.

'Jeasus! What did yer do that for, Ma?' he groaned, resting on one elbow.

Ma Malone glared down at him and moved the clay pipe to the other side of her mouth. 'Because you've kept me awake all the long night wit yer snorin'. Like a pig yez was and not just you, meladdo. All of yez!' She prodded him with the broom handle. 'Gerrup wit yez now. Yez work to go to and the rest of yez drunken eejits of brothers. Bejasus, but yer Pa would murder the lot of yez, God rest 'im! On yer feet now!'

He'd staggered to his feet cursing and trying to remember what day it was. On the sagging horsehair sofa against the far wall, Peader and Vincent sat with hands supporting heads. From the corner of the soot-blackened range that was devoid of blacklead, Franny, the youngest, slept on. It would be his turn to feel the business end of the broom next. Jake grunted as his Ma weighed into her youngest son, shrieking like a harpy and calling on the whole litany of saints to see how she was cursed with such a burden. He wished she'd shut up or at least lower her voice. He winced as he got to his feet and a memory stirred. There'd been a fight he remembered vaguely. Who was it who'd said that Franny Malone was as thick as pig shit? O'Rourke. Aye, one of the O'Rourkes and them bog Irish from Sligo. His da had come from Dublin and he wasn't going to stand for any insults from a Sligo man.

He pushed aside Seamus who was clinging on to the wooden draining board in the scullery as though life depended on it. Turning on the tap he bent and put his head beneath the cold flow. He felt like death and wished that he had another day's shore leave in which to recover. But he didn't and if he complained about it she'd belt him all the way down to the

Pierhead. He'd never met anyone with a temper like his ma. He shook the thick, dark hair from his eyes. Another bloody trip with not a drop of the hard stuff until they reached New York.

It was a silent and subdued band who'd made their way on the overhead railway to the Canada Dock. In turn they grunted as the Officer of the Watch checked them aboard. The ship was quiet, except for the tradesmen who were working against the clock to finish repairs. It was quieter than usual in the stoke-hold for the great turbines were silent. The only sound the clanking of the stokers' shovels as they prepared the furnaces to start the process of getting up steam.

Without a word to anyone, Seamus ducked under the bulkhead and moved towards the bunker. As a trimmer he was at the bottom of the hierarchy that comprised a skilled and efficient 'black squad'. He was glad the bunker was full. Nearing the end of a voyage when there was little coal left it meant bending and rising, bending and rising and his head couldn't have stood that. His mouth felt dry but there would only be water to quench his thirst. He drove his shovel into the pile of glittering anthracite and the air became thick with dust that clung to his lips, clogged his nose and irritated his eyes. Shovel after shovel was tipped down the chute to the coal-passer's barrow. His brother Peader's barrow. A barrow that would be emptied at the feet of Jake who would feed it into the hungry maws of the four furnaces, for Jake was classed as a skilled man. Aye, they worked well as a team as did Vinny, Franny and Declan Murphy, he thought before he resumed his task which he would repeat over and over again until the end of the four-hour shift. Then they would all collapse exhausted on to their bunks in one of the many 'glory holes' that existed all over the ship.

The trouble started when they had crossed the Mersey Bar, though none of them knew their exact location. They seldom even saw daylight. They had turned to for the middle watch still feeling under par and with four stokers short. Two of them had been wheeled aboard in barrows, too drunk to stagger up the gangway. All four were still sleeping off their excesses and were poorer by a day's pay for their breach of regulations. Their absence was something Jake fumed about for it meant he had two extra furnaces to contend with.

He thrust the ten-foot-long metal slice bar into the furnace. Stripped to the waist, his muscled torso glistened with sweat where coal dust and ashes had not adhered to it. His feet were shod in clogs to protect them from the red-hot debris. His face was seared by the heat from the open furnaces and his hands were scorched with the heat of the slice bar even though he wore canvas mitts. Ashes and clinkers showered down into the pit. He raked over the white-hot, fused impurities and spread the fire evenly. Teeth gritted, eyes narrowed to slits against the intense heat, he shovelled four heaps of coal into the furnace and slammed the door shut. His ears straining for the sound of the gong that timed all these operations and seven minutes were all that were allocated for each. Nor was it easy to hear the gong above the cacophany of furnace doors being banged shut, shovels ringing on steel and the roar of the drafts.

He moved on to the next furnace, ready to repeat the procedure. The weather had become choppy and it was no mean feat to keep a steady footing. As the bow plunged down, with arms working like pistons, he shovelled in the coal and slammed the door shut before the ship rose again. Failure to do so resulted in the coals spewing out.

He had just slammed shut the door of the last furnace and was preparing to move back along the row when a shower of red-hot coals fell around his feet. 'Jesus Christ Almighty! You nearly scorched the balls off me!' He glared at the stoker who was tending the next row. It was 'Shorty' O'Rourke. 'You missed the gong! Are yer bleedin' deaf as well as daft!'

'Shove the bloody gong up yer arse, Malone!' O'Rourke yelled.

'It's me slice bar that'll be shoved up your arse if yer can't keep time, yer ignorant thicko! You ask your Billy about what happens to them that are eejit enough to mouth off to a Malone.'

There was no interchange for three minutes while they shovelled and then it happened again, the coals burning through his moleskin trousers. He bellowed with pain and rage. 'Yer bastard! Yer did that on purpose!' he roared.

Heedless of the pitching and of the untended furnaces, he lunged forward with his slice bar and caught O'Rourke across the shoulder. The blow flinging the man back against the wall of the furnace.

His face twisted with pain and fury. 'I'll brain yer for that!' he screamed, raising his shovel and lurching forward with the roll of the ship.

The work carried on around them as they grappled and swung wildly at each other with slice bar and shovel. Peader Malone leaned on his barrow and shouted encouragement to his brother, ready to step in should Jake be felled. At the end of the row in the cavernous gloom he knew that Billy O'Rourke was doing the same.

As he watched the steam pressure gauge fall, the mate knew exactly what was happening and frowned. 'Bloody animals!' he muttered, looking at his watch and wondering how long it would go on. He had no intention of intervening for there was a standing order when the black squad fought. Close the hatches and stay clear. He'd heard a tale of one engineering officer who hadn't. He had never been seen again. It was rumoured that he had been brained with a shovel and his corpse tossed into a furnace. They could beat each others' brains out for all he cared. Just as long as they didn't take all night about it.

Chapter Seven

The strike had been short-lived but it had taken the presence of both the army and the navy to quell it. Damage to property had been heavy and the law-abiding citizens of the city had been shocked and scandalized. All the police officers who had gone on strike were dismissed and a new force recruited.

In the Mercer household Olivia's and Phoebe-Ann's peccadilloes had been forgotten as the evening of the soirée drew nearer and preparations reached fever pitch.

To her mounting chagrin Olivia found that more and more demands were being made upon her time and she raged about it to Phoebe-Ann whenever the occasion arose. As time progressed, Phoebe-Ann had found it the best policy to remain as quiet as possible. She had made the mistake of asking how the short hair was to be kept short.

'You really are a fool at times, Phoebe-Ann Parkinson! You either let it grow out or keep having it cut. Now I don't want to hear another word about hair, long or short. Damn Mrs Webster to hell and back! Why can't she use her own initiative instead of coming and annoying me with every little detail? I told her she had *carte blanche* but, no, she still annoys me with her stupid questions. Oh, I wish this whole thing was over and done with so I can have some time to myself without worrying about canapés, wines, flowers and musicians.'

Phoebe-Ann had tried to pour oil on troubled waters. 'Your new gown is beautiful; everyone will admire you and say how wonderfully well you've managed things.'

'Everyone will say how haggard I look. That's what everyone will say. And, what am I going to do about James? He's so morose he will put the dampers on the whole evening.'

'I don't think he wants to get involved, like.'

Olivia had paused and stared hard at her maid. 'How do you know that?'

'I talk to him, miss.'

'And he answers you?'

'Yes.'

'It's more than he does when I speak to him, or Papa either for that matter. So, he doesn't want to join us?'

'I don't think so. In fact I think he would prefer to just stay in his room.'

'Well, he can't. Not all evening anyway. How would it look? He'll have to show his face when people arrive, then he can do whatever he likes.'

Phoebe-Ann had sighed. He had been most emphatic, more animated than she'd ever seen him, when he'd said he wasn't going to be exhibited like a freak or be whispered about and he didn't care what anyone said, he was staying in his room. She'd agreed with him and had promised to plead for him. She'd thought how pitiful it was the way in which he hung on her every word, his eyes following her as she moved. Yes, pitiful. Often she wondered had he indeed lost his senses. Someone like him, educated, rich and handsome yet following her like a lap dog, as though she were the one who possessed those attributes.

When the evening of the soirée at last arrived, the

staff were exhausted both physically and mentally. In her ignorance of domestic procedures, Olivia had plagued them incessantly all afternoon.

Cook was still fuming from her last visit to the kitchen. 'The cheek of it! The brass-faced cheek of it! "There's not a lot of colour in them. Don't you think they look a little bit anaemic?" she says. My canapés are the finest in this city, though I say it myself, and her ma, God rest her, kept out of my kitchen and was always well satisfied, aye, even proud of my skills!'

'Oh, take no notice of her. She's like a cat on hot bricks. She doesn't know what to be at next.' Mrs Webster, whose own patience had been stretched to the limit, was for once openly critical of her employer.

Emily and Edwin exchanged glances as Phoebe-Ann burst into the kitchen, her cheeks flushed.

'I'll strangle her! I will! I'll strangle her!'

'Now what's the matter?' Emily demanded, wearily.

'Everything.' Phoebe-Ann sat down and blew a sigh through pursed lips. 'She's gone and changed her mind about what she's going to wear. After I'd gone to all the trouble of laying everything out and you know how long it took me to press that damned dress. That's not too bad, but she's hounding the life out of Master James. He doesn't want to have to stand in the hall and receive. He doesn't want to have anything to do with the entire thing, but she's gone on and on at him. It's a damned shame. It's a disgrace and the Master should know about it.'

Mrs Webster had regained her composure. 'Don't you think you're getting above yourself, Phoebe-Ann?' she queried in the rather cold voice she used when reprimanding those beneath her.

'He talks to me.'

'We know. I've been meaning to have a word with you about being so familiar.'

Phoebe-Ann opened her mouth to protest but closed it again as she caught sight of the warning look Emily shot at her.

'It may well do him good to meet people and if the Master is agreeable to it, and he would have instructed otherwise had he been of that opinion, then Miss Olivia has every right to cajole him. It is none of our business and it is definitely not your place to take sides!'

'Well, I for one will be glad when it's all over and done with,' Edwin put in, feeling a little sorry for Phoebe-Ann and for James Mercer. God help him, he was in no fit state to stand and make idle conversation with the old bores who were the Master's friends and the brainless idiots that were Miss Olivia's.

'She'll finish the night with a blinding headache and then I'll get no peace until I've calmed her down enough so she'll sleep. I can't see me getting to bed until about two o'clock tomorrow morning,' Phoebe-Ann said grimly.

Silence fell as the sound of voices raised in argument drifted from the hall. Phoebe-Ann pulled herself reluctantly to her feet. 'Oh, Lord! She's off again. I'd better go and see what I can do.'

Mrs Webster also rose. 'I'll come with you.' She was determined to see that Phoebe-Ann kept her place and did not speak out of turn.

It was Olivia and her father who were in the middle of a heated argument when the two women reached the hall. On seeing them Richard Mercer fixed his daughter with a piercing glare. He was not about to have himself talked about in the servants' hall.

'That will do Olivia! I want to hear no more about it. If James is not well enough . . .'

Olivia had no reservations about interrupting him. 'Of course he's well enough, Papa. He is just using his illness as an excuse. How will it look?'

'I do not care how it will "look". If your brother says he isn't up to receiving, and when I spoke to him he was very disturbed by the prospect, then I respect his decision and that is my final word. I'll hear no more complaints and arguments. Don't you think it is time you got dressed; it usually takes you at least two hours,' he added unkindly. How he wished that Adele had been alive. Everything would have gone so smoothly. There would have been no tantrums, no nagging and it was dawning on him that Olivia was proving to be quite useless at being a hostess. Had Adele been alive he would not even have been consulted as to whether or not he thought James was fit to receive company. She would have just quietly informed him, one way or the other, and then she would have made the appropriate excuses to their guests. He was thankful that Phoebe-Ann seemed to be coaxing Olivia towards the stairs. He was regretting that he had ever agreed to this soirée, but he had not entertained for so long that it had seemed churlish not to mark the victory.

It was Phoebe-Ann who had the blinding headache when at last at 7.30 sharp, Olivia, suitably attired, went down the stairs to stand with her father to greet the guests. With Mr Potter now retired it was Edwin in his best livery who stood ready to open the door. Phoebe-Ann and Emily, in their best black silk dresses and white lace caps and aprons, stood ready to take hats, coats and evening cloaks and attend to the wishes of those ladies who asked to 'just check my appearance. Such a windy night.'

I'm a nervous wreck, Phoebe-Ann thought. She just longed to creep up to the attic bedroom and lie down in the darkness and rest her throbbing head on the cool pillow. Of that there was no chance. Not for hours to come.

The house was soon filled with guests and, before the evening got under way, Richard Mercer proposed a toast: to the King and Queen and the gallant men who had fought and died for their country.

Emily, standing beside Edwin by the buffet, felt her throat constrict as she remembered her brothers. Phoebe-Ann was thinking of Rob and of James Mercer hidden away in his room, alone in the darkness. Edwin's thoughts were bitter as he thought of the mates he had lost and in his view it had all been a waste of time and nothing to do with king and country.

When Richard Mercer had finished speaking, there was little time to ponder such sentiments for they were all kept busy. Even young Kitty, resplendant in one of Phoebe-Ann's uniforms and drilled to an inch of her life in her duties by Cook and Mrs Webster, had been promoted for the evening. Her place in the kitchen taken by two of her younger sisters, hired just for the occasion.

It was almost half past ten, the evening was in full swing and they were all rushed off their feet when Emily found Phoebe-Ann under the stairwell, leaning against the wall, a hand over her eyes.

'What's the matter, Fee?'

'My head. Oh, Em, my head feels as though it's going to burst.'

'Now is a fine time to have a headache,' Emily

retorted a little sharply. Her own head was beginning to ache and she had little sympathy with her sister.

'It's more than just a headache. I feel really ill, Em. Honestly I do.'

Emily became more concerned. 'Go and ask Cook for something. You've no chance of getting to bed.'

'Don't I know it. I wish Mam had let me get a job in a factory. At least I wouldn't be standing here with my skull about to explode and my stomach in knots, but having to smile and be nice to fat old women covered in jewels. I would be in bed now with a cold compress over my head.'

'Well, you're not working in a factory so get down to Cook and just pray they all go home early.'

'Em, would you do something for me?'

'What?' Emily was cautious. She had enough work of her own to contend with.

'I promised Master James that I'd look in and see him. Bring him a bit of supper, like. He was upset earlier on, what with her tormenting the daylights out of him. Would you go instead?'

'He won't talk to me. You know he won't.'

'You won't need to talk. Just say I'm so busy . . . no, I'm detained and that you've come instead. Please, Em? I don't want him to feel left out.'

'He got out of having to make an appearance so why should he feel left out now?'

'He says things he doesn't mean sometimes but I know what he's really thinking. Oh, I can't explain it. I'm not much good with words. Please, Em, do it for me?'

'Oh, just this once. Don't go making a habit of it.'

'It will be better if you go. If Mrs Webster were to see me she'd read me the Riot Act again.'

'Go and get some tablets before they all start shouting for us both.'

As Phoebe-Ann disappeared through the green baize door, Emily wondered how she would go about filching titbits from the buffet without arousing suspicion. Then she remembered old Mrs Ferguson, a portly dowager who was virtually crippled with rheumatism and was unable to move about much. She'd fill two plates and take them both to her. Etiquette would prevent her accepting both plates.

As she deftly filled two china plates it was Edwin who noticed as he ladled out punch from a silver bowl. 'Who's making a pig of themselves?' he hissed out of the corner of his mouth.

Emily grinned. 'Mrs Ferguson.'

There was a lull in the proceedings.

'You can't fool me, Em. She wouldn't eat all that.'

'I know. The other one is for Master James. I promised our Phoebe-Ann I'd take it to him. She's got what I think is a migraine headache.'

'Her timing's rotten.'

'I know. It's probably Miss Olivia's fault.'

'I thought it was only the likes of them that got those bad headaches.' He jerked his head in the direction of a small group of middle-aged ladies who were deep in conversation. Probably discussing some topic that was of great interest to their sex, or so he deduced.

'She's had one or two before. Mam says she's highly strung.'

'Highly strung, my foot!'

'That's what I said.'

The group of ladies had finished their discussion and were moving *en masse* towards the buffet. Emily placed a damask napkin over the two plates and, with a bright smile, said, 'I hope you will excuse me. I must attend to Mrs Ferguson. She is a little tired.' The ruse worked. Instead of asking her to serve them they all nodded and smiled sympathetically.

The room was in total darkness when she entered and she was quite literally 'in the dark'. As her eyes adjusted to the gloom, she could make out a figure sitting in a chair beside the empty fire grate. She moved closer, puzzled, for he had his topcoat on.

'Are you cold, sir? Should I light the fire?'

He didn't answer.

'I've brought you something to eat from the buffet. Phoebe-Ann asked me to.'

The mention of her sister's name seemed to have an effect on him, for he rose and turned towards her. Although there was little light in the room she was shocked by his expression. His eyes were wild, his gaze darting around the room as though searching for someone or something and there was a marked twitch at the corner of his mouth.

'I'll leave your supper.' She began to back away, remembering that Phoebe-Ann had said he was upset.

Before she reached the door he had darted forward and caught her in a vice-like grip. 'We'll go away, Phoebe-Ann. Just you and me. We'll go away from all this noise, this terrible, terrible noise and all those staring faces. Faces looking at me, staring at me. Staring all the time. We'll go away. I'm ready. See, I've got my coat on, Phoebe-Ann.'

Emily struggled to free herself. It's me, Emily! It's not Phoebe-Ann!' she cried.

He appeared not to have heard her and pinned her against the door. 'Come with me, Phoebe-Ann. I'm rich. I'll take care of you. I'll marry you and then you'll be all mine and there won't be any noise and no staring faces. They all hate me, they do.'

Emily was really frightened now and she tried to cry out. She tried to pull away but his hold was too tight and then she felt his mouth on her skin.

'I love you, Phoebe-Ann. You love me too, I know you do. Don't leave me. We'll go away from here.'

'I'm Emily! I'm not Phoebe-Ann! For God's sake let me go!' she screamed. She managed to free one arm and tried to rake his face with her nails. Anything to make him stop what he was doing to her. 'I'll get your Pa! I'll scream so loud that everyone will hear me!'

She fought with all the strength she possessed. He was mad, she was certain of it, and that knowledge terrified her. His mouth cut off her screams until she tore her lips, bruised and bleeding, away, but her strength was failing. He was just too strong for her.

She kept on screaming until he pushed her across the bed and the breath was knocked out of her by his weight. She gasped and tried to call for help but her cries seemed to echo only in her head.

It could have been an hour or even two, or it could only have been a matter of minutes before he rolled away from her. She was never to know. He lay sprawled across the bed limp and she lay there too. Too shocked to move. Her throat was raw, her lips bruised and her whole body was aching. Just one thought penetrated her numbed mind. She had to get out before he woke . . . As she pulled herself upright a searing pain shot through her groin. Somehow she staggered to the door and then along the landing. She *had* to get to Phoebe-Ann's room and shut the door. Lock the door. Lock out James Mercer and what he had done to her. She leaned against the wall only half conscious. Deep, racking sobs shook her.

How long she stayed there she could never remember but it was Edwin Leeson who found her. He'd waited for her to return but when she didn't he began to feel anxious, although quite why he didn't know. When at last Phoebe-Ann appeared, he excused himself and, after being waylaid by three gentlemen, had got upstairs.

'God Almighty! Em! Emily, what happened?' He reached out to touch her rapidly swelling face.

'Don't touch me! Don't touch me!' she screamed at him, shrinking further against the wall.

Black fury chased away the concern that had filled his eyes. 'Who was it? Emily, tell me who did this to you?'

She gulped. 'Him. He . . . he thought I was Phoebe-Ann. I kept telling him . . .'

'James Mercer?'

She nodded.

He'd never felt so angry. He could have killed in that moment and not have cared for the consequences. 'The bastard! The bastard!' he yelled, smashing his fist against the wall, his anger futile, his wrath impotent and all the worse because of those very facts.

'He's mad! He's mad!'

'He'll swing for this, Em! I'll get him! The bastard!' Again the crash of his fist against the wall.

Emily sobbed harder.

Instantly he was all concern. 'I'll get someone. Will you be all right for a few more minutes?'

She couldn't reply.

When he returned he had both Phoebe-Ann and Mrs Webster with him. The housekeeper's eyes widened with horror as she took in Emily's face and her torn dress, the bodice almost completely rent down the front. 'Oh, dear God in heaven!'

Phoebe-Ann started to cry. 'Oh, Em! Em! What happened?'

Mrs Webster took the situation in hand. 'Phoebe-Ann, pull yourself together and go and get some cloths and anything cold you can find. Quickly girl! Move!' She placed her arm around Emily's shoulder. 'Let's get you to bed, Emily.'

Now that Emily was in safe hands, Edwin balled his fists into the pockets of his trousers. 'I'm going to get the Master.'

Mrs Webster turned on him. 'Oh, no, you're not! You will wait until the guests have gone.'

'To hell with the bloody guests! They should all know what that . . . animal has done!'

'Don't you dare announce to everyone what has happened here!'

His face was flushed dark red. 'Well, he's going to know,' he said and, before she could say another word, he'd turned on his heel and had stormed away.

Emily felt as though she were in a dream: a waking nightmare. Nothing was real, except the pain and the terrible feeling of guilt. Guilt that she had not fought harder. Guilt that in some way she had encouraged him, but in what way she didn't know. She let Mrs Webster undress her and slip her nightgown over her head as Phoebe-Ann appeared with a bowl, some towels and some lumps of ice wrapped in a tea towel. She'd spilt a good deal of the water, for her hands were shaking. She gnawed at her bottom lip as she looked from her sister's battered face to that of the housekeeper. 'I brought some ice.'

Mrs Webster placed the ice-pack against Emily's

right cheek. 'Get into bed now Emily and try to sleep.' She turned to Phoebe-Ann. 'Has Miss Olivia got anything that will calm her?'

Phoebe-Ann shook her head.

'Then go and ask Dr Coleman for something.'

Emily felt she would never sleep again. Although she felt totally exhausted, she was terrified to close her eyes. She lay down, staring at the sloping attic ceiling while her sister and the housekeeper whispered together. It was as though she didn't care any more what happened to her, as though it wasn't really she who was lying in the bed. It was someone else. Someone she was looking down on. Then Richard Mercer was beside her.

'Emily. Emily, can you hear me?' His tone was gentle but he couldn't hide the horror in his eyes. He'd gone icy cold when Edwin had taken him aside and told him what James had done. At first he'd refused to believe the lad. He was exaggerating. He wouldn't let himself believe that James was capable of rape, that most hideous of all crimes against women. But as soon as he saw her he knew it was true. 'Emily, was it my . . . son?' The words were as bitter as the bile in his mouth.

The movement of her head gave him the answer he dreaded.

'Oh, my God!' he groaned, for a second completely stricken before his composure was regained. 'Leeson, go down and tell Dr Coleman to come up here.'

'No! No!' Emily screamed the word. If she had to feel another man touching her she'd go insane.

'Hush. Hush Emily,' Mrs Webster soothed. 'It will be just a quick look and then something to make you sleep.'

Phoebe-Ann grabbed her sister's hand and

squeezed it tightly. To Emily it was like a lifeline. 'Oh, Fee! Fee! It was . . .' She choked on the words.

With tears pouring down her cheeks, Phoebe-Ann gathered her into her arms and held her tightly. 'It's all right now, Em! I'm here. Phoebe-Ann's here!'

Emily raised her face from her sister's shoulder. 'Oh, Fee! It should have been you. He thought I was you. He kept calling me Phoebe-Ann.'

Phoebe-Ann felt the room spin and her stomach churned, then a sickening blackness was closing down. She heard Mrs Webster's voice, there was a pungent smell in the room and the giddiness was fading.

'This is no time for you to be fainting! Send Kitty for Mrs Parkinson . . . I mean Mrs Davies. Just tell her to say she's needed urgently,' Mrs Webster instructed Edwin. Then she turned to Richard Mercer. 'I think you'd better go back downstairs, sir, before people start to speculate. Edwin, you'll have to manage as best you can until Phoebe-Ann can calm herself sufficiently to help you.'

He was openly mutinous. His concern was only for Emily. 'I'll not leave her!'

Mrs Webster drew herself up to her full height. 'It is not proper that you should be in the bedroom of a girl who is so obviously . . . distressed. There is nothing you can do to help her just yet.'

Emily looked up and for the first time realized what was going on around her. 'Do as she says . . . for me?'

The pain in his eyes was real. He wanted to hold her, calm her, reassure her but it was not what she wanted. He gave a curt nod and turned away. The two men left together. Once outside the room Edwin's anger flared again and he caught Richard Mercer's arm. 'It's not going to end here! I swear it's not!'

The older man looked down at the hand on his arm. 'We'll talk about it later. When her parents have been to see her and the guests have gone. I would appreciate it if you would try to keep this matter between ourselves, until Emily's parents have been.'

'I'll do it for her sake and her mam's but not for you!' He knew his words were insolent but he didn't care. He wanted justice for Emily.

Try though she may, Lily could get nothing out of young Kitty.

'I don't know what's up, missus, that's the God's own truth. But it's bad, I can tell you that. I haven't seen Emily or Phoebe-Ann for over an hour. Edwin's in a foul temper and so is Mrs Webster, an' Cook if it comes to that.'

Lily exchanged a worried glance with Albert.

'Get your hat and coat on, Lil. The quicker we get there the quicker we find out what's gone on and the sooner your mind will be eased.'

'Shall I go down the pub for the other two?' Kitty asked, hoping to sound helpful and having heard Lily mention the whereabouts of Jack and Jimmy on her arrival.

'No, you won't and don't be so hardfaced! Get yourself back: they'll be wondering where you've got to,' Lily snapped.

'I was only tryin' to be 'elpful, like.'

'Off you go, girl,' Albert directed quietly.

They walked quickly up Lonsdale Street and around the corner, Lily clinging to Albert's arm, thankful for his support. She had a sinking feeling in her stomach and she wondered what could be so wrong that they should both have been summoned on tonight of all nights.

111

'Just what have those two been up to? If our Phoebe-Ann's been throwing tantrums she'll feel the back of my hand and this time you won't stop me.'

'Lily, stop fretting and getting yourself into a state. Maybe there's been some sort of accident. A minor one,' he added hastily, seeing the consternation in her eyes. He could have kicked himself for saying it but he had only been trying to allay her fears. They walked the rest of the way in silence but occasionally he patted her arm, as though impressing on her the fact that he was there, giving her support. Like Lily he was certain it had something to do with Phoebe-Ann. Emily could always be relied upon to behave herself.

Nothing could have prepared them for the shock they both felt when Richard Mercer ushered them into his study and told them quietly and with sorrow in his voice what had happened. For the first time in his life Albert Davies felt a white-hot rage surge through him. Emily! Poor modest, hard-working, self-effacing little Emily! Before he could speak Richard Mercer was ushering them towards the door and he realized Lily was clinging to his arm and that she was shaking. Looking down he saw the tears coursing down her cheeks. 'Oh, Lily, love! What's to do? What's to be said, love?'

She shook her head. There was nothing either he or anyone else could do or say that would restore to her poor girl that which had been brutally torn from her. Her virginity, her innocence, her trust. In her heart of hearts she wished that her poor Emily was dead. Better dead than . . . this.

Before she went into the room, she made an effort to control herself, to steel herself for what was in store for her, the thing that all mothers dread. Albert

112

handed her his handkerchief and she wiped her face and straightened her shoulders.

'Will I come in with you, love?'

'No. Not yet. It's her mam she wants, no hurt intended.'

He squeezed her hand. 'None taken.' As he turned to open the door he was full of admiration for her. 'I'll wait here. In case she needs me,' he said flatly to Richard Mercer who nodded and walked down the landing.

As soon as she saw her mother Emily stretched out her arms. Instantly Lily held her tightly. 'Oh, Em! My poor little Emily! It's all right now, your mam's here and I'm taking you home. Do you feel up to it, love?' Her words were a hoarse whisper as she fought to control her own sobs.

Emily nodded and Lily gently brushed away the strands of brown hair that hung about her daughter's bruised face. 'You'll never have to come back here, I promise you. Either of you! Albert can go and fetch our Phoebe-Ann. She's coming home right now.'

Beneath the heart-scalding pity she felt for Emily a slow anger had started to burn. Anger that would gain strength until it would consume her, cloud her vision and her judgement.

Chapter Eight

It was nearly three o'clock in the morning when Edwin, unable to control himself any longer, knocked loudly on the door of Richard Mercer's study. He had inwardly seethed with anger for the rest of the evening and while the guests had departed. It had been left to Mrs Webster to tell Olivia that her brother had attacked Emily. Mr Mercer and the housekeeper had decided not to tell her the full extent of the attack. When Dr Coleman had heavily sedated James Mercer and seen to Emily, she had been driven home with Lily, Albert and Phoebe-Ann in a taxi cab.

Edwin had left Mrs Webster to clear up, aided grudgingly by Kitty and Cook. An air of dreadful foreboding hung over the house and there would be little sleep for anyone, he mused grimly. Kitty was the exception. She had been deliberately kept in the dark about the whole affair. 'Give that one the hint of the truth and she'll have it around the whole of Toxteth Park by morning!' had been Cook's prediction. She had also commented acidly that Kitty's ma had a mouth like a parish oven.

When he heard the summons, Edwin went in. The fact that his master looked old and haggard went unheeded. 'I've got to say it! What's going to happen to him?'

'I know what you think should happen and my first reaction was something along the same lines. I never wish to experience another night like this.'

'No doubt Emily would agree with you,' he shot back.

'I'm aware of that,' came the curt reply. 'I have to face the fact that my son . . . is not himself and probably never will be.'

'He's mad. Why don't you say it? Only a madman could have done . . . that!'

Richard Mercer ignored the outburst, but the word made him shudder. He had refused to even let himself think it. When Dr Coleman had told him that the best place for James was a mental hospital he had felt physically sick. 'He will be institutionalized.'

'Locked up.'

The older man nodded. 'I . . . I would be very grateful if you could see your way clear to keeping all this to yourself. I have my reputation, my business . . . I am a Justice of the Peace, as you know.' He pushed a sealed envelope across the desk.

Edwin's eyes narrowed and he drew in his breath sharply. 'You're bribing me to keep my mouth shut! I'd sooner starve than betray Emily like that! Keep your money and keep your job! I won't work in this house for another day!'

Richard Mercer leaned back in his chair wearily and passed a hand over his eyes. It was what he had expected but he had had to try. 'I understand you, Leeson, and, had you accepted, part of me would have despised you. I'm not insensitive to your outrage and your anger, but think of Emily. Think about how she and her family would feel if this got to court. Oh, the newspapers would have a field-day and even though they can't print her name, it wouldn't be long before someone found it out.'

Edwin twisted his hands in frustration. He was right.

'Work is hard to find these days.'

'I'll manage.'

'I don't blame you, but think about it. Your aunt is getting on in years and she relies on you.'

'I won't stay in this house!'

'I'm not asking you to.'

'Then what?'

'I'll give you employment within the Company. You're honest, diligent, efficient and loyal. Will you sail as a steward or a waiter on the *Mauretania*?'

Edwin was taken aback. It was something he hadn't expected.

'Think about it. Think hard. There is nothing either you or I can do to punish my son and little we can do for Emily either, except provide for her. It's work. Not highly paid work but I believe the tips can be good. You could provide for your aunt and you would not be under this roof, nor in contact with either me or Miss Olivia, who is as devastated as I am.'

'I'll think about it,' he said grudgingly, thinking that it had obviously been thought out carefully.

'Good.' The word was uttered with a sigh of relief. 'And there will be no gossip?'

Edwin looked down at him and realized that he despised this man. A young girl had been brutally attacked in his house and by his insane son and all he cared about was his reputation. His name and position. 'There will be no gossip as you call it, but not on account of you or Miss Olivia but because I won't heap all that on Emily's head. She's suffered enough.'

'Will you stay until I can find a replacement?'

'Only until the *Mauretania* docks,' he replied, not caring how condescending was his tone, how mocking was his attitude. As far as he was concerned Richard

116

Mercer was in his debt; it was not the other way around.

Emily had fallen into a deep sleep, aided by the medicine Dr Coleman had given her. Phoebe-Ann had slept in her mother's bed while Albert had tossed restlessly on the sofa. Lily had sat beside her daughter through the long hours of the night, her mind tortured by the fearful, dark images of James Mercer and her poor Emily. Images that wouldn't be banished no matter how hard she tried, and all the while her tears flowed freely.

Jack and Jimmy had been told and it had been left to Albert to talk them out of storming round to Upper Huskisson Street and beating James Mercer to a pulp.

'What good will that do? Apart from making you feel better? If I thought it would help Emily, I'd come with you and help you, but it won't. Neither will it help your mam for you'd be locked up by the scuffers and thrown into Walton Jail . . .'

'It would be worth it just to make that bastard pay!' Jimmy growled.

'It wouldn't. He's not in his right mind. What kind of satisfaction is there in beating a man who has lost his reason? Who can't understand what he has done? Let it be for your mam's sake. Aye, and Emily's.'

So they had remained at home nursing their anger and frustration.

At first, when she woke from her drugged sleep, Emily looked around the familiar room with surprise. She didn't remember coming home and why was Mam sitting in a chair beside the bed, her head on her chest, fast asleep? She tried to sit up and she groaned. She

117

felt as though she'd been beaten all over. Then she remembered.

The scream woke Lily with a jerk. 'Emily! Emily, stop it, love! It's all right, your mam's here. You're at home. Safe and sound.'

'Oh, Mam! Mam! Why me?' Then she remembered that he'd thought she was Phoebe-Ann.

'I don't know, Emily. I don't know. Who can tell what was going on in his twisted mind? Don't think about it any more. Promise me?'

'I can't help it,' she sobbed.

Never had Lily felt so helpless. She fought down her frustration. 'I'll make you a cup of tea and a bite to eat. You lie down now and rest.'

Emily lay back against the pillows. How was she ever going to feel normal again? Do all those things that other people do without even giving a moment's thought to: eating, laughing, singing. She would never laugh again. And work. How could she ever work again, and what would people think? She felt guilty and ashamed. She *must* have done something, said something. He wouldn't have just gone and attacked her like that. She forced the bile down, feeling the bitter taste in her mouth. People would point at her on the street. She would be called terrible names. Just the thought of it brought the blood rushing to her cheeks. And then there was Edwin. He'd been there. He'd found her like that. How was she ever to look him in the face again? She turned her head to the wall and closed her eyes. She wanted to die for what was the point in living? Her life had been ruined.

Lily bent over the range feeling like an old woman. Her shoulders and her back were aching, but the burden of grief she carried was the worst ache of all.

Albert had obviously gone out for his walk and there was no sign of either Jack or Jimmy and she wondered if they had accompanied him. She went through into the scullery and splashed cold water on her face. It helped to banish the numbness that had seeped into her body. When she returned to the kitchen the kettle had boiled and she spooned the tea into the pot from the red and black lacquered caddy, then she sat down, waiting for it to draw.

What was she going to do now? How could she coax Emily back to some semblance of normality after what she'd been through? She remembered something Emily had said last night. What was it? Something to do with Phoebe-Ann. That was it. He had mistaken her for Phoebe-Ann. Phoebe-Ann had been his intended victim. Her mind cleared. What the hell had Phoebe-Ann been doing to encourage him to think she would have welcomed his attentions? She'd heard her youngest daughter talking about him, boasting that she was the only one he would talk to. He ignored everyone else, including his own father. And she had said how sad it was that he followed her with his eyes. The little slut! The little tart! She must have encouraged him. It was the only explanation. In a flash she had crossed the room and had stormed upstairs. She flung back the bedroom door and the china jug and bowl on the washstand rattled.

Phoebe-Ann sat up, her short blonde hair tousled, her eyes still red and puffy from crying. The short hair only served to inflame Lily's anger. With two strides she had crossed the room and, throwing back the bedclothes with one hand, she caught her daughter by the hair with the other and yanked her from the bed.

Phoebe-Ann screamed in pain and terror. 'Mam! Mam, you're hurting me!'

'Not nearly as much as I'm going to, you little slut!'

'Mam! Mam, stop it! Please stop it!' Phoebe-Ann screamed.

'It's all your fault. You've been acting the whore with him, haven't you? Haven't you?' The sound of her hand as it struck Phoebe-Ann's cheeks, first the right, then the left, echoed around the room and the terrified girl shrieked.

'No! No, I haven't! I only used to talk to him. Oh, God, Mam, that's all it was! A few kind words!'

'Don't you take the Lord's name in vain and lie to me in the same breath, Phoebe-Ann Parkinson! Your pa must be turning in his grave and your brothers too, to see what kind of a harlot you've turned into! You thought you were on to a good thing, didn't you? Didn't you? You thought he was a gentleman. Did you think he would up and marry you? It was that, wasn't it? You thought you'd be like his bloody sister!'

'I didn't! I didn't! Oh, please, Mam, leave me be!'

Lily's anger and outrage had found an outlet, her reasoning impaired by rage. 'So you played the whore and where has it got you? Nowhere! Nowhere and, what's worse, your sister has had to pay for your stupid, sinful dreams! Your poor, innocent sister has been raped and ruined for life because of you!'

Phoebe-Ann had managed to tear herself away.

Lily's bosom heaved and her eyes glittered dangerously. 'Don't you think this is the end of it because it's not. I should have taken your pa's belt to you long ago, but by God I'll do it now! You'll regret the day you ever tried to copy Miss Olivia Mercer.'

'Mam. Don't!'

The cry was weak, yet it penetrated the red mist

that was dancing before Lily's eyes. She turned to see Emily clinging to the doorpost and behind her stood Albert.

'Lily, what's all this about?' he demanded in a tone she'd never heard him use before. Nor had she seen him look so grim as he took in the scene; Phoebe-Ann cowering against the far wall, her arms folded over her head as though to protect it, shaking and sobbing; Lily, her usually neat hair hanging in untidy strands either side of her face, trembling too.

'It's all her fault, the little slut! She's no daughter of mine!' Lily pointed to Phoebe-Ann with a stabbing forefinger. 'She's been leading him on; playing up to him, the poor mad sod. How was he to know what she was up to? She wanted to be a lady like his sister and she thought he'd make her one, so she led him on. It's her fault and I'll never forgive her. Never. I don't want her in this house. I don't want her near me.'

Fresh sobs racked Phoebe-Ann.

'Is what your mam says true, Phoebe-Ann?' Albert asked quietly.

'No! I swear by everything that's holy I didn't lead him on. I didn't want him to marry me. I didn't want to be like Miss Olivia. I only talked to him. I didn't even say anything or do anything I shouldn't have! I swear it!'

'Liar!' Lily screamed.

Albert caught her by the shoulders and shook her hard. 'Stop it, Lily! Do you hear me? Stop it. Look what it's doing to Emily, you screaming and swearing and blaming Phoebe-Ann! Stop it!'

All the anger drained from Lily as she saw the tears running down Emily's face. She burst into hysterical tears and clung to Albert. 'My poor girls. My poor girls. What did I do to deserve all this, Albert? God knows I've had my share of grief and trouble – why this?'

He patted her. 'I don't know, love. I just don't know. It doesn't seem right or fair but never mind all that. Everyone is upset.'

Jack and Jimmy had appeared on the landing and were surveying the scene with disbelief.

Albert took charge of the situation. 'Jack, lad, take your mam downstairs and give her a drop of brandy, she needs it. Aye, and one for Phoebe-Ann too. Oh, what the hell! Get us all one. We need it.'

Jack nodded, never thinking to question his step-father's authority.

'Phoebe-Ann go and get dressed and wash your face and then help Emily; your mam's in no fit state and she didn't mean any of this, she's just so upset and angry.'

Phoebe-Ann sniffed and nodded, still shaken, and for the first time wondered if her pity for James Mercer had indeed been construed by him into something far more sinister. A feeling that was to grow stronger and would be transformed into guilt that would turn to resentment which, in its turn, would be instrumental in ruining her life.

When everyone was much calmer and Lily had kissed Phoebe-Ann and when Emily had come down-stairs, pale and silent, Lily expressed one of her worries aloud. 'I don't know what you will do now. Neither of you are going back there.'

'I could get work in Tate's or Tillotson's, Mam,' Phoebe-Ann ventured timidly, not knowing how this suggestion would be received.

'Aye, maybe it would be the best thing for you. Maybe I was wrong forcing you to go back into

122

service. All this might not have happened if I hadn't been so set on you keeping your promise. I should have realized that things have changed.'

'How were you to know, Lil? You did what you thought was best, there's no use you feeling guilty about that.'

Lily managed a weak smile.

'I think you should go and see Mr Mercer when you're calmer. When we've all thought this thing through.'

'What for? I never want to set foot in that house again.'

'To see if he's willing to make some kind of compensation for Emily.'

'Like what?'

Albert shrugged. 'I don't know.'

'We don't want his bloody "hush" money,' Jack stated.

'No. Not money. Perhaps something in kind.'

'What? The least he can do is give her good references,' Jimmy put in.

'I don't doubt he'll do that. Perhaps he knows where she could get other employment.'

'They have stewardesses, Mam. I saw some on the day I went over the *Mauretania*.' Phoebe-Ann fell silent. Unwittingly she had reminded her mother about that awful day out with Miss Olivia, and she waited for Lily's wrath to descend on her.

'No. I don't want to do anything like that. I don't want to leave here.' Emily surprised them by the force of her objections.

'You won't have to. It's no life for a young girl, working like a skivvy for hours on end and being away from home and family,' Jimmy stated.

'Let's leave it for now. Leave it for a day or two

123

until we've all settled down,' Albert ended the discussion.

In the middle of the following week Emily agreed to see Edwin. He had called every day but she had resolutely stood firm in her determination not to see him. To all Lily's pleading and cajoling she had turned a deaf ear. Not even Phoebe-Ann's tearful urging had had any effect. It was Albert who made her change her mind. He had been quick to note how she had suddenly developed an aversion to men, himself and her brothers included. Indeed they were the only men within her immediate circle and vicinity but she seemed to shy away from physical contact and even their embarrassingly stammered attempts at apologizing for their loudness and often insensitive remarks appeared to make her shrink.

Jack had summed up their feelings. 'I find myself apologizing for being a man. One of the same breed as that bastard.' He always referred to James Mercer as 'that bastard'.

'No, lad. Not the same breed. Never that. But I know what you mean. I find myself watching every damn word that I utter while she's around.'

'It's poor Leeson I feel sorry for. I think he and our Emily had come to an understanding and now she won't even see him. He told me he gave it to old man Mercer straight. Wouldn't stay another day in the house. If he'd have had his way he would have had that bastard publicly branded and locked up and I agree with him. Except it would mean our Emily's name being tossed around every ale house in the city, and there's no way I'd have her go through that.'

Albert had nodded his agreement. 'Aye, but something is going to have to be done about it all. We can't go on like this for ever and young Edwin is very fond of her, I know that from the hangdog look on his face when your mam says, 'Not today.'

'Can't you have a talk to her? You're not as . . . well, not as close as us, if you know what I mean?'

'I'll try. All I can do is try,' Albert agreed.

After dinner that night the two lads made themselves scarce and Lily said the weather was so humid she needed a breath of fresh air. Preferably fresh, salt air and that it would do Phoebe-Ann good as well, her being stuck in that factory all day. Phoebe-Ann had been very fortunate indeed. She'd been taken on at the B&A, as everyone called the British American Tobacco Company. The wages were good and the work a lot easier than in other factories. Lily had sworn what she would do if she ever caught Phoebe-Ann with a cigarette in her mouth but Jack and Jimmy were very pleased when she brought home cheap cigarettes and tobacco for Albert's pipe.

'Sure you don't want to go with them, Emily? It's a fine evening,' Albert ventured as the two women were about to leave.

'No. No thanks.' Emily stared listlessly out of the window that looked on to the yard. It was an effort to do anything these days, her mind was so tired of going round and round over the same things.

'We'll bring you some peardrops. You like them,' was Phoebe-Ann's parting offer.

Albert stood up and walked over to where Emily sat. Dropping down on his hunkers he took her hands and held them, despite the fact that she tried to snatch them away. 'Emily, love, we've got to talk about this. Me and the lads can't spend our lives apologizing for being men, watching what we say, what we do. It's not natural and it's not right.'

125

'I know, but I can't help it.' She was still very uneasy.

'What is it that you hate the most? Come on, tell me now?'

'I don't want to think about it.'

'I know you don't, but try. Your mam's worried to death about you.'

'I just can't even bear to think about things I used to do.'

'Like what?' he coaxed, feeling he was nearing a breakthrough.

'The way I used to hug the lads sometimes. Link arms, things like that. I think I would be sick, really sick, if I tried to do anything like that now.'

He looked into her earnest face and felt defeated. It had affected her far more than he had realized. 'Well, we'll just have to think of a way round it.'

'I still love them. They're my brothers, but it's not the same any more.'

'I can understand that. Everything has changed, hasn't it?'

She nodded.

'And what about Edwin Leeson? He's called every day you know and he won't be able to come for much longer.'

For the first time he saw a glimmer of interest in her eyes. 'Why?'

'Because when the *Mauretania* comes back he's joining her. He refused to stay at his old job. He's going as a steward or a waiter or something. Won't you see him before he goes, Emily? The lad is very fond of you.'

'I can't. I can't. How can I face him knowing that he saw me like that? That he knew . . .'

'Emily, it's not your fault. None of it was your

fault, you have to get that out of your head right now. He doesn't think any the worse of you. He's worried about you, same as we all are. Won't you see him?'

She faltered. Was what Albert saying the truth?

'Look, just see him for five minutes. Your mam and me will stay in the room if you want us to.'

'I don't know.'

'If you don't try to fight this problem, Emily, it will never get any better, only worse.'

'How do you know all these things?'

'I don't "know". It just seems logical that's all.' He smiled at her. 'So, shall I tell him you'll see him later?'

She nodded.

'That's my brave girl. And, I've another idea. Tell me what you think of it?'

'What?'

'Well, when I first took your hands you tried to pull away and you kept on trying for about three minutes but now you've stopped. It's a small step, but it's a start. So, what we'll do every day, just you and me, no need to tell everyone, I'll sit and hold your hands. Just for a few minutes to start with and we'll lengthen the time a bit each day, until you feel quite happy about it.'

She didn't speak but the tears glistened on her lashes. How could she go on hating and despising all men when this man, her stepfather who had no need to care so deeply, bound by no ties of blood to feel outrage, was being so kind and good? She let him wipe away a tear with his index finger and steeled herself not to flinch. A new understanding, a new affection and respect for him was being born and the last thing she wanted to do was to hurt him. Was she on the road to recovery, she wondered, but then she realized that it would be a long, long time before the raw wound healed.

She had felt well enough to sit in the parlour with Edwin without the presence of either Albert or her mam. She gave him a thin, watery smile as she took the rather wilted-looking bunch of flowers he held out to her.

'They've drooped a bit with the heat. Sorry.'

'That doesn't matter. It's the thought . . . ' She placed them on the table and sat down, twisting her hands in her lap and praying he wouldn't try to reach out and touch her.

'Are you feeling better, Em?'

'A bit. Albert is good, kind . . .'

'Salt of the earth. Best bloke I ever met.'

They both fell silent and she thought how different it would have been in the days before . . . 'They said you're going away to sea?'

'Aye. I don't know how I'll get on but it's a job.'

'Won't you mind not being . . .'

'A butler?' he interrupted her. 'No. They're a dying breed. Soon be extinct like the Dodo,' he tried to joke. 'No. The big luxury liners are the thing of the future. Plenty of work and plenty of tips from rich Americans and, who knows, one day I might get to be a chief steward and that's better than being a butler.'

A memory stirred. 'Isn't that the ship that the Malones are in?'

'Right again. I don't expect I'll see much of them though, not that anyone in their right mind would want to see that lot. They'll be down in the engine room and I'll be in the dining room.'

'You're going as a waiter then?'

'Yes. I didn't fancy being a steward. Glorified skivvy

that. Hope I don't get sick. I wasn't on the way across the channel in the war and it was rough.'

She was feeling more at ease and less apprehensive that he would suddenly reach out and take her hand. 'How long will you be away for?'

'Just under three weeks at a time. We get shore leave in New York while we restock and coal.' What he didn't tell her was that rumour had it that the home port was to be changed from Liverpool to Southampton. He wasn't sure about it but he hoped it wasn't true. If it was, then he'd ask for another ship. He fiddled nervously with his collar. He had to ask her. 'Em, can I ask you something?'

Instantly she was on the defensive. 'What?'

'We did have an understanding, didn't we? I don't know how to say this . . . But has anything changed? I still love you, Em.'

She'd begun to tremble. Things had changed, how could they help not changing. But it was she who had changed, not him. 'Edwin, I don't want to hurt you, but don't ask me that, not yet, because I don't know. I just don't know. Maybe in time, maybe soon I'll get better and then . . .' She waved her hands helplessly as she fell silent.

He should have known better, he told himself. He had been a crass fool to even ask. Of course she needed time to get better, as she'd put it. He could have cut his tongue out. 'I'm sorry. I didn't mean to upset you. We won't talk about it again until you feel better. Just remember you're my girl and you always will be.' He reached out to take her hand but she pulled away from him. That gesture cut him like a knife, although he realized it wasn't meant to. She just couldn't help it. Mentally he castrated James Mercer as he did nearly every night.

'You get well and strong, Em. I'll see you when I get home.' His tone was light and his smile bright but both gestures were false and forced.

Chapter Nine

At the weekend a letter was delivered to Lonsdale Street. Lily turned it over in her hand, noting the fine quality of the paper, the neat black copperplate writing. She didn't have to guess who it was from. The paper and the writing, and the fact that they hardly ever received mail, told her plainly.

She sat down and passed it over to Albert.

'It's addressed to you, Lily.'

'I know, but I also know who it's from and I'm uneasy about it.'

Using the blunt edge of the knife, he slit the envelope open and drew out a single sheet of cream vellum and scanned the two lines of writing. 'You're to go to see him this afternoon with Emily, to discuss her future. That's what he says.'

'I thought it might be something like that. She'll not go.'

He sighed heavily. 'Who can blame her? But it's bound to be something important, tell her that. Something to her advantage.'

'Compensation?'

'Probably.'

'She'll not take his money and I won't blame her.'

'I understand how you feel, love, but she deserves something after what she's been through. And there's the fact that we're not going to drag his son or his precious name through the courts.'

Lily's heart was heavy. Was there to be no end to

all this heartache? Why couldn't they be left alone to nurse their wounds? Yet something forced her to demand some kind of retribution.

Emily refused point blank at first but, after an hour's coaxing and reasoning by Lily and Albert, she agreed to go. She did insist that they both go with her.

Edwin let them in. He smiled at Emily and his opinion of her rose. It took guts to come back here, he thought. He was thankful he would finish that evening. He only wished he could have gone into the study with her.

Richard Mercer greeted them curtly and indicated that Emily and Lily should be seated. He was a deeply troubled man. He would be profoundly grateful when this whole matter was cleared up, for a black cloud hung over the house. Mrs Webster was still her rather aloof and efficient self, hiding her thoughts and accusations beneath that mantle of cold formality she always wore. Cook he hadn't seen, nor the little chit with the frizzy red hair who had temporarily taken over Phoebe-Ann's job. Edwin was silent, but it was a brooding, accusing silence that made him feel guilty. Olivia had only been told that James had attacked Emily while the balance of his mind had been disturbed. He didn't tell her that the disturbance would probably never pass. Olivia could never have been told that her brother had committed rape. It was just too terrible a thing to explain to a young girl. It didn't cross his mind that Olivia was only a year younger than the girl who had suffered so terribly, and was the same age as Phoebe-Ann who had been told the shocking truth.

Olivia had wept copiously when James had been taken away with great secrecy and under sedation on the Tuesday night. That was an experience he never wanted to go through again. It would kill him. Of course he would visit his son, he told himself, but looking down the years to come he knew in his heart of hearts that the visits would become more infrequent until they would stop. Insanity was a terrible curse on a family. Even more so on a family as prominent as his, for he hoped Olivia would marry well.

He was patently aware that Olivia was shallow and totally selfish. That was in part his fault. She had demanded to 'get away from all this' as she'd put it, and he'd agreed with her that a cruise was a good idea. She had cried that she couldn't possibly put up with that Kitty or another succession of maids now that Phoebe-Ann had gone. Especially after the dreadful experience she'd just gone through. He had thought that perhaps it was best that the events hadn't touched her deeply. The *Berengaria* was due to sail for the Far East and he had duly booked her a state room. Now all that remained was to try to compensate Emily and he could try to pick up the pieces of his life.

He cleared his throat and fiddled with his watch chain. 'Emily, no words, no actions, no amount of money can compensate you for what you have suffered in this house, at the hands of my son. But in all honour I must try to recompense you.'

'Sir, I don't want your money!' Emily burst out. She felt cold. It was as though the atmosphere in the house had wrapped her in its icy folds and she fought down the rising panic.

Albert placed a steadying hand on her shoulder and she clasped it tightly.

'I wouldn't insult you with money alone, Emily. No,

what I am offering you is work.' He raised his hand to still the protestations he saw rise to her lips. 'My dear, departed wife has two aunts, maiden aunts, who live on Princes Avenue. They have a cook and a general factotum, both of whom are advanced in years. But they have no maid or housekeeper. Both have retired due to ill health. They have a small income but I pay for the servants. I'd like you to consider going to work for them. Your salary will of course be paid by me and there will be something invested for you, should you ever decide to marry or choose another path in life.'

Emily started to speak but he quietly interrupted her. 'There are no men in the house, except of course Mr Stockley who is as old as Mr Potter who has just retired.'

Albert squeezed Emily's hand. 'It sounds a fair offer, Emily, girl,' he urged, while wondering if Richard Mercer knew of her fear of men.

'Well, what do you say, love?' Lily queried. He was trying to make amends. He hadn't insulted them by offering a large sum of money. That would have appeared to have been a blatant attempt at bribery. Of course what he was offering was a sort of bribe. Nothing had been said but it was taken as read that no fuss would be made.

At last Emily nodded. She had to work, she knew that, and she hadn't relished the thought of factory or shop work. She'd been in service ever since she'd left school and she'd enjoyed it.

Richard Mercer breathed a sigh of relief and leaned back in his chair. 'Good girl. I'll write to Miss Millicent and Miss Nesta today. When would you like to start?'

Seeing how confused her daughter looked, it was

Lily who answered. 'Shall we say Sunday, sir? That will give me time to get her things sorted out.'

'Yes. Yes, indeed.' He looked a little perplexed. 'Er . . . I must say this. Both ladies are a little . . . eccentric, shall we say. They tend to adhere to old values.'

'Nothing wrong in that, sir,' Albert put in gravely.

'Perhaps I didn't put that very well. They adhere to the fashions of the early years of this century and sometimes those of the last one, too. Emily, I think you will be required to wear your skirts much longer, to cover your ankles.' He felt rather foolish. He should have let the girl find out their antiquated ways for herself but then she'd gone through enough without having to endure a dressing down for her immodesty, as he was sure Millicent would put it. She'd certainly come to no harm in that house. He'd always viewed Adele's aunts as a little bit strange. Harmless but slightly strange.

'I'm sure her mam will attend to all that.' Albert could see the interview was at an end and he felt it better to get them both out of the highly charged atmosphere.

'I should have asked him how much the investment was,' Lily said when they were outside in the street.

'Mam, I don't want to hear another word about that money. I don't want it!'

'You might do one day. Maybe you'll want to get married. It will be useful then, love.'

Emily turned to her mother, her gaze stricken. 'Oh, Mam, I'll never get married! I couldn't! I just couldn't!'

Lily patted her shoulder. 'Time is a great healer, Emily. Just believe that.'

*　　*　　*

Time was something that Edwin was short of. He left the house in Upper Huskisson Street on the Sunday night and the *Mauretania* docked on the Thursday, to sail again on Saturday. He had his uniform to buy from Greenburgh's in Park Lane. He had to sort out an allotment for his aunt, there were documents to be obtained, which inevitably meant running the gauntlet of a variety of officials and miles of red tape, and he wanted to take Emily out, if she'd agree. She refused but said she would go to see him off and with that he had to be content.

After a hectic week, at eight o'clock on Saturday morning he stood in the richly panelled first class dining room with hundreds of other waiters, stewards, cooks, bakers, scullions and bellboys, awaiting the arrival of the Cunard shore-side official and the Board of Trade official. Everything was alien to him and he felt a little daunted. On board this floating palace, as he perceived it to be, things were very different to all he had experienced on shore. He glanced around him thinking of the Malones but obviously the stokehold crew had a separate time and place for signing articles. A pungent aroma of beer and tobacco hung over the assembly. Obviously there were quite a few who were still recovering from their last night of shore leave and also some who had taken advantage of the hospitality of the Stile House at the Pierhead even at this early hour, he deduced.

'How long do we have to wait?' he enquired of a lithe, swarthy-skinned lad of about his own age who stood idly surveying the decorative plaster and stained glass of the domed ceiling.

'Until the Old Man and the Two Ringer decide to put in an appearance and the Company wallah of course. No show without punch,' he answered.

'The who?'

'The Captain, Second Steward and Cunard Official. What's yer name?'

'Leeson. Edwin Leeson.'

'Todd. Johnny, an' don't start singing that bloody song either! There's enough comedians on board as it is. Most people call me Todd.'

Edwin grinned remembering the old sea shanty entitled 'Johnny Todd'. 'It's my first trip.'

Todd rolled his eyes. 'God 'elp yer.'

'It can't be that bad?'

'Don't bet on it. The skipper's a birrof a tyrant. Comes round once a week to inspect all the glory holes.'

'Where's that?' It appeared to be a different language.

'Where we kip, like. Anywhere they can stick a few bunks an' a locker. Eh, up! Here they come.'

There was much shuffling of feet and gradually a silence fell as the Captain, accompanied by the Chief Steward and Chief Purser made their way to the table where the two officials who had preceded them were already shuffling wads of paperwork.

He listened while the Cunard Official read out the Statutory Conditions of Employment, to be honoured by all Company servants during voyage number 120 of the Royal Merchant Ship *Mauretania*. His concentration wavered as the latitudes and longitudes, rations and watering provisions in accordance with the Board of Trade scales were read out, plus the laws empowered to the Master over the crew for the duration of the voyage. Idly he wondered how order and efficiency could possibly emerge from the assembled motley crew who he judged to be about five hundred or more strong and not including engine-room crew. His deliberations were interrupted by a dig in the ribs from his companion.

'Told yer. Birrof a tyrant. "All members of the catering department to be in uniform at the wishes of the Master",' he repeated, *sotto voce*. 'He's a bloody marionette! Got to wear our bloody monkey suits all day!'

Edwin smirked at the description of the Captain as given by Todd. 'Don't you mean martinet? What happens now?'

'When yer turn comes, go an' sign on an' then its down to work. I bet yer only 'ere cos someone got a D.R. in 'is book.'

'What?'

'If 'e puts D.R. in yer Discharge Book you've 'ad yer chips. D.R. – Declines to Report. Bad behaviour. Dead bad behaviour. If yer mam or yer wife asks what it means, tell 'em it's Definitely Reliable.' He winked. 'Know what I mean, like?'

'I've got neither.'

'Aren't you the lucky one then.'

'The pay's not bad though. I didn't get £8.5s a month where I worked before.'

'Bet yer never 'ad ter work fourteen or sixteen hours a day for it though.'

'I did.'

'Not much of a bloody job then, was it. You'll gerra bit extra when we dock, like. What with yer dropsy an' all.'

'Can't you speak in plain English?'

'Don't get all airyated with me, la! Tips. Money from the bloods – passengers. Yer can spot the lousy tippers. Eats everything, asks for more, asks for the à la carte menu, drives yer up the wall with complaints and gives yer nothin' at the end of the trip. Some of them are real 'ardfaced too. Snap their fingers at yer as if yer were a bloody dog! Eh, up! It's our turn. See yer later in the Pig an' Whistle.'

'Where the hell is that?' Edwin was becoming infuriated by his own ignorance.

'Crew's bar in the fo'castle,' Todd grinned.

He wondered how he ever got through the first day and night. It was sheer pandemonium. There were people everywhere, crowding the alleyways and public rooms. Cases, trunks and other pieces of luggage were strewn about carelessly and children of all ages seemed to have suffered the same fate and had taken this lack of parental control as an opportunity to run wild. At least four cabins had been overbooked. One set of passengers had claimed the cabins while those who contest their right of occupancy sat determinedly on their luggage in the companionway and refused to move until the harassed Purser arrived to try to sort it out.

Stewards and stewardesses rushed around with lists in their hands and dazed expressions on their faces while trying at the same time to answer hosts of questions. The Purser's office was total bedlam and he was instructed in his duties by a short-tempered head waiter whose own problems included two new commis waiters and at least a dozen others in various stages of inebriation, one of whom had been locked up in a storeroom by the Master at Arms for his own safety and that of the passengers. He would be totally useless until the following day. 'And don't think you can lie in your pit all day if you're sick!' had been the final admonition from the head waiter.

Things did calm down once all the visitors had gone ashore and the three blasts on the ship's whistle denoted their imminent departure from Liverpool. He was hardly aware of the movement of the ship. He was told he soon would be when he commented on the fact to Todd who was on the same allocation as himself.

His new-found friend was far from happy. 'Two eights in the bloody annexe!' he commented, then seeing the look of mystification on Edwin's face he translated. 'I've got eight passengers at each sitting and the tables are at the end of the bloody room. I'll be worn out by termorrer!'

He had had little time to think after that. It was much like serving dinner at the Mercers', he thought, except that it was done at a breakneck pace. He also found that other duties were expected of him. He was expected to help the entrée chef and the vegetable chef and he had to carve for the buffet. At the end of the day there was a 'scrub out' of the kitchens. When he at last fell into his bunk he was exhausted.

He was awakened at six o'clock by the raucous blast of a bugle. Tea was brought round in a bucket by a bellboy and he was obliged to start the day with another 'scrub out', this time of a section of indoor deck. Then it was on with the first duties of the day.

It was a routine he quickly became used to and the crossing was uneventful. He was looking forward to going ashore in New York. His interest had been aroused by Todd who had a seemingly inexhaustible list of haunts.

' 'Ave yer got a girl back 'ome?' Todd asked one evening, when the work was finally over and they stood in the crew's bar.

'Sort of.'

'What kind of answer is that! 'Ave yer or 'aven't yer?'

140

'Yes.'

'Whats 'er name?'

'Emily.'

'Gorra photo of 'er?'

He shook his head. 'What about you?' He didn't want to dwell on his feelings for Emily. He knew she'd been concerned when she'd seen him off but she'd just held out her hand to say goodbye. He had hoped for more and there hadn't been time to hold a long conversation.

'Love 'em an' leave 'em, that's my motto. I live with me mam an' dad, our kid and me two sisters. Bring anyone home more than twice an' me mam starts askin' should she go an' book the 'all an speak ter the priest. She can't wait ter get rid of me. What does she do this Emily?'

'She's in service with two old spinsters.'

'Sod that for a lark! Was that what you did an' all?'

'Aye. We were in the same house until she moved.'

'An' you left an' all. Must 'ave been a bloody slave driver that fella,' Todd probed. He was no fool and Edwin had quickly realized this.

'I'd had enough. Wanted to see the world; besides, it wasn't the same after she left.'

' 'Ow many were there in the 'ouse?'

'Only three of them. The Master, his son and daughter.'

'Sounds like it was a doddle. What did yer up an' leave for?'

'No prospects.'

'No bleeding prospects 'ere either. Not unless yer lookin' for two rings on yer sleeve. That's about as high as yer can get, an' I wouldn't 'ave 'is job for a big clock! All that 'assle an' keepin' tabs on us lot! 'E can keep it!'

141

'No ambition then?'

Todd grinned. 'Oh, aye! Marry one of the toffs we gerron 'ere an' live in luxury all me life.'

'Fat chance of that I'd say.'

Todd became morose. 'Yer right. Most of them wouldn't spit on yer if yer were on fire. Drink up, only another day an' we'll be dockin'.' He grinned, good humour restored by the thought of shore leave.

Shore leave passed in a blur as he followed Todd from one drinking establishment to another, although he did make time to visit some of the shops. Most of them, however, were well out of his price range. He bought little souvenirs for his aunt and for Lily and Albert and Phoebe-Ann. For Emily he bought a little 'purse' as bags were called. It was an evening bag but he didn't care that she probably would never have occasion to use it. It was a trinket, a bit of finery. It was made of black satin and was worked with bugle beads and jet.

'That's a bit posh, like! She'll be after yer to take 'er to the Royal Court or the Adelphi so she can use it,' Todd remarked.

He shrugged and laughed. 'I might take her one day.'

'Yeah, an' I'll join the Band of 'Ope!' came the quick reply. 'Are yer comin' for a last pint of jungle juice then?'

The weather on the return journey was rough, but he thanked God that he obviously wasn't going to succumb to seasickness. As the storm increased in force the ship rolled and pitched and the sea crashed over her, wrecking the rails of the monkey island and tearing away two lifeboats. Her decks were completely awash and at times only her four funnels were visible above the foaming, churning water. Then she'd rise from the trough, her plates groaning and protesting beneath the weight of water before she plunged yet again into the next mountainous wave.

There were significantly fewer passengers in the dining rooms as the storm raged. Ropes were slung across the public rooms, table cloths were dampened so dishes wouldn't slide, but meal times were punctuated by the sound of breaking china and glass. Seasoned passengers moved with the roll of the ship. Walking when she dipped her bow, remaining stationary through the roll and rise before continuing their progress. Others ran a short distance, clung to the nearest solid fixture, then ran on again. But there were cases of broken bones. All these attempts at progress were pointed out to Edwin by Todd, accompanied by often hilarious comments. He also informed Edwin that the *Maury* had her own peculiar way of dealing with rough weather. 'Sort of a thrust, a dip and a dive into the sea and through it. Pitchin' an' sprayin' all over. They 'ave souls yer know, do ships. They're not just lumps of steel an' if yer don't believe me, ask the Captain. 'E says she knows 'e's in charge, like. Sounds daft but it's true. She's often soaked 'is best shirt by doin' 'er tricks, the dip and dive even when it's calm. I'm tellin' yer it's the God's own truth! Mind, it's at times like this that I'm glad I'm a waiter. I couldn't care less if the whole lot of them go down with seasickness, we'd 'ave no work. It's the poor bloody stewards I feel sorry for 'aving ter clean up after them. I'd stick a bloody bucket over their 'eads, save all the mess!'

By the time they reached the North Western Approaches Edwin felt he was a seasoned veteran. He'd had his baptism of fire, or should it be water, he mused. There were no new or strange procedures to face. Just the thought of docking in Liverpool and that was pleasant. He wondered how Emily had coped while he'd been away. He lit a cigarette and leaned over the rail of the promenade deck, staring down at the sea far below him. It was almost peaceful now after what they'd come through. He'd forgone the noisy companionship in the Pig and Whistle as all crew bars on all ships were called. He wanted time to reflect. It was a few minutes before he realized he wasn't alone. He turned and saw the strapping figure, chest bared to the cold wind, leaning against a ventilator. 'All right, mate?' It wasn't a question, just a form of acknowledgement that he knew the man was there.

The figure moved forward and he noted the soot-covered torso of a stoker.

'Not a bad night,' he ventured.

'I know you. Seen you before somewhere.'

He recognized the voice. 'Your name's Malone, isn't it?'

'Might be.'

Edwin shrugged. 'Suit yourself.'

'Got a light?' A cigarette was pushed under his nose.

He obliged. He knew their reputation and he didn't want any trouble. 'Can't be much fun working down there.'

'Don't expect it to be. Ever seen it. The stokehold?'

'No.'

'Didn't think yer had. Poncin' about up 'ere after the bloods.'

He felt his temper rise. 'It's no bloody picnic!'

'Ses you! Want ter go down an' see?'

144

To refuse the offer would be construed as cowardice, yet he had no inclination to go on a guided tour of the stokehold, especially not in his white uniform jacket. 'No thanks, I take your word for it. Hell afloat, so they tell me and you lot are the real grafters. The ship wouldn't be going anywhere without the black squad. Then we'd all be out of a job.'

Thus appealed to, Jake Malone grunted his agreement and they passed the remainder of the time in silence.

Chapter Ten

Emily had never met anyone quite like the two old ladies she had gone to meet for the first time the day after Edwin had sailed. As she knocked at the front door of the house in Princes Avenue she was very apprehensive.

The house had a look of faded gentility about it. Its pale grey paint was peeling slightly, the colour of the stucco had faded and the brasses were a little tarnished. A stooped old man had opened the door to her. When she'd given him her name, she stood in the gloomy hall while he disappeared along the narrow corridor. Old fashioned framed prints, draped in black crêpe, covered the walls. From what could be seen of the wallpaper that wasn't hidden by pictures, it was dark green overprinted with roses that had once been blood red. All the paintwork and the anaglypta that covered the bottom half of the walls was dark green. A bust of a man Emily didn't recognize stood on its column in the stairwell. A garishly decorated *jardinière*, containing an aspidistra, graced the foot of the staircase. The whole effect was sombre and exuded the air of a bygone age.

'You're to come in.' Stockley's reed-thin voice interrupted her thoughts.

He held the door open for her as she walked in and she acknowledged the gesture with a nod. Her first impression was of a very dark room, crammed with heavy furniture and bric-à-brac. Every surface was covered with china ornaments in varying sizes, dried flower arrangements, wax fruit and even small animals and birds under rather dusty glass domes. The ornately-framed mirror over the fireplace and all the pictures were again swathed in mourning crêpe and she wondered who had died. The heat from the fire that burned in the hearth was oppressive and unnecessary, she thought.

'What's your name, girl? Is that letter for me?'

Millicent Barlow spoke in a clipped, authoritarian voice. She was older than her sister and no-one was allowed to forget it by word or deed. She was tall and thin. Her greying hair was parted in the centre and tightly scraped back into a bun which was covered by a white lace cap. She wore a black silk dress that heightened the waxy colour of her skin. The dress was old-fashioned, the high buttoned collar covered with jet beads. She reminded Emily of a much thinner version of old Queen Victoria.

She held out the letter and stood, eyes downcast, while it was read. Miss Nesta, she observed from under her lashes, was small and plump and had once been a very beautiful woman and a remnant of that beauty still clung to her. Her complexion was fair, her cheeks retaining a pinkish tinge like that of a faded rose. The blue eyes were wide and Emily thought she saw a glimmer of amusement in them. Like her sister, her hair was taken back and covered by a cap, but a few tendrils had escaped or been allowed to escape, and it was noticeable that her hair curled naturally. Her dress of dove grey moire was in the high buttoned, fitted style of the Edwardian era and a white, lacy shawl was draped around her shoulders. They were like relics of another age, Emily thought.

But they posed no threat to her and she had liked Miss Nesta on sight.

'He speaks very highly of you, does my nephew, so why has he sent you here to us?' Millicent Barlow's grey eyes were piercing. She didn't believe in beating about the bush.

'I . . . I thought he might have explained . . .' She felt the blood rushing to her cheeks.

'What did you do wrong? Come along I insist on frankness?'

'Nothing ma'am. I did nothing wrong.'

'Don't fuss the girl, Millie! If dear Richard thinks she will suit us, she will. You wouldn't have wanted him to send us someone who had done something dreadful, would you?'

'Dear Richard, my foot! How long have we been asking him for more help? Now, if dear Adele were still alive . . .' She produced a scrap of a lace handkerchief and dabbed her eyes.

'Now Millie, don't upset yourself. You know it's not good for you.' Miss Nesta began to reach out towards her sister.

'Don't fuss me, Nesta! You know how I hate it!'

Nesta Barlow looked hurt and Emily felt sorry for her.

'I'm sorry if I'm intruding on your grief, ma'am.' Emily gestured towards the black-garlanded over-mantel. 'I wasn't told that you'd been bereaved. May I ask who has died?'

Miss Nesta uttered a little gasp and Miss Millicent's eyes showed her shock, but it was she who spoke. 'Why our dear Adele of course! Didn't *that* man tell you?'

Emily stared back in confusion. Adele Mercer had been dead for years and years. 'But . . .'

Miss Millicent waved her into silence. 'We won't dwell on it, it's too upsetting. Do you know your duties?'

'Yes, ma'am.' She was puzzled, but Miss Nesta gave her a lovely smile. She smiled back. They were both a bit odd but she had warmed to Miss Nesta and she'd probably grow to like Miss Millicent once she'd got used to her.

'That dress won't do. Only paupers and loose women show their legs. You'll dress properly in this house.'

'Yes, ma'am. I understand. I've had my uniforms lengthened.'

Lily had spent the last two nights adding six inch strips to the hems of her black working dresses and when she'd tried them on she'd wondered how she would ever manage to cope with the long skirts constantly threatening to trip her up. 'Humour them,' had been Lily's advice. 'You'll have to get changed before you come home; you can't go walking the streets like that. It's so old-fashioned everyone will die laughing,' had been Phoebe-Ann's advice. Lily had tutted in annoyance.

'Good. Now get along, Emily. Cook will inform you where everything is kept. We rise early and retire early. Prayers are at nine a.m. sharp. This is a Christian household.'

They didn't belong to this century, Emily thought with amusement as she went downstairs. Family prayers every morning had gone out with the death of the old Queen nearly twenty years ago. The same antiquarian order prevailed in the kitchen and she sighed. There would be no Goblin vacuum cleaners in this house.

Cook was a wizened old woman but a kindly soul.

149

Over a cup of tea she told Emily something of the family history. The old man had been a sea captain and a fierce disciplinarian who ruled the household with a rod of iron when he was at home. Miss Nesta had been a real beauty but he had refused all offers for her hand, despite the protests of Nesta and her mother. By the time he died their mother too was dead and Nesta's beauty had faded. The former suitors had all been married for years by then. Millicent Barlow was a lot like her father but destined to be a spinster, Cook added. 'She bosses poor Miss Nesta around something awful at times and Miss Nesta is such a sweet soul.'

'Why do they still have all the mourning up for Mrs Mercer?'

'Lost track of time in that respect. They wanted time to stand still. Adele Mercer's father was their brother and they doted on them both. It shattered their little world when she died. She used to come here every week without fail and brought Master James and Miss Olivia when they were young. Oh, those were the days. This house used to come alive. It was just what was needed – the sound of children's laughter.'

At the mention of James Mercer Emily felt sick and she hoped Cook wasn't going to question her further.

'So, you see they are a bit odd but there's no harm in either of them. A word of warning though. Never, never move anything. Not a picture or a vase or a knick-knack. They know where every single thing is and if they're moved there's hell to pay. The last girl made that mistake, apart from which we couldn't afford her.'

'Don't they . . . I mean . . .'

'Have any money? Not much. They have this house

and a small allowance Mr Mercer makes up to a decent amount and he pays our wages. I've been with them since they were girls, and Mr Stockley too. Just the two of us left now. Sad really, there used to be a big staff when the old man was alive. I started as a scullion and Stockley as a footman. Aye, it's sad.'

Emily warmed to the woman and as she looked around the old-fashioned kitchen she felt at ease. More at ease than she'd felt since she'd left Upper Huskisson Street. Oh, they were eccentric but she liked them both, especially Miss Nesta. 'I'd better make a start then,' she said, getting to her feet.

'Your being here will make a difference, Emily. It will make life easier for us.'

Emily smiled. 'Just as long as I don't move anything.'

She settled in well. The work was not too hard or demanding, once she'd given everywhere a thorough 'bottoming' as Lily always called a good clean out. She found that Miss Millicent's bark was worse than her bite and that Miss Nesta had a streak of mischief in her. They both lived in the past which she found odd. They had no wireless and no newspapers were delivered, so events in the world outside passed unnoticed and unmarked. It was an atmosphere whose tranquillity suited Emily. The quiet charm was balm to her battered spirit and she began to look forward again.

She had been there two weeks when one afternoon she decided to sort out the linen cupboard which was situated on the top landing. She knew that the linen was really the responsibility of a housekeeper, but as there wasn't one she supposed she'd have to do it. Miss Millicent was out. Once a month she ventured from the house by taxi, to the committee meeting for the Society for Distressed Gentlewomen. She said it did her good, made her count her blessings for there but for the grace of God, not to mention the benevolence of Richard Mercer, went herself and her sister. Miss Nesta did not accompany her. 'I was never very good at committees and things,' she said airily when Miss Millicent's forthcoming outing was explained.

Emily assumed Miss Nesta was in the drawing room, so she was startled to see her disappearing through the door that led to the attic. She followed her.

'Is there something I can do for you, Miss Nesta?'

Nesta turned around, her hand going to her mouth, her eyes darting along the landing. 'Oh, you won't tell Millie will you? She doesn't like me to come up here.'

'Not if you don't want me to.'

Miss Nesta beckoned her into the room. 'Shut the door, Emily. Now, if you promise not to tell Millie I'll show you my special things.'

Emily was mystified and curious. 'I promise.'

'Then open that trunk for me, please.'

Emily did as she was bid and was surprised to see no accumulation of dust on the lid of an old cabin trunk. Inside were layers and layers of tissue paper and small muslin sachets of lavender and lemon verbena.

Miss Nesta had sat down in an old wicker chair. 'Take them out.'

Under the tissue was a froth of cream lace and faded pink satin. It was a ballgown that had once been beautiful.

'Oh, Miss Nesta, it's lovely!'

'Yes, it is. I call this my "yesterday chest". Take them all out, I want to look at them.'

Emily shook out the folds of a blue organza looped up with bows of blue satin ribbon, then a buttercup yellow silk festooned with ecru lace. 'Oh, they're beautiful! Are they yours?'

The old lady nodded, her expression wistful, her eyes misty.

'You must have looked gorgeous.'

'I did. Mama used to say, "Nesta, you look just like a princess." There should be some other things.'

Emily delved into the trunk again. At the bottom was a pair of embroidered satin slippers, so small they could have been made for a child, and a fan of painted silk stretched between ivory ribs. Little silver tassels decorated the handle. Half a dozen dance-cards, silk tasselled and all full, were the last items. She passed them to Miss Nesta who fingered them lovingly.

Emily smiled at her. 'I bet you were the belle of the ball.'

'Oh, indeed I was. I never had an empty dance-card like Millie sometimes did. I was always the centre of attention and all those handsome young men would make such a fuss of me that Mama said it would turn my head.' Her blue eyes were misty as though she could visualize again those happy, far off days.

Emily felt so sorry for her, remembering what Cook had told her. 'Did you . . . did you ever want to get married, miss?'

'Yes. Oh, yes I did, Emily. And I could have had my pick too.' She sighed. 'But they were never good enough or wealthy enough. Papa always found fault . . . ' Her words died away and Emily was sorry she'd asked. It had been tactless of her.

'If only he had given me the chance . . . . I would have been so happy I know I would, and I'd've been a good wife too.'

153

'I'm sorry. I didn't mean to pry.'

Miss Nesta smiled, a smile full of regret. 'I know you didn't. I like you Emily, you're a good, kind girl. Do you have a young man?'

She nodded.

'And will you marry him?'

'I don't know, miss.'

'Oh, you should, Emily!'

'It's not all that . . . easy.'

'Does your mama not approve of him?'

'Yes. At least she would, but . . .'

'But what?'

'It's hard to explain.'

'Don't you love him?'

'Yes. But . . .'

'Then marry him, Emily! Time is so precious. It slips away and all that is left is . . . memories.' She stared down at the objects in her lap, stroking the satin slippers gently. 'Memories. Memories are dry and dusty and sad.'

Emily felt so sorry for her. 'Maybe I will marry him one day,' she said softly.

Miss Nesta consciously pulled herself out of her reverie. 'Will you put them away carefully, dear?'

'I will. They are so lovely.'

The old lady got to her feet. She held out the fan. 'I'd like you to have this, Emily.'

'Oh, Miss Nesta, I couldn't!'

'Of course you can. It's not valuable. I insist!' She pressed it into Emily's hand. 'As a reminder that youth and beauty and hope don't last for ever. They tarnish, like the silver tassels on this fan.'

Emily took it. 'I'll treasure it, Miss Nesta, I promise.'

Miss Nesta didn't seem to have heard her. The

familiar vague expression was back in her eyes and she walked slowly to the door, leaving Emily kneeling on the floor surrounded by the finery that was like a tissue of half-forgotten dreams.

It was Saturday afternoon and Emily was still at work when Edwin called at Lonsdale Street. Phoebe-Ann was resplendent in her new autumn coat of violet bouclé, with a matching hat. She was ready to wander around the shops in town with her friends, something they did every Saturday afternoon, although they didn't always buy things. They just enjoyed looking and planning and gazing enviously in the windows of the more exclusive shops whose prices were far beyond their reach. They also enjoyed being admired by the young men who congregated on corners for this purpose.

'How did it all go, lad?' Lily asked, indicating that he should sit down.

'Not too bad once I'd got used to things and found my way around and learned the language,' he laughed. 'Here, I brought you these.' He handed out small packages to everyone. Emily's gift he had tucked inside his coat.

'You work too hard for your money to go buying everyone presents,' Lily protested.

He grinned. 'I gathered that it was sort of expected, but I wanted to anyway,' he added hastily.

'Oh, Mam! Look at this, isn't it great?' Phoebe-Ann was delighted with the small bottle of cheap perfume.

'Bought on Fifth Avenue where all the best shops are.' He had actually bought it just around the corner but it was close enough, he thought.

'Just imagine – all the way from New York! Alice will be green with envy.'

'And at all costs Alice must be made to be green with envy,' Albert joked before intercepting a frown from his wife.

Phoebe-Ann dabbed a little behind her ears and leaned forward towards Edwin. 'Does it smell heavenly?'

'I don't know about that, but it's nice.'

'If you're going out Phoebe-Ann, then go. All this nonsense is giving me a headache.'

Phoebe-Ann ignored her mother although Lily's sharp tone upset her. Mam always seemed to be getting at her lately and she couldn't forget that awful scene when Lily had beaten her. Mam would always attribute some of the blame to her, even though Emily insisted she didn't. It was so unfair, too, but there were nights when she lay in bed, listening to Emily's breathing, when she would turn over and over in her mind all the things she'd said to James Mercer. Had she led him on? Had he misconstrued her sympathy? Had those words – meant only to show that she understood and pitied him – been taken as tokens of growing affection? The doubts always magnified in the hours of darkness and sometimes they fired her imagination until she began to believe it *had* been her fault and that she would be punished for it, and she'd had to stop herself from waking Emily and telling her she was sorry, so very, very sorry. But, when daylight came, it chased away the shadows of guilt and she felt stupid for becoming so hysterical, for blowing it all up out of proportion.

She smiled at Edwin as she placed the violet hat over her short hair and picked up her bag. 'See you all later on.'

'Will it be all right for me to go and meet Emily from work, Mrs Davies?'

Lily smiled. 'It's a bit early yet and I'd wait on the corner of the street. Miss Millicent and Miss Nesta are a bit old-fashioned.'

'As well as being odd?' Edwin grinned.

'You've heard then?'

'Emily wrote to me. The letter was waiting when we got to New York.' He wanted to ask how Emily was. Did Lily think she'd be more responsive to him now, but he couldn't bring himself to ask.

'Have a cup of tea and tell us what it's like, this going to sea,' Albert stated.

He took the cup Lily handed him. 'Hard work. Even harder if you get seasick. I was lucky, it didn't affect me, although we came through quite a storm on the way home. I saw lads who could hardly stand, their faces green, but having to work just the same.'

'Did you see anyone you knew?' Lily asked, for half the men in the city went away to sea.

'Only Jake Malone.'

'God! You could have done without that I'll bet!'

'He didn't seem that bad. He was sober of course. I don't envy him. It's a living hell down there. I went and took a quick look. A picture straight from hell it was. I don't know how they stick it, but apparently they are the finest black squad afloat.'

'I heard that they're going to convert the *Maury* to oil,' Albert put in.

'It's a rumour that's been going around for a while. Ever since she went back into service after the war. The *Aquitania* is oil-fired, and the *Berengaria*, and they don't need half the manpower. A lot of jobs would be lost. There's a rumour that Southampton will be the home port soon.'

'What will you do then?' Lily asked.

157

He shrugged. 'Go with her I suppose, though I won't like it.'

Lily said nothing but began to stack the dirty teacups.

She looked the same, he thought with relief, as he saw her walk down the street. He stepped into the roadway so she would see him clearly. If only . . . if only she'd run to him, throw her arms around him.

'You're home,' Emily said shyly, looking up at him.

'I called to see your mam first. She told me to wait on the corner. Are they that bad?' he tried to sound jaunty.

She laughed. 'No. They are both lovely to work for. Oh, Miss Millicent can be a bit of a pain at times but Miss Nesta is a sweet old thing. It's such a shame; she showed me the beautiful clothes she wore when she was young and she must have been a beauty. Her pa would never let her marry and when he died she was too old. Beautiful dresses they were, packed in tissue paper and she insisted on giving me a fan.' She chattered on hoping to hide the awkwardness she felt. 'I don't think Miss Millicent would approve of you calling for me, though.'

'What about you, Em? Would you approve?'

She shrugged.

'Will we go for some tea? I've got something for you and I'd like to give it to you, well, somewhere sort of private.'

Panic bubbled up. Oh, no! What if he was going to ask her to marry him? What if the 'something' was a ring? What would she do, what could she say to him?

He sensed her fear. 'I'm not going to spring any surprises on you, Em. Honestly.'

She breathed deeply. She was going to have to overcome this feeling, for how could she hurt him? He had done nothing wrong. 'All right then,' she agreed.

She chose a little café at the very top of Bold Street where it merged with Renshaw Street, and they ordered tea and scones. When the tea arrived, she poured and started to make idle conversation.

He thrust the small package across the table. 'I know it's a bit of a useless thing, but I like it and I thought you would too.'

She undid the wrapping and exclaimed in delight at the beadwork and declared she'd never seen anything so fine, then she rebuked him for buying it. 'It must have been so expensive.'

'Maybe one day you'll find a use for it. We might have a night out at the theatre.'

'Us, at the theatre?'

'Why not?'

'We don't go to places like that. I mean it's people like Miss Olivia . . .'

'We can always make it the Hippodrome then?'

She smiled at him. 'Maybe one day.'

He wanted to reach out and take her hand but he controlled himself. 'Can I take you out tonight; it is Saturday?'

She looked into his eyes and fought down the panic she was feeling. 'Where to?' she asked. He'd never know how hard it had been to speak those words.

A slow smile spread across his face, a smile tinged with relief. 'Anywhere you like. You choose.'

She knew Phoebe-Ann was going dancing but she didn't want to join the throng on the dance floor of the Rialto or the Grafton. That would mean holding his hand, letting him encircle her waist with his arm.

159

'Shall we go to the music hall?' There she would be safe. He would sit beside her but in a separate seat.

'Fine. Which one?'

'The Trocadero?'

'I'll pick you up at seven.'

She smiled. 'I'll bring my evening bag.'

Chapter Eleven

Early in the New Year Albert had a letter from his cousin, Megan, asking could her son, Rhys, possibly stay with them while he looked for work and lodgings. Things were bad in the pits and he'd set his heart on coming to Liverpool to find work.

'No need for him to look for lodgings, he can live here, it's only right. He's family,' Lily said, seeing an opportunity to repay Albert for every act of love and kindness he'd shown them all since she'd married him. And she was worried about Phoebe-Ann. Ever since she'd been taken on at the B&A she'd become very forward in Lily's opinion. Three nights a week Phoebe-Ann went out with her friends from work. She spent hours before the mirror on these nights and if Lily commented on it there was always some remark or retort that bordered on insolence. And she'd caught her with face powder on.

'I just don't want to see her going to the bad,' she told Albert.

'Lily, you're being too hard on the girl. She's young, she wants to enjoy herself, she'll settle down in time, you see.'

'All she thinks about is dolling herself up and going out.'

'What's wrong with that?'

'It's the company she keeps. I've heard tales about that Alice Wainwright.'

He sighed. He wasn't very keen on the girls

Phoebe-Ann chose as her friends but it wasn't his place to say so and besides it would only worry Lily more. He'd also kept from her the fact that Jimmy had confided in him that he was thinking of emigrating.

'I have to say this, Albert, she's a flirt. I've watched her – even with Edwin Leeson. She's courting trouble. You'd think she'd have learned after our Emily . . .'

'Now, Lil. I think we agreed that that wasn't her fault.'

'Sometimes I wonder, I really do.'

'Don't be daft. She's just naive. She really doesn't know that she's . . .'

'Courting trouble. I worry about her. I wonder where she'll end up.'

'She's not that much of a fool. She has got a bit of sense.'

Lily shook her head. 'No she hasn't. Our Emily has always been the sensible one. At least when they worked together, I knew Emily would keep an eye on her, but look what happened and I'm not at all certain that Phoebe-Ann was blameless.'

'We could go round and round like this all night, Lily. Leave her be, she'll be just fine. She'll meet a nice lad and get wed and settle down, see if she doesn't.'

'I just hope she doesn't start acting up when Rhys arrives, that's all.'

Albert pursed his lips and looked thoughtful. Maybe Rhys's arrival would be timely. Maybe Phoebe-Ann and his young cousin would be attracted to each other. He pulled himself up. There he was seeing them down the aisle and they hadn't even met each other yet!

'He'll be very welcome, Albert, you know that.'

'Who will be welcome?' Phoebe-Ann asked, coming into the room. A smart little purple cloche hat covering her short hair, the matching coat over her arm.

'Albert's cousin is coming to stay with us.'

Phoebe-Ann looked interested. 'What's he like? How old is he?'

Lily shot a glance at her husband.

'He's as old as Jimmy and the last time I saw him he was in short britches. Strictly brought up if I know anything about his mam and dad.'

Phoebe-Ann looked uninterested. Probably a strait-laced country yokel, no fun at all.

'Come here to me,' Lily demanded.

Phoebe-Ann looked wary. 'What for?'

Lily got up. 'What's that you've got on your face?'

'Nothing, Mam.'

'Don't lie to me, Phoebe-Ann Parkinson!'

'It's only a bit of rouge. Everyone wears it now. You're so old-fashioned. Alice's mam doesn't carry on at her.'

'That's because she's usually in the snug of the Grecian with her cronies, knocking back milk stout! I don't like you mixing with her, she's common.'

'Mam! What a thing to say. You're a snob, that's what you are!'

'Don't you dare speak to me like that!'

Phoebe-Ann knew she'd gone too far. 'I'm sorry.'

'I should think so too.'

'And where are you off to? Dancing, is it?' Albert tried to make peace.

'The Rialto, there's an exhibition on. All the dances from America.'

'I wouldn't call all that dancing! Kicking your legs up and waving your hands!'

'Oh, Mam, please don't start again.'

'Go on and enjoy yourself,' Albert grinned, catching Lily's arm and forcing her to sit down opposite him.

When Phoebe-Ann had gone, Lily tutted but Albert smiled. 'Perhaps Rhys's coming might be the making of her. He just might be the right one.'

'I should be so lucky! Oh, maybe you're right. Perhaps I'm getting to be an old misery, it's just that I keep thinking of poor Emily.'

'They say lightning doesn't strike twice in the same place, Lil. Stop worrying, love.'

Rhys Pritchard was a dark-haired, dark-eyed, well-built young man in his early twenties and as soon as Lily was introduced to him she liked him. As soon as Rhys was introduced to Phoebe-Ann he fell in love with her. He was quiet by nature and even a little shy in the company of girls. It stemmed, he supposed, from not having any sisters and mixing solely in the company of men. Phoebe-Ann was unlike any girl or woman he had ever met. She dazzled him with her hazel eyes, her short, shining hair, her lithe figure and her vivacity. She was like a bright star, he thought. His eyes followed her every movement and he wondered how soon he could ask her out. He'd been brought up strict chapel and was eager to observe the proprieties, especially as he was a guest in the house, a stranger to the family, except Albert.

He broached the subject with Jimmy who was the same age as himself and the more garrulous of the two brothers. He was also the one who had offered to help him in his quest for work.

They travelled together on the overhead railway on Monday morning. It was bitterly cold, with frost sparkling on roof tops and pavements, glittering like diamonds in the light from the street lamps, for it was not seven o'clock. The atmosphere in the carriage was heavy with tobacco smoke and the smells which had impregnated the working clothes of the men and boys crushed together on the wooden seats.

'Don't get too upset if you aren't taken on, like. It's just a matter of either "first come, first served" or "if your face fits"; depends which blockerman it is.' Seeing the puzzled expression on Rhys's face he added, 'The foremen; they wear bowler hats.'

'I'm used to that sort of system. If the gaffer likes you, you get steady work.'

'What's it like down the pits?'

'Terrible. You've got to have worked down them to really understand.'

'At least here you can see the sky and breathe fresh air, though it's not so bloody fresh. Full of soot and muck an' God knows what else.'

'Jim, do you think your mam and Albert would mind if I asked Phoebe-Ann to come out with me?'

Jimmy raised one eyebrow. 'You don't believe in hanging around, do you? She'll lead you a dance, I'm warnin' you.'

'Will they mind though? They won't think I'm being forward, like?'

'Mam won't mind and I shouldn't think Albert will either. Good bloke your cousin. Best thing that ever happened to our mam, marryin' him. 'Ere, tell the driver it's not the end of his bloody shift so what's the 'urry?' he yelled to no-one in particular as they were all thrown forward when the driver applied the brakes a bit too harshly. There were other such comments as men thrown together disentangled themselves and their metal lunch boxes and billy cans.

'Bloody maniac! Look at the state of me "carry out"!' the man next to them grumbled, looking morosely at a large 'doorstep' of bread that had been wrapped in old greaseproof paper and stuffed in his coat pocket.

'What about Phoebe-Ann?' Rhys persisted.

'I'm tellin' you she'll lead you a dance.'

'I don't care.'

'Like a lamb to the slaughter. Well, ask her if you're so set on her. She likes dancin' and goin' to the cinema. Thinks she looks like Mary Pickford – some 'ope she's got!' He laughed at his own joke but seeing Rhys hadn't joined in he stopped. 'You know, the one who's just married Douglas Fairbanks.'

'I know who she is. Now you mention it, Phoebe-Ann does look a bit like her.'

'Oh, God! There's no doin' any good with you!' Jimmy rolled his eyes in mock despair.

'I can't ask her until I get a job.'

'Don't suppose you can. You can't take that one out on fresh air. Come on, it's our stop – Gladstone Graving – pneumonia corner!'

It was nearing the end of the week before Rhys was taken on and he'd begun to despair of ever getting work or asking Phoebe-Ann out. Day after day he'd joined the crowds of men looking for work on the docks and he began to wonder if he had been rash in his optimism that a city the size of Liverpool could offer work.

Saturday came; he had two days' pay and, after Lily had flatly refused to take a penny for his keep, he plucked up courage.

The lads were out helping Albert, who had a rush job on, and Lily was down the street with a neighbour who had been taken ill. Emily had not come in, which left him alone with Phoebe-Ann who was pressing a skirt with the flat iron.

'That's nice. Is it new?' he asked awkwardly.

'No.'

'Oh.' He was at a loss. Should he pay her more compliments or . . . Oh, in for a penny in for a pound, he thought. 'Phoebe-Ann, would you, will you . . . There's a new film on at the cinema in Clayton Square; will you let me take you?'

She stopped ironing and stared at him. 'Tonight?'

'Yes.' His heart was racing.

She hadn't really paid him much notice. Oh, she'd scrutinized him closely at first. He was handsome but so quiet and sort of gawky. It was the first time she'd ever heard him utter so long a sentence. She was in a quandary. She'd planned to go to the Locarno with Alice and Ginny, but she hadn't been to the cinema for ages.

'Mary Pickford's in it. You look like her, Phoebe-Ann,' he ventured.

She smiled and fluttered her long lashes. 'You're only saying that to flatter me!'

'I'm not! I mean it! You do!'

'All right then but I'll have to tell Alice I've had a change of mind.'

He was elated. 'Yes, yes of course. Shall I go and tell her?'

'No. You could take a note to her though.' He looked so eager to please her she thought. He would be like putty in her hands. 'I'll just finish this; I'll wear it tonight seeing as you like it,' she smiled.

*   *   *

He was ready long before she was. He'd taken the note to Alice who had looked him up and down and then smiled condescendingly and he decided he didn't like her. He smiled good humouredly when Jack, Jimmy and Albert made jokes about being a 'fast worker'. Lily had given him a genuine smile and had said, 'Don't you let her play you up. She's a flighty little madam at times.'

When Emily had arrived home he'd smiled at her while Lily explained he was waiting for Phoebe-Ann and if she didn't hurry up it would be no use in going at all. The film would be half over. He liked Emily. She was a quiet, self-effacing girl but he suspected that she was holding something back.

Phoebe-Ann made his heart sing when she slipped her arm through his on the way to the tram stop. She made him feel proud and important. Yes, that was it. Important. Something he'd never felt before. He bought her a quarter of lemon drops and a quarter of Everton Mints because she couldn't make up her mind.

'Oh, Rhys, you're so generous,' she said, gazing up at him.

'You can have anything you want, Phoebe-Ann,' he'd replied, wishing he could afford chocolates and even jewellery. But perhaps one day, he mused.

She had enjoyed herself, she thought with some amazement. She hadn't expected to.

'If you were old enough I'd take you for a drink. Somewhere really posh, not just a pub,' he said when they were on their way home.

'Would you – really?'

'Yes.'

She slipped her hand in his. She knew she was being very bold but she didn't care. There was no harm in him. He wouldn't get what her mam called 'ideas'. 'What about afternoon tea? The Imperial Hotel is very nice. By Lime Street Station.'

'Fine.' It sounded expensive but he felt reckless.

'Tomorrow?'

'It's Sunday.'

'So?'

'Don't you go to chapel or church? It's the Lord's Day.'

'Of course we do! We go in the morning to St Nathaniel's. I'm talking about the afternoon.'

'Won't they be closed?'

'No! It's an hotel!'

'I don't know. What would your mam say?' He'd never heard of anyone going out to a place of entertainment on a Sunday.

'She won't say anything. We're not going to an alehouse or somewhere common like that!'

He was reticent. At home they went to chapel at least twice, sometimes three times and, in between, it was considered proper to either read or walk in the hills beyond the valley. His mam had never done anything like what Phoebe-Ann was suggesting. 'Couldn't we go next Saturday afternoon?'

Phoebe-Ann was annoyed. What was the matter with him? He'd seemed so nice. A bit quiet but nice and now he was all pious and disapproving, as though she'd suggested they do something really shocking. 'I've made arrangements for next Saturday.'

'I'm sorry if I've upset you but I have my principles. I can't help the way I am but I do . . . I am . . . fond of you.'

169

She looked at him from under her lashes, wondering how far she could push him. 'You could take me to the Imperial one night. We could have a drink.'

He was relieved that she was willing to compromise. 'Yes, that's what we'll do. Do they serve tea in the evening?'

'No. A glass of sherry wouldn't hurt and I've often been told I look older than I am.'

'You mean?'

'Oh, don't be such a killjoy!'

'I'm not!'

'You are! Oh, I suppose I'll have a glass of lemonade if you're going to make such a fuss!' At least it would be a night out, she thought, and the Imperial was a very smart and snobby place. Wait until she told Alice and Ginny about this. She smiled up at him, good humour restored.

When Lily heard of the proposed outing she shook her head. 'Do you honestly think they'll let you in?'

'Why shouldn't they? There's nothing wrong with our money – Rhys's money.'

'Have a bit of sense, girl. Even in your best clobber you still look what you are – working class!' Jack said dourly.

'Nothing wrong with that, is there?' Rhys asked.

'No. Unless you want to get into the Adelphi or the Imperial. Only the toffs go there and I don't want you to look a bloody fool being turned away!' Jimmy answered. 'You're not going to make a fool of him, our Phoebe-Ann!'

'Too right I'm not, because I'm not going! I'm not going anywhere with him ever again! I hope you're all satisfied now!' she cried, her cheeks flushed. Snatching up her bag she flounced upstairs.

170

'I wasn't being awkward, Rhys, lad. I just didn't want you to be humiliated,' Jimmy said.

'She's got ideas above herself! I don't know what gets into her at times!' Lily felt sorry for the lad. He looked so downhearted. She was angry with Phoebe-Ann because she had hoped the friendship would blossom. 'She'll get over it, Rhys. Give her a day or two and ask her again,' she advised.

He smiled. He didn't know how to cope with Phoebe-Ann but it didn't make him love her less.

When he returned to Lonsdale Street on Monday lunch time after having no luck at the docks, Rhys was dispirited. He'd take anything he thought. Anything. As he walked disconsolately, hands in pockets, head down, he almost collided with three thickset drunks who staggered around the corner.

'Gerrout of me way!' one yelled at him.

He wanted no trouble. 'Sorry, mate!'

'Who're yer callin' mate? Yez not me mate!'

He ignored them and walked on.

Lily was standing on the pavement, a brush in her hand. 'Take no notice of them! Drunken pigs! It's the brothers Malone, the Mona Street Mob, three of them at least and by the look of them they've been paid off.'

Rhys looked after the three staggering figures. 'Paid off?'

'Aye. They all work in the stokehold of the *Mauretania*. Come on in and I'll get you something to eat.'

Albert looked up as Rhys entered, while Lily informed him of the current state of the Malones, adding some acid comments on what she'd do if they were any relation of hers, which she thanked God they were not.

171

'Would there be jobs there?' Rhys asked.

'Where?'

'The stokehold. The *Mauretania* was it?'

Lily was horrified. 'You don't want to work there!'

'I'll take anything I can get. Where would I find out?'

Albert looked perturbed. 'The Labour Pool I should think. At Mann Island.'

'Will you come with me?'

'Oh, Albert, don't let him go! I'd have nightmares thinking of him working down there and with that lot!'

'Lily, I just want to work and I'm used to coal.'

Albert stood up and reached for his cap. 'We can try but don't expect too much.'

The clerk at the Pool informed them that it was their lucky day. 'Not Irish are you?'

'No, Welsh. Is that a problem?' Rhys replied.

The man grinned. 'No but I can't say "the luck of the Irish", can I? Also most of the black squads are Irish, well, Liverpool Irish.'

He went on to inform them that there were two jobs going on the *Maury*. It appeared that there had been a fight on the homeward journey, yet another fight, he corrected himself. The protagonists had been discharged.

'Wouldn't have been named Malone by any chance?' Albert enquired.

'Right first time. Seamus Malone and Frank O'Rourke and it's not the first time they've tried to brain each other either!'

Albert looked grim. He knew that the black squads usually worked in family teams and he guessed that neither the Malones nor the O'Rourkes would take

172

kindly to anyone who filled their brother's shoes. He looked at Rhys and his heart sank. The lad looked as though he'd won first prize in a raffle. He stood back while the forms were completed and the clerk handed Rhys his copy. 'Take this to the Registrar of the Mercantile Marine; they'll issue you with your discharge book.'

'Where's that?'

'Royal Liver Buildings.'

As they crossed the cobbles of the Pierhead, Rhys looked exuberant. 'Wasn't that a piece of luck then? Do you think Phoebe-Ann will change her mind and let me take her out before I go?'

'I think she might well do that. She's a nice girl really, just a bit highly-strung, so her mam says.'

Rhys looked thoughtful. 'I suppose she needs to be treated rather specially then?'

Albert nodded. 'But don't let her get the upper hand, lad. Be firm but kind. She'll respect you for it in the end. And you'll respect her feelings.'

'My intentions are honourable. I know it's all been very quick, but I know she's the girl for me. If I work hard and . . .'

Albert caught his arm. 'Hold your horses, boyo! Think about your mam. Send her what she's due, isn't that why you came here?'

'Yes, but she'll understand about Phoebe-Ann when I tell her.'

'I don't understand about Phoebe-Ann. God above! You've only taken her out once and you want to go hurtling into an understanding!'

'I don't want an understanding.'

'You don't?'

'No. I'm going to marry her.'

173

Albert stared at him in astonishment before he wondered just what Phoebe-Ann would think of that and he hoped there would be no trouble.

Chapter Twelve

Albert's hopes had been dashed. Rhys, bolstered by the fact that he now had work, plucked up courage to ask Phoebe-Ann out on Friday night, his last night before he sailed. She had politely refused. She pointed out that she had made prior arrangements. Albert had watched the lad's face fall and he had to agree with Lily that Phoebe-Ann was becoming a flirt.

Lily had been furious with her daughter and had pushed her into the scullery. 'If you have any sense in that empty head of yours you'll accept the lad's offer! Far better than going out with your so-called friends and kicking up your legs in common dance halls!'

'Mam, I'm not going out with him!'

'Why not? What's the matter with him?'

'He's so stuffy! Look at the way he took notice of our Jimmy.'

'He had sense and so did Jimmy. You'd have been mortified if you'd been asked to leave the Imperial and so would he. You still fancy yourself as a lady like Miss Olivia Mercer, don't you? And you know how that ended up.'

'It's not fair the way you keep throwing that up at me, Mam! It wasn't my fault!'

Lily was not deterred. 'You're getting too big for your boots lately. He's a decent lad from a good home and now he's got a job. Not a job that we would have liked for him, but it shows he is a worker. And he'll work damned hard. He doesn't smoke or drink or gamble. What more do you want?'

Phoebe-Ann wanted to cry out that it was because of those virtues, which in her opinion made him dour and no fun at all, that she wasn't remotely interested in going out with him, but she didn't dare. 'He can't string two words together and the way he dresses . . .'

'What have clothes got to do with anything? That's just typical of you. You'd go out with a tailor's dummy as long as it had the "right" clothes on it. Have the sense to look under the clothes and see the man. Fancy feathers count for nothing in the end and you'll do well to remember that, miss!'

'You're matchmaking. You've been planning this all along, you and Albert. That's why he's come to live here, isn't it? Well, I'm not going out with him again.' And she turned and stormed out of the scullery, leaving the door wide open and Lily standing rigid with anger, her hand itching to slap her daughter. He was everything that she would have looked for in a son-in-law but obviously Phoebe-Ann didn't view him in the same light. He was obviously not sophisticated enough, although that was no bad thing.

As she walked quickly down the street, her heels tapping loudly on the pavement, guilt nagged at Phoebe-Ann. She understood that her mam wanted to see her settled, to see both herself and Emily married to decent, hardworking men, especially since all that trouble at the Mercers'. That hadn't been her fault. It hadn't. Nor was she going to enter into an 'understanding' with Rhys Pritchard just to set her mam's mind at ease. It wasn't fair of Lily to even think she should. Her mind went back over the time she had spent at the Mercers'. She often tried to recall all her words and actions, to reinforce the fact that she was utterly blameless, but she could never manage to completely dismiss this nagging guilt and now it increased her annoyance.

Her face was set and the frown lines had deepened in her forehead when she reached Alice's house. It was always untidy no matter what time of the day it was and Phoebe-Ann wrinkled her nose with distaste at the strong smell of cabbage that lingered everywhere.

'What's up now, your face is like thunder?' Alice greeted her. She was small and inclined to plumpness that would in time run to fat.

'Oh, it's Mam!' Phoebe-Ann plumped herself down on the sofa, after first pushing aside a pile of unironed clothes.

Alice turned back to the mirror and continued applying the oxblood lipstick to her lips. 'She got a cob on again?' she mumbled.

'So have I. She keeps pushing me at Rhys Pritchard. She thinks he's the perfect man for me.'

'He's a big drip,' Alice stated. 'Quite good looking but a drip just the same.'

'That's just what I mean. Look at the carry on when I wanted to go to the Imperial.'

'The feller on the door wouldn't 'ave let you in.'

'He might have. It would have been fun, but our Jimmy had to go and put his oar in and spoil it.'

She wondered if she should beg some lipstick from Alice then changed her mind. Even if, later on, she were to rub it off with her handkerchief Mam would still know. She had eyes like a hawk and then there would be the handkerchief to explain away. It wasn't worth it. She did accept Alice's offer of a 'touch of

177

rouge' that could be explained as rushing home to be in on time. 'I'm not going to let it ruin my night out,' she stated firmly, removing her hat and drawing a piece of black ribbon from her bag. She'd spent hours sewing sequins on it in the privacy of her bedroom. 'How do you think this looks?' She tied it around her forehead, making a neat little bow above her left ear.

Alice was suitably impressed. 'Dead classy, I'd say. It's like that one we saw in the Bon Marché that they were asking a small fortune for. Where did you get it?'

'I made it.'

'Honestly?' Alice was suspicious and a little envious. Phoebe-Ann always managed to look so smart. Alice didn't know how she did it either because Phoebe-Ann didn't have as much money to spend on herself as she did. Also Phoebe-Ann was tall and slender; she'd look good in a sack. Not like herself, small and dumpy with hair that wouldn't lie down flat and smooth and shiny like Phoebe-Ann's.

'It took me hours to sew these things on but it was worth it. I wish I'd bought some of that glittery material.'

'Oh, shut up! You make me sick. I suppose you can make your own frocks, too?' Alice retorted but with a smile that softened her words.

'I can if our Emily helps me.'

Alice was teasing two curls forward against her powdered cheeks. 'Your Emily wouldn't approve of that glittery stuff. She's like your mam; you wouldn't think she was only a bit older than us. She looks dead old, especially in those awful frocks she has to wear for work. Catch me goin' out lookin' like that!'

Phoebe-Ann opened her mouth to protest, then closed it. She couldn't tell Alice why Emily had suddenly become so quiet and dressed so dowdily, even though Alice was her best friend. But it was as though Emily was trying to look plain on purpose these days. Sometimes she felt exasperated with her sister, then at others she felt guilty. She hadn't encouraged James Mercer. She'd been kind to him that's all. Still, she couldn't rid herself of the feeling that he wouldn't have forced himself on her. Would he have had to, she often mused? Then she'd shudder. She hadn't known he was bordering on insanity.

'Are you ready then? We'll get caught in the crush if we're late,' Alice reminded her.

Crowds of people were milling around the entrance to the Rialto, and Phoebe-Ann felt her heart begin to beat faster. 'I wonder who we'll meet tonight?'

Alice poked her in the ribs with her elbow. 'Could be "Mr Wonderful" or it could be Mr Rhys Pritchard.'

'He wouldn't come here, would he?' Then Phoebe-Ann laughed. 'You're a tease Alice Wainwright!'

They left their coats at the desk and then went into the ladies' powder room, which was crowded with girls elbowing each other for room in front of the large mirror that extended across one wall.

'Would you look at the gob on that one!' Alice whispered, indicating a very plain girl in a bright green dress. 'If I looked like that I'd go round with a bag on me 'ead.'

Phoebe-Ann thought this was very unkind and said so.

'Oh, it's all right for you. You look like a fashion model. Come on, it's too hot in here an' all that cheap scent is gettin' on me chest.'

They had managed to get a seat at a table near

the edge of the dance floor. That way they could appraise the dancers and yet be clearly seen by hopeful admirers.

'What time is this cabaret thing going to start?' Alice asked.

'Eight o'clock but it must be nearly that now. I wish I had a watch.'

'We don't really need to watch all this "show-off" dancin'. We know the basic steps anyway, we've practised them often enough at lunch times.'

'It's bound to be different. They've come all the way from America.' Phoebe-Ann clasped her hands tightly together and closed her eyes. 'One day I'm going to go to America. You should hear the tales Edwin has to tell about New York and the places he's been.'

'I'll bet, and I'll bet the only places he's seen the inside of are bars and knocking-shops.'

Phoebe-Ann was shocked. 'He's not like that! Mam would never let him go within a mile of our Emily if she thought he did . . . things like that.'

Alice made a rude noise with her mouth. 'Me mam says that's all men think about and if they can't get it with decent girls then they get it with the other kind.'

Phoebe-Ann was glad she'd at least lowered her voice but she felt her cheeks burning. 'Shut up, Alice! Look, here they come! Oh, look at her dress! Next pay day I'm going to get some of that glittery material no matter what Mam says.'

For the next half hour she was enthralled by the expertise of the dancers and she took in every detail of the girl's costume: the loose-fitting bodice, the wide sash tied around her hips, the ends of which trailed almost to the floor, the handkerchief hemline that sparkled with a silver fringe that swayed so alluringly, the silver bracelet worn above the elbow and through which was threaded a flimsy scarf, the short dark hair encircled with a band of silver which sported two white ostrich feathers.

Phoebe-Ann's eyes sparkled, her cheeks were tinged with colour and her foot tapped in time to the music. She made a pretty picture and one that was not lost on a young man on the other side of the floor. Jake Malone had had a few drinks but he was far from drunk. It had been Vinny's idea to come here tonight. At first he had been scornful, as his brothers were, but then when Vinny had implied that a 'bit of skirt' might be forthcoming, he'd changed his mind. As he'd stood surveying the crowd he'd begun to think it was all a waste of time and that he looked like the 'nancy' he had been called by Seamus as he and Peader and Franny had gone off for a heavy night's drinking. 'Fine bleedin' pair we look,' he said peevishly.

'God, there's no pleasin' some people! Have a bit of patience will yer.'

'I'm a bit short on that just now. Go an' get the ale in, I'm spittin' feathers.'

When Vinny had shouldered his way towards the bar and he'd seen her, Jake's annoyance fell away. She looked like something out of a book or a film, he thought. Strangely, he didn't start to strip her with his eyes which was what he usually did when he first met a girl. 'Who's she?' he asked nodding in Phoebe-Ann's direction as Vinny came back with the drinks.

'How the hell should I know, I haven't got second sight!'

'I think I've seen her before but I can't remember where.'

'Yer soft get! Do yer think you'd forget someone

181

who looks like that?' Vinny, too, was looking interested.

Jake downed his pint in one and shoved the empty glass at his brother. 'Keep yer hands to yerself. I saw 'er first!'

'Where are yer goin'? It's your bloody shout!'

Jake ignored Vinny's question and, as the music and the dancing exhibition had stopped, he pushed his way towards her. 'Can I have this dance, girl?' he asked, feeling awkward.

Phoebe-Ann turned a dazzling smile on him, but it was a smile that instantly faded when she realized who it was asking her to dance. 'Er . . . no. No thanks.'

'Why?' he demanded feeling even more awkward. It hadn't entered his head that she would refuse him.

'Oh, Lord! Let me think up an excuse,' she prayed. Yet he didn't look drunk. In fact he didn't look too bad at all. 'Um . . . er . . .' she stammered, casting an imploring glance at Alice who was trying to smother a grin. That annoyed Phoebe-Ann. 'Yes. I'll dance with you.' Her smile returned and, from the corner of her eye, she saw the look of astonishment on Alice's face.

To her surprise he wasn't a bad dancer. 'Come here often?' he asked.

She glanced up at him. 'Can't you do better than that? It's not very original.'

Cocky with it, he thought, but it only made him admire her. 'I think I've seen you before.' He hesitated. He wished she wouldn't keep looking at him like that, smiling in a sort of secretive way. It unnerved him. At least she wasn't afraid of him. Most girls were, especially those who lived in their neighbourhood.

'But you can't remember where,' she forstalled him.

182

'If you're goin' to be a smart arse . . . sorry.' He missed the beat and stumbled. He had never found himself apologizing before; she was having a peculiar effect on him. Or was it the beer? he wondered.

'I've seen you before. You're Jake Malone aren't you and the last time I spoke to you, you could hardly stand up.'

'You spoke to me? When? Where?'

'On the street, months ago. Why do you get into that state?' She could sense she had the upper hand in this conversation and he was holding her as though she were made of glass.

'What state?'

'Falling down drunk. You were disgusting.' She could feel Alice's eyes on her and gave a tinkling laugh. A few more heads were turned in their direction and she liked the stir they were causing. It wasn't often that Jake Malone was seen dancing and sober at the same time.

'If you worked in that hell-hole you'd get falling down drunk, too.'

'I've been on the *Mauretania*,' she said imperiously.

'Gerrof!'

'I have! Miss Olivia Mercer and I were taken on a tour by the Chief Electrical Officer. Her father is a director of Cunard.'

He didn't know if she was just pulling his leg. 'So, where is Miss Mercer tonight then?'

She shrugged. 'Off on a cruise, so I believe.' Then she felt a little sorry for him. 'I worked for her. I was her maid.' She laughed again at the thought of feeling sorry for Jake Malone. Yet he was quite handsome, his clothes were smart and he had a brute strength that she found attractive. He was completely the opposite of Rhys Pritchard, she thought.

'Don't you work there any more then?'

'No. I work at the B&A.'

'What's your name?'

'Phoebe-Ann Parkinson.'

Even her name was different, he thought. Not just plain Mary or Maggie. 'Where do you live?'

'Lonsdale Street.'

He thought for a moment. 'Was it your mam who married that bloke, Davies?'

She nodded.

'Me mam said you were a stuck-up lot.'

She should have felt annoyed but she didn't. 'That's what you told me the last time we met. You bawled across the street that our Emily and me were a "stuck-up pair of judies".'

'I never did!'

'You did. I was stone cold sober at the time, even if you weren't.'

'Ah, for God's sake will you give it a rest with the drink an' all!'

The music had stopped and she withdrew her hand from his. It was announced that the next dance would be the Charleston and everyone was invited to try their newly-learned skills.

'Sod that for a lark! I'm not prancin' around like a bloody eejit! Will you have a drink?'

She looked uncertainly in Alice's direction. She'd never had a drink bought for her before. She'd only had a couple of glasses of sherry in her life and Mam would be livid if she found out. That thought made her reckless. 'I will.' It was quite a heady feeling. Sort of very adult, sophisticated.

As he guided her towards the bar, people drew back. His reputation went before him. Everyone was staring at her and whispering behind their hands and she felt very important.

'It's your turn to buy the ale but I see yer bagged off,' Vinny remarked acidly.

'You watch your mouth, mellado! This is Phoebe-Ann and I'm not havin' you blackguard her! Here, make yer name Walker an' get me a pint. What will you have?' He found he was even watching how he spoke to her. He pushed a coin at Vinny and it glinted gold in the light. It felt good to see the expression on his brother's face and that of the men in the vicinity. He'd show them all he was worth a bob or two and no-one was going to call him a tight arse.

Phoebe-Ann thought quickly but she couldn't call to mind a sophisticated drink. 'I'll have a small brandy, please.'

'Bejasus! She's not soft is she! Act daft an' I'll buy yer a coalyard!' Vinny commented before moving quickly out of range of his brother's boot and in the direction of the bar.

'Take no notice of him. Don't know 'ow to talk to decent folk. Is anyone taking you home, Phoebe-Ann?'

'I don't know. I came with my friend.' She was feeling a little guilty at leaving Alice and also a hint of apprehension had crept in. Mam would brain her if she saw her with him and what if he got fresh with her? How would she handle that?

'Can I see you home then?' he persisted.

She bit her lip, not knowing what to say.

He misinterpreted her gesture. 'We'll get a cab.' He applauded himself. That had been a brilliant stroke. Only the toffs travelled in taxi cabs and he could see she was impressed.

'Really? In a taxi?'

'Of course. Nothin' but the best for my judy . . . I mean girl,' he hastily amended.

'Who said anything about me being "your" girl?'

He looked down at her, his eyes begging her not to turn him down. She was different was this one. She had a bit of class and he'd never felt like this about any girl before. 'I didn't mean . . . I only meant . . .' For the first time in his life Jake Malone was lost for words.

Phoebe-Ann was quick to notice his embarrassment and a feeling of power surged through her. 'You can see me home and then I'll think about it.'

He looked like a puppy dog, she thought, with his dark eyes and adoring expression. Suddenly she realized that she would be able to twist him around her little finger if she wanted to. The feeling of power increased in magnitude.

He ran his finger around the edge of his collar. He'd willingly work in hell itself if it meant he could have her to hold and kiss, to show off, to lavish affection and gifts on. She was so beautiful and she had a certain aura about her. He wondered where he'd heard that word before; he wasn't even sure of its meaning. He was still staring down at her, holding her hand, when Vinny arrived back with the drinks. 'Go an get that feller on the door to order me a taxi cab!' he instructed in a voice loud enough to turn the heads of all the people in front of them. Phoebe-Ann rewarded him with a smile and a muttered, 'Oh, Jake, you're *so* extravagant!'

'All right Rockerfeller! What did yer last servant die of!' Vinny retorted, annoyed that everyone was looking at them.

He was instantly grabbed around the throat. 'Shut

yer gob an' do as yer told! An' don't show me up in front of me girl!' he added.

'Don't gerrof yer bike! I'm goin',' Vinny retorted when the pressure on his throat was released. As he moved back he cast his brother a mocking glance. 'Wait till me mam hears you've gone all soft over a judy!'

Jake ignored him but a frown crossed Phoebe-Ann's face as she remembered Ma Malone's fearful reputation.

'Take no notice of him, me mam's all right. She'll like you.'

Phoebe-Ann just smiled. She had no wish at all to be 'liked' by Ma Malone. That realization brought her back to earth. Oh, well. She'd make him drop her at the bottom of the street and she needn't see him again if she didn't want to; but that was the strange part of it – she did want to see him again.

Part II

Chapter Thirteen

It was in the company of Edwin and Todd that Rhys had his first experience of New York, as he had no wish to accompany his fellow members of the stokehold on a bout of heavy drinking. He had been allocated to the O'Rourke team, a fact that had pleased neither the O'Rourkes nor the Malones. In the brief periods when he had time to think he considered it a blessing that conversation was limited by the noise and the concentration required to carry out the work in the allocated time. After a few days he had formed the opinion that the majority of the black squad were best left well alone. He had received Edwin's message with gratitude for he'd no wish to wander a strange city by himself.

It was the first time he'd felt totally clean and human and he said as much to Edwin as they walked from the pier towards the subway.

'I thought it was bad down the pit but I've never worked so hard or so fast. I'm sick of the sound of that blasted gong and as for the heat! It defies words.'

'Any trouble from the Malones?' Edwin asked.

'Not really. A few words, a few curses but I think they disliked me just because I was with the O'Rourkes. I think they'd have taken the same attitude with the Angel Gabriel. Not that I was made welcome by the O'Rourkes, having filled their brother's job. They're a murderous lot, all of them. I keep my mouth shut and my head down, best way to get on.'

Edwin didn't envy him either the job or the company. 'Well, time to forget it all for a bit. We'll go for a quick drink first. I said I'd meet Todd. You'll like him. He's a bit of a comedian but then so are half the crew.'

Todd was suspicious of Rhys. 'You sure we won't end up in clink?' he asked Edwin, eyeing the burly young Welshman warily.

'Positive. He's not really like any of them, that's why he's coming with us instead of spending the next few days in a paralytic stupor in some Irish-American bar.'

'Why did yer sign on then?' Todd asked. He'd never met a member of the black squad whose sole aim in life wasn't to stay permanently plastered.

'No choice,' Rhys replied. 'No other work to be had and I've got to pay my keep, send back money to Mam and then I thought I'd get something for Phoebe-Ann.'

Todd shrugged and pulled a face. 'Always a judy at the back of it somewhere. Isn't she your Emily's sister?' The question was directed at Edwin.

He nodded.

'I thought so, there's not many called Phoebe-Ann. Isn't there a street called that?'

Edwin nodded again. 'At the back of Mill Road Hospital.'

It was the first time Rhys had heard anyone refer to Emily as 'your Emily' and he wondered again at the rather cautious relationship between Edwin and Phoebe-Ann's sister. Mentally he noted to question Edwin on it later.

'Come on then, let's get the necessary shopping over and then we can get down to the serious business of enjoying ourselves. Where's it to be then?'

Rhys finished his drink. 'Wherever the best shops are. Nothing but the best for Phoebe-Ann.'

'I thought you said your cash was spoken for,' Todd said.

'It is – most of it.'

'Then it's no good goin' up to Fifth Avenue. No use goin' up there even if you'd been paid off. Did yer gerra sub?'

Rhys nodded but looked disappointed. He'd particularly wanted to buy something that would impress Phoebe-Ann. That would show her that he thought she wasn't just any girl.

'I know where there are some good stores. Not too expensive but not the five and dime stores either,' Edwin put in, feeling sorry for Rhys.

'What's wrong with the five an' dimes then? Me mam an' me sisters think the stuff I get them is great.'

'I'm not saying it isn't, but it's sort of like buying stuff from Woolworth's in Church Street instead of Bunnies or Lewis's.'

'Well, if he wants ter go buyin' stuff from places like that 'e'll 'ave ter get promoted pretty bloody quickly!' Todd remarked sarcastically.

Rhys was like a child let loose in a toy shop as he gazed in awe at the exclusive shops on Fifth Avenue. Yet at the same time he was disappointed, wishing he could have afforded some small thing for Phoebe-Ann with a posh label inside or printed on the wrapping paper or box. It was with real regret that he let Edwin guide him around the corner and towards the smaller, less expensive stores.

'Start as yer mean t'go on. If yer spend the earth on them, they'll expect yer to go on spendin' yer last brass farthin' on them,' Todd warned sagely.

Both Todd and Edwin wandered aimlessly between the counters as Rhys deliberated between a pair of fancy gloves embroidered on the back and fingers with tiny flowers, and a smart-looking pink, lilac and white scarf which the assistant assured him was 'genuine imported French chiffon'.

'Well if it's French it would 'ave ter be imported, wouldn't it? Unless we're in the wrong country,' Todd stated and encountered an icy glare from the assistant before he wandered back to Edwin.

Edwin had bought Emily a small brooch which Todd admired and then reluctantly passed over the appropriate number of dollars for a similar one for his mother. 'I feel a right dope wanderin' around 'ere,' he commented. 'People might get the wrong idea. 'Ope no-one sees me.'

Edwin laughed. 'Who's going to see you and besides, if they do, they'll be here for the same reason as us. Getting things to take home.'

'I just wish 'e'd make up 'is mind, that's all. Wastin' good shore leave with all this shoppin'.'

'Oh, leave him alone. It's his first time away and he's really smitten with Phoebe-Ann and she's giving him a hard time.'

'Oh, aye! Playin' 'ard ter get?'

Edwin nodded.

Todd brightened. 'Wouldn't bother me 'ead then if I were 'im. 'E should give 'er a wide berth. Eh up! There's a turn up for the book.'

'What?'

Todd managed to look grave and mischievous at the same time. 'Somethin' yer never likely ter see again.'

'What are you going on about now?'

Todd jerked his head in the direction of the next

counter but one. 'Jake Malone. Sober an' buyin' women's stuff.'

Edwin followed his gaze and was amazed to see Jake Malone neatly turned out and indeed sober and with no less than two assistants parcelling up what looked like a dress, and a dress made of bright blue, filmy material edged with silver fringe. 'You can bet that won't be for his ma,' he remarked with amusement.

'Must 'ave got 'imself a tart, like. She must be off 'er rocker whoever she is, or as 'ard as nails!' Todd hissed.

'He must know her quite well. I mean a dress is sort of personal.'

'Of course it's personal; it's somethin' ter wear, isn't it.'

'You know what I mean. It's something you'd buy your wife, not your girl. It's sort of like buying underwear. Not really "proper" unless you're married.'

Todd grinned. 'Maybe 'e 'as gorra wife on the side, that no-one knows about.'

Rhys, who had finally settled on the scarf, also stood watching the spectacle until Todd nudged him and said, 'Look at somethin' else. We don't want 'im ter think we're spyin' on 'im. Ger 'im dead narked an' 'e'll start on us, an' yer don't want that.' He directed his last words at Rhys.

They all began to take a close interest in a counter on which a variety of haberdashery was displayed. Rhys thought it strange that Malone hadn't mentioned the fact that he had a girl, but then why should he? He belonged to the 'opposition' and, besides, whenever women were talked about it was with such coarseness that it shamed him to think about some of the terms they used. Then he remembered Edwin's remark. No, it wasn't decent to buy clothing for a woman, except gloves, bags and such like, unless it was for a wife or mother and the blue dress certainly couldn't have been for Ma Malone.

'You're off your head Phoebe-Ann Parkinson, and besides that your mam will kill you!' Alice stated in shocked tones as they sat in the warm shunshine in St John's Gardens at the back of St George's Hall on Saturday afternoon.

Phoebe-Ann tossed her head. 'I don't care! I like him. I know people say awful things about him but he's not like that with me.'

'Just because he took you home in a taxi an' left me on me own, lookin' like a fool.'

'I've said I'm sorry about that, but I had no choice, did I?'

'So, what went on then for you to get all soppy over a Malone?'

'Nothing "went on". I'm not like that!'

'You're probably the first girl he's had who isn't!'

Phoebe-Ann didn't want to think about other girls. Jake had been so eager to please her, she had been very flattered. When she'd asked him to drop her at the bottom of Lonsdale Street he hadn't made a fuss. He'd just gazed at her and asked could he see her before he sailed or would she go and see him off. That request she'd refused because she knew Albert, Emily and her mam were going to see Rhys and Edwin off.

He'd looked so hurt that she'd kissed him on the cheek and said, 'I will think about being your girl, Jake.'

'I've never met anyone like you, Phoebe-Ann, an' that's the truth. An' if yer were my girl I'd spend me last farthin' on yer. Nothin' but the best of everythin'.'

196

She'd let him kiss her and she'd been surprised by the feelings that his lips evoked. Instead of being completely in control of the situation, she'd found herself trembling and clinging to him. With surprise and regret she'd drawn herself away from him, murmuring that she dare not be late in.

'Just wait till yer see what I'm goin' ter bring yer from New York, Phoebe-Ann. Will yer come an' meet me when we dock?'

'If I can. I might be at work, but I'll try. I promise,' she'd said as she alighted from the cab on the corner of Bloom Street.

She'd had to steady herself before she'd gone in, in case Lily saw that there was something amiss. They had all been engrossed in getting Rhys packed up and she'd slipped upstairs almost unnoticed. She did like Jake. She liked him a lot and she had tried to analyse her feelings, something she wasn't in the habit of doing very often. Was it because he was so unlike Rhys? Was it because he, who was feared by so many, treated her like a princess – a feeling that gave her immense pleasure. Or was it that she was attracted to his raw masculinity? Could it be that she was falling in love? Really in love? she'd asked herself. Only time would tell.

'So, when are you goin' to see him again?' Alice asked.

'I said I'd try and get down to meet him when he comes back, if I'm not at work that is.'

Alice shook her head. Phoebe-Ann was mad. Even her mam, who wasn't half as fussy as Mrs Davies, would go absolutely crackers if she were to announce that she had taken up with Jake Malone. 'They'll kill you, and you know what old Ma Malone is like. The whole street is terrified of her.'

'I'm not going out with Ma Malone, am I?' Phoebe-Ann shot back, but she knew Alice was right. Mam would kill her. 'You're going to have to help me, Alice.'

Alice looked suspicious. 'How?'

'By backing me up. I'm going to have to tell them I'm out with you, or around at your house.'

'Don't go getting me involved! I'm not getting blamed!'

'Oh, Alice! Don't be mean!'

'I'm not being mean! My mam will batter me. Your mam will batter me an' all, that's after she's killed you first!'

She could see that Alice was going to be awkward. 'I'm not asking you to do much. You never come round to our house and Mam never sees your mam. It's just in case. I'll give you my new headband and I'll even help you make a dance dress.'

Alice faltered. What Phoebe-Ann said was true. She probably wouldn't be called on to verify Phoebe-Ann's whereabouts by Mrs Davies, she never went to Lonsdale Street, and she did so much want a dance dress. She'd seen some lovely material and fringe. 'Oh, all right!'

Phoebe-Ann smiled at her. 'Come on then, we'll get to Blackler's before they close if we hurry and we can get it cut out tomorrow.' She was expansive with her enthusiasm. After all, what else was there to do until the *Maury* came home?

For five days Phoebe-Ann occupied the thoughts of two men in the stokehold of the *Mauretania*. Rhys laboured and sweated in the bunker, shovelling coal down the chute into the barrow of the cantankerous Billy O'Rourke. He pictured Phoebe-Ann's face when he gave her the scarf, all done up in its pretty wrapping paper. He'd ask her out that very night and he'd take her somewhere 'posh', like he'd promised. He could just see her eyes light up and she'd give him one of those dazzling smiles. It was a hope and a dream that sustained him through the brutal shifts and one he took with him to his narrow metal bunk.

Jake Malone's thoughts were running far ahead of those of Rhys, as he braced himself against the searing heat of the furnaces, part of his mind intent on the sound of the gong. When he finished his shift, he often went up on deck for some fresh air to clear his head of the stink of sulphur and coal gas. Up on deck, back against a ventilator, head and chest bared to the Atlantic wind, he pictured Phoebe-Ann dancing in his arms in the blue dress. She was like a vision, something he thought he'd never have for his own. He remembered the soft feel of her skin and her lips, the perfume that clung to her hair, and he felt dizzy with longing. But it was a longing tinged with a strange tenderness. He prayed that she'd meet him when he docked, that she'd say she would be his and then . . . Then he'd ask her to marry him. That realization had shocked him. He'd never considered marriage to anyone. All life had consisted of was work and then getting into a stupor to obliterate the brutality of that work. All he'd ever known was hard work, harsh words, blows and he'd learned all three from a tender age. There had been no gentleness in his life. But there was now and he wanted to protect it, to own and cherish it.

As the cold wind whipped through his dark hair, he let his imagination, constrained for so long, run riot. He could see her in a white satin dress, her face framed by a cloud of tulle and orange blossom, smiling up at him. He'd take her back to their own little house, which would be clean and bright and would smell of her perfume. Simple, childlike dreams he thought, nothing too grand or complicated. Their own little house, unlike the only home he'd ever known. It was always untidy, dirty and overcrowded and filled with the smells that clung to them all, and the stench of boiled cabbage and the midden in the yard. No, nothing like that would do for Phoebe-Ann. A nice little place of their own. No Vinny, Seamus, Peader and Franny swearing, arguing, belching, snoring or Ma shrieking like a harpy and swearing with the best of them when she felt like it and snoring as loudly too, after a few bottles of stout. His vigils became a habit that he looked forward to. The pictures and dreams became more vivid and Phoebe-Ann became more deeply entrenched in his heart.

Phoebe-Ann had scoured the *Echo* each night for news of the *Mauretania*, so much so that Lily had remarked on it. She'd also remarked on the fact that Phoebe-Ann was spending a great deal of time at Alice Wainwright's house to which Phoebe-Ann replied, 'I told you I'm helping her make a dress. We're not out on the town or anything like that. Honestly, Mam, you're never satisfied. If I'm out too often you complain and if I'm not you still moan.'

'Oh, I suppose you're right. At least it's a harmless pastime.'

'Is it for anything special?' Emily intervened.

'Not really. She had her heart set on a new dance dress and she couldn't afford to buy one. Not a really nice one, that is. She saw one in the window of George Henry Lee that she likes.'

'You've got her as bad as yourself. George Henry

Lee's, I ask you! What's the matter with C&A or Sturla's? They're good enough for me and your sister.'

Phoebe-Ann hadn't answered. She had no wish to antagonize her mother over such a simple thing when she might well have to face much bigger issues in the future. But she wouldn't dwell on that either.

Lily picked up the discarded newspaper and scanned the lines of print. She never read the society column but a small photograph caught her eye. 'Well, fancy that!'

'What?' Emily asked.

'Miss Olivia Constance Mercer . . . engaged to the Honourable Edward Arthur Wakeham,' Lily read aloud, skipping the more eulogistic description.

'She was bound to marry someone like that, an honourable or a sir,' Albert interrupted.

'Is he handsome?' Phoebe-Ann enquired, pleased for her former mistress, yet thinking how much Olivia's future would differ from her own.

'He looks as though his shirt collar is choking him,' Emily commented, peering over her mother's shoulder.

'It does, doesn't it? Makes his eyes look sort of froggy. And he looks so old!' Phoebe-Ann giggled. He must have pots of money for she was certain that Olivia Mercer would have fallen in love with someone much younger and far more handsome and dashing.

'Don't be such a cat, miss! He's probably the steadying influence she needs. Unless she's changed, and I doubt that. Probably it's been "arranged" by her father.'

Phoebe-Ann said nothing, determined not to upset Lily.

*   *   *

To her delight she found that the docking of the *Mauretania* coincided with her lunch break. The passengers would disembark at the Pierhead and then the ship would tie up in the Canada Dock. It would be a bit of a rush but she'd make it, even if it were only for five minutes or so. She couldn't let him down.

She changed out of her overall in the toilets, took off the turban and brushed out her hair. She'd told the supervisor she had important family business but that she wouldn't be late back. Both the tram and the train seemed interminably slow and she gazed out of the window as the train rattled along above the dock road. There was a fine view of all the docks, the river and even the Wirral bank of the Mersey, but she didn't notice it. She could just make out the time on the five-sided clock tower and breathed a sigh of relief when she alighted at the Canada Dock.

She ran from the station to the dock gate where she was stopped by a policeman.

'Sorry, luv, can't let you through.'

'I'm meeting my . . . boyfriend.' She looked up at him with what she hoped was her most appealing smile.

He grinned. 'That's what they all say. You'll have to wait here. Got my orders.'

She glared at him. He probably thought she was one of the 'Maggie Mays' who hung around the dock gates. The thought infuriated her. Couldn't he tell the difference between a decent girl and one of *them*? She looked around and for the first time hoped that Albert hadn't decided to come to meet Rhys. There was no sign of him or his cart and she was relieved. Two women, with young children clinging to their skirts, stood on the other side of the gate. They were poorly dressed and the children had runny noses and shabby clothes. Obviously wives she thought, sniffing disdainfully. Fancy coming to meet anyone looking like that, and they could have cleaned the kids up too. It didn't occur to her that these women came to meet their men to try to wrest a few shillings from them before it was wasted in the pubs that could be found on every corner along the whole length of the dock road.

She began to walk up and down, peering through the dock gate. Supposing she'd missed him? He'd think she didn't care and she hadn't meant what she'd said. Then she heard her name being called. She hadn't planned in any detail what she would do or say to him, but she found herself running towards him, arms outstretched, her heart racing.

He caught her and swung her off her feet. 'Phoebe-Ann! You came! You came!' He looked into her sparkling eyes and a wave of pure joy swept through him.

'I haven't got long. It's my dinner time.'

They both ignored the rowdy cheer that came from a group of men coming out of the dock, followed by the jeers and taunts of the rest of the Malones. Nor did she see the envious glances of the waiting wives.

'I'll see you back,' he offered as she tucked her arm in his. 'I've missed you,' he ventured.

'I've missed you, too, Jake. I haven't been out at all. Alice said I'm a real misery.'

He hadn't expected her to stay in every night and he was filled with gratitude. She'd waited for him. She hadn't gone off dancing or anything like that. It must mean something. He thrust the parcel towards her. 'I bought you this.'

She was surprised. 'What is it?'

'Wait and see. I hope you like it.'

'You won't mind if I don't open it here, will you?'

He was a bit disappointed but then he thought it might be a bit awkward and someone was bound to make some comment that would be repeated to his ma. 'No. Will you wear it tonight?'

'Now I'm really curious. Tonight?'

'Yes. Where would you like to go?'

'There's a couples night on at the Grafton, and we're a couple aren't we?'

That made him smile. 'We are too.'

'I'd better meet you outside.'

He nodded. He was going to be in for enough stick from his brothers as it was. Better to meet her outside the dance hall.

She left him at the factory gate. She reached up on tiptoe and kissed him. 'I'll see you tonight, Jake, and I'll wear it – whatever it is. I promise.'

He watched her walk away and his heart almost burst with love and pride. She was his girl and, what's more, she'd waited for him without being asked to do so. That surely meant she was serious about him.

'So yer 'ome then. Where's the rest of yez?' Ma Malone greeted him as he walked into the tiny cramped and cluttered kitchen.

'Down the Caradoc. Where else?' he said.

She grunted and then looked at him suspiciously. 'Why didn't yer go wit them? Is there somethin' the matter wit yez? If yez 'ave got a dose of the pox then yez can get out an' stay out!'

'Will yer shut yer gob! I 'aven't got nothin' like that! Can't I come 'ome once in a while without havin' ter face a bloody inquisition!' He slipped back into the thick accent that he had consciously suppressed with Phoebe-Ann. 'What's ter eat?'

'Boiled bacon an' it's not ready yet. Yez'll 'ave ter wait.'

'Bloody boiled bacon. Can't yer do anythin' else!'

'Not on the allotment yez leave me.'

He knew she wasn't left short of money. All his brothers and himself left an allotment but most of it went on stout and horses. 'I want me shirt doin' for ternight.'

'I want doesn't get!' she snapped.

'Do I 'ave ter do it meself!' he yelled, his patience exhausted. Fine home-coming this.

'Don't think yez can shame me to the neighbours, meladdo! Where is it? I'll do it later.'

He produced the shirt, rolled up in a ball.

She glared at it. 'Jesus, Mary an' Joseph! Look at it! 'Ave yez been cleaning them boilers wit it?'

'I just want it for tonight. I've got a new collar.'

'What's all this in aid of then?'

He sighed. He supposed it would be easier to tell her because as soon as the rest of them arrived home it would be common knowledge. 'I'm goin' to meet me girl.'

Ma Malone's beady dark eyes filled with suspicion. He'd never mentioned any girl before and he'd never wanted a shirt washed and ironed for the occasion either. 'What girl?'

'Someone I met before I sailed.'

''As she gorra name?'

He was loath to tell her. He didn't even want Phoebe-Ann's name to be mentioned in this house. It would be tantamount to sacrilege, so high was the pedestal he'd placed her on.

She noticed the hesitation. That was a bad sign. This looked serious. She'd always sworn she'd never

205

share her kitchen with another woman nor was she happy about the fact that her sons could show affection to anyone but herself. 'I just 'ope she's a good Catholic girl that's all or be God neither of yez will set foot in 'ere.'

Jake was taken aback. It was something he had never even considered. He had loved Phoebe-Ann from the minute he'd set eyes on her, and he'd never even given a thought to what religion she was. Now that he had to think about it he decided it didn't matter. He never went to church nor did any of his brothers nor Ma. It was years since she'd crossed the doorstep of any church and the priest never came near the house to see why not either.

His silence was not lost on his mother and she glared at him. So, that was it. A bloody Protestant. She'd soon sort this one out. 'Where are yez goin' now?'

'The ale'ouse. I might get some peace an' quiet there.'

'I'll have to come home with you first,' Phoebe-Ann explained to Alice.

'Why?'

'Don't be so thick! I'm going to have to say I've borrowed your dress. How else am I going to explain this away?' She tapped the parcel she was carrying. It had caused a sensation when she'd finally opened it in the toilets at break time.

'It's not me who's the thick one, Phoebe-Ann Parkinson! They'll take one look at that and know it's not been made with stuff from Blackler's and look at the style of it.'

'I promised I'd wear it tonight.'

'Tough luck!'

'I'll just take it in and take it upstairs, then before I'm going out I'll put my coat on. That way they won't get a good look at it. It's so gorgeous and I did promise.'

Alice shook her head. Phoebe-Ann was letting herself in for a heap of trouble and what's more she herself was getting tangled up in the web of lies Phoebe-Ann was intent on spinning. 'Don't blame me if you get found out and your mam belts you.'

Phoebe-Ann tossed her head. 'I'm beginning not to care anyway.'

Alice shrugged. When Lily Davies found out she was certain that the explosion would be heard all the way to the Pierhead. If Phoebe-Ann had chosen to fall in love, why on earth hadn't she picked someone like that drippy Rhys? Anyone would be better than Jake Malone. But, as she looked at her friend, Alice realized that Phoebe-Ann was indeed in love or infatuated. Either way it spelled storms ahead and she didn't intend to get caught in the subsequent maelstrom.

'You're late tonight,' Lily observed when Phoebe-Ann finally arrived home.

'I went home with Alice; she's letting me borrow her new dress for tonight.'

Lily looked up. 'What's so special about tonight?'

'Nothing really. Just a dance at the Grafton.'

'Isn't Alice going?'

'No, she's not feeling well. I'm going with Ginny,' Phoebe-Ann lied, hoping her cheeks weren't going to flush and give her away.

'She must be feeling ill if she let you borrow a dress she hasn't even worn yet.'

207

'She has worn it. She had it on the other night.'
More lies, but she was in too deep now. 'Where's
Albert?' she asked to change the subject.

'In the yard with Rhys. They'll be in in a minute.'

She had totally forgotten about Rhys. 'How did his
trip go?'

'Not too bad. Damned hard work he said it was.
Much harder than down the pit. Well, let's have a
look at this frock then? You've both spent enough
time on it, it should be a creation of wondrous
beauty.'

Phoebe-Ann hesitated, thinking what Alice had said
about the dress.

'What's the matter with it?' Lily asked. 'Has it got
no back in it or – worse – no front?'

'No!'

'Well then, let's see it, this copy of a George Henry
Lee model gown.'

There was no way out. Phoebe-Ann undid the
parcel and shook out the folds of gentian blue crêpe-
de-chine.

Lily was very impressed. 'By, you've made a good
job of it the pair of you! A fine job indeed. I think
you're both wasted in that factory. You should take
up dressmaking.' She turned as Albert and Rhys
entered the kitchen. 'Would you look at this, Albert.
Our Phoebe-Ann and Alice Wainwright made it.
Copied it from one they saw in the window of George
Henry Lee's. I was saying they should take it up as a
trade.'

Albert smiled broadly at Phoebe-Ann and she
blushed and smiled back.

Rhys's gaze was riveted on the dress. It couldn't
be! It just couldn't be! But it was. It was unmistakable.
He felt sick. It had been Phoebe-Ann who Jake

Malone had been shopping for and the fact that it was a dress made him feel worse. Surely . . . surely Phoebe-Ann hadn't let Jake Malone touch her or take liberties with her! He sat down suddenly.

Lily was all concern. 'Rhys, what's the matter?'

He managed a smile. 'Still not used to the ground under my feet not moving, that's all.'

Albert laughed. 'Still feels as though he's at sea.'

Rhys wished he was still at sea, for all the brightness and hope had gone.

As soon as he was able, Rhys approached Phoebe-Ann on the subject of Jake Malone. He'd tried to ignore it but he couldn't. It kept eating away at him. In a rare moment before he sailed he found himself alone with her.

'Can I ask you something, Phoebe-Ann?'

She looked up from ironing a blouse and he remembered how only a short time ago he'd first asked her out. She'd been ironing then, too, he thought.

'What?'

'Where did you get that dress?'

'Which dress?' she asked impatiently.

'That blue one you said was Alice's.'

She was taken aback. He worked with Jake and she wondered if Jake had been boasting. 'Someone bought it for me. I couldn't tell Mam that, could I?'

'Jake Malone bought it. I saw him and so did Edwin and Todd.'

'Oh, so I suppose half the crew of the *Maury* know about it, too!' she snapped.

'No. Just us three and him.'

'He's got a name!'

209

He got up and walked to the window, hands thrust deep into the pockets of his trousers. 'Why him?'

She slammed down the flat iron and threw the blouse over a chair. 'Well, why not? I didn't know I needed your permission. I like him!'

He turned towards her. 'Phoebe-Ann, I work with them! I hear the way they talk about women and girls and it makes me sick. They're so crude and coarse! All they care about is one thing.'

'Jake's not like that!'

'He is. He's no different to the rest.'

She began to wonder if he was speaking the truth but she pushed the doubt to the back of her mind. He was just jealous. 'He is! You're jealous of him.'

He came towards her, his eyes pleading. 'Yes I am jealous, Phoebe-Ann. I don't want you to throw yourself away on the likes of Jake Malone.'

'What I do is my business,' she interrupted angrily.

'Phoebe-Ann, I care very much what happens to you. Put a stop to it now, please? What kind of a man buys a dress for a girl who isn't even his betrothed, let alone his wife.'

How dare he? Phoebe-Ann fumed. How dare he speak to her like that? He wasn't even related to her. Before she could start to berate him he caught her hands.

'Phoebe-Ann, I love you! I have loved you since the minute I set eyes on you. You're so beautiful and so sweet. Don't let him drag you down into the mire that he and his brothers wallow in.'

She snatched her hands away. 'I'll go out with whoever I wish and I don't believe you! You're jealous and angry that I don't love you.'

He turned away from her. She'd thrown his

declaration of love and devotion back in his face and it hurt. It hurt deeply. But even more bitter to bear than her rejection was the fact that she'd obviously given her heart to Jake Malone.

Chapter Fourteen

Emily noticed the difference in Phoebe-Ann almost from the first time Rhys had gone away to sea. At least she thought it had something to do with that. It had changed Rhys too; he seemed quieter, more withdrawn and surprisingly he hardly ever spoke to her sister unless it was necessary. She'd mentioned the fact to Edwin but he had been as confused as herself. He had come to the conclusion that they had had some kind of a row, for any attempt to bring up the subject of Phoebe-Ann with Rhys was hastily cut short in such a way that he was not allowed to question Rhys about it.

Whatever had passed between them, it certainly hadn't affected Phoebe-Ann, Emily thought. She went around with her head in the clouds most of the time and spent a good deal of time with Alice or at Alice's house. Emily guessed that Alice had a boyfriend on the *Mauretania* for, when that ship docked, Alice always wanted Phoebe-Ann to accompany her to the dock. When it was away, Phoebe-Ann spent most of her time cheering Alice up. Or at least that's what she said she was doing and she had no reason to doubt her sister.

As the summer wore on she worried less about Phoebe-Ann for she had other things on her mind. One was Edwin and the other was Miss Nesta Barlow.

She was far more at ease with Edwin now. She could tolerate him holding her hand and giving her a quick kiss on the cheek or forehead, but nothing more.

'I still feel as though I can't . . . Oh, you know what I mean!' she'd tried to explain to him, when after they'd been to the cinema he'd tried to hold her and kiss her.

'I thought that with time you might be more . . . comfortable. You are still fond of me, Em, aren't you?'

'Of course I am. You know that will never change. It's the thought of . . .'

'Don't think about it if it upsets you.'

They'd been silent for a while before he'd taken her hand. 'Emily, I want to marry you one day. I mean it. I'll provide for you, I'll be good to you. I don't earn bad money, although I will be away for most of the time.'

She hadn't replied. She'd thought how much she would have looked forward to that, once.

'Just think about it. I'll wait, Em, until you're ready. You know me: "Old Dependable".'

The tears had sprung to her eyes. He was so patient. 'You shouldn't have to wait, Edwin. It's not your fault. It's mine.'

'It's not been a year yet, Emily. You've got to give it time, like Albert says. Maybe I'm rushing you.'

'No, you're not. If . . . if things had been different I'd have wanted to get engaged.'

'Do you?'

She felt so guilty. Was she being fair to him, making him wait? Yet her one dread was that he would get tired of waiting and find someone else. She'd tried to imagine what life would be like without him for she missed him while he was at sea. If she looked at it like that the future was bleak indeed. She *was* being a fool. She took a deep breath. 'Yes. Yes, I do.'

213

He fought down the impulse to catch her in his arms and kiss her. 'Do you really mean that, Emily?'

'I do.' She desperately wanted him to feel that she cared enough to make the commitment and yet she took comfort from the fact that some engagements could be long. Very long sometimes.

'Oh, Em! I do love you. I want to hold and kiss you.'

She smiled. She had to try for both their sakes. She reached out and touched his cheek. 'Then what's stopping you?'

He held her as though she were made of glass and gently kissed her on the lips, yet despite all his gentleness and care, he felt her cringe and try to draw away. He was filled with compassion and admiration for her. She was trying to be so brave. 'When will we tell everyone?'

'I don't know.'

'Let's wait until I come back next trip. I'll bring you a ring or would you sooner choose one here?'

'You choose one for me. That way it will be special.'

She meant it, but she also was aware that it would give her more time to compose herself and to fend off all the questions that would be asked about when the actual wedding would be and she knew she couldn't face that just yet.

The problem with Miss Nesta was amusing up to a point and she encountered it the day after Edwin had sailed. It was Miss Millicent's monthly outing and she'd seen her off in her taxi and returned to the house.

'Emily.' Miss Nesta beckoned her into the drawing room and she wondered if another trip to the attic was forthcoming. She had become quite fond of the 'yesterday chest'.

'Will we be going up to the attic, Miss Nesta? I could take a tea tray up.'

'No, but thank you, you're a very willing girl, Emily. There is something you can do though.'

'What is it?' Nesta Barlow looked like a mischievous child, she thought.

'Take this.' The old lady held out what looked like a folded envelope and inside it was a half crown and on the inside of the flap were two words, 'Sea Breeze'. Emily was mystified. Did Miss Nesta want some soap or other toiletry. 'What is it?'

Miss Nesta looked around. 'It's a bet. I want you to find a bookie or some such person and place that bet for me.'

Emily's mouth dropped open. 'Miss Nesta! A bet!'

'Hush!' She smiled. 'My brother, Tom, taught me how to do it. To study form. Of course I can't have a racing paper or anything like that but I sometimes borrow Stockley's paper. He doesn't know of course. I pretend I want it for the news.'

Emily was still mesmerized. Was she hearing all this?

'I used to do it quite often when Tom was alive. It used to be our secret. I got great satisfaction from it because Papa detested betting and gambling. It was my way of paying him back, you see. He never knew, more's the pity, and quite often I won. Millie would have a heart attack if she knew,' she whispered.

A smile spread across Emily's face. It was too absurd. Miss Nesta – a secret gambler.

'I always win on horses that are named Sea or Ocean or are in some way connected with the sea and ships.' She rubbed her hands together. 'Oh, Papa would hate it and besides it's so exciting and I don't have much fun. It's poetic justice, too, that I do win so often. Now, not a word to anyone, Emily. It will be our secret and if I win you shall have some of my winnings.'

'But Miss Nesta, I don't know any bookies!'

'But you must do.'

'I don't! Honestly!'

'Then ask your brothers or Mr Davies or your young man, but you'll have to be quick. The race is at three o'clock and Millie will be back at four thirty.'

'Edwin is away and my brothers are at work, and it's illegal.'

'Then ask Mr Davies. Now hurry up, Emily.'

All the way home she kept laughing to herself. Miss Nesta, of all people, gambling on a horse race! She could imagine Miss Millicent's face.

Albert was in the yard when she dashed in.

'What's up, Emily?'

'Do you know any bookies?'

'What?'

'Do you? It's not for me – it's for Miss Nesta. Look.' She held out the envelope.

'Miss Nesta Barlow?'

'I know it sounds crazy but it's true. She wants this on the three o'clock at Haydock. Apparently her brother taught her how to do it and she used it as a way to get back at her father for refusing all the offers of marriage. He hated gambling.'

'So do I.'

'What am I to do? I can't disappoint her.'

Albert looked perplexed. 'Ask your mam.'

Lily was as dumbfounded as Albert but in the end she said, 'Go and see Florrie Harper. Her Harry knows a bookie. But don't get caught! I don't want to see the police round here and us all dragged off for illegal gambling. What's the world coming to Albert? The likes of a lady like Miss Nesta gambling on horses!'

'Well, they are a bit odd the pair of them but I never thought she'd do anything like this. It beats all, Lil, it certainly does.'

To everyone's amusement and astonishment the horse won, and Jimmy was duly sent down to 'Black Jack' Costello for the winnings which Emily smuggled to Miss Nesta the following day. The old lady rubbed her little hands together in glee. 'How much is it, Emily?' she whispered.

'Two pounds ten shillings, miss.' She passed over the money.

'Here, this is for you. I knew I could trust you and I think you will be lucky for me.' She handed Emily the ten shilling note.

'Oh, I couldn't take all that, Miss Nesta!'

'Don't be silly. It's for "services rendered" and I did promise you you should have something.'

'I can't take ten shillings!'

'Yes, you can. I'll hear no more arguments.'

Reluctantly Emily took the money and tucked it inside her dress. 'What did you mean by me being lucky for you?'

'Oh, this is just the start. You see, for years I haven't had anyone to take the bets for me. Mary got too old, then she got sick, so until you came I couldn't indulge my little "fancy". Then I had to be sure I could trust you but you were so understanding about my yesterday chest that I knew you wouldn't fail me and I was right.'

'You mean you're going to . . . ?'

'Yes. Only once a week, mind. I'm not greedy and I really don't have any use for the money. If I started buying things Millie would get suspicious.'

Emily didn't know what to say. 'But . . . but what do you do with your winnings?' she asked, before she realized that it wasn't her place to ask such a question.

Miss Nesta tapped the side of her nose with her forefinger. 'That's my little secret.'

Emily shook her head wondering just what she'd let herself in for. It was against the law, so she realized that some proper arrangements would have to be made with 'Black Jack' Costello or both she and Miss Nesta Barlow could end up in court.

When Edwin returned she had accumulated nearly thirty shillings she told him laughingly.

'You're having me on, Em! You don't mean that she's got a regular arrangement with "Black Jack" Costello to back horses?'

'She has. The day before the race she writes down her horse on a bit of paper, I wrap it up and put it under the bootscraper by the gate and then he strolls past, bends down to tie his bootlace and picks it up. She only bets on horses whose names are connected with the sea though.'

'What about her winnings?'

'Same thing, except I watch for him passing, then nip out and pick it up before anyone else does.'

He roared with laughter. 'I just hope Costello's trustworthy.'

'He has to be. Our Jack and Jimmy have sworn they'll shop him if he starts any tricks and, besides, she has agreed that he takes his "commission", as she calls it, out of the winnings.'

'How often does she win?'

'Nearly all the time. I swear I don't know how she does it and our Jimmy says Costello doesn't either but he's glad all his customers aren't like her.'

'The old man must be spinning in his grave!' Edwin whooped.

'That's her intention.'

'What does she do with the money? Surely her sister would notice anything new or extra?'

'That's the odd part. I don't know. I asked her but she wouldn't tell me. I do all the dusting and cleaning and I've never come across a hidden hoard. Maybe she puts it in the bank.'

'Don't be daft, Em. Miss Millicent would find that out and so would old man Mercer. Maybe she's got other vices that she spends it on. She's a rum old thing if ever there was one. I wouldn't have credited it.'

'Well, she's not hurting anyone.'

He became serious. 'You make sure you're careful, Emily. You could both go to jail you know. She knows it's illegal and so do you and you'd be accused of "receiving" or "aiding and abetting", sorry about the pun.'

'I will and so will "Black Jack". It's his skin as well. Mam was mortified but everyone else thinks it's a huge joke. Except our Phoebe-Ann. I honestly don't think she knows what's going on, her head is full of cotton wool. Have you seen Alice Wainwright hanging around the docks with anyone from the Maury?'

'No. Should I have?'

'Just that the way Phoebe-Ann talks Alice must be practically engaged to someone on her. I don't know who.'

Edwin recalled the day they'd seen Jake Malone sober and shopping but then dismissed the memory.

'And talking of engagements.' He drew a small box from his pocket and handed it to her.

She took it from him and gulped. The moment had arrived. There could be no putting it off now and really she should try to be happy about it. She was, she told herself. She'd been the one who had agreed to the engagement, to be otherwise wasn't being fair to him. She was just being stupid. She opened it. A gold ring set with a tiny sapphire nestled inside. 'Oh, it's lovely, it really is!'

'I thought seeing that you've got blue eyes that it would be nice, like. A bit different.'

'Shall I wear it now?'

'Do you want to, Em?'

She nodded, not trusting herself to speak, as he slipped it on her finger.

'I love you, Emily.'

'And I love you.' She laid her head on his shoulder. She did love him. She did, but she knew she should have felt happier than this, that there shouldn't be that curious feeling in her stomach as though it were awash with ice water. She felt that the smile was nailed to her face.

'When will we tell them all?'

She raised her head. 'What's wrong with right now?'

He got up, pulling her with him. 'At the rate you and Miss Nesta Barlow are going you'll have saved up enough for the wedding before me.'

Their announcement was met with cries of joy and surprise from Lily, Albert and Jack. Jimmy, Rhys and Phoebe-Ann were out.

Lilly searched her daughter's face with relief. Emily had obviously overcome her terrible experience at the

220

hands of James Mercer and she was so relieved. She'd always liked Edwin Leeson and the announcement couldn't have made her happier. She just wished Phoebe-Ann would find herself someone decent like Edwin. She said as much as she hugged him.

Albert pumped his hand and Jack slapped him on the back and made jokes about Emily making an honest man out of him and was he going to give up this wild life at sea.

'Only if you're going to pay my wages, Jack.'

Jack was glad that Emily had got herself a decent bloke. Mam would worry less and that would make things easier for Jimmy and himself, for they were both talking about emigrating.

'This calls for a celebration. Jack, get down to the pub and bring our Jimmy and Rhys back home and get a bottle of something.' Lily went for her purse but Albert forestalled her by pushing a note into Jack's hand.

'And if you see our Phoebe-Ann tell her to come home now. In fact go and call at that Alice's and see if she's there. She spends more time there than here these days,' Lily called after him.

She turned to Emily. 'Have you thought of a date yet?'

'Don't go rushing them, Lil,' Albert laughed.

'No. Give us a chance, Mam.'

'Well, I'm just so pleased and happy for both of you that whatever you decide I'll agree with. A big do or a quiet one.'

'I don't want a big do, Mam. Just something simple.'

'Aye, leave all the grand stuff to Phoebe-Ann when it's her turn,' Edwin added, seeing the look of apprehension in Emily's eyes. He didn't want to rush her.

'Oh, no doubt she'll want a showy affair. Probably want to invite the whole street,' Emily laughed.

'Then she'd better start saving up for it instead of spending all her money on clothes. Clothes mad, she is, and nothing but the best since she and Alice Wainwright got into this dressmaking.'

When Jack returned it was with Jimmy, Rhys and Phoebe-Ann who looked decidedly put out.

'Try and look happy for your sister,' Lily hissed.

Phoebe-Ann was annoyed because she'd planned to meet Jake outside the Gaumont cinema and she'd had to beg Alice to go and tell him she'd been called home for some emergency and Alice hadn't been too happy about it. She selfishly wondered why Emily couldn't have waited until tomorrow to announce her engagement but she smiled and kissed her sister on the cheek and said the appropriate words and admired the ring. She was happy for Emily, of course she was, she just wished she could have told them all about herself and Jake. Especially as she'd seen the look of disapproval on Rhys's face. She'd been tempted to but Alice had talked her out of it. If they would just give him a chance they'd see how he'd changed she'd argued with Alice.

Alice had grimaced. 'He might have changed but the rest of them haven't.'

The following night, when she met him and told him of Emily's engagement and the fuss that was being made he'd put his arm around her and had drawn her closer to him. 'You wait, Phoebe-Ann, we'll show them all.'

'What do you mean, Jake?'

He cleared his throat. 'When we get engaged.'

She looked up at him. 'Will we?'

'Of course we will. I want to marry you Phoebe-Ann. I love you. I want to give you everything. We'll have a place of our own, all fixed up posh, like. You'll have a ring with real diamonds in it and . . .'

She caught his enthusiasm and her heart was singing. 'And a white satin wedding dress and a long white veil and we'll be so happy!'

He held her tightly. Yes, she'd have all that and more. 'I know what we'll do. We'll go and see Ma, right now.'

She drew back. 'Now?'

'Yes. I'm fed up with the others taking the mickey out of me and me ma poking fun with her sly digs. Once they see you Phoebe-Ann they'll know, and they'll learn to watch their tongues in future.'

She was very apprehensive. Ma Malone had a fearsome reputation and yet if she was going to marry Jake then she'd have to face the old harridan sooner or later. She supposed it might as well be sooner. 'All right, let's get it over with. Do you honestly think she'll like me, Jake?'

'How can she help it?'

When he walked into the kitchen with Phoebe-Ann, it was as though Jake was seeing his home for the first time and with new eyes, especially as Phoebe-Ann shrank closer to him.

She was trying not to show the disgust and shock she felt. The room was not only untidy but dirty. The curtains at the window were grey, the battered sofa and chairs were stained and greasy, and the oilcloth on the floor was broken and cracked and could have been either brown or grey. The table was covered with sheets of old newspaper, stained with tea. The range was filthy and the overmantel crammed with all kinds of odds and ends, covered in a thick film of sooty dust.

Only Peader and Vinny were at home. Vinny was asleep, slumped over the table, an empty jug of beer at his elbow. Peader looked up at her with blood-shot eyes.

'Ma, this is Phoebe-Ann. Me girl.'

Ma Malone looked at Phoebe-Ann, taking in the fashionable clothes, the short blonde hair and the look of disgust that Phoebe-Ann couldn't hide. 'An' what kind of a name is that? I can't remember no saint bein' called that.'

'Don't you start, Ma!' Jake warned.

'I'll start if I want to. It's my house an' you remember that!'

Phoebe-Ann made an effort. 'It's nice to meet you Ma . . . Mrs Malone. Jake has told me so much about you all.'

'Sure is that right? Isn't that a wonderful thing altogether? Do yez hear that Peader, yer eejit brother has been tellin' the whole world about us all.'

Jake glared at his mother. 'Me and Phoebe-Ann have come to tell you somethin'.'

'An' what's that then?' Ma Malone faced them both, her hostility apparent in her voice and demeanour.

Phoebe-Ann clutched at Jake's arm. 'Maybe we'd better wait for a more . . . suitable moment.'

Jake, having resolved to inform his mother of his intentions and having steeled himself for her reaction, shook his head. There would never be a *suitable* moment.

'Is it struck dumb the pair of yez are?' Ma demanded, having taken an instant dislike to the smartly dressed girl at her son's side. So, this was the one all the fuss was over and not just in the matter of clean shirts either. She quickly deduced that Phoebe-Ann was one of those women who were determined to 'improve' their man. In her eyes that would be to reduce Jake to a silent, awkward, timorous man in a very short period of time indeed; to shame him in the eyes of his family and make him an object of fun or pity to the neighbours. Well, this bold, painted rossi would have to deal with her first and there was no way she would allow any son of hers to be 'improved' in such a way.

'We're gettin' engaged!' Jake blurted out.

'Good on yer, lad! Let's 'ave a bevvy on that!' Peader cried, then cursed as Ma belted him across the side of his head.

'Shut yer gob an' yez has 'ad enough ter drink!' she yelled at him, snatching the jug away from him. She placed her hands on her hips and squared her shoulders. 'Is that what yez 'ave come to tell me. Well, let me do the tellin' now! If yez think I'm goin' to be doin' a jig wit delight yez can think again! I'm havin' no painted Orange hussy in my house!'

'I'm not Orange!' Phoebe-Ann shot back with some spirit.

'Well yer not one of *us*! Yer a bloody Proddy an' it's the same thing!'

Jake was shaking with anger and humiliation. 'You've not set foot in church for months an' it's bloody years since yer went to Mass, so you've no room to talk like that!' he yelled.

Ma took a few steps forward, wagging her forefinger menacingly at them both and, despite his anger, Jake stepped back a pace while Phoebe-Ann clung to his arm. 'That's got nothin' ter do with it. She's one of *them* an' what's more she's trouble. Yez 'ave only got to take one look at the face paint an' the skirt halfway up 'er arse, showin' everythin' she's got, ter see she's trouble!'

All Phoebe-Ann's resolve drained from her at the coarse description. She tugged at Jake's arm, tears pricking her eyes. How had she ever been stupid enough to believe that Ma Malone would have been even halfway civil to her? She was a horrible, crude, common woman and she hated her.

'Ah, leave the ol' bag! Take no notice of 'er, we're gettin' out of here!'

'Aye, go on the pair of yez! Gerrout of me house! Get yer Orange hussy out an' don't bring 'er 'ere again!' Ma screamed after them as Jake slammed the front door with such a force that it echoed down the entire street.

Phoebe-Ann burst into tears. 'I tried, Jake! I did try! Why did she have to say all those . . . terrible things about me?' she sobbed.

'Ah, don't let the old bitch upset you, Phoebe-Ann.' Jake felt he could have murdered his Ma. He must have been mad to have taken Phoebe-Ann home. What had he expected? 'I'm sorry. I really am.'

She sobbed harder for, as well as the realization that she had not been welcome in the Malone household, she was aware that Jake would not be welcome in hers either, but for very different reasons. 'What will we do, Jake? My Mam won't like you either but not because you're a Catholic,' she added, reminding him, as if he needed reminding, of his Ma's shrieked bigotry.

'We don't need them – any of them! You'll have your own place, like I promised you, with all the fancy stuff you want.'

Phoebe-Ann's dreams of floating down the aisle in

a cloud of white satin and tulle were disappearing. 'But what about the wedding? No-one will come.'

'Me brothers will, even if it's in the Registry Office.'

She remembered Lily's wedding and the grim austerity of Brougham Terrace and she felt cheated. 'We could go to St Nathaniel's. It would be quiet and I know our Emily won't let me down.'

Jake seized on her words, still smarting from Ma's insults. 'And what about that bloke that works with the O'Rourkes? That Welsh feller? Rhys. Aye, that's his name.'

'No, no, he won't come but our Emily's fiancé, Edwin Leeson, might.'

'There you are then. There'll only be my Ma and yours missing. You'll have your big day and we'll show them. Together we'll show them all!'

She raised her tear-streaked face to his. 'Yes, we'll show them.'

The following week Miss Nesta gave Emily a sovereign.

'But you haven't won anything.'

'I know but I want you to have it. An engagement gift if you like.'

'Oh, that's very kind of you, miss.'

'Now don't tell Millie. All she's worried about is you leaving us.'

'I won't be doing that for a long time, miss.'

'Good. Now run down the path with this.' She pressed the familiar envelope into Emily's hand.

Emily grinned to herself as she pushed the paper under the bootscraper, looked around and then went back inside. She hoped she would be 'lucky' for Miss Nesta today; she was a sweet old thing.

She'd only just reached the kitchen when the sound

of the door knocker reverberated through the house. She frowned. Who on earth was that? And was it absolutely necessary to hammer like that, loud enough to wake the dead?

Her heart dropped and her stomach turned over when she opened the door and was confronted by 'Black Jack' Costello and two burly, grim-looking men. She knew instinctively they were plainclothes policemen.

'Do you know this man, miss?'

Emily started to stammer. 'I . . . er . . .'

'We've been watching both of you for a while now. Very interesting little pantomime it has been too. And what's today's choice?' He waved the envelope at Emily and she blanched. 'China Clipper was it?'

'Emily! Who is at the door?' Miss Millicent Barlow's curt demand galvanized Emily. 'I'm not quite sure, ma'am,' she called, praying that she could think of some excuse or explanation.

Miss Millicent was not to be fobbed off. She pulled the door wide open and glared at the three men. 'All hawkers and tradesmen round the back! Can't you read?'

'We're policemen, ma'am. Detectives.'

'Well what are you standing on my doorstep for and who's he?' Miss Millicent pointed at Costello.

'I think we'd better come in, ma'am.'

'What on earth for?'

'It's to do with your maid. We don't want a public scene, do we, ma'am.'

'Emily, show them into the back parlour. The *small* back parlour.' She was not being intimidated in her own house.

As they all walked in Miss Nesta appeared.

'No need to fuss Nesta. They're the police. At least, two of them are. You'd better come too.'

Nesta Barlow gave a little cry and clapped her hand over her mouth.

As they filed into the room Emily looked with trepidation at Miss Nesta. It was a serious offence they faced.

'We have reason to believe that your maid and this person, one Jack Costello, known as "Black Jack" Costello, have been engaged in illegal gambling.'

'Don't be ridiculous!' Miss Millicent interrupted.

'We have been watching them, ma'am. A uniformed officer first brought them to our notice. She puts the bet under the bootscraper, he picks it up and if there are any winnings he puts them under the said bootscraper, she comes out and collects them. And here's the proof. Caught red-handed.' He thrust the envelope at Miss Millicent.

'Not Emily! I don't believe it!'

Emily bit her lip. How could she inform on Miss Nesta?

Costello looked sheepishly from Emily to the detective. It didn't matter much to him if she denied it or not. He'd been nicked and that was that. Occupational hazard.

'Oh, dear! Millicent, it's all my fault,' Nesta Barlow blurted out, twisting her hands together.

'Don't interrupt, Nesta!'

'But Millie, it is! You see it's not Emily's fault at all. They're my bets.'

Millicent Barlow looked at her sister as though she'd gone mad, the detectives looked mystified but Emily's relief was obvious.

'It's true, Millie.'

229

'You mean . . . you . . . you've been . . . ?' Miss Millicent stammered.

'Tom taught me how to do it and I had such fun and I know Papa hated it and that he'd be turning in his grave . . .'

'Nesta Barlow! You . . . you wicked, wayward . . . Oh, the scandal!' Miss Millicent sat down abruptly.

The two policemen looked at each other. This was turning into a nice mess. The sergeant cleared his throat. 'So, let me get this straight: your maid, Emily Parkinson, was acting on your instructions?' he inclined his head towards Miss Nesta.

'She was.'

'Nesta Barlow! How could you?'

'Oh, it was easy, Millie. Mr Costello and I had an "arrangement".'

'We know that, ma'am, but did you know it was illegal?'

'I think so. I never kept the money though.'

Miss Millicent who had been leaning back, her hand over her eyes, sat upright. 'What money? Oh, don't tell me you compounded everything by actually winning money!'

Emily thought Miss Millicent was about to faint, but Millicent Barlow was made of sterner stuff.

'Yes, I did win. Quite often too. You see I always picked a horse with a name that was connected to the sea and ships and they never let me down. It's all to do with Papa . . .'

'Nesta! I don't want to hear another word!'

Again, speculative glances were exchanged by the policemen. Quite obviously the old lady was a bit strange.

'So, where is this money?' Miss Millicent demanded.

230

'I gave it away. It was no use to me and I didn't do it for the money anyway.'

Emily breathed a sigh of relief. She was still 'an accessory after the fact' but at least Miss Nesta hadn't said she'd given her money which would have been called 'receiving'.

'Who did you give it to?' Miss Millicent asked stridently.

'I don't like to say.'

'Oh, my sainted aunt!' Miss Millicent exploded.

'I'm afraid we'll have to know, ma'am.'

'Oh dear. Can I whisper it to you?'

'You have been carrying on this low . . . common deceit for months and now you are overcome with false modesty! You'll tell us all – no whispering!' Miss Millicent stated.

'I gave it to . . . to . . . low women.'

Millicent Barlow uttered a scream. 'Oh, dear God! Don't tell me you've been walking up and down Lime Street or Canning Place! I just can't bear it! I can't!'

'Don't be silly. Stockley took it.'

'That's almost as bad! Oh, he hasn't been consorting with . . . !'

'No. He took it to a very nice lady in the Salvation Army, you know, they wear lovely bonnets and sing quite a lot.'

'I know who they are, Nesta!'

'They have a home where those . . . er . . . tarts, can go, if they want to stop being . . . er tarts.'

'Nesta Barlow! Wash your mouth out with carbolic soap!'

Emily was having trouble concealing her amusement and so was Costello. The two policemen looked decidedly uncomfortable.

'This Stockley person, can he verify all this?'

'Oh, yes. He's been with us for years. Now what will happen?' Miss Nesta seemed only mildly distressed.

'Oh, what will Richard Mercer say when he finds out about all this!' Miss Millicent was shaking her head.

'Is that the Richard Mercer of Cunard?'

'Yes, he's our nephew. The husband of our dear departed niece, Adele. Thank God she's dead, Nesta Barlow, so she can't see how depraved you've become.'

Miss Nesta looked bemused. 'Oh, she knew, Millie. Sometimes she gave me money herself. She said it was such a good cause.'

Millicent Barlow didn't think she could stand any more shocks and said so.

The detectives huddled together, whispering, while Emily looked down at her feet and Costello looked around the room, eyeing up the furnishings.

Again the sergeant cleared his throat. 'Under the circumstances, we feel that there is nothing to be gained by prosecuting this matter further. But, you must swear never to indulge in such actions again, ma'am.'

'Oh, I do! I promise on the grave of my mama! She was the dearest person in my life!'

'What about him?' Miss Millicent pointed at Costello.

'If he sets foot within a mile of here, he'll be nicked!'

'Black Jack' Costello looked as though he'd come into an inheritance, mentally swearing never to have anything to do with daft old bats like Nesta Barlow.

'I think you should show these kind officers out Emily, after giving them a drink, if they will partake of one. I feel quite ill,' Miss Millicent instructed.

Emily nodded, much relieved.

Miss Nesta made to follow her.

'Not you, Nesta! I have quite a lot of things to say to you before I retire to my sickbed!'

Emily cast a consoling look at Miss Nesta as she closed the door. Miss Nesta was full of surprises for a lady from such a sheltered background. The whole episode would keep the family amused for weeks, she thought.

Chapter Fifteen

Despite Jake's offer to 'stand by her', Phoebe-Ann decided she'd tell her family alone. Jake had promised to buy her a ring, an expensive ring, in New York and she hoped that she could make them understand that Jake had changed. Also things may not deteriorate into a full-scale row if he wasn't beside her. She'd manage better on her own, she told him.

Before he'd sailed they'd gone to look for rooms, but she'd been disappointed with the ones offered until Alice's mother unwittingly provided the solution by telling her that old Mrs Garner had gone to live with her daughter and that, if anyone got in quick, they would have a good little house. 'Got its own privy an' wash house,' Mrs Wainwright had told a very bored Alice but a very interested Phoebe-Ann.

Phoebe-Ann hadn't even bothered to go and see the house, instead Jake had given her the money and she'd gone straight to the landlord and, by lunch time that day, number fourteen Florist Street was hers and Jake's.

Her spirits had lifted when she'd gone to see it and planned how she could transform it. It wouldn't cost a fortune, she told Jake. A lick of paint, and Great Homer Street market was a wonderful place to pick up things cheap and nice pieces of second-hand furniture could be had from pawn shops. By the end of the day she was in high spirits as she kissed him goodbye at the landing stage.

'Oh, it will be wonderful, Jake.'

He held her close, unable to believe his luck. He'd gone along with all her proposals for the house and his admiration of her had increased, as had his pride. He'd be someone to be reckoned with. A nice place of his own, all done up and kept spick and span and a smart wife to boot. Of course they'd all jeer at him going 'posh' but to hell with them! For the first time in his life he'd have respect. People would look at him when he came home from sea or when he took Phoebe-Ann out and they'd nudge each other and say 'There's Mr Malone with his wife. Nice, respectable couple they are.' Yes, Phoebe-Ann had given him much more than just her love.

'Just wait until they all see the ring I'm going to get you Phoebe-Ann. It will make your eyes stand out.'

' 'Ere! Lover-boy! Get yer skates on or the Chief will 'ave yer guts fer garters!' Vinny Malone shouted as the usual crowd of last-minute drinkers rushed out of the Stile House and towards the waiting liner whose stentorian whistle blasts fortunately drowned out the rest of Vinny's remarks.

'Bye, Jake! Take care!' Phoebe-Ann called after him.

'You've put me ma in a right black mood,' Vinny complained as they made their way up the crew gangway.

'Tough shit! We've just been an' put down the rent on a house an' we're goin' to get married when I get back. So, tell 'er to stuff that in her bleedin' old pipe and smoke it!'

'Jesus! She'll murder yez!'

'Aye, an' you an' all 'cos you're goin' to be me best

235

man and just because I'm givin' you that honour, you can lend me the money for the ring. In fact, you can all chip in, seein' as you're so lucky gettin' a girl with a bit of class for a sister-in-law. That rent money nearly cleaned me out but she was set on it.'

'What rent money?' Peader asked, catching the last of Jake's words.

' 'E's goin' to marry that judy from Lonsdale Street. Wants me to be best man. Wants us all to lend him a few bob towards the ring, she's just cleaned 'im out.'

'You bleedin' eejit! She'll bleed yer dry if yer let 'er! I've met 'er sort before!'

Jake lunged at him. 'Don't you talk about Phoebe-Ann like that!'

'Oh, for God's sake don't you lot start before you're even on board! Get below before I have to dock your pay!' the Master-at-Arms yelled at them.

'Don't expect us all ter come round callin' on yer. You'll be lucky if me ma lets us go to the weddin'!' Franny stated.

Jake aimed a blow at him. 'Listen to Mammy's baby! Shit scared of his own shadow!' he jeered.

Franny Malone lashed out at him but Peader and Vinny pulled them apart. 'We'll none of us 'ave any bloody money if you two don't pack it in!'

Phoebe-Ann watched until the tugs had the *Mauretania* well out into the river, then she turned away to make her way home. Some of her enthusiasm had waned, she thought, as she got off the tram and began to walk up towards Lonsdale Street. Then she brightened when she thought of the house in Florist Street. That would show Mam that she really did mean to get married and that she didn't care whether they approved of Jake or not.

236

In a way she was glad that everyone was at home when she walked in.

Emily smiled at her. 'You've been up to something, Fee. You've got that look on your face.'

'I've got something to tell you all.'

Albert and Jack stopped mid-conversation. Jimmy put down the *Echo* and Lily wiped her hands on her apron.

'What is it? Out with it?'

'Our Emily's not the only one who's getting married. I am.'

'What!' Lily was so surprised she dropped the spoon into the teapot along with the tea.

'And I've got a house of my own, in Florist Street.'

'Just hold on a minute, miss! Start at the beginning. Just who are you going to marry?'

Phoebe-Ann looked around at the curious faces and prayed for courage. She took a deep breath. 'Jake Malone.'

The silence was deafening.

'Well, say something?' she pleaded.

Lily sat down. 'I didn't hear that right, did I? Someone tell me I must have misunderstood?'

'No, Mam, you didn't.'

Something inside Lily snapped. 'Phoebe-Ann, you can't mean that you've been going around with the . . . that blackguard? How long has this been going on?'

Phoebe-Ann held her ground. 'I love him, Mam, and he's not like . . .'

The rest of her words were cut off by Lily's hysterical laughter. 'You love him! You love that drunken, worthless, useless sot! No-one but that old battleaxe of a mother could love him! Have you seen

237

the state of them? Never sober! Have you seen the state of the house and her!'

'Yes, Mam, I have and I hate her but you're wrong about Jake.'

'Phoebe-Ann you're not serious? They're hooligans and villains of the first order! They've got the whole of Mona Street terrified of them!' Jack yelled.

'You won't even let me explain about Jake!'

'You're right! He doesn't need any explaining, the whole bloody neighbourhood can "explain" about Jake Malone!' Jimmy cried. 'You're not going to disgrace us all by marrying the likes of him!' Jimmy's fist crashed down on the table, making the cups clatter.

'I am! I am going to marry him!'

'Your da would disown you and so will I if you go on with this!' Lily cried.

'Why can't you give us a chance? Jake isn't like the rest of them!'

'I don't want to hear his name again!' Lily yelled at her.

'I didn't expect you to be happy about it but at least . . .'

'Happy! I'd be happier if you were dead rather than married to him!' Lily interrupted.

'Phoebe-Ann, don't you think you should give this thing more thought? It's a big step marriage, to anyone, but someone like him, you can't really know him.' Albert's voice was the calmest and Phoebe-Ann turned to him.

'I do know him! I've been seeing him for ages and I have thought about it.'

'Dear God in heaven! Why didn't someone tell me? Why hasn't someone seen them together and warned me weeks ago?' Lily groaned, before jumping to her

238

feet, sparks of anger glittering in her eyes. 'Oh, I can see it all now! You've been up to your tricks again, haven't you? You've been lying to me! You haven't been at Alice Wainwright's, you've been out with him! You've been parading around the town hanging on the arm of Jake Malone! Oh, God help us all!' Lily burst into tears. Her worst fears had been realized. She'd always prayed that Phoebe-Ann would never let her pretty, naive little head be turned by some useless 'no mark'. Now it had happened. Phoebe-Ann was so trusting she'd believe anything. She'd obviously got carried away by her daydreams and the fact that her sister had got engaged. Jake Malone! Satan himself couldn't be much worse than any of the Malones!

Albert rushed to comfort her.

'You listen to me our Phoebe-Ann! If I see you with him I'll break every bone in his body, I swear I will!' Jack yelled. He had no intention of becoming the butt of numerous jokes or pitying glances from the regulars of the Grecian.

'And I'll help him!' Jimmy added and for the same reasons.

'Stop it! Stop it!' Phoebe-Ann placed her hands over her ears and burst into tears.

Emily hadn't said a word, she was too shocked, but now, seeing both her mother and sister in floods of tears, she moved towards Phoebe-Ann. The habit of protecting her younger sister instinctive. 'Stop yelling, all of you!'

'Oh, Em! You understand, don't you?' Phoebe-Ann pleaded.

'No. I don't.'

Lily threw off Albert's comforting and restraining embrace. 'You see, even your sister is shocked but she still protects you! Your poor sister who was raped because of your stupidity! Now you're consorting with trash and you're too dense to see where it will all lead or maybe you don't care about hurting us all again!' Lily screamed, too angry to care if her words were like blows.

'You've always blamed me for that, mam, haven't you? You've never forgiven me! It wasn't my fault but you never believed me! You never believed me!'

'Why should I when all you ever do is lie to me?'

'I haven't lied to you. I *was* at Alice's, except when Jake was home.'

'Don't you dare to even speak his name in this house, Phoebe-Ann Parkinson!' Lily was beside herself with rage and sorrow.

Phoebe-Ann broke down again while Emily looked around in despair. 'Come upstairs with me,' she urged her sister.

Albert was again holding his sobbing wife but she broke away from him. 'If she's going through with this then she's not staying in this house for another minute! I don't care where she goes, she can live on the streets for all I care! If she won't give him up then she goes and what's more she'll be no daughter of mine!'

Phoebe-Ann tore herself away from Emily. 'I don't care! I don't care what any of you say, I love him and I'm going to marry him and one day you'll be sorry!'

'It will be you who'll be sorry! You'll have a terrible life with him and don't say I haven't warned you!'

'Lily, Lily love! Calm down!' Albert cried.

'I'm going! I'm not staying here. I hate you all!' and wrenching open the door Phoebe-Ann ran out.

Emily cast a despairing look at her stepfather.

He nodded and she ran after her sister, catching Phoebe-Ann at the back gate.

'Fee! Fee, wait!'

'Oh, Em! What can I do? What can I do?' Phoebe-Ann's cheeks were tear-stained.

'You can give him up,' Emily said quietly.

'I love him! He's not like Mam says he is! The others might be but he's not. Oh, Em, he's so good to me and he idolizes me!'

'Oh, why him?' Emily groaned.

'I don't know. Why do you love Edwin?'

Emily held her sister in her arms. She was shocked and upset that Phoebe-Ann had chosen to marry into the worst family in the whole neighbourhood but Phoebe-Ann was terribly upset and terribly determined. 'Oh, Fee! What will you do?

Phoebe-Ann tried to pull herself together. 'I'll go to Alice's. Mrs Wainwright will let me stay there until Jake comes home.'

'You really do mean it. You love him.'

'You don't think I'd go through all this if I didn't, do you?'

Emily felt defeated. Utterly defeated. Phoebe-Ann had always been naive but this! To tear the family apart and for someone like Jake Malone. It was beyond belief. 'Oh, Fee! You poor little fool.'

Phoebe-Ann wiped her eyes on the back of her hand. 'You won't desert me, Em, will you?'

'You know I won't, but please think about it, Fee! Think about all it means.'

'I have. I know what I'm doing. I'd better go now.' She released herself from Emily's arms. 'I'll be at Alice's if anyone . . . needs me.'

Emily watched her open the yard door and her heart was heavy. What kind of a life was Phoebe-Ann letting herself in for? She was like a pretty butterfly but she fervently prayed her glory would last longer than a day.

Phoebe-Ann turned. 'Will you do something for me?'

'You know I will, if I can.'

'Will you come to my wedding and be my bridesmaid?'

Mam would be furious but she couldn't let Phoebe-Ann be alone on what should be the happiest day in any girl's life. She nodded. 'Of course I will but I'll have to keep it a secret.'

The yard door closed and Emily leaned her forehead against it, the tears falling down her cheeks. Was it always to be thus, she wondered? Twice Phoebe-Ann had managed, unwittingly, to turn her life upside down. Firstly with what she believed had been innocent conversations with James Mercer and now by her determination to marry a man who was reviled by everyone, a determination that had torn apart a happy family. Still her heart bled for her sister and she prayed that Jake Malone had changed and that he appreciated what Phoebe-Ann was giving up for him.

Twice Emily had tried to broach the subject with Lily but each time she had been cut short by her mother's bitter words. Phoebe-Ann had chosen between decency and a loving family and a no-good drunkard and Lily wouldn't hear her name mentioned in the house. Even Albert had turned a deaf ear to all her pleadings for he was angry that Phoebe-Ann was causing Lily so much anguish.

She went to see Phoebe-Ann at Alice's, taking her sister's clothes. But it was a strained, uneasy meeting and Phoebe-Ann was immovable in her determination. On her way out Mrs Wainwright had taken her aside.

'I've tried to talk to her, Emily, but it's no use . . . 'E's a drunkard an' worse, they all are. But she just won't 'ave it. Even our Alice can't make 'er see sense. I couldn't see her walking the streets with nowhere to go, could I? I 'ope your mam won't hold that against me.'

'No. I think she's really relieved you took her in Mrs Wainwright. She's just praying Phoebe-Ann will change her mind.'

'Your poor mam must be heart-scalded. Tell her I was askin' for her an' Phoebe-Ann's fine here.'

She'd thanked the woman, who meant well.

All the joy Phoebe-Ann had felt before Jake had sailed had evaporated and with it all her bravado. She felt alone and friendless. Even Alice and her mother thought she was mad. Why couldn't they just have given him a chance?

When he finally arrived home with a beautiful ring, the sight of her face told him what had happened even before he had to ask.

'To hell with the lot of them! We don't need them. We're happy. Look, put this on and we'll go and see the minister or priest or whatever he's called. Fix up a date.'

'I didn't think it would be that bad, Jake. I really didn't. It was awful. Everyone yelling and screaming at me, except our Emily, and Mam throwing me out.'

'You've not changed your mind, have you?'

'No. No, of course not.'

'That's my girl.'

'It's just that . . .'

'What?'

'It doesn't seem so bad for you.' She thought it

grossly unfair that she had borne the brunt of the upset.

'Don't bet on it. Me ma's already got our Seamus, Peader and Franny on her side. I've only got our Vinny. He told her to sod off, that he'd do what he liked and if he wanted to be my best man and in a Proddy church, she wasn't going to stop him.'

Phoebe-Ann sighed heavily. So, it wasn't just her family, although she really didn't care very much about the rest of the Malones.

'Let's go and see the vicar, is that what he's called?'

She smiled. 'Yes. You just call him Mr Laird, not Father Laird.'

'And we won't tell any of them when it's to be so they can't spoil it. Except our Vinny of course.'

'And our Emily. She said she'd be my bridesmaid.'

'There you are then. They'll all come round in the end, see if they don't.'

She didn't care if Ma Malone never 'came round' but she cared deeply that her mam would.

'Can I see Phoebe-Ann please, Mrs Wainwright?' Rhys asked, looking imploringly at the woman. He knew he was a fool to even have come but he was so shocked and disturbed that to have done nothing to try to stop Phoebe-Ann was unthinkable. He wondered how he'd not heard of it in the stokehold but then he ignored the Malones and went out of his way to avoid Jake.

Mrs Wainwright tactfully took Alice's arm and steered her towards the scullery on the pretext of a mountain of dirty pots and dishes that would need their combined efforts to render clean. It would also give the excuse of clattering them loudly to cover the sound of any arguments.

'I suppose you've come to look down your nose at me and say I'm mad?' Phoebe-Ann snapped, openly hostile to him.

Rhys shook his head. Until he'd seen her he'd hoped he could succeed where the others had failed, but as he took in the set lips, the jutting chin and the defiance in her eyes he knew his mission was impossible. 'No. I came to say that . . . that I still love you Phoebe-Ann and I always will.' He twisted his cap between his hands, fighting down the urge to take her in his arms and kiss her until all thoughts of Jake Malone were obliterated.

Phoebe-Ann relaxed, she even felt sorry for him. 'I'm sorry, Rhys.'

'Don't pity me! The one thing I can't take is pity. I'll have to work beside him knowing that you belong to him, but I'll manage. I don't need anyone's pity. I just came to tell you that . . . well, if anything goes wrong, I'll be here. I'll still love you.' He was thankful for the noises issuing from the scullery. He had his pride, he wanted no-one to hear his words except Phoebe-Ann. He also knew he could not run back to the valley. That would be like telling the whole world that he was devastated because of her. No, he would continue to work in the stokehold and he'd keep his pride and dignity and nurse his sorrow in silence.

There were tears on Phoebe-Ann's lashes as she thanked him and impulsively kissed him on the cheek. She had expected him to be angry and dismissive and his words had moved her. Moved her but not made her budge an inch from her decision.

Emily was let in on the secret but sworn to secrecy, as was Vinny Malone.

'No-one is going to spoil her day more than they

have done already,' Jake informed his brother and Emily who had both made the short journey to Alice's with great stealth.

Seeing Phoebe-Ann with him Emily began to wonder if all her sister had said was true. He was sober, clean and well-turned out and even his speech was far more refined than his brothers'. Perhaps they had all misjudged him. Then she remembered seeing him on the day of Lily's wedding. She sighed. Phoebe-Ann had made her decision.

'There will be just me and Phoebe-Ann, Emily and you, our Vinny, and the vicar. After the bit of a service we're going to Reeces' for a slap-up meal. You are both invited.'

Vinny looked impressed but Emily bit her lip.

Phoebe-Ann looked with pleading at her sister, so she nodded. What harm could a few more hours do?

'And you'll both be welcome at our house, won't they Phoebe-Ann?'

'Yes. I hope you'll both come and visit me.' This was directed more to Emily than Vinny because, although she was grateful for his support, she didn't particularly like him.

Emily smiled at her. She would have to sneak round, Mam must never know.

'So, when's the happy day, like?' Vinny asked, rubbing his hands together in anticipation of a drop of the hard stuff to seal the arrangements.

'The beginning of the month. November the fifth at ten o'clock.'

'Oh, that's great. Guy Fawkes day an' if me Ma finds out there'll be more than fireworks goin' off. But me lips are sealed. Now let's 'ave a bevvy on it.'

Phoebe-Ann glared at Vinny.

'Have one for me on the way home. Alice's Mam don't keep any booze in the house,' Jake grinned.

Vinny looked disgusted and, as he left, Emily heard him mutter, 'Right bleeding do this will be. More like a wake than a weddin' an' the gob on 'er when I mentioned a bevvy. Me ma's right.' Although Emily didn't agree with him she had to smile. Phoebe-Ann had already worked wonders on Jake Malone.

As the weeks went by, Lily was sure that Emily knew something although she denied it. Each time Lily questioned her she said, 'Mam, if you would only go and see Phoebe-Ann yourself, she'll explain . . .'

'No! I'll never speak to her again until she comes here and tells me it's all off and that she's learned her lesson.'

'You know she won't do that. But she is all right and Mrs Wainwright told me to tell you that she is doing everything to try to talk her out of it.'

'It's a bit late now. I should have put a stop to her running around with the likes of Alice Wainwright, then she'd never have met that . . . that "no mark"!'

'Oh, Mam, you couldn't have stopped her. She's grown up.'

'She's not twenty-one. I could stop her and I could do it even now.'

'Then why haven't you?'

'Because Albert said what good would it do. I'd have had to take her before the justices and the scandal of that! Then as soon as my back was turned she'd only run off to that place in Scotland, Gretna something or other, or worse, maybe even leave the country. It's been done before and she's such a trusting little fool. I just keep praying she'll come to her senses and come home.'

247

Emily had patted her mother's shoulder. 'You do still worry about her, even though you say you don't.'

'How can I help it, Emily? She's my own flesh and blood. I was so angry, I still am, but if she were to come in here now and tell me she was coming home I'd be the happiest woman in the whole of this city. All I can do is hope that by cutting her off she'll stop and think.'

It was on the tip of Emily's tongue to say that maybe they had misjudged him, that he did look as though he'd mended his ways, but then Lily would know she had seen him and spoken to him and that was something she couldn't let happen, both for her mam's and Phoebe-Ann's sakes.

'Mam, if you'd just see her.'

'Don't! Don't Emily. I won't hear another word.'

Emily had turned away, knowing it was a lost cause.

Chapter Sixteen

Phoebe-Ann had no white satin wedding dress or long veil but an ivory coat and dress with a matching hat. The big bouquet she'd always envisaged was reduced to a small posy but at least it was a proper wedding, she told herself, in a church and not a drab, bare room.

Emily felt so sorry for her sister as she stood beside her in the otherwise empty church. Nothing had turned out right for Phoebe-Ann. They'd often day-dreamed about what kind of weddings they would have in the days before so much tragedy had over-taken them.

From the money Miss Nesta had given her, Emily had bought the happy couple a very nice eiderdown and bedspread in cream-coloured heavy cotton overlayed with deep pink roses. She'd bought them from Sturla's Department Store and they'd kindly wrapped them up, too. Phoebe-Ann had been so delighted that she had insisted on putting them on the bed at once. Jake had noted that it hadn't crossed Vinny's mind to buy them any-thing.

When the service was over and Phoebe-Ann was the new Mrs Malone and had been duly kissed by her new husband, her sister and her new brother-in-law, Emily had reluctantly excused herself, leaving the newlyweds and Vinny to enjoy their solitary wedding breakfast at Reeces'.

'Did everything turn out satisfactorily?' Miss Millicent asked when she returned.

'Yes, thank you, miss.'

'Let's hope it continues like that.'

'Oh, I'm sure it will, Millie.' Miss Nesta looked wistful. 'Such a pity for so few people to attend, though I really do admire your sister, Emily.'

'Why?' Miss Millicent asked sharply of her sister.

'Because she has the courage to follow her destiny.'

Miss Millicent tutted. 'Destiny, indeed!'

Miss Nesta looked knowingly at Emily. 'Was she lovely? Is she happy?'

'Yes, she looked lovely and I think she is happy.'

'When will she tell your mama?'

Emily frowned. 'I don't know, miss. I don't think she is going to tell her at all.'

'Why not?'

'What is the point, miss? She knows Mam won't entertain him and she's gone and done what Mam forbade her to do – married him.'

'Oh, dear.'

'I feel so sorry for your poor Mama,' Miss Millicent said.

Miss Nesta smiled. 'Let's not dwell on it. Have you and your young man set a date yet, Emily?'

'No, not yet. There's been all this fuss over Phoebe-Ann, I don't think Mam could stand coping with me as well.' She began to place the dirty teacups on the tray. Her excuse was so feeble but only she knew that.

The meal at Reeces' had been lovely, despite the fact that Vinny's table manners left much to be desired and his loud comments had made her cringe, Phoebe-Ann thought as she folded her clothes and slipped on the new nightdress. Jake had persuaded her to have

250

a 'bit of a drink' to celebrate, for the restaurant only served wines which both he and Vinny had derided. She'd agreed. After all it was a *special* day. She'd had three sherries and had felt very light-headed as they'd walked for the tram home. Jake and Vinny had been very merry – not drunk, just merry, she'd told herself; after all, it was a celebration. The effects of the sherry had worn off, leaving her with a slight headache and a deepening feeling of apprehension.

Of course she knew all about the 'birds and bees' as Lily called it, but she didn't know what it would be like in reality. She'd dreamed, imagined, but not too deeply. Alice had hinted that it wasn't in the least bit wonderful, not that she'd had personal experience, she'd added hastily. She'd once heard her mam confiding in her Aunty Edna that she planned all the meals and made mental shopping lists while 'it' was going on. Phoebe-Ann had been dismayed. 'It can't be that bad!' she'd cried. Alice had shrugged. 'Sometimes it's worse, so I've heard.'

Phoebe-Ann had remembered Emily and how she'd looked that terrible night and now that image of her sister – bruised, beaten and shaking with shock and horror – filled her mind. What if it *was* so awful? What if it was always violent? What would she do? What *could* she do? She tried to clear her head. No, it just couldn't be like that. Mam had never looked . . . shocked or bruised. She realized that she was shaking and it wasn't just because the room was cold.

She climbed into bed, the icy smoothness of the new sheets serving to increase the shivering. She pulled the blankets and coverlet up to her chin. The romantic dream she'd cherished had never really taken her further than the altar. She'd never really thought about this aspect of marriage. Mentally she shook herself. 'Don't be such a little fool!' she scolded herself. She loved Jake and he loved her. It would be wonderful, it wouldn't be like Emily's nightmare experience. She closed her eyes wishing she could get all thoughts of Emily and James Mercer out of her mind.

Her eyes opened wide as Jake came into the room, but she closed them tightly as he began to undress. Her cheeks burned with embarrassment and she wished he would switch off the light. She had never seen a man naked and she couldn't bring herself to open her eyes.

At last the room was in darkness and he got into bed, his hands reaching for her. She turned towards him, still trembling. He grunted, thinking it was desire that had overwhelmed her. She began to relax as he kissed her, thinking what an idiot she'd been. What was there to fear? He loved her.

His kisses and caresses became more passionate, almost rough in his urgency, and, suddenly, panic washed over Phoebe-Ann. He was hurting her. She cried for him to stop but he ignored her and the panic deepened. It *was* going to be the same for her as it had been for Emily! This disregard for her feelings, her needs, her dreams. Where was the tenderness, the gentleness, the soft, sweet caresses? This was how it must be for everyone she thought, only no-one had ever told her. She tried to lash out, to push him away but he was too strong and now he seemed to be in the grip of a power that was driving him to do terrible things to her. This wasn't the Jake she loved, this was someone else. He was pushing himself into her and she began to fight him, screaming in pain and fear.

With an effort Jake pulled away from her. 'What's the matter?'

'Stop it! Stop it!' she screamed.

'What's wrong? You're my wife, Phoebe-Ann, I love you and this is . . . this is . . .' He couldn't find the right words to explain to her that this was normal.

'You're hurting me! It's horrible . . . it's just like what . . .' she stopped, suddenly remembering he didn't know about Emily and James Mercer.

'I didn't mean to hurt you, Phoebe-Ann.'

She began to cry softly and Jake looked at her with a mixture of frustration, disappointment and bewilderment. He'd known she was a virgin but he'd never expected this rejection, this fear.

Phoebe-Ann swallowed hard. Only hours ago she'd promised to 'love, honour and obey' and she'd heard him say the words 'with my body I thee worship'. That made it right. It was bound up with marriage. She was his wife now and it was his right. Slowly she nodded. She would just have to try to cope with it. Maybe, maybe in time she'd even enjoy it, after all she'd been so eager to marry him and she'd known what marriage entailed, so why was she feeling like this? It was something to do with Emily and James Mercer, that much she realized. Something to do with the feelings of guilt that invaded her mind in the dark hours of the night. But she must try not to think like that. This was her wedding night, she was supposed to be happy.

She lay with her eyes closed, her arms around his neck and when he entered her she bit back the cry of pain. Her body was rigid, her nerves taut, although she didn't realize it, and when Jake rolled away from her she felt bruised and somehow violated. Two teardrops crept from beneath her lashes and slid down her cheeks. Oh, why hadn't Mam told her it would be like this? She'd believed that it would be like . . .

like what? She hadn't let her imagination go this far. She wished she could talk to Emily but she knew she could never, ever confide in her sister, it would only hurt her. She wished she could talk to her mam, ask her advice, invite her sympathy. But Mam wasn't even speaking to her. She wished she could tell Jake about Emily, maybe then he would understand why she had suddenly been overcome by this awful fear and revulsion. It was out of the question. She would never subject Emily to that, for she couldn't be certain that Jake wouldn't tell his brothers.

Jake lay staring at the ceiling, feeling dismayed and a little annoyed. What the hell had got into her? She'd been eager to get married. She'd never before rejected his advances, so why now? After all they'd been through to get wed now she had gone all cold and rigid, as though he was raping her. She couldn't be afraid of him. It must be something to do with the way her ma had explained things to her. Or maybe she hadn't explained at all. Perhaps she'd been left to find out from other people, but however she had learned about it she must have known what it entailed. All the other girls he'd been out with had, but then she was different. He'd put her on a pedestal, but would she prove to be as cold as a marble statue? Maybe it was because he'd been too eager, but he'd been patient long enough. No, it was just because it was the first time for her. She hadn't known what to expect. Next time things would be different.

Next time and the three times after that were just as bad. Phoebe-Ann was unable to disassociate herself from Emily's experiences although she tried hard. The nagging guilt grew out of all proportion until she started to believe that this was her punishment for what she believed was her part in Emily's tragedy. Each time she lay stiff, biting her lip to cut off the cries and each time she'd cried herself to sleep. She still loved Jake, she told herself, and in every other aspect their marriage was good. If only she didn't have to share the same bed. All she needed was some time and patience, she would get used to it, she *would* get better, she vowed.

Jake had tried to be patient with her but he was not a patient man, nor could he understand her rejection of him. She said she loved him and he had to admit that things between them were fine, until they went to bed. Because his patience and tolerance were strained he began to feel annoyed. What more did she want of him? He'd virtually given up the drink, he'd alienated his family, he'd given her everything she'd wanted, they'd even married in *her* church and now . . . now she couldn't bear him to make love to her. Oh, she'd been eager enough for his kisses and embraces before, although because he had respected her he'd not touched her. Had she really only been looking for someone to provide her with a place of her own, a ring on her finger and the title of 'Mrs'? No, it hadn't been like that at all, he told himself. She'd fallen head over heels in love with him. She wasn't a 'gold digger'. Despite all his reasoning the seeds of doubt had been sown and they refused to be dislodged. Well, she'd have plenty of time – he was sailing again soon and when he returned things were bound to be better. 'Absence makes the heart grow fonder' Vinny always joked about his girls. He knew her heart and soul were his, he just wished her body was too.

Albert was worried about her. 'Why don't you go and see her, Lily? Give it one last try?'

'It won't work. She has always been stubborn when she's set her mind on something; she's like her da, and she's obviously set her mind on him. God help us all! I'd only go and lose my temper with her and I'll not have Mrs Wainwright with her ear glued to the door, nor would it be fitting for me to be laying down the law in her house. In her way she's been good to Phoebe-Ann. At least I've known she has a roof over her head and something to eat.'

'Look, if you won't go and see Phoebe-Ann, why not go and see him? I'll come with you.'

'Him! I'd never lower myself to speak to any of them!'

'Then his ma? Now, before you go up in the air, think about it. She's probably not happy about the whole thing either. For different reasons, of course, but she is his mother, whatever we think of her. She must have some concern for him.'

'Concern! That's a word she doesn't even know. How can she when she's managed to bring up a tribe of hooligan drunks?'

'She's a widow, like you were. Perhaps she just couldn't do as good a job with her lot as you did with yours.'

'She'd have done better if she'd stayed out of the pub, and I haven't done all that well, have I? Oh, you're such a good man Albert Davies, you look for goodness in everyone, even Ma Malone.'

'Then go and see her? Have a bit of a talk with her, see if you can both forget your differences and talk the pair of them out of it? Tell her it will be the biggest mistake he'll ever make, as it will be for Phoebe-Ann.'

Lily thought about it. She couldn't see what Ma

Malone could object to in Phoebe-Ann, except her religion. She was a far better class of girl than any of the Malones deserved and in her view the old harridan should be grateful, but Albert was usually right. 'Oh, I suppose it's worth a try. I'll swallow my pride then.'

'Do you want me to come with you?'

She smiled tiredly. 'No. I think I can manage her on my own.'

'Then I'd go round soon, while he's away. While the rest of them are too, although I believe one can't find work.'

'That one was sacked by Cunard for brawling!'

'The offer still stands.'

She patted his hand. 'No. You've your work to attend to. You can't go turning down work because of our Phoebe-Ann. Oh, what did I ever do without you?'

She told none of the family what she intended to do, for she wanted no more arguments. So, the following morning she made her way to Mona Street, her face set in lines of determination. It was the last thing she would do for Phoebe-Ann. If this failed then she'd just have to get on with it. She'd insisted on making her bed; she'd have to lie on it no matter how uncomfortable it got, and she didn't doubt that it would grow very uncomfortable, for whatever kind of 'changes' she'd wrought on Jake Malone they certainly wouldn't last long, of that fact she was certain.

She grimaced at the dirty curtains, the tarnished knocker, peeling paintwork and dirty step. The woman had no pride in her home, that much was obvious. She was thankful she knew few people in Mona Street, but most of the houses were well-tended. Like everyone else, there wasn't much money

257

coming in and their homes did not boast fancy furnishings, but what they had was kept clean and if there wasn't meat on the table every day, their steps were donkey-stoned as were the flags in front of each terraced house. It must be dreadful to have the Malones for neighbours, she thought. She rapped smartly on the knocker and folded her arms. If needs be the whole forthcoming conversation would be held on the doorstep. At least then the whole of Mona Street would know of her opposition to this mismatch.

After knocking again and waiting she became impatient. She was certain there was someone in and she hadn't steeled herself to come here and not get a reply of some sort. She walked up the street, around the corner and down the entry until she came to the back door, swinging on its broken hinges. She pushed it open and looked at the yard with disgust. It was full of rubbish: bottles, an old cushion, bits of rags and old newspapers. Ashes and clinkers from the range were scattered around, the midden was full to overflowing and here and there were bits of food in various stages of decay. The place must be alive with vermin, she thought with a shudder as she kicked a rotting cabbage stalk out of the way.

The back door was open and she could hear sounds from within so she hammered on it loudly. 'Mrs Malone! Are you in there Mrs Malone?'

Ma Malone appeared, her hair hanging in greasy untidy strands around her face, her grubby blouse sleeves rolled up to the elbows and voluminous black skirts covered by a very dirty and wet apron. 'What do yez want? I'm doin' me washin'. Who let yez in 'ere?'

At least she did wash things Lily thought, although judging by the state of the apron it was after a fashion that couldn't be compared to her own wash. She tried not to notice the smell wafting from inside the house. 'I want to talk to you. I tried the front door but got no answer so I came around the back.'

'Oh, did yez now? An' who the 'ell are you?'

'I'm Lily Davies. Phoebe-Ann's mother. You do know that our Phoebe-Ann and your Jake are planning to get wed?'

Ma looked at her with hostility. Snooty-lookin' bitch she was. Now she knew who that toffee-nosed little hussy took after. 'So?'

'So, I've come to talk to you about it. I don't suppose you're any happier than I am about it, though she's too good for him.'

'Is she now. An' what about my lad? Workin' 'is fingers to the bone so he can buy 'er fancy stuff. Never bought 'is poor old ma anything like that.'

'That's as may be, but I'm not having it.'

'You're not 'avin' it! You're not 'avin' it! What do I get out of it then? A bleedin' toffee-nosed, painted Orange floosie, that's what I get!'

Lily's temper began to boil. 'We're not Orange! We're Church of England!'

'It's the same thing. Yez all the bloody same. Proddies! Orangemen! God blast the lot of yez to hell an' back!'

Lily was hanging on to her temper and her dignity. 'I didn't come here to discuss religion.'

'Well, I'm discussin' it an' no-one asked yez to come and yez standin' on me step so I'll say what I like! She's a tart and an Orange one at that!'

'My girls are not tarts! If Phoebe-Ann seems like one then it's because she's been associating with the likes of him! Trash! Drunken, ignorant, Irish trash the lot of you! I pity your neighbours that I do.'

Ma took a step forward, her eyes glittering malevolently. 'Gerroff me step before I take me brush to yez!'

The fact that she was on Ma Malone's territory and not her own increased Lily's anger. Why had she come here? She must have been mad to have thought she could reason with this old harpy. Bog Irish trash she was. 'And you can tell our Phoebe-Ann she can get herself home unless she wants to live in the sty with pigs like you, you low, dirty, bad-mouthed old fool!' She turned away, shaking with fury, not caring if the whole of Mona Street were in their back yards listening.

Ma Malone started to laugh, a horrible, cackling sound full of derision and venom. 'Go on get out wit yez! Yez is too late anyway.'

Lily had reached the door but she turned. 'What's that supposed to mean?' she yelled.

'Yez has come too late. They're married. Two days ago an' there's nothin' yez can do about it, so bugger off and leave me alone! It's bad enough that I've got a flamin' Orangeman's daughter in me family without yez comin' 'ere blackguarding me and mine! Bugger off!'

Lily fled into the entry. It wasn't true! Phoebe-Ann couldn't have been such a fool. Not her dainty, fastidious Phoebe-Ann married to that monster! She slid on some rubbish and fell, grazing her hands and knees, but she got up and hurried on. The quicker she left Mona Street the better. All she wanted to do was to get home. Home to Albert. He'd know what to do now. Home to her clean and tidy house before her heart broke in two.

Albert had been thinking about her proposed visit all morning. And the more he thought about it the more he told himself he had been a fool to let her go alone. Even the old woman had a terrible reputation. What if she attacked Lily? It had been known to happen. Ma Malone's neighbours could testify to that. There was a fresh wind coming off the river that threatened rain, but he hadn't noticed as he'd unloaded the cart at the dockside and then loaded up again.

As he drove between the city and the dockside he pondered the situation more deeply. If Lily's attempts failed, he'd just have to try and talk her round to accepting the fact and try to make the best of it for he was certain that, once the initial novelty had worn off, Jake Malone would revert to his old ways, if, indeed, he had abandoned them. Phoebe-Ann wouldn't know how to start to cope with such a husband and would need all the support she could get. The one blessing was the fact that Jake Malone would spend most of his time at sea. He prayed that maybe the honeymoon period would be extended because of that, if they managed to get to the altar, and he sincerely hoped they didn't.

It was nearly lunch time when he'd finished his last load. He looked up at the lowering sky and the heavy, scudding clouds. He'd go back for some dinner. Lily would probably need some support. He had no load to pick up until two o'clock when the Harrison boat would be in. He'd go via Mona Street. He might just be able to judge what kind of success, if any, Lily had achieved. A lot could be gleaned from the faces of women standing on their doorsteps jangling with their neighbours.

It had started to rain heavily by the time he reached Myrtle Street and the wind was whipping up the litter and debris. He pulled his cap lower over his forehead and turned the collar of his coat up, fumbling for the piece of old sacking he kept under the seat for such occasions and regretting that he hadn't taken notice of Lily and got one of those oilskins the deck hands on the ferries wore. He'd be soaked by the time he got to Lonsdale Street.

There were no gossiping women on their doorsteps in Mona Street and, as he turned the corner into Faulkner Street, some pieces of old newspaper blew across the road. With a high-pitched whinny, the horse reared up in fright. The next instant he was being thrown from side to side as the horse bolted, its iron-shod hooves slipping on the wet cobbles and adding to its terror.

He tried desperately to get control of the terrified animal, dragging on the rein until his shoulders ached, yelling at the top of his voice as people scattered for safety. At the corner of Bloom Street and Upper Canning Street a policeman threw himself bodily into the road and, risking life and limb, hung on to the bridle for grim death. The horse was a Clydesdale, capable of pulling three times its own weight and Albert knew from experience that unless stopped it would career on until exhausted. Runaways were frequent with so much horsedrawn traffic.

He was still being flung about but he could see that the policeman hadn't lost his hold and he prayed that the pressure on the bit would slow the horse down. He heard the copper shout, he heard the scream, he saw the tangle of arms and legs and the blur of dark blue material and he flung himself across the foam-flecked, heaving flanks until he caught the edge of the heavy collar. He dragged on it with all his strength and gasped with relief as he felt the animal's pace slow. Hanging on to the coarse black mane with one hand he managed to grasp the head-collar and jerk it back sharply. He was thrown backwards, his head jolting painfully, but it had stopped. It stood shaking and quivering and covered with sweat. He slid down from its back, throwing the rein to a man who had run from a shop doorway.

He was panting, his chest tight with the exertion, as he ran back to where a crowd had gathered around the figure on the ground. Two more policemen were running up the street, their capes flapping behind them in the wind. He hoped the poor copper wasn't too badly hurt.

He pushed his way through the crowd and as he saw the shocked faces turn away, he knew his hopes had been dashed. He stared down at the crumpled figure and with a cry of horror fell to his knees. It couldn't be! It couldn't be! His hand shook as he reached out and drew the limp and broken arm away from the battered, bleeding face. 'Lily! Oh, dear God! No! Lily!'

His cry brought tears to the eyes of all those watching.

One of the policemen pushed forward. 'All right, move away now. Who is it?'

A woman standing at the front of the crowd shook her head, tears coursing down her cheeks. 'It's his wife, lad! It's his own wife!'

Jimmy came for Emily and as soon as she saw him standing on the doorstep, his cap in hand, she knew something terrible had happened. He'd told her bluntly. There was no other way.

She clung to his arm all the way home, quietly sobbing. It had been Miss Millicent who had put her own coat around Emily's shoulders and told Jimmy to get her home at once.

'Our Jack's on his way home, too.'

'Oh, Jimmy, where's Albert? Is she . . . where is she?'

'At home, Em, and so is he. Even the scuffers couldn't make him leave her.'

'But how . . . why?'

'I don't know, Em. They just came running up the street for me, I was on my way back. His horse bolted.'

She went straight into the parlour for that's where they had laid Lily. Albert was kneeling beside the sofa, his face white and drawn and he was clinging to her hand. A policeman stood by the empty fireplace. Her hand went to her mouth as she took in the scene. Her mam. Her poor mam lying there all broken, her face bleeding. Her best blue coat all torn and dirty. 'Mam! Oh, Mam!' she cried softly.

Jimmy put his arm around her and he was fighting back the tears. It was a few minutes before she dragged herself away from him and bent down beside her stepfather. 'How . . . ?' She covered his hand with hers and he looked up at her with haunted eyes.

'Bolted . . . didn't know . . . thought it was a . . . copper . . .'

'Where had she been?'

He just shook his head. He couldn't think of anything except the fact that she was dead and he'd killed her.

'Try and get him upstairs, miss. Get the neighbours in to see to your mam,' the policeman urged her.

She couldn't see him for the tears that were blinding her. 'Come with me, Albert, please?'

'I'm not leaving her. I can't leave her! It was me . . . it was my fault!'

'No it wasn't, man. You tried but you couldn't stop

264

the blasted animal. It was an accident. A terrible accident. You can't blame yourself. For God's sake, get him out!' the constable hissed at Jimmy.

It took both Jimmy and a devastated Jack and the constable to get him to his feet and upstairs, while someone went for the doctor and someone else went for Mrs Heggarty who would lay Lily out.

Emily sat at the kitchen table, her head in her hands, her throat rough and dry, her eyes burning. Mrs Harper stood beside her, patting her shoulder ineffectually, too stunned herself to believe what had happened. Mrs Rowe from further down the street was making a pot of strong tea.

Emily couldn't conceive that her mam had gone. That she'd never hear her voice again. Never see her smile or laugh or cry. She sobbed into the table cloth until the policeman came downstairs.

The three women looked at him expectantly.

'The doctor's given him something to make him sleep. We'll need to get a proper statement from him later on, when he's a bit more himself, like. The woman from down the road is in with your mam and these ladies will stay with you, love, won't you?'

Mrs Harper and Mrs Rowe nodded.

Emily's vision was blurred. 'What . . . what was she doing there?'

'Don't know, love. Is there anyone else you want us to get in touch with?'

How could she think clearly at a time like this? Her mind was in shock, her whole body numbed.

'Well, I'll get off then. I'll come back in the morning or maybe tonight.'

She looked up at him as he replaced his helmet. Would things be clearer by tonight? Would they ever be clear at all?

'Hang on a minute!' Mrs Harper called and he turned back.

Emily looked up at her blankly.

'Emily, what about your Phoebe-Ann?'

Until that moment she had forgotten that she had a sister.

Chapter Seventeen

Alice went home with Phoebe-Ann after the police had called at the factory and she'd been called into the manager's office. She'd been in no fit state to go home alone. Alice sat her down in the chair by the range and made a pot of very strong tea and heaped four spoonfuls of sugar into both their cups. They'd both had a terrible shock. She was scared because Phoebe-Ann hadn't broken down and cried. All the colour had drained from her face and she'd let Alice lead her to the tram stop and then on to the tram and up the street. It wasn't natural, Alice thought. She should cry. She should let it all out.

'Here, drink this up. It will be good for you.'

Phoebe-Ann took the cup and drank.

Alice gnawed at her lip and wondered if she should go for her own mam, but they'd told her not to leave Phoebe-Ann alone. She began to wish that Jake Malone had been home, or that someone, anyone, would call in. 'What will you do?' she asked.

Phoebe-Ann stared at her. 'What?'

'Will you go round and see them all?'

'Who?'

Alice was getting really frightened. 'Albert, your Emily, Jimmy and Jack, them.'

'And Mam. You forgot Mam.'

Alice got to her feet. 'Phoebe-Ann, don't you under- stand? It's your mam who's . . . dead. She got trampled by a runaway. Albert's horse. Don't you understand?'

Phoebe-Ann's face crumpled and Alice let her breath out slowly with some relief. This she could cope with. 'Come on, luv, let it all out now. 'Ave a good cry.' She put her arm around her sobbing friend and Phoebe-Ann clung to her.

'It's my fault! It's all my fault!' she sobbed over and over.

'It's not! Don't be daft, how could it be your fault his bloody 'orse bolted?'

'I'll never see her again, Alice, and she was mad at me. I never even told her I'd got married. Oh, Mam! Mam!'

'Hush now, it's all right. She'll understand now.' Alice tried to comfort her. 'When will Jake be home?'

'Not for ages. Oh, Alice, why isn't he here now when I need him?'

Alice thought it was typical of bloody men, never where they were really needed. 'He wasn't to know either, was he? Will I take you up to our house or should I take you back . . . there?' She hoped Phoebe-Ann would ask to go to their house. Her mam would know what to do next.

'I want to go home, Alice! I want to go home!'

'Come on, I'll get your coat and take you round.' She felt sorry for Phoebe-Ann. She didn't know how she'd cope if it were her mam, but then Phoebe-Ann had caused so much trouble by insisting on marrying Jake Malone, and she wondered how she would be received in Lonsdale Street.

When Alice pushed open the kitchen door and gently shoved Phoebe-Ann inside, Emily got to her feet. Within seconds the two sisters were clinging together

268

and sobbing while Alice, feeling she could do no more, quietly left.

When they had both calmed down a little, they sat on the floor in front of the range, still clutching each other's hands tightly.

'Oh, Em, what will we do now? I'll never be able to tell her I'm sorry, so sorry!'

'She never knew. She never knew you were married. Oh, poor, poor Albert.'

For a second Phoebe-Ann forgot her own grief. 'Where is he?'

'Upstairs. Our Jimmy and Jack are trying to get him to tell them what happened. Oh, I wish Edwin were here.' Emily felt the burden of her grief and that of Phoebe-Ann's was too heavy for her shoulders. She wanted Edwin to comfort her: his arm around her shoulders, his voice telling her he'd look after her. But all she could see was Lily's broken and bleeding body. Fresh tears welled up in her smarting eyes.

'Can I see her, Em?' Phoebe-Ann asked, a sob in her voice.

Emily nodded. At least Phoebe-Ann would be spared the sight she'd seen. Mrs Heggarty had fixed Lily up and had arranged her hair so the cuts and bruises didn't show too much. At least Phoebe-Ann would see her mam the way she remembered her. 'She's in the parlour, but I don't think I can . . .'

'I'll go on my own, Em. I want to tell her I'm sorry.'

Emily was still sitting on the floor when Jack came down, his face haggard with grief and pity.

'How is he?'

'Taking it hard. Blaming himself.'

'It wasn't his fault. Every day there is someone hurt or killed by runaways.'

'I told him that and Jimmy did too and the doctor and that young copper, but it's no use. He keeps saying he shouldn't have let her go on her own: he should have gone with her, then it could never have happened. That's all he says over and over again. Or he did until whatever it was the doctor gave him quietened him down. But he won't sleep. He's fighting it. Will you go and try, Em? You and he always got on well together.'

She got to her feet. Yes they did 'get on' as Jack put it, but it was more than that. He'd become a real father to her. She'd been so young when her da had died and then for all those years there had only been Mam and he'd helped her so much after her experience – more than he'd ever know.

'I'll go up to him.'

Jimmy got up and left the room when she went in. Albert looked at her with stricken eyes as she sat on the bed and took his hand.

'It wasn't your fault. Please, please don't blame yourself? You can't. We . . . I . . . we all need you and love you so much.'

It broke her heart to see his lips trembling. 'We'll all manage. She . . . she wouldn't have wanted us to . . . ' She couldn't speak, the sobs choked her and she sat holding his hand tightly while the teardrops fell on the coverlet.

She had been certain he was dropping off to sleep, that he was at last letting go, that he'd stopped fighting the drug he'd been given. It was the best thing for him. Tomorrow, things would be better, she thought. But they'd never be that again, not without Lily, not without her mam. She fought hard to control the sobs in case she disturbed him. If he could just get some sleep. She wondered tiredly would any of them ever sleep again.

She jerked upright, eyes wide open as the shouts and screams reverberated through the house. The noise woke Albert and he tried to get out of bed.

'No. Lie down. I'll go and see what's the matter. Lie down. I'll come back, I promise.'

As she flung open the kitchen door she saw Phoebe-Ann with tears streaming down her face and livid red marks on her cheek and Jack grimly holding Jimmy back.

'What's she doing here? That little bitch killed Mam as sure as if she'd been driving the cart!' Jimmy yelled, beside himself with rage and grief.

'What?' Emily cried.

'Who let her in?' Jack asked grimly.

'I did, she went in to see . . . Mam.'

'She killed her! She killed her an' I'll lay her out with me bare hands!' Jimmy yelled.

Emily was horrified, thinking Jimmy had lost his reason.

'Get her out of here, Em. I can't hold him for much longer. Just get her out!'

Emily caught her sister and pushed her into the scullery and slammed the door. 'You'd better go, Phoebe-Ann. I don't know what's the matter with him, except that he's so upset he can't know what he's saying.'

'Phoebe-Ann held her cheek. 'He hit me! He hit me!'

'He didn't mean to. He's upset. Go on, get home.'

'I don't want to. I don't want to go back to that empty house. I don't want to stay there on my own.'

'Get Alice to stay with you. I can't leave them, not now. I might be able to get round later. Go on. Get home and I'll come later on.' How she was going to manage it Emily didn't know but she managed to push Phoebe-Ann out.

Jack had Jimmy pinned down in a chair, but his face was still contorted with rage.

'She's gone. You've gone and upset Albert. He was nearly asleep. Why did you have to go and start on her? And you hit her!'

'If I'd have known she was here, I'd have thrown her out myself,' Jack answered.

'She's just as upset as we are.'

'She's got every right to be!' Jimmy yelled, trying to get up.

'Christ Almighty! Will you pack it in, Jimmy! You belting our Phoebe-Ann isn't going to bring Mam back,' Jack bawled at his brother.

'Stop it! Stop it, both of you and now isn't the time to be swearing, you know she hated it. What's the matter with you both?'

Jack had given up the struggle but some of Jimmy's anger had gone. 'Mam had been to Mona Street, to see that old bitch, Ma Malone. To see if they couldn't put a stop to our Phoebe-Ann and him getting married.'

'If she hadn't gone up there this wouldn't have happened. And if Phoebe-Ann hadn't been so bloody thick as to want to marry the likes of him, Mam wouldn't have needed to have gone at all. It's all her fault. She killed Mam,' Jimmy blurted out.

Emily felt sick. No wonder Jimmy had hit Phoebe-Ann. But on the heels of this realization came the knowledge that if she'd told Mam that Phoebe-Ann was married, Lily wouldn't have gone to Mona Street. Guilt was added to her burden of sorrow and shock. She felt herself sway and she grabbed at the back of the chair.

272

'Sit down, Em. God knows we've all been through enough today.'

She sat down. 'You can't blame her entirely, Jack.'

'Why not?'

'Because . . . because Phoebe-Ann is married and I stood for her. If I'd have told Mam, she wouldn't have gone there, so I'm as much to blame.'

Jack groaned. 'Is there no end to it at all? She's caused so much trouble . . . I wish she'd have gone and chucked herself in the bloody river and then we would never have had to cope with all this.'

Jimmy glared at Emily. 'Why didn't you tell her? Why didn't you bloody well say something?'

'Because I promised Phoebe-Ann I wouldn't. Oh, Jim, don't start on me because I do feel like chucking myself in the river right now! How am I going to live with all this? How am I going to tell Albert? It will kill him.'

'Don't tell him, not yet. He can't take any more. Don't even mention our Phoebe-Ann to him. As far as I'm concerned I hope I never set eyes on her again. I hope she's happy with what she's done and I hope he gives her a dog's life. She deserves it.'

Emily looked ahead to the long years of bitterness that the future seemed to hold. She couldn't go and see her sister; Jimmy would kill her rather than let her go. Never had she wished that Edwin was home more than she did then.

Phoebe-Ann had waited all night for Emily to come and, at last, when she heard the chimes of the church clock at midnight, she knew she wasn't coming. She wanted to die. She wanted to crawl into bed and die. She hadn't known Mam had gone to see Ma Malone until Jimmy had roared at her. In fact now she was

273

wondering about the whole sorry mess she'd made of things. But then she thought of Jake and longed for him to be home. She didn't want to be on her own, but she was and there was nothing she could do about it, for she dared not go back to Lonsdale Street. She had to stay and face things she didn't want to face at all.

Alice forced her to go to work the following day and she'd gone and worked mechanically, never acknowledging the nods and words of condolence from the other girls and women. That night she'd made Alice promise to stay with her for she couldn't face another night alone.

Mrs Wainwright had agreed. 'Left on 'er own she'll go off 'er 'ead an' do somethin' to herself, shouldn't wonder. God, but I wouldn't like to live with what she's got on her conscience.'

Most of the neighbourhood knew the full story by this time and also the fact that the funeral had been set for two days later, after the inquest which would be just a formality. Fatalities from runaways were common enough. Accidental death would be the verdict.

Alice, prompted by her mother, had offered to go to the funeral with Phoebe-Ann but she'd said no. She hoped she stood more chance of being reconciled with her brothers and Emily if she went alone. Mrs Wainwright had lent her a black jacket and hat, both old-fashioned and too big, and she had her good black skirt. She looked ill and dowdy as she made her way to the church in which she'd been married so short a time ago.

She was surprised by the number of neighbours who had turned out and there were one or two carters, associates of Albert's, who had also come. Their black bowler hats and best Sunday overcoats looking odd

274

amongst the mainly black shawls of the women and the jackets with black armbands of their male neighbours, many of whom had taken time off from their work and would therefore be short in their pay packets.

She sobbed all through the service and she couldn't bring herself even to look at the coffin or Albert or the rest of her family. Then, when it was over, she filed out with the rest and got the tram to Toxteth Park Cemetery.

It was a cold, damp day and a heavy mist hung over the cemetery and seeped into the thin jacket, making her shiver. She longed to stand with Emily who was clinging to Albert, sobbing quietly, while Jack and Jimmy stood rigidly at Albert's side. Fresh spasms shook her as she heard the dreadful, final sound as the first handfuls of soil fell on the coffin. The sound shrieked at her that her mam was dead and it was all her fault.

When she looked up, she saw the people drifting away and only Emily stood by the open grave, the grave diggers leaning on their shovels, a respectful distance away. She moved forward.

'Emily.'

Emily looked up.

'Em, I'm sorry . . . It's my fault . . .'

Emily couldn't speak.

Phoebe-Ann drew closer, praying that Emily wouldn't turn away from her. 'Em, say something . . . please?' she begged.

Through burning eyes, their lids swollen from crying, Emily looked at her sister. She should hate her but how could she? She was as much to blame. She held out her hands and Phoebe-Ann seized them like a lifeline.

'Oh, Emily! What am I going to do? How can I live with all I've done?'

'How can we both live with it, Fee? I should have told her?'

'Oh, I wish the *Maury* was back.'

'So do I. Oh, so do I,' Emily answered tiredly.

Emily managed to slip around to see her sister a few times, without the knowledge of her brothers. She went at night when it was dark so she wouldn't be noticed by the neighbours. She'd given in her notice to Miss Millicent and Miss Nesta who were both reluctant to accept it.

'If you ever change your mind, Emily, come back to us,' Miss Nesta had said, pressing an envelope into her hand. It contained five, crisp, white five-pound notes. 'For your future, Emily,' she'd whispered.

'And if there is anything at all we can help you with, don't hesitate to come to us,' Miss Millicent had offered, handing her a parcel which she later found to contain a white damask table cloth and napkins. She'd written a 'thank you' note to them both with tears in her eyes at such generosity.

She was to keep house now in her mother's place and she knew that she was the only one who could help Albert through his grief. Both her brothers had gone back to work; they couldn't afford not to now for, until Albert had recovered enough to resume his business, there was only their money coming into the house as they'd both refused to allow Emily to use the money Miss Nesta had given her.

'I want no arguments, Em. It's yours. She gave it to you for when you have a home of your own and there's an end to it,' Jack had stated.

She had given up hope then that she would ever

have a home of her own and at that time she didn't want one. This was her home, it always would be. Edwin would agree and if he didn't . . .

She went down on the tram with Phoebe-Ann when the *Mauretania* docked. Together, they stood waiting at the Canada Dock gate, both in the black of mourning for they had both dyed all their clothes.

Edwin was first off and when she told him, he took Emily in his arms and held her tightly. 'My poor, Em. My poor, poor Em, having all that to bear on your own. I'm sorry love, she was a wonderful woman.'

She knew if she broke down now she would never stop crying so she held it all back.

He stood with his arm around her shoulders until he saw Rhys pushing his way ahead of the crowd of stokers and trimmers.

When Edwin told him, Rhys's shocked gaze went to Phoebe-Ann. She looked so haggard and thin. Before he had time to speak, Edwin had taken his arm and was pulling him aside.

When she saw Jake, Phoebe-Ann uttered a cry and, elbowing her way into the crowd, ran straight into his arms.

He looked down at her with undisguised horror. 'What's up? What's been going on here?' He looked across at the other small group: at Rhys whose face was like thunder, Edwin who couldn't disguise the enmity he felt and Emily, red-eyed and accusing and also dressed in mourning.

'Ask your wife!' Rhys spat at him, before Edwin pulled him backwards. He wanted no confrontations here. Emily was upset enough already.

'What's up, girl? You look like you need a drink?'

Phoebe-Ann couldn't speak so she let him guide

277

her across the road and into the smoke-filled bar of the nearest pub.

'Get that down you,' Jake instructed, annoyed that his homecoming had been so miserable.

Phoebe-Ann downed the drink and gasped and coughed.

'Come on, tell me what's been going on?'

In a flat, expressionless tone she told him.

'Ah, God! The poor feller!'

'But don't you see, it was my fault! She'd been to see your ma.'

'What's that owld biddy got to do with all this?'

'Mam went to see her to try to get her to stop the wedding.'

'But we were already wed, me ma knew that. Our Vinny can't keep his trap shut after he's had a few drinks. She's not speakin' to me, so the rest of them tell me. Not that I care.'

'My mam didn't know.'

'I thought your Emily would have told her.'

She shook her head.

'I wish I could trust me brothers like that. Rent-a-gob, that's our Vinny. Oh, what a bloody mess. Still, she was all right with you, your Emily, I mean?'

'She is but the others . . . '

'Oh, sod the others! I'm home now so cheer up. We're wed, all legal, like, so no-one can do anything about that. You're my wife,' he added with pride. Her loss hadn't really touched him deeply and he couldn't see how Phoebe-Ann was to blame for a bloody horse bolting. It could have been anyone's horse. It could have happened in Lonsdale Street, so what was all this fuss over?

She wondered how he could be so offhand about it. Didn't he realize that, apart from Emily, her whole

278

family had cut her off? She leaned back in the chair, suddenly so very tired and utterly wretched.

'You look worn out. We'll get off home and we can both have a bit of a lie down, like.'

A spark of anger flared. She had just told him her mam was dead and her family had ostracized her and all he wanted to do was take her to bed. 'No, we won't! Is that all you can think of Jake Malone? Is that all, at a time like this?'

He stared at her. 'What did I say wrong?'

She got to her feet. 'If you don't know, then I'm not going to tell you!'

'Oh, that's nice, isn't it! That's a nice welcome 'ome! Why don't yer just say "sod off"!'

'Stop that!'

'You're me wife and I won't be able to get home as much in future!'

'What do you mean?'

He hadn't meant to tell her like this, but the way she had rejected him had annoyed him. He'd seen the smirks and nudges and heads nodded in their direction. If she was going to carry on like this he might as well go and make his peace with his ma, have a few bevvies with them all. 'This is the last time the *Maury* will sail from Liverpool. It's Southampton from now on, an' if you're going to have such a cob on then . . .'

She didn't wait for him to finish. She'd been staring at him in horror; now she turned and, pushing her way through the crowd, ran out into the street, leaving him standing looking after her with a mixture of annoyance and bewilderment on his face.

Chapter Eighteen

It was hard to believe that Mam had been dead for almost a year, Emily thought. Now it seemed as though she'd always run this house, always coped with Albert, who was growing more and more withdrawn and morose, still unable to come to terms with the fact that he had been instrumental in Lily's death.

Jack and Jimmy talked about nothing else but emigrating to America and she knew that when they had saved up enough money they would go. But saving was the hardest part although she fully intended to insist that they take the twenty-five pounds Miss Nesta had given her. After all there was still the money Richard Mercer had invested for her.

Edwin still came home as often as he could, but the travelling to and from Southampton meant he wasn't home for very long. They'd spoken about the future but it didn't look too hopeful. Work was getting harder to find in the city and, for Edwin and others, there was little choice but to stay at sea. It was work, even if it did mean they had little time with their loved ones.

Emily had told him that when Jack and Jimmy finally left she couldn't leave Albert on his own. He'd agreed with her but had silently wondered if he could persuade them both to move down south. He'd see more of her that way but his hopes weren't high. She went every Sunday to take flowers to Lily's grave and

Albert joined her. His grief had healed a little but he'd never be the same man, they both knew that.

Life for Phoebe-Ann hadn't improved. Jake did make the effort to get home when he could, but the days and nights were long. She had seen her brothers twice on the street and both times they had cut her dead, crossing to the other side of the road. Emily came when she could but that wasn't often because it had to be dark and the evenings were getting longer. She was at work all day. Sometimes she thought that if it hadn't been for her work and Alice and Ginny she would have gone mad. She'd changed; it would have been a miracle if she hadn't. She'd grown up and she'd become quieter. Jake couldn't, or wouldn't, understand how she felt and he even seemed to have given up trying lately.

He'd been full of profuse apologies after that first row when he'd come home well past midnight, singing and staggering up the road and collapsing in the lobby. But on his last shore leave they'd had another row.

Jake's disillusionment was increasing. He'd hoped that, while he'd been away, Phoebe-Ann would have overcome her initial distaste for love making. She hadn't.

She'd tried to explain to him but he couldn't grasp what she was saying.

'It's no use you goin' on an' on about all these feelings an' imaginings, it's not solvin' anything, is it? I'm not a bloody mind-reader nor a bloody monk either! You're my wife an' that's that!'

'Can't you understand that I can't help it? I don't want it to happen, it just does! Something just . . . snaps in my head and I feel so . . .'

Jake's eyes narrowed as a thought crossed his mind. 'Who's been talkin' to you, Phoebe-Ann?'

'No-one!' she shot back, praying he hadn't heard something about Emily. 'You know how they've all been acting since Mam died! And, that's another thing, I thought you'd be more sympathetic, more understanding!'

'I am!' he retorted hotly. It wasn't his fault that she had this problem and now she was accusing him of not being sympathetic. All right, he was sorry about her mam, but she should be getting over it now. It wasn't the end of the bloody world. He stared at her hard. The pretty, laughing, loving girl he'd fallen for was changing and not for the better. Was this what he'd changed his whole life-style for? Why he'd given up all his pleasures; the happy nights spent drinking with his brothers. All right, so they often had too much to drink – nothing to moan about. So, he'd chased other women, again encouraged by his brothers. Aye, they'd had some good times together. If she was going to carry on like this every time he came home . . . He shrugged. 'I've said I'm sorry about your ma a hundred times, now come 'ere and let's kiss an' make up.' He'd winked meaningfully, thinking a light-hearted approach might work.

'You see! You haven't even been listening to me! How can you think I feel . . . loving, when I can't get it out of my head that it's partly my fault that Mam . . . ?'

Jake's patience had snapped. 'Oh, for Christ's sake, don't start on that again!'

'Where are you going?' Phoebe-Ann had cried as he'd snatched up his coat.

'Out! That's where I'm goin'! I'm goin' to find somewhere where I can 'ave a bit of a laugh an' a joke, instead of havin' to listen to you whingeing on about your ma or your bloody "problem"! What's got into you, Phoebe-Ann? You've changed. Or were you always like this and I was so bloody thick I never noticed?'

Stung by his callousness, Phoebe-Ann glared at him. 'I was the thick one, Jake Malone, to think I could expect consideration and understanding from you! To think I could change you. Make you into someone halfway decent! Go on! Go out with your drunken brothers or friends! I don't care!'

When the door had slammed behind him, she'd sunk down in a chair and, dropping her head in her hands, she'd cried. 'Oh, I wish things were different! I never expected it would be like this! Oh, Mam, I'm sorry!' she'd sobbed, yet she knew what Lily's response would have been. She would have to get on with it and hope things would improve.

He'd come home in the same condition as before and that night, after he had tried to placate her, things had once again deteriorated.

'You're doin' this on purpose, aren't you? Tryin' to punish me?' Jake cried when she'd fought against his embrace, the familiar revulsion washing over her.

'I'm not! I'm not!'

'You are! You're makin' me pay for the way your bloody family treat you and for goin' out with me brothers!'

'It's got nothing to do with that!' she cried.

'I've tried, Phoebe-Ann, you can't say I haven't! I'm a man an' I have needs an' rights too. You can't go on pushin' me away!' Jake's pride was hurt. No-one knew the way things were between them, at least he hoped not, but Vinny and Peader had made some pointed observations that were too near the truth for comfort.

'Jeasus! Look at the gob on 'im! Mustn't be gettin' 'is share at 'ome!' Vinny had yelled.

'She keepin' yer short, Jake, lad?' Peader had put in, after there had been a bit of a row between them.

Jake felt a cold sweat break out on his body. If they ever found out the truth, his life would be hell. That thought increased his annoyance with Phoebe-Ann. She was making a bloody fool of him! Denying him his rights, making him beg like an eejit for something that was his due. He'd stared down at her. There were lines forming on her face. She was cold and unfeeling and selfish . . . Her face, with its elfin features, alabaster skin and wide blue eyes, reminded him of that of a china doll and it was just as set and hard. A great wave of anger and frustration had engulfed him. He'd given her everything and she'd given him nothing in return. Heedless of her cries and protests, he'd crushed her to him and taken her, roaring in pain as she'd raked his neck and shoulders with her nails. Then she'd gone quiet and rigid and he'd hated that even more than her attempts to fight him. It was as though she didn't even care enough to summon the energy to reject him and in his anger he'd used her roughly and called her every obscene name he could think of.

Next morning, he had hardly spoken to her and she'd maintained what she hoped was a cold, dignified silence. When he returned that evening her nerves were still raw, her body still aching and her self-esteem still badly bruised by his taunts. She had let fly at him with all her pent-up anger. He'd yelled back, again accusing her of being cold, unnatural, selfish and a bloody misery to boot and had then stormed out, gone drinking with his brothers and come home blind drunk. She'd screamed at him, calling him every name she could think of and then, exhausted, she'd gone to the bedroom, barricaded the door with a chest, and cried herself to sleep.

Things had got a little better before he left, but not much. Tiny seeds of doubt had been sown in Phoebe-Ann's mind and loneliness, boredom and resentment were helping them grow. She'd also had to contend with her mother-in-law, who, emboldened by the fact that she had managed to turn Vinny against her as well as all the others, now sought to regain Jake's affections and money by bullying Phoebe-Ann.

Alice had persuaded her to accompany her into town on Saturday afternoon. 'For heaven's sake make more of an effort with yourself Phoebe-Ann! You used to be so smart and fashionable!'

'That's just it. I "used" to be. There's no reason for it now. I'm a married woman and he's never at home so what's the point in getting all dressed up to the nines just for work or to come back here?'

'Oh, there's no doing any good with you these days! Just because you're married doesn't mean you have to look a hundred. There's nothing wrong with going to the pictures with me and Ginny either.'

'People would talk.'

'What people and what would they have to talk about? Don't be so thick. Get your best frock on and we'll go and do some window shopping, like we used to. Or proper shopping; you're not short of a bob or two what with your wages and what he leaves you. And tonight we'll go to the Gaumont and I'm not taking no for an answer!'

Phoebe-Ann smiled and agreed, but the old

excitement had gone. What was the point in dressing up just to go and look in shop windows at clothes that it would be pointless buying when she would have no occasion to wear them?

She hadn't made much of an effort with herself and Alice commented on the fact. 'Honestly, what's happened to you? Your hair needs cutting, it's straggling on the ends. That style needs to be kept tidy. That lipstick doesn't suit you at all, it makes you look washed out and where did you get the frock – the rag bag?'

Ginny nudged her. 'Shut up and stop gettin' at her.'

'It's for her own good.'

'Alice, I know you mean well but what's the point of it all? I've said all this before so let's leave it at that. When I feel like dressing up, I will.'

Alice shrugged. 'When's he home next?'

'Thursday but it will be late when he gets in. It takes hours from Southampton.'

'Going to Lime Street to meet him?'

'No. He said he won't know exactly which train he'll be on. There's an early one and a late one. No point in me hanging around Lime Street for hours.'

'Do they have bars on those long distance trains?' Ginny asked, she having never been further away from Liverpool than a day trip to Llandudno.

Alice glared at Ginny. What a tactless thing to ask. 'Yes, but I can't see them serving to third class people.'

Phoebe-Ann glared at them both. Just what were they implying? That Jake would head for the nearest bar as soon as he left the ship?

'Let's go and look what they've got in Val Smith's. I'm sure I heard someone say they've got some

286

gorgeous little caps that completely cover your hair, made in that glittery stuff. The latest thing they are.'

Phoebe-Ann looked interested and Alice was quick to notice. If she could just get Phoebe-Ann interested in herself again it would be a start. She was certain that things between her friend and Jake Malone were far from rosy.

They were all peering into the window of the large and very fashionable millinery establishment when two young ladies, dressed in the height of fashion and carrying hat boxes, came out. The pavement was crowded and Phoebe-Ann stood back to let them pass. Then a smile lit up her face. One of them was Olivia Mercer.

'Miss Olivia!'

Olivia turned. 'Phoebe-Ann Parkinson, is that you?'

'Yes, miss, but it's not Parkinson any more. I'm married.'

Olivia looked her up and down. 'Oh, you poor thing! It doesn't suit you at all, Phoebe-Ann. You don't look the same person. You were always so bright and attractive. What have you done to yourself? No, I definitely think being married doesn't suit you. What does he do, your husband?'

Phoebe-Ann was so shocked she stammered that he went away to sea, whereupon Olivia enthused effusively about her cruise until her friend caught her arm and reminded her that they had another appointment.

'The bitch! The snotty bitch!' Alice cried indignantly as the pair drove off. 'Fancy saying that to anyone. She's got a nerve! Not "How are you?" "How nice to see you." No, she goes and insults you!' She could see the dazed, hurt look on Phoebe-Ann's face. 'Let's go and get a cup of tea. Lyon's is the nearest.'

Olivia's words rang in Phoebe-Ann's head and she peered at herself in the shop windows they passed on their way to the tea rooms. Did she really look so dull and drab? Maybe that's why Jake had preferred the company of his awful brothers. She'd been too upset about Mam and everything to care much about how she looked. He should have understood that, but she was finding that 'understanding' wasn't one of Jake's strong points.

'Alice, she's right,' she admitted over the tea table.

'I told you you were letting yourself go, but she still could have put it in a nicer way, especially as you haven't seen each other for years.'

'I think I will spend some money on myself and I'll come out with you tonight, too.'

'Thank God for that! She's just decided to join the human race again,' Alice smiled.

She'd bought a new dress and hat and shoes and she was walking from the tram with Alice, Ginny having left them for she lived in the opposite direction.

'Don't look now but your dear mother-in-law is coming down the street,' Alice remarked caustically.

'Oh, blast! There's nothing I can do to avoid her.'

'You'd better speak to her.'

Phoebe-Ann stared at the small, malevolent figure with distaste.

'Sure, if it isn't her ladyship, me daughter-in-law. Been out spendin' our Jake's money I see.'

'I have been spending my own money. I work for it.'

'Yez should stay at home like a proper wife. There's no need for yez to work, wit that posh 'ouse an' all.'

'What I've got and what I do is my own affair.'

'Oh, Miss high an' bloody mighty!' Beneath the outward scorn Ma was suspicious, always looking for something she could use against Phoebe-Ann, but having had little contact with her up to now there hadn't been much. She decided to change tactics. 'I suppose yez want to be lookin' yer best for himself comin' home on Thursday then?' She poked at the parcels Phoebe-Ann was holding.

Phoebe-Ann was annoyed to think that she knew the movements of all her sons. 'As it happens I'm going out with my friends tonight and I fancied some new things.'

'Did yez now an' where are yez off to?'

Inwardly Alice groaned. Phoebe-Ann had walked straight into that. Sometimes she was such a fool.

'To the cinema with Ginny and me. No harm in that is there?' Alice snapped.

'I was speakin' to the organ grinder not the monkey!' Ma shot back. 'Yez 'ardfaced madam.'

'As I said, what I do is my own affair.' Phoebe-Ann realized too late what her mother-in-law had been fishing for and had found. She nodded curtly and turned away, followed by Alice.

Ma Malone watched them. Jake had been a fool to marry and even more of a fool to get himself tied up with that bold rossi.

'You'd better go and meet him on Thursday before she gets down there and puts her two pennyworth in,' Alice advised.

'She wouldn't do that. She never goes to meet them.'

'That's because they never manage to stagger home the first night or if they do they're too drunk to hold a conversation. But I'd go, she's a wicked old bitch. She'll be running down there so fast you'd think old Nick was after her.'

Phoebe-Ann nodded her agreement. One thing she had realized was that you never underestimated Ma Malone.

Lime Street station was crowded with relatives waiting for the train from Southampton for the *Mauretania*'s crew were mainly Liverpudlians. Phoebe-Ann wore her new outfit and had had her hair trimmed, and Alice had said she looked just like her old self and he was sure to appreciate it.

The train arrived in a cloud of steam and people started milling around the ticket barrier. She'd looked for Emily but hadn't seen her. Then she remembered her saying Edwin didn't like her being down here so late at night. She peered into the crowd, scrutinizing the faces. She began to get irritable. Why couldn't he have been in the first wave off instead of leaving her standing waiting while all around her there were happy reunion scenes? But then he wasn't expecting her to meet him.

It was Vinny she spotted first, laughing uproariously and hanging on to Franny and her face clouded with annoyance as she saw the group behind them: Peader, Jake and Seamus. All more or less holding each other up. Seamus had obviously spent most of the night in some pub before coming to Lime Street and buying a platform ticket. They were all a bad influence on Jake, she thought, her temper rising, as Vinny and Franny staggered towards her.

' 'Ere's the welcomin' party, Jake, me boyo!' Vinny shouted.

'Shut up, Vinny Malone, everyone's looking at you!' she snapped.

'Dat's not very welcomin', like, is it?' Franny peered at her closely. 'Yez'll do no good with 'er, Jake, she's gorra cob on!'

Jake had managed to free himself from his brothers. 'You look nice, Phoebe-Ann,' he said affably, despite the fact that for most of the journey home his brothers had mocked and derided him about his wife's airs and graces.

'Don't you touch me! You're drunk – all of you!'

'Oh, aye, that's a great welcome that, I must say!' Peader put in.

'You mind your own business!' She took Jake's arm. 'We're going home.'

'Not before 'e's seen me ma. I've got me instructions,' Seamus interrupted.

Phoebe-Ann glared at him. So, she'd sent Seamus down here to bring him to see her first. No doubt to tell him a pack of lies about her going out with Alice and Ginny. 'I said he's coming home with me, now!' A group of people had lingered to watch the argument. It offered a small diversion, but a policeman was also making his way across to them. 'How dare you make a show of me like this, Jake Malone!' she hissed, pulling at his arm. 'You're a disgrace! You're disgusting, that's what you are!'

He pulled away from her grip. 'If yer goin' to carry on like this I'm goin' ter see me ma.'

The policeman was within earshot. 'Jake, please?'

'Leave him alone,' Seamus interrupted.

'You mind your own bloody business, Seamus Malone! Go on, clear off!'

'I'm not havin' you speak to me brother like that.' Jake was also getting annoyed. Who did she think she was coming down here and showing him up in front of everyone – brothers and shipmates and their families?

'Are you coming home?' Phoebe-Ann was near to tears but she wouldn't let them have the satisfaction of knowing that.

'When I've seen me ma.'

'Having trouble, miss?'

She looked up at the policeman and then at Jake. 'No, officer, but I'd be glad if you could see me to the tram stop?'

'Yer not goin' off with a bloody scuffer!' Jake yelled.

'You go to hell, Jake Malone!' she yelled back while the rest of his brothers tried to calm him down, for the constable had taken out his whistle and truncheon and they had no intention of spending the night in a cell with their heads cracked.

She thanked the constable and began to walk towards St George's Hall. The tears fell freely now. She was angry, hurt, disillusioned and ashamed. God knows when he'll get home and in what state she thought, but did she really care? The answer was unclear for, when he was drunk, she found Jake utterly repulsive.

'Phoebe-Ann! Phoebe-Ann!'

She turned at the sound of her name being called and, dashing away her tears with the back of her hand, she saw someone waving to her from the other side of the road. It was Rhys. She didn't know whether to be glad or sorry.

He crossed over. 'Where are you going? It's too late for you to be here alone.'

'I'm going home.'

'Where's Jake?' Even now he found it an effort to speak of Jake Malone.

'I don't want to talk about him!'

He understood. He'd seen young Franny Malone staggering along the corridor of the train with a bottle in his hand. He'd also heard him arguing with the guard until Peader had appeared and smoothed things over to prevent them being thrown off the train.

'Where's Edwin?' she asked.

'He managed to get off early and caught the earlier train.' He fell into step with her. 'How are things, then?'

'Same as usual. How are things at . . . home?'

'Albert's getting more and more withdrawn. I wanted him to go back home, to live with my mam, but he won't. Says he won't leave . . .' He stopped. He was going to say 'Lily' but he thought it would be tactless and she looked as though she had enough to bear. His heart went out to her. If only. If only . . . 'No sign of our tram,' he said.

She shrugged.

'Oh, what the hell! Let's get a taxi, it's only money.'

Before she could protest, he had hailed a passing cab which drew into the kerb alongside them.

'Where to, la?'

Rhys opened the door for her. 'Florist Street, then Lonsdale Street.'

The driver nodded. The Southampton train was in.

From the other side of the wide street, at the doorway of the 'Royal', Seamus Malone shook his brother. 'Oh, that's nice, isn't it? There's yer wife gettin' in a taxi with some feller!'

Jake peered in the direction of his brother's stabbing finger. All he saw was the back of a man climbing into a cab. 'I can't see her, yer bleedin' liar!'

'Well, I saw 'er!'

Peader shoved the pair of them inside. 'Shurrup! Yer wastin' good drinkin' time!'

Phoebe-Ann was silent as they drove through the dark streets and Rhys felt so sorry for her.

'Do you get out much?'

'I go to work and sometimes I go to the pictures with Alice, and our Emily comes round when she can, but that's supposed to be a secret.'

'I know.'

'Do you?'

'Of course, but the others don't.'

'I saw them a couple of times and they cut me dead.'

'They were very bitter Phoebe-Ann but I think they both regret it.'

'Did they say so?' For the first time that evening she felt hopeful.

'Not in so many words but Emily said they ask if she's heard anything about you. If you're all right, if he's treating you well.' He felt awkward and yet annoyed. Quite obviously she was upset and he'd seen the rowdy group in the pub doorway. He felt he could have throttled Jake Malone. 'That's when she told me she goes to see you.'

'But she hasn't told the rest of the family?'

'No, but give them time. If they are still interested in your welfare they'll come round, stands to reason doesn't it?'

She managed a smile, wishing she could tell him how much she longed to be able to visit them, to air her grievances, to share her hopes, to be part of a caring family once more. She missed them all. She admitted she was lonely and at that moment, after Jake's desertion, she just wanted to go back to Lonsdale Street to be comforted and supported. Instead she said, 'It was good of you to see me home, Rhys, and in style,' she added, thinking of her only two other taxi rides. One on the night of the riots with Olivia Mercer and the other with Jake on that fateful night at the Rialto.

When they reached Florist Street and the cab stopped he got out and helped her out.

'Thanks, Rhys. It was very good of you. You might have known that I didn't want to come back on my own.' She was too miserable to try to pretend that everything was fine. 'I really do appreciate it.'

'I know. I told you once that if you ever needed . . . help . . .' He left the rest unsaid.

She nodded and gave him a sad little smile, then she turned and walked the few yards to her front door.

He hadn't come home that night and she'd been glad of the fact. She'd slept fitfully and gone to work tired, her eyes dark ringed. When she got home she found him sitting at the kitchen table, a half-empty bottle of rum beside him. Her heart plummeted.

'I see you've come home then.'

'It's my house, isn't it?'

She ignored him and took off her coat and hung it on the peg behind the door. 'I'll get you a meal, it may help to sober you up.' She muttered the last words under her breath.

'I heard that an' if I want to drink in me own house I will!'

Oh, Lord! He was going to be difficult and she didn't know how to handle him. 'What did your ma have to say?' She hoped her tone was light.

'I don't remember much.'

'Maybe it's just as well then.'

'What's that supposed to mean?'

She was losing her patience. 'Anything you want it

to mean! I suppose she told you she'd seen me with Alice and Ginny? Well, just like I told her, I'd been buying a new outfit and I was going to the pictures with my friends. You can't expect me to stay in every night of the week while you're away.'

Now he remembered just what his ma had said and all the taunts and innuendoes concerning Phoebe-Ann that his brothers had made on every voyage since he'd been married. At first he'd ignored them, telling them they were just jealous and they didn't know what they were missing by not having a wife and a nice home. Lately he'd often pondered their words and their meanings, especially as she was so dull and miserable lately and now she seemed to be turning into a nag. His patience was getting thin. All she seemed to do was moan and complain and spend his money. 'Yes, I bloody well do expect you to stay in. You're a married woman an' I'm not slavin' away, pullin' me tripe out in that bleedin' stokehold so you can tart yourself up and go wastin' me money!'

'I used my own money! I didn't spend a penny of yours!'

'And that's another thing! You can give that job up. I can provide for you . . . I'm not havin' everyone sayin' I can't and that you have to go out to work. Yer makin' me look a bloody eejit who can't support a wife!'

Phoebe-Ann had a vision of what kind of a life his words portrayed and all the anger, frustration and disillusionment broke loose. She slammed the pan down on the table. 'I'll go out to work if I want to! I'm not staying in this house day in and day out by myself! I'll go mad if I do. I want to be with other people, not sitting here staring at the walls or waiting until you fall in!'

He got to his feet. 'Now you listen to me, girl! I've given you all the things you wanted, an' I'm not havin' it thrown back in me face. Me ma warned me and she's right. Bleedin' me dry like a leech and then showin' me up in front of everyone. An' our Seamus saw you gettin' in a taxi with some feller!'

'It wasn't just "some feller" and your bloody Seamus hates me and always has done! But she put him up to it. I'm not stupid, she's wicked, that's what she is, and you're all too thick to see it!'

He uttered a roar like a lion and lashed out at her, catching her across the side of her head. With a scream she fell backwards into the fireside rocker. A red mist danced before Jake's eyes as he remembered Seamus's words and his ma's. A cheap floosie, that's what his ma had called her. 'Runnin' off with some-one else on yer first night 'ome, too,' Seamus had bawled at him when he'd tried to defend her. How was he to know what she was up to while he was away? Out with her friends at the pictures. Did he believe that, Seamus had jeered. He'd been a bloody fool and now the neighbourhood would be splitting their sides laughing to see Jake Malone being given the runaround by a bit of a girl.

He caught her by her hair and dragged her to her feet. He'd show her who was the boss in this house. She needed knocking into shape properly this time. A hiding to make sure she knew that. He hit her again and again, her head snapping backwards and forwards like that of a rag doll until at last he released her and she fell in a crumpled heap on the floor. He kicked her inert form. That would teach her she couldn't make a monkey out of him. He should have done that long ago. She needed keeping in her place like his ma had said.

He picked up the bottle from the table, shrugged on his jacket and slammed out. Now he felt his pride had been restored and he'd go and tell his ma that he *was* the master in his own home.

Emily and Edwin had decided to go for a walk as it was a pleasant evening and they had little chance of being alone in the house.

'How is Albert?' Edwin asked as they turned the corner.

'Much the same. My heart aches to see him sitting staring into space. He's turning into an old man. It's pitiful.'

'Rhys was telling me he wants him to go and live with his mam, back in Wales.'

'I know, but he won't go. I've asked him. Rhys has begged him and so have Jack and Jimmy.'

'It would solve a lot of problems if he were to go, Emily.'

'I know. When those two finally have enough money, they'll go.'

'How soon do you think that will be?'

'I don't know. I think Jimmy would go now but Jack's more cautious. Says he wants enough money behind him to last a while, in case they can't find work.'

'If Albert went to live with Megan, what would you do?'

'I don't know.'

He put his arm around her and drew her towards him.

She reached out and touched his cheek gently. 'I know we don't get much time to ourselves. You're very patient, any other man would get annoyed.'

He drew her closer, heedless of the fact that

there was quite a bit of activity still going on in the street.

She didn't draw away from him and the fact surprised her. Usually she was very self-conscious about public shows of affection.

'Oh, Em. I'm a bit tired of being patient.' He cupped her chin in his hand and tilted her face upwards and then gently kissed her.

Again, she made no attempt to draw back and yet again she was surprised at herself. The feeling of panic was absent. She felt a slight fluttering of the old fear but, as he continued to kiss her, it faded and was replaced by a deep tenderness. A feeling of belonging and . . . freedom! His lips were banishing the terrible dark memories and she relaxed. Her body felt feather-light and she could have continued to float, wrapped in this wonderful cloud of love and relief. A blessed warmth crept over her.

It was he who drew away first. 'We could get married, Em. If Albert went to live with Megan, we could get a place near Southampton.'

She sighed deeply. Now she wanted to be with him, to love him, to tell him about the new warmth she felt, but his words had forced the practicalities into her mind.

'It's a big step, and what if they decide to bring the *Maury* back to Liverpool?'

'There's not much chance of that.'

She was her old, practical self again. 'What will happen when they convert her to oil?'

'A lot of the black squad will be laid off. Rhys has been worrying about that. He said if it happens it would be better for Albert to go to Megan and he'd try for work in the pits again. Which would leave just you and me.'

She squeezed his arm. 'It's not that I don't want to get married. It's just that I can't . . . won't leave Albert. He was so good to me.'

Edwin sighed. They were going round and round in the same old circle. Albert wouldn't move and she wouldn't leave him. Heaven alone knew when Jack and Jimmy would finally leave. He supposed he could move in with them but he'd wanted her for himself. He'd wanted them to have a place of their own, no matter how humble. They deserved it, even if it wasn't near Southampton. He'd get the train back like all the others did, like Jake Malone did, but then he and Phoebe-Ann had their own house. There would be little privacy with Albert, Rhys, Jack and Jimmy.

'Where's he going?'

His train of thought was interrupted by Emily's question and he saw Jake Malone walking unsteadily towards Melville Place, obviously en route to Mona Street. 'His ma's by the look of it.'

'What's he got in his hand? It's a bottle. He's drunk!'

'What's new?'

'Poor Phoebe-Ann.' Emily stopped walking. 'Oh, Edwin! Something's wrong! I know it is!'

They looked at each other and then he grabbed her hand and they began to run.

She'd dragged herself into a sitting position but her head was throbbing so badly she couldn't hold it up, nor could she see very clearly. As the door opened she shrank back.

'Oh, dear God in heaven!' Emily screamed, dropping to her knees beside her sister. 'Did he do this?'

Edwin also bent down. 'I think we'd better get her to the hospital.'

'No.' The word was barely audible her lips were so swollen.

'And the police!' Emily raged. 'He should be locked up!'

Again there was the feeble cry from Phoebe-Ann.

'She can't stay here, that's for certain. Let's try and get her to her feet.'

Gently, they both eased Phoebe-Ann upright and she clung to Emily, shaking all over.

'Home . . . home . . .' she whispered.

'It's all right, Phoebe-Ann, you're not staying here. We're going to take you home now. Can you walk?' Emily asked.

'Emily, run back and get one of the lads. I think we're going to have to carry her.'

'What if he comes back?'

'I'll brain the bastard with the poker!'

She was out of breath when she reached Lonsdale Street.

'What's wrong?' Jack demanded.

Emily fought for breath.

'Is it Edwin?' Jimmy prompted.

'No. No . . . it's . . . Phoebe-Ann!'

'What's wrong with her?' Rhys demanded, sensing from Emily's demeanour that there was in fact something amiss.

'Whatever it is, it's nothing to do with us,' Jack stated.

Colour suffused Emily's cheeks. 'Don't you dare to stand there and tell me you don't care about her, Jack Parkinson! She's still your sister, your flesh and blood!' Emily screamed.

'Emily, what's wrong?' Rhys pressed.

'He . . . That drunken pig has beaten her half to

death! You should see her poor face! We saw him, he was on his way to Mona Street.'

'I'll kill him! I'll kill him with my bare hands!' Rhys yelled, the blood of anger flooding his face.

'You'll have to wait your turn, lad! Me and our Jack first! Whatever she's done, she's our sister and no yellow-bellied Malone is going to get away with laying one finger on her, let alone belting her! Get your coat, Jack!'

'Cowardly bastard! Beating a woman, no, a slip of a girl who can't fight back!' Jack growled.

'He's done it this time! Not content with making a show of us all by marrying her, now he has to beat her up. He'll never raise a hand to her again or anyone else either when I've finished with him!' Jimmy vowed.

'You stay here and get your breath back, Em.'

'No, Jack. I'm coming with you. She needs me!'

'She needs us all and we'll not desert her,' Jimmy said, pushing Rhys out of the door.

When they saw Phoebe-Ann they were all shocked and horrified. Then fury overtook them all.

'I'm going up there and I'm going to beat him senseless!' Jimmy, the most volatile, yelled.

'Don't be a bloody fool, Jim! You can't go on your own,' Edwin said.

'He's right. Just hold on a bit. Let's get her home first, then we'll sort him out,' Jack added.

Rhys was shaking with the sheer force of his anger. He'd always thought Jake Malone was an animal and now he had proved it. He'd take great pleasure in smashing his face in, the way he had smashed Phoebe-Ann's. His beautiful Phoebe-Ann. He would never have touched her no matter what the provocation, but he was certain she hadn't courted Jake Malone's violence. He didn't care about himself, all he wanted right now was to see Jake Malone taught a lesson.

All the former animosity towards Phoebe-Ann had been dispelled by the sight of her injuries. Emily put her to bed and applied cold compresses to the swellings which were distorting Phoebe-Ann's face into grotesque proportions. She feared that her sister would be disfigured for her nose looked as though it had been broken and she'd lost some teeth. Her heart ached for her sister. Poor, silly, naive Phoebe-Ann who'd always been the beauty, who'd always been so proud of her appearance. She'd really believed that she could change Jake Malone into a decent man. What a cruel price she had paid for that belief.

Even Albert had been stirred from his apathy and helped her with the cold compresses. It was a while before Emily realized that the house was silent. 'Where is everyone?'

'Gone to sort out Malone, aye, and all his brothers if needs be.'

'Oh, no! They'll all get hurt.'

'What else did you expect, Emily? They couldn't just ignore this and it's about time someone taught that lot a lesson. I shouldn't wonder if most of the men in Mona Street don't give them a hand. It's been long overdue.'

'But you know their reputation and there's five of them!'

'And there's four of them and they're all mad. Bloody mad. Don't worry, Emily.'

She looked down at her sister. Oh, was Phoebe-Ann never going to stop causing her so much trouble and heartache?

* * *

303

'I'm not taking on the five of them and on their own ground, that's just bloody stupid. You're asking to get your head cracked open,' Jack stated as Jimmy ranted and raved about what he would do to all the Malones. 'Use your brains for once!'

'Jack's right,' Edwin put in. 'They'll all be fighting drunk by now and that old harpy has been known to lay a man out with that brush of hers.'

'So, now you're all frightened of an old woman too?' Jimmy jeered.

'And now we're fighting amongst ourselves!' Rhys stated hotly.

'So, what shall we do?' Jack tried to calm Jimmy down.

'By the time he's boasted about what he's done, he'll feel man enough to come back. He's no scruples.'

'What if he doesn't?' Jimmy asked.

'He will.'

'If he doesn't, I don't care what you say, I'm going up to Mona Street beat the hell out of him, by myself!'

'All right, if he doesn't come back, we'll all go. We'll have the element of surprise. They won't be expecting us. Does that suit everyone?' Edwin asked.

They all nodded.

They hadn't long to wait until they heard the drunken shouts and curses.

'He's not on his own,' Jack remarked.

Rhys peered out from behind the lace curtain. 'There's three of them.'

'The other two must have passed out.'

'Nearly even. Four to three,' Jimmy said grimly.

'Let me deal with that bastard?' Rhys asked.

'No. She's my sister,' Jimmy argued.

'For God's sake don't start again!' Jack hissed.

If the neighbours heard the yells and screams and the crashing and splintering of furniture, no-one came to their doors. Those doors that had been open when the Malones had turned into Florist Street had been quickly slammed shut and curtains were tightly drawn across all the windows. Those curtains didn't twitch when Seamus Malone staggered out of the front door with blood pouring down his face. Nor did they move when Peader appeared in an even worse state and limped painfully up the street.

A constable on his beat glanced at the four dishevelled and bloody figures who turned into Crown Street and then continued on his way after uttering, 'Good night, lads.' Nothing for him to get involved in. They sorted most of their own difficulties out in this neighbourhood and he'd spotted Seamus Malone hanging on to a lamp-post, trying to wipe the blood from his eyes. Always trouble that lot, he mused. Still, this time it looked as though Seamus Malone had met his match. It was a thought that gave him great satisfaction. Pity all five of them couldn't have learned a lesson, he thought. Still, five to four would have constituted an affray and he'd have had to intervene. He turned the corner and strolled on.

Jake Malone lay on the floor of his own kitchen unconscious. His inert form lying at an awkward angle, the blood drying on his face. He'd never cause trouble for anyone again. He'd never work again. He'd never walk again for Jimmy Parkinson's boot had crushed the vertebrae at the base of his spine.

Chapter Nineteen

Next morning Emily awoke heavy-eyed and weary. Phoebe-Ann had tossed restlessly for most of the night, moaning in pain. Her face was even more swollen and the bruising was starting to show: a mass of purple, blue and black patches. She was unable to open her mouth very wide and Emily had had to spoonfeed her with soup. She wished Phoebe-Ann had let them take her to the hospital, if only to reassure them that there were only cuts and bruises, that no unseen damage had occurred, but Emily was determined to send for the doctor, no matter how much it cost.

When she went downstairs she found Albert already up, dressed and with the kettle on.

'How is she, Emily?'

'A mess. I'm going to send for Dr Whelan, there must be something he can do for her. How are the others?'

'A bit stiff and sore. Cuts, bruises, but nothing broken.'

She sat down and passed her hand over her eyes. 'Oh, what will happen now? She can't go back to him.'

'She's still his wife, she's legally bound to him.' Seeing the look of astonishment on Emily's face, he hurriedly carried on, 'I'm not saying she has to go back to him. I'm just pointing out a fact. If he wants to be awkward about it he could demand that she goes back, but he'll have learned his lesson. He'll not touch her again. He probably never expected to be the one who would get the worst hiding – aye, and his brothers, too. You know, in a peculiar way, it might be the making of them both. She might have grown up and realized that marriage is not a bed of roses and he might now realize that he can't carry on the way he did when he was single.'

'You could be right but, oh, it's such a mess; a terrible mess. Mam should have dragged her before the justices, got her made a ward or whatever it was.'

'Aye, and it was me who told her not to do it,' Albert added, regretfully.

Emily was sorry she'd brought the subject up, but what he said was true. Phoebe-Ann was still legally his wife. If he came round causing trouble, demanding that Phoebe-Ann go home, she couldn't see that her sister had any other course open to her but to go back.

Jack was the first to appear, followed by Rhys, then Jimmy.

'You all look as though you've gone ten rounds in a boxing match at the stadium,' Emily said.

'I feel as though I have. How is she?' Rhys asked.

'Not too good.'

'I think I'll go and see her, if you think it will be all right?' Rhys asked.

'No. She doesn't want to see anyone but I'm going for Dr Whelan, I don't care what she says.'

'If it's any consolation to her, she can't be feeling half as bad as he will, or Seamus or Peader Malone.'

'I just hope she won't be disfigured. You know what she was like about her looks, and she was a very pretty girl. How was Edwin when he went home?'

'Much like the rest of us. He said he'd stop by this morning.'

Emily looked at them and then at Albert. 'Albert, would you go for Dr Whelan, please? You and I are the only ones who look respectable and I'll have to see to Phoebe-Ann. I'm going to try to get some breakfast down her although it will have to be with a spoon again. If anything, she looks worse today than she did last night.'

Albert got up and reached for his jacket and cap but their attention was directed to Edwin as he came hurrying into the room.

'Ma Malone's on her way down the street with Vinny and Franny in tow,' he announced.

Emily looked apprehensive. Now what? More trouble? Had they come to demand that Phoebe-Ann go back to Jake? Hadn't they had enough? Hadn't they all done enough without coming looking for more trouble? She dashed into the scullery and came back with the yard brush gripped tightly in her hands.

'Emily, what's got into you?' Albert asked, looking perturbed.

'I've just about had enough of them all against Phoebe-Ann, including Jake, and now she has the nerve to come round here! She's at the back of all this, you can bet on it! Never happy unless she's creating mayhem!' And before any of them could stop her she'd flung open the door and marched into the lobby.

The front door was opened just as Vinny was about to hammer on it and he stepped back as the brush was thrust in his face.

'You can take yourselves back to that hovel you call home or so help me I'll lay the lot of you out! Get off my doorstep!' Emily yelled. All the anxieties and worries of the last twelve hours were banished, dissolved in the tide of righteous anger that made her shake with its force.

They were all dumbfounded. This was something they hadn't expected.

'Go on, clear off before I get the lads to shift you, like they shifted the rest of your fine, upstanding, courageous sons! You've got a bloody nerve coming here at all!'

Ma Malone recovered from her surprise far quicker than her sons did. 'I'll 'ave the law on yez. Y'murderin' bitch!'

Emily shoved the brush towards her until the bristles were almost touching her face. 'I'll be murdering you, you evil old besom and not before time either! Someone should have given you a good clout years ago! So, if you don't clear off, it will be me!'

Vinny and Franny stepped backwards as Jack, Jimmy, Rhys and Edwin appeared behind Emily, but Ma Malone held her ground.

'Don't think yez can frighten me, yer 'ardfaced little bitch! You've gone an' crippled me son, do yez hear me! Yez 'ave crippled him for life!' She stabbed a bony finger at the men.

Emily thought it was all part of her ploy to intimidate them. 'Serves him right! He's nearly crippled my sister. Oh, wasn't he the big, brave feller, belting the daylights out of a girl! Well, he got what was coming to him so now you can all get back to Mona Street, because you don't terrify us the way you do your neighbours. If you don't shove off then these two will be going home in the same state as the other three went home last night! Clear off!'

Edwin's estimation of Emily rose. He'd never seen her so angry and with her eyes flashing, the determined set of her lips, she reminded him of Lily.

309

' 'E never came home last night! He's in the Royal Infirmary! You crippled 'im, you bastards!' Ma Malone shrieked, almost beside herself with rage.

Jack and Jimmy pushed past Emily. 'You heard her, clear off! It serves him right. Now get the hell out of it, back to your own midden!'

Vinny Malone pushed the seething figure of his ma out of the way and squared up to Jimmy. 'Listen, you pair of thickos! She's tellin' the truth. You crippled him. You done somethin' to his back an' they say he won't ever walk again! He's paralysed!'

'So sue us! I said clear off, are you deaf as well as bloody daft!' Jimmy roared back.

'I'll 'ave the law on yez all!' Ma screamed.

Jack was unimpressed. 'Go on then, get the scuffers. Just how are you going to prove it? It's his word against ours.'

'And our Seamus and Peader,' Vinny growled.

'I said against ours – me, Jimmy, Rhys, Edwin, Emily and Mr Davies. We'll swear blind we didn't go over the doorstep last night.'

'Look at yer faces, them cuts and bruises will show them!' Franny shot back.

'So, we had a family argument. Lots of families have bust-ups. Go and get the scuffers then. They won't bloody well come and you know it! You've caused them too much trouble in the past. They'll send you off with a flea in your ear. They'll probably be thankful that someone finally sorted you lot out. Bugger off, the lot of you, before I put you all in the "Royal"!' Jimmy took a step forward, as if to emphasize his point.

Ma Malone was speechless with fury, so livid she was purple in the face.

Vinny glared at them all, then grabbing her arm, pulled her away.

'Go on, clear off and don't come here again! You've done enough harm to this family. Our Phoebe-Ann's lying upstairs with her face so battered me poor mam wouldn't even recognize her. He deserves everything he got!' Emily called after them.

They all stood watching as, with some difficulty, Franny and Vinny dragged their mother up the street. Their progress was made even more humiliating by the fact that every woman in Lonsdale Street was on her doorstep to watch. It was a momentous occasion to see the dreaded Malones bested and slinking home.

'Do you think they will go to the police?' Emily asked, as they all returned to the kitchen.

'No. They know the police wouldn't be interested. Like I said, they'll probably all be as delighted as the residents of Mona Street must be. We saw a copper last night and he saw us. He must also have seen the Malones. They would have to go that way home,' Jimmy said.

'I wonder, was she telling the truth?' Albert asked.

'She's probably exaggerating, but even if she wasn't he deserves it,' Jack said grimly.

'Oh, it just gets worse,' Emily sighed. The anger had gone, leaving her feeling weak and a little light-headed.

'It's not finished yet either,' Edwin said and they all turned questioning eyes towards him. 'You realize that you won't be able to go back, Rhys? You can't work in that stokehold again. They'll kill you and I mean that. It's no exaggeration.'

Emily sat down as she let this statement sink in.

'He's right, Rhys. It would be suicide. They'd brain you at the first opportunity and no-one would raise a hand to stop them. Even the officers don't intervene when the black squad fight. You know that,' Jack said gravely.

Rhys nodded slowly, seeing for the first time that his love for Phoebe-Ann, and his retaliation for her injuries, had put him in this position. He'd have to go back home, for there were no jobs to be had in Liverpool. 'What about you, Edwin?'

'I don't have to work with them. I'll just watch myself when I'm ashore and I've got mates who'll look out for me. No need to worry about me.'

Emily stared up at him with fear in her eyes.

He placed a hand on her shoulder. 'Don't worry. I'll be careful. But Rhys will have to go back unless he finds a job.'

Albert nodded. 'Best write to your mam, lad. I'm sorry, but there doesn't seem to be any way around it. Times are bad. Ships are being laid up.'

Rhys felt defeated. It wouldn't have been so bad if Phoebe-Ann had been free. He would have willingly taken her back with him but he would have to go alone. She was still married and there was no way around that. Maybe it was best that he leave for if she decided that she must go back to Jake he didn't think he could stand it.

'Come back with me, Albert?'

Albert shook his head. 'I can't. I can't leave here, you know that, lad.'

Rhys didn't press him further but his heart felt like a lump of stone.

There was little Dr Whelan could do for Phoebe-Ann he informed Emily. 'You did the right thing with the cold compresses. There are no deep cuts, the swelling will go down and the bruising will fade. Broken noses

312

can't be set I'm afraid, but at least neither her jaw nor cheekbones have been fractured. She'll have to see a dentist about her teeth, but not until all the swelling has gone. The man should be prosecuted and locked up!' he finished angrily.

'There won't be any need for that, Doctor. He won't touch her again.'

He nodded. He'd seen the cuts and bruises on the faces of her brothers.

'Will she be disfigured?'

'It's hard to tell. I don't really think so, in the long term, but you'd better prepare her just in case.'

Emily wondered how she was to do that. Phoebe-Ann had always been proud of her looks so it would be doubly hard. It was as if worry after worry was being piled on her and she wondered how she would cope. But she had to. Mam had coped with far worse things than this.

Rhys had made a last, desperate attempt to find work, any work. He'd haunted the Labour Exchange, the Employment Pool, the docks, the railway yards, but in a city where unemployment was rife, there was nothing.

He begged to see Phoebe-Ann before he left and, despite her sister's protests, Emily had shown him into the bedroom and then left them alone.

Phoebe-Ann turned her face to the wall. She didn't want to see the look of shock and horror on his face. She looked hideous. She'd asked Emily for a mirror and now she wished she hadn't. She would never look in a mirror again, she'd sworn as she'd sobbed.

'Phoebe-Ann, I've come to say that I'm leaving. I'm going home.'

She still kept her head turned away from him.

He reached out and took her hand. 'I don't want to go. I'd willingly stay here but they'd kill me the first opportunity they got. There's no work to be had – God knows I've tried – so I've got to go back.' Gently he touched her cheek.

'Don't! Don't!' she cried.

'I don't care how you look. I still love you and I'm glad he's crippled.'

Emily hadn't told her that and, forgetting her injuries, she turned towards him.

'Aye, I'm glad,' he repeated grimly, fighting down his shock at the sight of what Jake Malone had done to her face.

'How?'

'Something to do with his back. I saw Jimmy knock him down and he was on the floor when we all left.'

'Oh, Rhys! I feel terrible. Everything is my fault. Mam, Albert, our Jack and Jimmy getting hurt and Edwin and now . . . now you've got to go back and he's . . . crippled.'

'You mustn't talk like that, Phoebe-Ann.'

'But it *is* my fault! It *is*!' she sobbed.

He took her in his arms. 'Hush now, *cariad*, everything will turn out fine in the end.'

She clung to him. 'How can it? How can it? I wish I were dead, I really do! I've caused so much trouble!'

'Don't say things like that! Don't! Promise me you won't do anything foolish?'

She couldn't answer him.

'Phoebe-Ann, if you don't promise, I'll stay! I don't care what the Malones do to me, it would be as nothing if I thought you'd harm yourself.'

She couldn't have anything happen to him, she thought. It would be as if she'd killed him. 'I won't. I promise.'

'That's better.' He kissed her tenderly on her forehead. 'Oh, Phoebe-Ann, I'd give anything, anything to turn back the clock! If only you hadn't married him.'

'But I did.' The words were choked.

'If ever there's anything . . . anything at all, I can do for you, Phoebe-Ann, will you come to me?'

'Oh, Rhys, I don't know why you are bothering with me, after me being so cruel to you. I'm not worth it.'

'Yes, you are, Phoebe-Ann and I'll never forget you!'

After he'd gone, she lay back and her mind wandered over the events of the last year. One short year and so much misery in it. She was too afraid to look forward, for the future just didn't bear contemplating.

As the days and weeks passed, Phoebe-Ann regained her strength, physically, but mentally she was exhausted, battling with all the conflicting emotions. The swelling and the bruising gradually disappeared and her face didn't look half so bad, although her nose didn't look quite right. She'd gone to the Dental Hospital and they'd been very kind and understanding and they'd worked wonders. Emily said she now looked just like her old self but she knew that that the girl was dead. She would never be the same again.

Alice called frequently and she'd helped Emily to reassure Phoebe-Ann that she wouldn't be scarred. After almost a month, between them, they'd considerably lightened Phoebe-Ann's spirits.

On the following Friday, Alice called on her way home from work. 'How's the patient today then?'

'A bit down in the dumps. She keeps examining her nose,' Emily replied.

'She's going to have more than her nose to worry about.'

'Why?'

'I heard he's coming out of hospital tomorrow.'

'She's not going back there, Alice.'

Alice looked uneasy. 'Will you come with me while I tell her?'

Phoebe-Ann was staring morosely out of the window that overlooked the side of Bloom Street.

'You can't stay up here for ever; it's about time you got yourself downstairs and even out of the house,' Alice scolded, but in a kindly way.

'I can't! I can't go out! Everyone will be looking at me and talking about me. I must be the scandal of Toxteth!'

'Don't flatter yourself. Besides, once they've all seen that you haven't grown another head they'll forget all about you and start on someone else. I think everyone sympathizes with you. Florrie Harper said you must have been a saint to put up with him for so long and that they'd all felt like cheering when your Emily chased Ma Malone. Your Emily's a bit of a heroine in Mona Street, an' the lads as well of course.' She grinned at Emily.

'Alice has got something to tell you,' Emily stated quietly.

A shadow crossed Phoebe-Ann's face. 'What?'

'He's coming out of hospital tomorrow, so I heard.'

Phoebe-Ann looked stricken. 'I can't . . . I won't . . . !'

'You won't have to go back there unless you want to,' Emily reassured her firmly.

'Where will he go?' Phoebe-Ann asked.

'Back to his ma, I suppose. He can't see to himself. They've given him some kind of a chair with wheels, but someone will have to push him around, a bit like a baby in a pram.'

Emily looked disturbed. She couldn't see Ma Malone pushing him around the streets for everyone to mock and gloat at their predicament and say, 'Serves them right.'

'I suppose if he gets awkward about it, he could demand that you go back, Phoebe-Ann. You're still his wife.' Alice repeated what her mother had said that morning.

'I'm not going back to him! I'm never going back to him! I should have listened to you all when you tried to warn me. Oh, I was such a fool!'

Emily said nothing. It wouldn't help Phoebe-Ann now for her to say 'I told you so'.

Alice had no such reservations. 'Yes, you were a fool and you should have listened but it's too late now. Still, never mind, I can't see that he'd want you to go back.'

'Why not?' Emily questioned.

'Well, things are sort of reversed now, aren't they? Phoebe-Ann's the strong one and he's the cripple, an' I should think he's terrified of your Jack and Jimmy.'

Emily thought she had a point and, by the look on Phoebe-Ann's face, she knew her sister felt the same way.

Chapter Twenty

All Jake could remember was walking back into the house and seeing the four of them wading in with fists flying. He remembered Jimmy Parkinson hitting him in the face and he'd stumbled. He remembered a wave of pain washing over him and then nothing until he'd come round in the austere, white-tiled ward in the Royal Infirmary. His ma and Vinny were standing by the bed but the first person he'd asked for was Phoebe-Ann until his ma reminded him what had happened. He'd been given something to quieten him and he'd slept but the next morning a doctor, accompanied by a sister and a nurse had come and told him that he'd never walk again. They'd used fancy words and terms that he didn't understand, trying to explain what had happened to him. In the end he'd just blurted out 'What the hell is all that supposed to mean?' and they'd told him.

At first he hadn't believed them but as he'd tried to move his legs, so hard had he tried that the sweat stood out on his forehead, and they'd not moved an inch, he'd realized it was the truth. He'd raged and cursed and finally wept like a child. He'd sworn and damned Phoebe-Ann and her brothers to all the torments of hell. Then he'd sunk into a black depression which hadn't lifted at all. He had been sorry he'd beaten Phoebe-Ann and he really didn't mind the fact that her brothers had come to exact retribution, but had the bastards needed to cripple him? He'd alternated between moods of fury and dire self-pity until they'd told him they could do no more for him.

He demanded they take him home in an ambulance; at least people would see how badly he'd been hurt and wouldn't mock, he hoped. It was a vain hope. The residents of Mona Street hated them all so much they were all on their doorsteps grinning and pointing.

Vinny and Franny helped to get him indoors.

'Get him in the house, the pair of yez, before they all choke laughin',' Ma snapped and the front door was slammed behind them. It was a hollow, ominous sound, like the door of a prison cell closing and he'd grown to hate the house, for it had become his prison.

As the dreary, tedious days passed, he watched his brothers with something akin to hatred as they moved effortlessly around and came and went as the mood took them. Something he would never do again and they took it so much for granted, too, he thought bitterly.

After four weeks he thought he'd go mad if he didn't get out of the house. 'I'm bloody sick of these four walls. Can't one of you get me out for a bit?' They'd all just arrived home and he felt even more trapped.

'If yez think I'm pushin' yez up the street wit them all standin' on their bloody doorsteps and skittin' me, yez 'ave got another think comin'!' Ma announced. 'One of youse lot can take him, I've got enough on me 'ands.'

'Sod off! I'm not pushin' him! Be like pushin' a bloody pram!' Seamus stated. 'He got himself into this by marryin' her in the first place! Bejasus! We warned him often enough.'

'That's a nice thing ter say, isn't it!' Vinny snapped.

'It's the bleedin' truth, an' now we'll have to support him too! He can't work.'

'What's all this "we"? You haven't been doin' much work yourself lately,' Vinny shot back.

'Not for the want of tryin'. There's no bloody work to be had.'

'Shut yez bloody gobs, the pair of yez! It's not much ter ask, is it? Look at all the extra work I've got with him,' Ma stated hotly.

Jake felt as though they were talking about him as though he wasn't even in the room or as if he were mentally retarded.

'I didn't effin well ask to be crippled!' he bawled.

'Well you are and there's nothin' you can do about it,' Peader yelled at him. They were all still smarting with humiliation, for most of the black squad, and in particular the O'Rourkes, had done nothing but poke fun at them. 'I'm goin' to fix that Welsh bastard. It wasn't his quarrel. He'll have to come back some time, he'll lose his job.'

'He's gone. Back to where he came from,' Seamus announced.

'Shit scared, I'll bet!' Peader mocked.

'What good will it do beatin' any of them up now? Just lose our jobs, like Seamus, an' things are bad enough,' Franny said gloomily.

'Listen ter the little yellow bastard!' Peader mocked.

Ma lashed out with the wet cloth she was holding, catching Peader across the face. 'Don't you call 'im a bastard! He was born in wedlock like yez all were! If yer da was 'ere he'd belt yer. If 'e was 'ere he'd sort yez all out!'

'I'm sick of hearin' that! It's all yer ever whinge on about and have done for years! Iffen yer da was 'ere!

320

Iffen yer da was 'ere!' Peader yelled at her, holding his cheek, which bore the red mark where the cloth had caught it.

'Shut yer bloody gob or it'll be me brush that yez'll get across the head and not a bit of rag!'

Jake felt weary. His battered spirits cried out for some peace and solace but all they ever did was scream and yell at each other.

'I'm glad I'm goin' back tomorrow. To get away from you two at least!' Vinny cried, before he stormed out.

'Where are yez goin' now? I can't move 'im by meself,' Ma shouted after him, as Franny, Peader and Seamus all reached for their jackets.

'Down to the ale-house. I'm not stayin' here to listen to you moanin' and whingein' all day,' Peader flung over his shoulder at her.

When they'd all gone she stared down at Jake with annoyance. 'Get no bloody 'elp from any of them.'

'Ma, I didn't ask to be stuck in this chair.'

'An' I didn't ask for all the extra work. I get no peace. Our Seamus is right, yer shouldn't 'ave married the bitch. Yer don't see 'er runnin' to look after yez. She 'asn't even 'ad the decency ter ask after yez.'

'I shouldn't 'ave belted her,' Jake muttered.

'Yer shouldn't 'ave married her. What am I goin' ter do when they've all gone off? Our Seamus is no bloody good, he's no 'elp an' he's got no money either.'

'You'll just have to manage, won't yer?' he snapped at her. 'You'll have to stay in more.'

'Stay in! Stay in! That's all I do. I can't 'old me head up now an' all this washin' because yer can't stop yerself from doin' everythin' under yer. It's worse than when yez was a babby.'

321

Jake burned with humiliation. 'You're a bloody-minded, bad-mouthed, old bitch!'

'Start callin' me names, meladdo, an' I'll not lift a finger to 'elp yer. Yer can sit in yer own muck all day an' night!'

Jake looked around for something to throw at her but there was nothing within reach. Instead he glared at her with such intense hatred that she slammed out of the room.

She stuck it for three days after they'd gone back to sea. As she'd predicted, Seamus was no help to her at all. She saw the years ahead of her stuck in the house, loaded down with washing and extra chores, for a nurse had come in to see him and had told her that the house was a disgrace and that if she didn't clean it up, she'd have the Board of Public Health down on her. She'd told her to use more bleach and Jeyes Fluid unless she wanted them all to go down with typhoid fever or dysentery. The hardfaced bitch had also told her to change Jake more often; he was getting sores that would turn bad if left. She'd fumed and ranted and raved for hours after the woman had gone. Well, she'd had enough of it. He wasn't her responsibility any more. He had a wife. She could look after him. She'd done her bit, now it was that stuck-up, Orange, floosie's turn, whether she liked it or not.

'We're goin' out,' she informed Jake.

He looked hopeful, thinking the nurse's words had had some effect, despite all her ravings to the contrary. 'Where?'

'Out, I said. An' yer keep yer eyes straight ahead of yer. Ignore them all! I'm not havin' yer shame me.' She had started to pile together the old strips of sheets

322

and towels on the table, together with the things the nurse had left her. She looked around for something to put them all in. Rummaging behind the sofa, she pulled out an old sugar sack and began to stuff them all inside it.

'What are yer doin'?'

'I'm gettin' yer things together.'

'What for?'

'I've had enough of yer! Yer goin' back to yer wife!'

He looked aghast. Hadn't he had enough to put up with, enough humiliations. 'I'm not goin'!'

'Yez are!'

'You wait until our Seamus gets in! You wait until the others come home!'

'An' what good will they do? Nothin'!'

She dumped the sack on his knee.

'You effin, evil, old cow!' he yelled.

She cuffed him hard over the head. 'Don't yez speak to me like that! I've put up wit yer since yer were born, it's 'er turn now!'

Emily stared in astonishment at the spectacle on her doorstep. 'What's this?'

'Where's 'is wife?' Ma demanded.

'Why?'

Albert appeared behind her. 'What do you want?'

'He's 'er responsibility now, not mine. It was yer brother who put 'im in this chair, so now yer can get on with it!'

'Oh, no, you don't! He's not staying here!' Emily cried.

'I'm not sayin' 'e is. They've got that posh 'ouse. She can take 'im 'ome.'

Emily was acutely aware that the curtains were twitching up the entire length of the street. She also felt a pang of sympathy for Jake Malone. 'You can't just dump him here!'

'I can, an' I am!'

'What kind of a mother are you? Haven't you got any feelings for him? He's your own flesh and blood!' Emily demanded.

'An' he upped and married her after I'd told 'im he was bein' a bloody fool! It's his own fault he's like this. I've had enough! He's turnin' me house into a bleedin' 'ospital an' bag-wash an' it's stinkin' ter high heaven an' all!'

'I would have thought it did that before this,' Emily retorted.

Ma Malone glared at her. 'Yer can say what yer like, 'e's not comin' back with me!' And with that she turned and stumped away.

Emily and Albert looked at each other.

'We can't leave him on the doorstep,' Albert said quietly.

'How is she going to take it? What will she say?'

'I'm not paralysed in me head an' all!' Jake roared at them.

'No, you're not. Give me a hand with him?' Emily asked Albert.

They left him in the kitchen while Emily went upstairs for her sister and Albert returned to the yard where he was mending a harness.

'What was all the noise about?' Phoebe-Ann asked.

'It was your mother-in-law.'

'What did she want?'

Emily sat down on the bed. 'She brought Jake round and left him. He's in the kitchen.'

'No! No! I won't see him! I won't!'

'I'm afraid you'll have to Phoebe-Ann. She said he's your responsibility now and she's right.'

324

'I don't want anything to do with him!'

'Phoebe-Ann, you've got no choice, I'm afraid. He is your husband. He can't hurt you now. In fact, I feel quite sorry for him.'

'Sorry?'

'Yes. It must have been awful for him to be dumped here. She just walked away and left him. Fine mother she is!'

'Em, I don't want to go back.' Phoebe-Ann was near to tears.

'I know what you've been through, and we're all sorry it happened, but I know what Mam would have said.'

'What?'

'You took your vows, freely, in a church and before God, to love, honour and obey, in sickness and in health, for better or for worse. You've *got* to take him back, there's no other way!'

Phoebe-Ann began to cry and Emily felt sorry for her, but the time for tears and recriminations was past. He couldn't stay here, it just wasn't possible. Not only for his sake but she knew her brothers would turn him out. 'Stop that and pull yourself together! You're not a child, you're a married woman. You've got to grow up, Phoebe-Ann.'

'How can you say that to me after what he did to me?' Phoebe-Ann wailed.

'I know it's hard, terribly hard, but, as I've already said, he can't hurt you now. He'll depend on you, not the other way around. You'll have to be the strong one from now on.'

'I don't want to be!'

Emily was getting annoyed. 'For heaven's sake, Phoebe-Ann, grow up! He's your responsibility and what's more you'll have to be the bread-winner from now on, too. Dry your eyes and come down with me while we try and sort this out.'

Reluctantly, Phoebe-Ann wiped away her tears. Emily had never spoken to her like that before. Didn't she understand how terrified she was of him?

Some of her fear diminished when she saw him. He looked as though he'd shrunk. Or was that because he was sitting in the chair?

'I'll make you both a cup of tea and then you can sort it all out between you,' Emily said firmly as Phoebe-Ann sat down.

Neither of them spoke until Emily had made the tea, poured it and then left the room.

'I didn't want to come here. That old bitch brought me!' Jake blurted out, frustration and bitterness gnawing at his insides.

'How . . . how are you?'

'Don't ask bloody stupid questions! I'm crippled, that's how I am and by your bleedin' brother!'

'You beat me! You beat me senseless! What did you expect?'

'Lots of men belt their wives every day but they don't end up a cripple.'

'Then they should do! I don't want to go back there with you. My nose was broken and you knocked out some of my teeth!'

He looked away. For the hundredth time that day he wished he'd never laid a finger on her. He wished he'd never even set eyes on her.

'Emily says you can't stay here. Our Jack and Jimmy won't have you.'

'Then we'll have to go back to Florist Street, won't we? You're my wife. You were quick enough to get me to the altar and spend my money, so now you can look after me. "In sickness an' in health",' he mocked.

Phoebe-Ann knew there was no other course open to her. She forced herself to think of practical matters. 'What will we do for money? Will the Parish give us anything?'

That was something Jake hadn't even thought of and it added to his humiliations. Jake Malone on the Parish! 'Don't you think I've got enough to put up with without bein' on the Parish? You can work.'

'How can I work and look after you at the same time?' she demanded hotly.

'I don't know but we're *not* going on the Parish!'

'We'll have to move. The rent is too dear and, besides, I won't be able to get you up the stairs, not on my own,' she added curtly. She didn't care if she was being cruel. He had no right to demand anything of her.

'Then you'll have to go out and look for rooms, won't you?'

Tears were threatening to overwhelm Phoebe-Ann. She'd thought life was as bad as it could be, now she knew different. She'd have to spend the rest of her life in some drab rooms, always short of money, always working and always having to look after him. Her stomach churned when she thought of the things she would have to do for him. Wash him, dress him, change his soiled and stinking linen. Oh, she couldn't even think about that!

Emily helped her to get him back to Florist Street and as she'd unpacked her things, straightened up the place and made them a meal, Phoebe-Ann began to realize just how much work was involved in looking after him. The fact that Jake burned with resentment and frustration was lost on her. All she did was complain about her woes: that she wasn't strong enough to be dragging him on and off the sofa or in and out of the chair; that her head ached from the stuffy atmosphere, laden with unpleasant odours; that her hands were chapped and raw with so much washing and scrubbing. In those first weeks they did nothing but yell at each other and Phoebe-Ann often thought of Rhys and bemoaned aloud the fact that she would have been far happier had she married him. A fact that infuriated Jake even more.

As usual it was to Emily that she turned. 'We'll have to move and where am I going to find a job that will leave me time to see to him as well?'

'You need some rooms on the ground floor, something not too expensive, but with a wash-house or the use of a wash-house. You can't take his stuff to the bag-wash. You could bring it here if you had to but that would mean you living nearby and I don't know of anyone who has rooms to let.'

'Even if I found some, how would I pay for them?'

'I could go and see Miss Millicent and Miss Nesta.'

The thought of once again being surrounded by beautiful things, in a clean house that didn't smell of carbolic, Jeyes Fluid and worse odours, made Phoebe-Ann look hopefully at her sister. 'Would you, Em? Would you explain?'

Emily smiled. 'I'll go and see them. It will be a start.' She wondered if Phoebe-Ann would ever stop relying on her. Probably not, but at least she was being positive about things now.

The house looked exactly the same, she thought as she knocked. The door was opened by a young girl whose hair was untidy and whose apron was grubby.

'I would like to see the Misses Barlow, please.'

'What's your name?'

'Emily Parkinson.'

The girl nodded, indicated that she should go in and then disappeared in the direction of the drawing room, to return and state 'You're to come in.'

Emily thanked her, thinking there was not much finesse about her.

'Emily! Dear Emily!' Miss Nesta cried.

'Thank you for seeing me, miss.' She smiled at Miss Millicent.

'How are you, Emily? How are things at home?' Miss Millicent asked.

'I'm fine, miss, thank you. But I've come to ask a favour of you.'

'Sit down,' Miss Nesta instructed.

'Thank you, miss, but I'd sooner stand. It doesn't seem right.'

Miss Millicent nodded approvingly. 'You always had such impeccable manners, Emily. Which is more than can be said for that little chit. I don't know what domestic staff are coming to these days or where Richard finds them. Highly unsuitable all of them.'

'It's about work that I've come.'

Miss Nesta clapped her hands together. 'Emily, you're coming back to us! Isn't that wonderful, Millie?'

'No. No, miss. I'm sorry, but I wasn't asking for myself.'

They both looked disappointed.

'It's for my sister. Phoebe-Ann was Miss Olivia's maid, before she was married.'

'But she's married, so why does she want to work here?' Miss Nesta enquired.

'Didn't I hear that there was some trouble? Didn't

he turn out to be a dreadful person?' Miss Millicent quizzed Emily.

She nodded. 'He did. He beat her badly.'

'Oh, the beast!' Miss Nesta cried.

'Quite. Has she left him?' Miss Millicent asked dryly.

'No. You see he is now crippled. He can't walk or stand or do anything for himself, so she needs to work to keep the house going. But she also needs a job where it will be possible for her to go home in the day to see to him. A job that will be near so she won't have to waste time travelling.'

'I see. How dreadful for her. Do sit down Emily, you are giving me a crick in my neck looking up at you. Never mind the proprieties.'

Emily sat on the edge of the chair Miss Millicent indicated.

'If she worked for Richard Mercer then she will be suitable, no doubt about that, and we do live near and, of course, we would have no objections to her slipping home. But I'm afraid we can't pay her very much. Not as much as she would get in a factory or shop.'

'She knows that, but she couldn't possibly work in a shop or a factory, they'd never let her take time off. She'll just have to manage.'

'Won't she get any help from the Parish or whatever charitable organization sees to these cases?'

'She's got her pride, Miss Millicent. I've told her I can let her have a bit now and then, to help out.'

'You always were such a kind girl, Emily. Well, it's settled then. Tell her to come and see us.'

Emily rose and smiled at them both. 'Thank you. You're so good and kind. I knew you'd help, if you were able to.'

'And what about your young man, Emily? How is he?'

'Quite well, thank you.'

'Haven't you set a date for the wedding yet?' Miss Nesta enquired

'Nesta! What a thing to ask. It's none of our business. You've been associating too much with the dreadful girls Richard keeps sending us.'

'I don't mind, miss. It's difficult you see. He won't move in with us and I don't blame him. We'd not have much privacy. Albert . . . Mr Davies, is not himself at all.'

'Such a shame,' Miss Nesta murmured.

'Don't interrupt, Nesta.'

'And I won't leave him. He was so good to me after . . . after I left Mr Mercer's employ. His nephew, Rhys, begged him to go and live with his mother, back in Wales, but he wouldn't go. So, you see, it's difficult.'

'How upsetting for you, and now your sister is burdened with this dreadful man. His mother has the most awful reputation, so Sally, the last girl we had, told me.'

'I'd better be going and thank you so much for being so understanding.'

'We did say that you were to come to see us if you needed anything, Emily.'

Emily smiled at Miss Millicent, thankful they had at least taken one burden from her. All she had to do now was find Phoebe-Ann some decent rooms.

As she walked back to Lonsdale Street she wondered if she would ever be free of all the demands made on her. Would she ever marry Edwin and have a place of her own, a life of her own without having to shoulder everyone's troubles? But when she examined the situation closely, she realized sadly, as she had often done before, that Phoebe-Ann was to blame for all the misfortunes that had overtaken them.

Chapter Twenty-one

Phoebe-Ann managed to find rooms in a house in Liffy Street. They were clean, which is all that could be said of them, she told Emily sourly.

'What more did you expect for the money? As long as they aren't crawling with bugs or riddled with damp, that's the main thing. You've got some lovely furniture and things. They will look nice when you've fixed them up.'

'I can't take all my things. There is only one bedroom and a big living room that I have to use to cook in as well.'

'Is there a range?'

'Yes, but there's no inside privvy. Some of those houses have them.'

'We've never had an inside privvy! Even fourteen Florist Street didn't have that luxury, Phoebe-Ann!'

'There's no wash-house either. Just a line in the backyard.'

'Then you'll have to bring the washing here and maybe our Jimmy will fix up a rack in the living room for you, like mine.

'You don't have all the stuff I have to wash, and after I've done a day's work at Princes Avenue too.'

Emily had looked at her sister with annoyance. She was always complaining these days. All the softness had gone from her face, and lines were forming on her forehead and at the corners of her mouth, for she never smiled now. Emily sighed. Phoebe-Ann didn't have much to smile about so she shouldn't be hard and impatient with her.

'If I give you some money you can buy new sheets and towels and use all the old ones for him. That way you won't have to wash every day. You can just put them in to soak.'

Phoebe-Ann looked grateful. 'I don't know what I'd do without you, Em. Not many girls have sisters who are so good or so patient.'

Emily laughed. 'Is my halo slipping?'

It was that very night, after Phoebe-Ann had gone, that Jack and Jimmy announced that they had finally saved up enough money to emigrate.

Although she was glad for them, Emily felt as though she'd been physically struck. Only now did she realize how much she depended on them. Oh, Albert was working again, not as much as he used to and usually only mornings, but it brought in enough money so they'd been able to manage. It wasn't just their money she'd miss though, it was their company and their support.

'It's taken you long enough to save up so I shouldn't feel so miserable. It's not as if you've just dropped it on me out of the blue. Oh, but I'll miss you both.'

'We've thought about it for a long time, even before Mam died, and we have been ages saving up, you know that, Em,' Jack reminded her.

'I know and I know there's not much in the way of prospects here. So, when will you go?' she asked.

'We went down to the shipping office today. The *Aquitania* is the first ship available. We'll be going next weekend. I know it's a bit short notice, but maybe it's better like that and we'll be going from Southampton.'

'Oh, I'd forgotten that. I wish you were going from Liverpool. We could wave you off but I don't think we can afford to go to Southampton.'

Jimmy put his arm around her. 'It would be a bit of a wasted journey and, besides, you'd be miserable all the way back.'

'What will you do when you get there?' Albert asked, looking at them sorrowfully. He'd become very fond of them both.

'Get somewhere to live to start with, then get a job.'

'There's some very rough neighbourhoods.'

'There are in every city, Albert,' Jack replied. 'But do you remember Blanco Kimnel who lived down Lowther Street? He went out about five years ago and he's doing great now. His mam gave me his address and said to look him up, that he'd help us find work. He sends her a "fistful of dollars" each month, to use her words.'

'That's a relief. I won't worry so much about you now,' Emily said. 'I suppose I'd better start and get all your stuff together. Don't you need papers and things?'

'Aye, we'll have to sort all that out this week. At least we won't have time to go getting cold feet,' Jimmy answered.

No-one had much time to think about their forth-coming departure. Emily was kept busy washing, ironing and packing while Jack and Jimmy sorted out all the red tape. Albert watched them sadly, thinking yet another part of his life was ending. They'd become the sons he'd never had and they'd been companions as well.

'I wish I was going with them. I'd give anything to just sail away from everything and everyone and start a new life,' Phoebe-Ann sighed. She'd come round to go to Lime Street station with them.

'Don't you think I've wished that too, except that I wouldn't want to go without Edwin.'

'You? I thought you were happy here, Em?'

'I'm not really complaining, but it would be nice just to sail away with Edwin. No more worries, no more responsibilities.'

'At least Edwin's not crippled. There's nothing in the future for me to look forward to.'

Emily was sorry she'd spoken and she hoped Phoebe-Ann wasn't going to break down at the station, because she knew if she did, then she would too and that would upset her brothers.

Before they left the house Emily brought out a bottle of whisky and all the men had a small glassful. They all had misty eyes, too. She'd surreptitiously tucked a five pound note into Jack's pocket, some of the money Miss Nesta had given her. He'd protested but she'd been adamant. 'I've nothing else to give you. It's my going away present. Take it.' They'd both kissed her and she had swallowed hard, fighting back the tears.

There was the usual crush at the station: people waiting for trains to arrive, others waiting to board, all anxiously glancing up at the clock. They all wore their best clothes, for it was a special occasion. Despite this, Phoebe-Ann looked dowdy and untidy and Emily looked at her sadly, thinking how smart and pretty she'd always been, and she wondered if her brothers were thinking the same thing. If they were they gave no sign of it as they hugged them both. They then shook Albert's hand and Edwin's. He'd been granted extra leave as his Aunt Sarah had died.

'Just don't forget to put pen to paper once in a while,' Emily instructed them.

'It won't be that often, Em. You know we were never much good at letter writing.'

'Don't you dare lose touch, Jack Parkinson. Don't go disappearing off the face of the earth or I'll come and find you.'

'Don't worry about them, Emily. I'll look them up each shore leave.' Edwin laughed and was rewarded by a smile of gratitude from Emily.

'Now see what you've gone and done. He'll be spying on us and reporting back,' Jimmy joked.

They all laughed but for them all the tears were very close to the surface.

'I wish I were coming with you,' Phoebe-Ann said miserably.

'So do I, but there's no use dwelling on things.' Jack hugged her and she clung to him until Emily gently prised her away.

'Better get aboard. I think I heard the last call.' Edwin called their attention to the fact that the train was preparing to leave.

Emily clung to them both, tears in her eyes. She'd probably never see them again, she thought. 'Take care of yourselves and good luck,' she whispered.

'We'll send for you all when we make our first million,' Jimmy joked.

The little group stood huddled together watching as the two men walked quickly down the platform. They turned and waved before they got aboard and then they leaned out of the window, waving until they were lost in the clouds of steam as the train pulled out.

I'll always remember them like that, smiling and waving, Emily thought. Just as she remembered Harry and Rob, proud and smiling in their uniforms.

They were all downcast as they turned to leave, but Phoebe-Ann was more forlorn than anyone else. It was as if her youth, her dreams and her happiness were disappearing in that cloud of steam. She didn't want to go back to Liffy Street, back to him, back to that stinking mess that even now made her retch at times. So she seized eagerly on Edwin's offer of a drink before they went home. They all needed cheering up, he said.

As Emily linked her arm through his, he looked down at her. 'If only . . .'

'I know, but don't say it or he'll be upset if he hears you and think he's being a burden, which he isn't.'

He sighed. 'Oh, Emily, how much longer?'

'I don't know, but something will turn up, you see.'

Whenever she could manage it, Phoebe-Ann went round to spend half an hour with Alice. It was the only break she got from Jake or work. He had been openly hostile to the idea but she'd ignored his protests.

'Why don't you come out with us one night? No-one could object to you having a few hours' enjoyment,' Alice suggested.

'I couldn't. Even if he didn't make such a song and dance about it, I couldn't afford it.'

'Ginny and me will treat you.'

Phoebe-Ann thought of the days when Jake had been at sea and she'd had her job at the B&A. She'd had money then. Money of her own to spend how she wished. It was a bitter, depressing fact that now she never even had a few shillings to spend on herself. 'No, that wouldn't be fair.'

'What if I paid one week, Ginny the next and you

the third week, that's fair? You could save up a few coppers each week that way. You need cheering up, Phoebe-Ann. God, I don't know why you haven't gone round the bend yet, stuck with him and the only break you get is going to work.'

'You don't have to remind me, Alice. I know what a mess I've made of my life,' Phoebe-Ann flashed back at her friend.

'I didn't mean to remind you and you know it. Haven't I been your best friend through thick and thin?' Alice looked hurt.

Phoebe-Ann nodded. 'I'm sorry I snapped at you, but I'm so tired and so sick of . . . Oh, of everything!'

'There you are then. You need a break and once a week isn't too much to ask. A few hours on a Sunday night to go to the pictures or maybe for a quiet drink.'

Phoebe-Ann thought about it. Oh, how she longed to have some time to herself, when she could forget about Jake and the terrible life she now lived. Time when perhaps she could dress up, go out and even pretend she was a single girl again, without a care in the world except how she looked. Oh, how long ago those days seemed now and all her youth, all her beauty and vivacity had gone with them. 'All right, I will.'

Alice began to smile but then, as Phoebe-Ann's face dropped, she frowned. 'What's the matter now?'

'I haven't got anything decent to wear.'

'Can't you borrow something from your Emily? I know she doesn't dress in the height of fashion but she's got some nice things. A bit plain, like, but better than you can afford,' Ginny said.

That hurt Phoebe-Ann so much that she felt the tears prick her eyes. Ginny was only stating the truth, she thought; she shouldn't be so sensitive. But everything she had was worn and washed out. She hadn't had anything new for months. She couldn't afford to buy anything so she'd have to ask Emily for a loan of something. What would she do without Emily, she thought. Whenever there was a crisis in her life Emily had been there, helping, comforting, supporting. No-one could have a better sister. She wished Albert would go back to Wales and give Emily some freedom and happiness with Edwin.

She called to see her sister on the way home.

'Have you got time for a cup of tea and a scone?' Emily asked.

'Just a quick one. If I don't get back soon he'll start ranting and raving.'

'He's no better then?' Emily asked as she pushed the kettle on the hob and began to butter a fresh scone. Albert sat reading the *Journal of Commerce* to see what ships were due in and if there would be work in the offing. Many ships were lying idle now for times were getting harder. Rhys had written telling him of the miners' strike and the fact that he was looking for alternative work, so things were just as bad back home.

'No, although sometimes I can't help but feel sorry for him. That's until he starts yelling at me, telling me it's all my fault.'

'Take no notice of him. He's bound to feel like that. Tell him he's lucky that you do look after him, his ma wouldn't. That should shut him up.'

'I do but it doesn't stop him. In fact it seems to make matters worse.'

'How are the two old ladies?'

Phoebe-Ann smiled tiredly. 'Both fine. I love working there, Em, it's so clean and so quiet.'

'I know, they're dear souls.'

'Miss Nesta often gives me things to take home and so does Cook and last week Miss Millicent slipped me a half crown and told me to get something for myself. She thought I needed cheering up. If only I could stay with them, live in.' She sighed. 'I've come to ask you a favour. Every time I come here I seem to be asking for something.'

'Isn't that what sisters are for? What is it?'

'Alice has persuaded me to go out with her and Ginny each Sunday night.'

'It will do you good and surely he can't object to a few hours.'

'Alice said we'll take turns in paying so I will have time to save up a few coppers each week, but I've nothing to wear and I can't afford to buy anything. Most of my stuff I get from old Leiberman's or down Paddy's Market.'

Emily felt so sorry for her. Reduced to buying second-hand clothes from the pawnbroker and Paddy's Market. 'Of course you can. Go up to my room and pick something, anything.'

'You really don't mind then?'

'Oh, for heaven's sake, Fee, what is there to "mind" about?'

When she'd gone upstairs Albert looked at Emily. 'I hope she appreciates you.'

'I wish I could help her more.'

'I could give you a few bob if it would help.'

She smiled at him. 'I could make her a dress. She doesn't have time to sew. Material doesn't cost that much. I hate to see her reduced to buying second-hand clothes. Mam would go mad. I know we often had second-hand and even third-hand stuff when we were kids and there was only Mam's wages to keep us all, but we're both women now.'

'Your mam couldn't have seen how things would turn out, Emily.'

'No, she couldn't. Hush, here's Phoebe-Ann.'

When Phoebe-Ann walked into the kitchen with Emily's burgundy-coloured two-piece and pale pink blouse wrapped carefully in brown paper, Jake demanded to know where she'd been.

'I've been sitting here by myself for hours. I'm hungry and thirsty but you wouldn't care about things like that!'

She ignored his complaints and began to spread some dripping on a slice of bread she'd cut from the loaf.

'I'm sick of bloody dripping, isn't there anything else?'

'No, and you're lucky to get this. My wages aren't on elastic!'

'It's all right for you, you eat up there in Princes Avenue, you don't eat this muck.' He knocked her hand away and the plate and the bread fell on the floor.

Phoebe-Ann gritted her teeth and picked it up. 'You can eat it, muck and all now, because there's nothing else.' She slammed the plate down on the low table beside him.

He ignored her words. 'What's in the parcel?'

'Something our Emily lent me.' She poured the boiling water on to the tea leaves, leaves that had already been used once.

'What for?'

Phoebe-Ann placed her hands on her hips as though girding her loins for a battle. 'Because I haven't got anything decent to go out in, that's why! Because I spend all my money keeping you!'

He glared up at her. He'd give anything just to get out of this chair for a few seconds. Then he'd show her she couldn't speak to him like this. All the affection he'd had for her had turned to festering hatred. 'I said what for?'

'Because in future I'm going out with Alice and Ginny on a Sunday night, for a few hours away from you and this . . . this hovel!'

'If you've got money to waste then you can give me better food!' he yelled.

'I haven't got money to waste. It will take me two weeks to save up a few pence. Scrimping and saving, doing without anything to eat myself. I deserve to go out. To get away from you once a week!'

'And what do I deserve? I deserve better than you screaming at me, starving me, leaving me alone all day!'

'I come home twice in the day to see to you.'

'It's your duty. It's your fault I'm in this chair!'

Phoebe-Ann had had enough. 'It's your own bloody fault and I'm sick of listening to you whining. I hate you! I bloody hate you, Jake Malone! You should be grateful for what I do for you. I've a good mind to take you around to your ma and leave you there, the way she dumped you on me. And if I want to go out and spend the money I work for, I will! I want some enjoyment and I'm going to have it!'

'You whore! That's what you are, a whore! You can't get anything from me so you'll go out and find yourself a man – any man! Goin' out with Alice an' Ginny!' He laughed derisively. 'You bloody liar! I hope you get the pox, you whoring bitch!' he yelled at her, the veins at his temples throbbing with the force of his anger.

Phoebe-Ann snatched the plate he was holding and

threw it with as much force as she could muster against the range, where it shattered into dozens of pieces. 'There! Now you can starve, Jake Malone! And, what's more, you can sit in your own filth all night, I'm going to bed!'

'You bitch! You bloody little bitch!' he was almost sobbing with rage. 'I'll make you pay for all this! One day I'll make you pay!'

She sat down on the edge of the bed and undid the parcel with hands that shook. She could kill him, she could. She'd let him stew for the night. Usually she washed him and changed him and got him on to the low camp bed beside her bed, but tonight he could sit there all night. That would teach him to be so evil-minded. How dare he say such things to her when she'd given up everything for him?

As she hung up Emily's clothes, the tears spilled down her cheeks. What had she become? She'd sunk as low as him. Swearing and screaming, like his ma. No, she'd never sink as low as Ma Malone, never. She had to try to maintain some dignity, some self-respect, but it was so hard being tied to a man like him. Tied and trapped for the rest of her life. She leaned her head against the wardrobe door. She was twenty-one years old and her life was over. What would Mam have said, what would Lily have advised her to do? Make the best of it and not sink to his level, that's what Mam would have said. But there wasn't anything to make the best of.

She thought of Rhys and a fresh wave of sobbing overtook her. She should have married him, he would have been good to her, he still loved her. He'd told her that before he'd gone away. If only she could leave Liverpool, leave Jake and run away to Rhys. It was impossible and that made it all the more bitter a pill to swallow. She was still married and both Rhys and his mother were strongly religious people.

She wiped her eyes and drew the curtains and began to get undressed. In future, she'd ignore all his taunts, all his complaints, all his swearing. She'd be silent and dignified and each Sunday she'd get herself dressed up and have a few hours of freedom. Perhaps that, in a small way, would help to compensate for being trapped in this sham of a marriage. But tonight he could sit in the kitchen, that would teach him to call her a whore.

Chapter Twenty-two

Jake became increasingly bitter and harder to live with as the months passed, but Phoebe-Ann argued and fought tenaciously to keep those few, precious hours on a Sunday evening. She swore to Alice and Emily that without them she would go completely mad. But, as the weeks turned into months, those few precious hours of freedom only served to increase her resentment. She envied both Alice and Ginny: their jobs, their money, the time they had to themselves, unburdened and carefree, and the fact that they were always more smartly dressed than she was. Emily was generous with her clothes and had made her two dresses and a skirt but the resentment built up week by week and there were nights when she lay staring at the ceiling wishing she could just leave Liverpool, go anywhere as long as she was far away from Jake Malone and Liffy Street.

Emily felt sorry for her but her constant complaints were beginning to irritate.

'There isn't much more I can do for her,' she said to Edwin.

'She shouldn't expect you to. You've already done more than most sisters would do. And, when it comes down to it, Em, if it hadn't been for her we would have been married long ago. It started years ago. I know she meant no harm, that she was just trying to help James Mercer, but just lately I seem to keep having the same thoughts. She's always been a burden to you, Em, and she probably always will be.'

As Emily had had a particularly trying day, she silently agreed with him instead of defending Phoebe-Ann as she usually did.

Phoebe-Ann had had a trying day, too. She'd got up with a headache, Miss Millicent had been awkward over the household accounts which had reduced Miss Nesta to tears, and Cook was snappy because her rheumatism was causing her a lot of pain. When she'd gone home to give Jake his lunch, he'd cursed and sworn at her from the minute she'd set foot in the door. It was only Monday and she had six whole days and nights before she could escape for a few hours and pretend she was single and free. She'd made him a cup of tea, some paste sandwiches and had slammed out again. When she'd finished work she'd walked home with a heavy heart. The day or the work wasn't over for her. Miss Millicent and Miss Nesta would sit down to an appetizing supper, set on a table covered with a crisp white damask cloth and laid with fine china. Then they'd sit in their comfortable, warm, clean drawing room and read or embroider, cocooned in peaceful silence, away from the harsh, noisy, dirty and distressing reality of life. If she'd been able to live-in, she would have shared that tranquillity and luxury but for her it was back to those depressing rooms, drudgery and *him*.

As she walked down the street she saw Mrs Elston from next door, standing on her doorstep, arms folded over her ample bosom. Phoebe-Ann gritted her teeth. She'd have to pass the Elston house so there was no way of avoiding the woman. 'Cold and damp again, Mrs Elston,' she said tiredly.

Mrs Elston jerked her head in the direction of

Phoebe-Ann's house. 'Comes ter somethin' when I've got to stand on me doorstep in this weather to get a bit of peace an' quiet.'

'What do you mean? What's been going on?' Sometimes when Jake yelled at her, Mrs Elston would hammer on the adjoining wall with the brush, so she assumed he'd been making a lot of noise. Probably cursing and swearing to himself.

'Sounds like there's hundreds of them in there, havin' a do, instead of just five.'

'Who's in there with him?' Phoebe-Ann felt the stirrings of annoyance followed by trepidation.

'The whole tribe of them. His flamin' brothers, that's who!'

Phoebe-Ann's eyes narrowed. Ever since the day she'd pushed him up Florist Street, none of the Malones had ever come to see him. 'Oh, they are, are they! Well, they can just clear off. They've never been near since she threw him out, so they needn't think they can start now! I've got enough to put up with with him!'

Mrs Elston settled herself more comfortably against the door post. This looked very promising indeed. She'd wait until Phoebe-Ann Malone had gone in, then she'd give Madge Hamilton a knock. Aye, it promised to be a real good slanging match. First bit of excitement in the street for months.

By the time Phoebe-Ann stalked into her living room her cheeks were flushed and her eyes glittered dangerously. She glared around at them all. They seemed to dominate the room and Jake was sitting in the middle, looking as though he'd backed the winner in the Grand National.

'Just what the hell are you all doing here?' she snapped.

'I told yer she'd 'ave a cob on, didn't I?' Franny said, trying to hide the bottle he was holding.

'Can't we come and see our brother now, seeing as it's his birthday an' you never bring him round to see us?' Seamus remarked sarcastically.

She'd forgotten it was his birthday. 'If you want to see him, and it's taken you all long enough to remember that you've got a brother, then one of you can push him back to Mona Street. Maybe his loving mother would like to see him as well, as it's his birthday.'

'Don't you start on me ma. She's gettin' on now an' he's your responsibility,' Peader answered.

Phoebe-Ann laughed cuttingly. 'Getting on! It doesn't stop her from getting herself down to the Grecian every night, does it? Nor did it stop her getting thrown out last week. Drunk and disorderly, so I heard!'

'What me ma does is her business,' Jake muttered. 'You never remembered me birthday.'

Phoebe-Ann laughed again. 'And she did? So, where's the card and the present then? Or have you already drunk it?'

'She always was a bloody misery; didn't even get a bevvy in when they got engaged,' Vinny muttered.

'You keep your mouth shut in my house, Vinny Malone!' She could see that she was going to have trouble getting rid of them and for a moment she was afraid, remembering that she had neither Jimmy nor Jack to support her now. She glared at them all and then, turning, she went into the bedroom and slammed the door.

As she took off her uniform and put on her old, faded dress and equally faded pinafore, she could hear them muttering, punctuated by bursts of coarse

349

laughter. How she hated them all and how dare they think they could invade her home whenever they felt like it, birthday or no birthday. But how could she stop them? And they'd all been drinking. Wasn't Jake hard enough to cope with without a drink inside him? Nor was he used to it now. There was no money for drink.

She wondered should she stay in the bedroom until they'd gone, but then anger flared. Why the hell should she? It was her home, she worked to pay the rent, to keep food on the table and a fire in the range. She went without even what in the past she would have considered the bare necessities to keep a roof over their heads. She was cold, hungry and thirsty. No, she wasn't going to stay skulking in the bedroom waiting for them to leave. If needs be she'd have to use desperate measures to get them out. She marched purposefully back into the other room.

'Right. You've seen him, you've all had a good moan about me, so now you can clear off home or to the ale-house, I don't care which. I've been working all day to keep him and I've got things to do.'

'We'll go when we're ready,' Seamus stated ominously.

'Aye, they'll go when I say so,' Jake added, emboldened by their presence. They'd put her in her place.

Phoebe-Ann stared malevolently at Jake. Once she wouldn't have known what to do next but now things were different. She'd put up with so much, suffered so much that all the gentleness in her nature had been buried under the brittle shell that had formed around her heart. 'I'm going to give you one last chance to tell them to go, Jake Malone.'

'Sod off!'

'Right, you asked for it! Don't say I didn't warn you. Tell them to get out and not come back – ever!' She folded her arms and waited for the answer she knew wouldn't come.

'They can come here any time they want to! You leave me all bloody day with nothing to do but stare at the effin walls and talk to meself!'

She didn't reply. Instead she grabbed the chipped enamel basin and began to fill it from the sink in the corner of the room. From the shelf that was fixed above the sink she took a large bar of carbolic soap and a pile of clean rags.

'What's that for?' Franny asked, eyeing the bowl of water.

She studiously ignored the look of horror on Jake's face. 'To wash his dirty arse, unless you want to do it? He's been sitting here since lunch time so he's bound to be in a nice mess. Here!' She shoved a piece of old towelling towards Franny, who shrank back.

'Are you all so bloody squeamish that you can't take the sight of the mess?' She dragged the old piece of blanket from across Jake's knees; she was past caring how he felt. She pushed his hands away and tried to unbutton the old trousers he wore, faded almost to white by the constant washing and bleaching. Her eyes bored into Jake. 'Tell them to get out now or so help me I'll not see to you for a week!' she hissed.

'That's enough. Come on, we're going. You're not going to humiliate him like this, you hard-hearted bitch!' Seamus snarled.

Phoebe-Ann straightened up. 'Get out! Go on, get out of my house and if any of you set foot in here again then I'll have the law on you!'

'You ugly, evil, whore! I should have killed you! I should 'ave bloody killed you when I had the chance!'

351

Jake screamed at her, beside himself with shame and hatred.

Phoebe-Ann turned back to him. 'Pity you didn't. It would have been worth it, knowing you'd swing at the end of a rope and then you'd burn in hell for ever!'

'You'd better watch yourself, girl. We'll not forget this,' Seamus growled from the doorway.

Phoebe-Ann picked up the bowl and threw the contents at him. He cursed as the water drenched him and then he stormed out.

She didn't even bother to clean up the mess, she just slammed into the bedroom and threw herself on the bed. Oh, God! What had happened to her? She'd just acted like Ma Malone. Screaming and swearing and threatening to humiliate Jake like that. Where had all her decency, her sensitivity gone? She knew the answer. When she had started to sink into the mire, becoming like them. She was lowering herself to their level, the gutter, but how had she let herself become so degraded? Again she knew the answer. It had all begun the day she had taken up with Jake Malone. When she'd started lying and deceiving everyone, herself included. When she'd married him despite everyone's attempts to stop her. And her mam had paid such a high price for her determination to try to spare her the utter misery she now endured.

'Oh, Mam! Mam, I'm sorry! What's going to become of me, Mam? How can I go on like this?' she sobbed into the pillow.

Albert saw them walking back up Myrtle Street and he'd wondered where they'd been. He ignored the taunts and jeers but kept his eyes ahead and flicked the reins to make the horse hurry on. For a second he wondered savagely why the horse couldn't have bolted now and trampled the whole tribe of them beneath its hooves. It would have been good riddance. Then he sank back into the apathy that plagued his waking hours.

He was halfway up Lonsdale Street, his chin on his chest, deep in melancholy thought, so he didn't notice Franny Malone lurking on the corner of Bloom Street. Franny grinned to himself. They were all the same that lot, looking down their noses at everyone. No wonder she was such a bitch, that Phoebe-Ann. He'd bring them down a peg or two. At least he'd bring the old feller down. His fingers closed over the ball bearings in his pocket. He always carried them in case a game of penny and two farthings was in the offing. As the horse drew level, he threw them into the road and turned and ran quickly off down Bloom Street.

The animal slipped twice, reared up, plunged down and slipped again, falling heavily on its side with a high-pitched scream of pain. Albert, taken completely by surprise, was flung from the driving seat of the cart and landed on the cobbles. He cried out as the pain shot through his right leg.

The neighbours came running from their houses and Florrie Harper went for Emily.

'What happened? Did anyone see what happened?' Emily cried, bending over Albert whose face was white.

'It was no bloody accident!' Bill Withington said grimly, holding up a ball bearing. 'Who ever did it needs a dozen strokes of the cat.'

'Will someone help me to get him inside?' Emily begged.

Two men stepped forward. 'Better get an ambulance, don't think we should really move him,' one advised.

Emily looked up imploringly. 'Then will someone get one for God's sake!'

Bill Withington hurried off towards the emergency phone at the bottom of the street and Florrie came out with a grey blanket.

'Put this around him, love, he's shakin'. By, but the shock could kill him. The wicked sod should swing! 'Ere, Fred Murray, go and get someone to put the poor 'orse out of its misery. Don't stand there gawpin', shift yerself!'

Someone had gone for Edwin and he arrived at the same time as the ambulance, the vet and the police. The whole street was out and he had to push his way through the crowd.

'How is he, Em?'

'Oh, thank God, you're here! I think he's broken his leg and I don't know what else.' She was kneeling on the cobbles with Albert's head in her lap.

'The ambulance is here and . . .' His words were cut off by the single crack of a pistol shot as the vet put the writhing animal out of its pain.

Emily shuddered and he put his arm around her.

They got Albert into the ambulance and both Emily and Edwin followed.

'Can I take some particulars, miss, please?' The policeman stood beside Emily.

'What?'

'Can't you leave it until later? You can see how upset she is,' Edwin said curtly.

'I'll give yer some!' Bill Withington shouted.

The constable turned, getting out his notebook.

'Someone put ball bearings in the road. It was deliberate and I think I saw one of the Malones legging it down Bloom Street.'

'Oh, aye, which one?'

354

'Couldn't be sure. It might have been the youngest, Franny, or Vinny.'

'Franny is the youngest,' Florrie Harper interrupted.

'You couldn't be absolutely certain about it?' the policeman pressed.

'Not absolutely but it was one of them.'

The constable closed his notebook.

'Well, aren't yer goin' round there to arrest him? Mr Davies could 'ave been killed,' Florrie demanded.

'No proof.'

'I said I saw him!'

'But you can't be absolutely sure. That's no use, it wouldn't stand up in court. I'll go round and see that lot, though; bloody pests the whole tribe of them. I'll come back later to get a statement, miss,' he said to Emily.

'Neither use nor flamin' ornament!' Florrie muttered, glaring at the retreating back of the constable.

Albert was kept in overnight to be sure he wasn't concussed. His leg had been set and he'd been given something for the pain which made him drowsy.

'Can we take him home tomorrow?' Emily asked the sister.

'Come tomorrow morning. I think he'll be fine. It's the shock though at his age.'

'He's not that old. He looks it but he's not.'

The sister smiled. 'Then he should get over it.'

As they left the hospital and walked down Pembroke Place Emily shook her head sadly. 'What harm had he ever done anyone? Why do a terrible thing like that?'

'If it was one of the Malones then they don't need reasons. They're just bad through and through.

355

Rotten to the core, all of them. Inflicting pain and suffering on an old man and a poor dumb animal. Someone should horsewhip them!'

'He didn't need this. He's never been right since Mam died and now . . .' She turned anxious eyes to Edwin. 'Now I'm afraid of what this will do to him.'

'He's strong, Em. In body, I mean, so let's hope everything will turn out right. Let's get you home, you've had a shock yourself.'

'Do you think I should call in and see our Phoebe-Ann? To see if she knows anything about this, why they did it.'

'No. She's got enough to cope with and besides they've never set foot in Liffy Street to see him, so it can't have anything to do with him or Phoebe-Ann.'

Emily nodded. What he said was the truth. She felt so weary. Poor Albert, why did he have such rotten luck? He'd never hurt anyone.

Chapter Twenty-three

Albert recovered slowly and Emily was worried about him. He just seemed to have given up, she told Edwin. At least he had been doing a bit of work and he had been more cheery, but the accident had pushed him back to where he'd been just after Lily had died.

'Why don't you write to Rhys? Maybe if he came to see him he might be able to do something? I know what you're thinking, Emily. That I just want Rhys to take him back to Wales and off your hands, but that's only a part of it. You're worrying about him and waiting on him hand and foot and it's wearing you out. What are you going to do for money?'

'We've been managing on what he had saved up, that and what you've given me. You don't have to leave me an allotment you know.'

'I'd sooner leave you something. At least then I know you aren't going short.' What he didn't say was that by leaving her the 'allotted' amount it would ensure that, if he was lost at sea, she would have a small pension. She'd wanted to use the money Richard Mercer had invested for her but he wouldn't hear of it. 'With Christmas nearly on us, I don't want you having to scrimp and save. But think about writing to Rhys, will you?'

She'd nodded, but as she watched Albert become more withdrawn her anxiety for him made her sit down and pen the letter to Rhys.

*   *   *

The following week he arrived and came striding up Lonsdale Street.

'Rhys Pritchard! Why didn't you let me know you would be here so soon?' she cried as she opened the door to him.

'I wanted to surprise you.'

'Come on in, don't be standing on the step. You look very well, quite prosperous in fact.' She smiled, noting the good quality cloth of his suit and topcoat.

'I touched lucky. I'm in business now. Didn't Albert tell you?'

'I think he mentioned something about you changing your job, but that was all. What sort of business?'

'Undertaking.'

She looked at him with astonishment. 'Never! How did you get into that? Isn't it . . . morbid?'

'Old Mr Hughes died and his brother, Mr Dylan Hughes, wanted an assistant. They had no family, see. Mam was speaking to him after chapel and she asked him would he be willing to train someone and he said it would depend. The long and short of it was that Mam talked him into training me. It's not morbid really; you learn to detach yourself from that side of it and you'd be surprised how interesting it is.' He laughed. 'No, I'm not going to give you a detailed account. At least I'll always have work. It's a service everyone needs in the end.'

'I suppose it is. Anyway, it's good to see someone getting on.'

'How is he?'

'Not good. He just doesn't seem interested in anything. I have a terrible time getting him to eat.'

'Let's see if I can cheer him up. I may even be able to talk him into coming back with me.'

She led him into the kitchen where Albert sat staring into the fire, a rug over his knees.

Rhys was shocked by his appearance. He would hardly have recognized him. He looked like an old, old man. His hair was nearly white and his face so lined and careworn that it made his heart bleed for him. 'What's all this I hear about you not wanting to eat, Albert Davies?'

Albert looked up and a smile spread over his face. 'Rhys! Rhys, lad, it's good to see you!'

'How are you?'

'It shook me up that fall, it really did. My leg is stiff and the doctor says I've got rheumatism. You're looking very well. Your mam wrote to me about you, but I can't remember what she said.'

Rhys grinned and proceeded to fill Albert in on the details of his new career, while Emily made some tea, smiling at them both. It was good to see Albert looking so bright and Rhys looking so well. Edwin had been right. Rhys's visit might well be the making of Albert. She knew she shouldn't think so, but she couldn't help but wish that Rhys could persuade Albert to go back. She wasn't being selfish, she told herself. She was sure that Albert would be happier with Megan, away from all the painful memories here, back in the place he'd grown up in, in a close community bound by a common language and culture. And now that Rhys appeared to be quite affluent, Albert would have a better lifestyle than she could afford.

Later that night when Albert had gone to bed, Rhys broached the subject of Phoebe-Ann. 'How is she, Emily? I want the truth.'

'The truth,' she repeated as she sat down opposite

him. 'The truth is hard, Rhys. She manages to get out on a Sunday evening for a few hours but the rest of the time she spends working, worrying and looking after him. How she copes I don't know. They hate each other but are tied to each other. He, because no-one else will look after him, his Ma stuck it for a while then she got fed up and dumped him on Phoebe-Ann – and she *is* his wife. "In sickness and in health",' she finished.

'How do they manage for money?'

'She works for Miss Millicent and Miss Nesta and I help out when I can, but that's not often these days. I really don't know how she makes ends meet. He refuses to go on the Parish and I can't say I really blame him. There are times when I feel sorry for him.'

'You feel sorry for him after what he did to her?'

'It must be awful to have to be washed and changed like a baby.'

Rhys didn't want to think of Phoebe-Ann having to do such menial and disgusting chores. He thought of her small, soft hands, her sweet curving mouth, her beautiful hazel eyes and her shining blonde hair. No, she shouldn't be tied to a monster like him and have to do everything for him. 'Do you think I could go and see her?'

'Wouldn't it be better if she came here?' She was thinking of Jake and of Phoebe-Ann. What effect would it have on them both? Rhys, tall, straight, handsome and well dressed, going to see those depressing rooms and what Phoebe-Ann had been reduced to.

'Will she come?'

'We can ask. I'll go tomorrow lunch time. She comes home to see to him twice a day.' She stood up.

'She's changed, Rhys. It was something she couldn't help. Not with the kind of life she has.'

'Is that a way of warning me, Emily?'

'Yes. Don't expect to see the girl you knew.'

He sat staring into the fire long after Emily had gone to bed. It was so ironic, he thought. Now he could offer her a good home, pretty clothes, security, but she was tied to Jake Malone. When Jake had been able to give her those things he had had to send most of his money home. He sighed, getting to his feet. Tomorrow he'd try and persuade Albert to go back and he'd see Phoebe-Ann, probably for the last time, and he'd have to hide his feelings and not betray by a look or a word that he'd noticed any change in her.

Albert proved to be stubborn. He thanked Rhys for his kindness and that of Megan. He knew they could give him a good home and he sometimes thought it would be good to go back, but then he'd think of Lily lying in Toxteth Park Cemetery and he couldn't leave her.

'But she'd understand, Albert. She would only want the best for you and she's not really there.'

'She'll always be there.'

'What I meant was that only her body is there, her soul is with God and she'll be watching over you. She'd be happy to see you at home amongst your own people. People who care about you, people you grew up with.'

'I just can't, Rhys. I can't explain it. But I can't leave Liverpool.'

'And what about Emily? It's time she and Edwin were married. They've waited long enough. She won't leave you, she cares about you too much. Edwin would get a place near Southampton, he wouldn't

361

have to waste two days of his leave travelling, but she won't hear of it.'

Tears sprang to Albert's eyes. She was a good girl, Emily. More loving that any natural daughter and he was so fond of her and that was another reason why he didn't want to go. But, as Rhys put it, he was being a selfish old man.

'Won't you even think about it?' Rhys pressed.

'I will. I'll think about it.'

Rhys smiled. 'Don't be too long about it. I've only got a couple of days before I have to go home.'

He didn't have any degree of success with Phoebe-Ann. She came the following night after supper and he was shocked by her appearance, nor could he hide that shock. Emily had warned him but he'd never expected to see her looking so old and downtrodden. Her hair was clipped back and it was lustreless and untidy. Her skin had the unhealthy pallor of malnutrition. The corners of her mouth drooped down and there was a tracery of lines at the corners of her eyes. Between her brows there was a deep, horizontal line caused by the constant frown she wore. Her clothes were drab and shabby and her hands were rough, red and workworn. His heart went out to her when she tried to smile. Emily had tactfully left them alone.

Phoebe-Ann stood twisting her wedding ring around nervously, trying to be cheerful, trying not to let him see how ashamed she was of her appearance.

'I don't need to ask how you are, Phoebe-Ann,' he said gently.

'Then I won't say I'm just great, Rhys. I'm not. I'm tired and weary and I'm so sick of being a drudge. She sat down by the fire and turned her head away from him so he couldn't see the incipient tears. 'I don't want to sound as though I'm whining either. It was all my own fault.'

He sat opposite her, longing to reach out and take her in his arms, to hold her, to say she would never have to worry again, that she would never have to spend her days and nights working. Instead he asked, 'Is there no-one who can give you a break?'

She laughed. It was a harsh, abrasive sound that made him cringe. 'Even his own mother refused to do what I have to do for him and, after I saw them all off, none of his brothers will come near again. There is no-one, Rhys. It's as simple as that.'

He reached out and took her hands. 'Oh, Phoebe-Ann what have they done to you? They've turned you into a bitter, worn-out woman. Where's the pretty, spirited laughing girl I knew?'

His words tore at her heart. 'She's dead, Rhys! She died the night he beat me up and you and Jimmy, Jack and Edwin went round to sort him out.' She withdrew her hands. 'It doesn't matter now.'

'It matters to me, Phoebe-Ann!'

'It shouldn't do, for there's nothing you can do. Nothing I can do either. Haven't you heard the saying, "Marry in haste, repent at leisure"?'

He felt so helpless. 'There must be some charity, some institution that could help.'

'There is. The Parish or the workhouse.'

'No, I didn't mean anything like that. He was a sailor, can't the Sailor's Society help?'

'Only if he had died at sea. I enquired. I have tried, Rhys. I've asked everyone I can think of and some Miss Millicent told me about, too. I don't qualify. But I get out for a few hours on a Sunday and our Emily's

363

good. I think if I didn't have her I'd have thrown myself in the river long before now.'

Again he reached for her hands, shocked. 'Promise me you'll never even think about that, Phoebe-Ann?'

'I can't promise you that, Rhys. You don't have to put up with it all and it would be so easy. A few short steps from the landing stage and the undertow is so strong that I'd be . . . gone in a few seconds.'

He caught her by her shoulders and pulled her to him. 'Stop it! Stop it, Phoebe-Ann!'

She began to cry softly, then as the sobs shook her he held her closer and stroked her hair.

Until she'd spoken the words she hadn't thought about it, but it would be easy. A few steps over the chain-link rail, a few seconds and she'd never have to go back to that house again. She'd never see him, hear him or smell him again. And she was so sick of the smell of him. The stench hit her every time she walked through the door and it symbolized just what her life had become: a stinking, rotting mess.

'Phoebe-Ann I'm not going back until you swear you will stop thinking like that. Even if it means I have to stay here for ever, I will.'

Her sobs quietened. She couldn't keep him here, it would only make her misery harder to bear, like having a jewel dangled under her nose – something so wonderful but something she could never have. She pulled away from him and wiped her tears away.

'I wouldn't do it. I was just thinking aloud.'

'Promise me?'

'I promise. Even a miserable life is better than no life at all and, besides, I'd be afraid I'd burn in hell if I did that.'

He was relieved. For a few brief moments he had been quite determined never to return home.

'I'd best be getting back. I said I wouldn't be long.'

'What did you tell him?'

'That I was coming over here, that's all.'

He wanted to give her all the money in his wallet but he felt that that would only humiliate her. Instead he mentally noted to leave it with Emily and he'd keep on sending her money for as long as she would need it. At least if some of the financial worries were lifted things might be better for her. And, he couldn't bear to see her dressed in cast-offs. He gently traced the outline of her cheek with his fingers. 'Oh, Phoebe-Ann . . . If only . . .'

'I know! I know!' she interrupted sharply, turning away from him and reaching for her coat. She wanted to scream and rage that life was so unfair, that she now loved him but it was too late. Too late. The words echoed in her head, mocking her.

'You're not going back until you've had something to eat.'

Phoebe-Ann turned at Emily's words and wondered how long her sister had been standing in the doorway, but Emily was bustling about, setting the table.

'I can't, Em.'

'Yes you can. Half an hour more won't hurt him. How long is it since you ate?'

Phoebe-Ann shrugged. 'Lunch time, I suppose.'

'You see, if I don't keep my eye on her . . .' Emily addressed herself to Rhys, trying to lighten the atmosphere. It was so charged with emotion that you could cut it, she thought.

'I'll walk you back. It's too late to be out alone,' Rhys offered.

It was on the tip of Phoebe-Ann's tongue to say, 'Who would be bothered with a hag like me?' but she stopped herself. She didn't want him to think she was looking for pity. She had to try to hang on to some dignity.

She made him leave her on the corner. She didn't want him to see the squalor she now lived in.

'Phoebe-Ann, you know that you only have to call and I'll come running. Whatever is the matter. You won't forget that, will you?'

'No, Rhys, how could I?'

He pulled the collar of her worn coat up around her ears. It was a tender gesture. 'Take care of yourself.'

She was so close to breaking down that she couldn't trust herself to speak, so she nodded and turned away and began to walk quickly up the street. She didn't look back. She couldn't. It would have been just too much to bear.

He watched her go and wondered if he would ever see her again. He shivered as a blast of the icy wind rushed around the corner. At least she'd promised him never to harm herself, and with that he would have to be content, but it was cold comfort. His heart felt like a lump of solid ice as he retraced his steps to Lonsdale Street.

He had been gone a week, Phoebe-Ann thought as she closed the door of the house in Princes Avenue behind her and prepared to make her way home. In a few days' time it would be Christmas but she had nothing to look forward to. She wouldn't join the crowds in Church Street or Bold Street or London Road, doing their shopping, buying gifts for their loved ones.

She had neither the money nor the inclination. Nor would she join the throng on Christmas Eve when the Christmas tree would be erected in Church Street and the Salvation Army would play carols. There would be no goose, no plum pudding or bunloaf as there had been when her mam had been alive. Now there was no Mam, no Jack or Jimmy. Just Jake. She'd probably go to see Emily in the afternoon but Emily was so happy that it almost made her cry to see her. Albert had promised Rhys that after the holiday he would go back, and early in the New Year Emily was finally going to get married.

Then there would be no Albert and no Emily. Edwin was already talking about looking for a place in Southampton. She dreaded even to think about what her life would be like without Emily living so near at hand. She'd be alone. Totally alone. No, she wasn't looking forward to Christmas.

She walked up Liffy Street with her head bent against the wind that held a promise of sleet or snow. When she reached the junction of Dove Street and Liffy Street she almost collided with someone and, looking up, she saw a swaying Vinny Malone.

'Where have you been?' she snapped.

'What's it got to do with you?' He peered at her through bloodshot eyes and the smell of the liquor on his breath made her wrinkle her nose.

'I thought I told you never to set foot in my house again!'

'Miserable old cow,' he muttered as he staggered off.

Pig! That's what he was, that's what they all were.

As she walked into the living room she smelled the liquor. So, he had been here. She took off her coat and turned to Jake. 'I see that drunken sot of a brother of yours has been here while my back was turned.'

'It's supposed to be bloody Christmas an' I'll get nothin' from you!'

She stared at him hard. His eyes were glazed and a trickle of saliva ran down his chin. She felt sick. He was drunk. If he had been able to get on his feet he would be staggering, like Vinny Malone. 'You're drunk!' she screamed at him. A tide of anger, frustration and hatred surged through her.

'What if I am?'

So, Vinny Malone thought he could come round here and make her life even harder, did he? This was the end. She'd taken all she could take. She began to snatch up all the bits of clothing and the old towels and rags.

'What are yer doin' now?'

'Just what your ma did! I've had enough of you, Jake Malone. She can have you back and if she won't let you in then you can stay in the street until you freeze to death. I don't care! I've had enough!'

She reached out for the handle of the wheelchair but he lashed out, catching her across the side of her face. She screamed and struck back at him. He tried to fend off the blows with his arms but Phoebe-Ann's fury had given her strength. He roared with pain as her fingers twisted around his hair and with what strength he had in his upper body he grappled with her, dragging himself half out of the chair. She released the grip on his hair and pushed him away and he fell out of the chair and backwards against the range.

She backed away from him, her breath coming in short gasps. It would take all the strength she had left to get him back in the chair but she'd do it. She'd meant what she said: Ma Malone could look after him from now on. She began to pull and heave at him. 'Damn you, Jake Malone!' she grunted. Then she realized that his eyes were closed and that he was heavier than usual. She let his weight go and he fell back, his arms limp, his wasted legs tucked under him. He'd passed out! Now what was she going to do? She felt like bursting into tears. She would just have to try again. She bent over him and then gave a cry of horror. He wasn't breathing! He was dead and she'd killed him! Panic took hold of her. She backed away from him and, wrenching open the door, ran out into the night without either coat or hat.

Chapter Twenty-four

Emily and Edwin had been sitting making paper chains to decorate the Christmas tree that Edwin proposed to buy on Christmas Eve, after they'd done the last minute shopping in St John's Market. There was a good fire and Albert was dozing as they talked about the future.

'Do you think you'll like it, Em? It will be a strange town.'

'I suppose I'll get used to it and I'll have you home for two extra days. No more spending all those hours on the train. I wrote to Jack and Jimmy today. I suppose by the time they get it we'll be married or very nearly.'

'The mail doesn't take that long. The *Maury* carries the mail and she only takes five days, less most times, and the *Berengaria* and *Aquitania* are just as fast. They'll have time to write back.'

'I hadn't thought about it being so quick.' She laughed. 'I know what our Jack will say: "About time too".'

'They're doing very well out there. They work damned hard and soon they'll have a nice little business. A proper builder's yard too. I never thought I'd see the day when Jack and Jimmy Parkinson would be gaffers. Last time I was around there they'd just taken on their first bricklayer.'

'They would have to. Neither of them know the first thing about it. I'd hate to see a house they built.'

370

Edwin laughed. 'The house that Jack built! It just shows what can be done with a bit of cash to start with. Jimmy says he's glad now they waited and saved. A bit of cash, a bit of gumption and a bit of enterprise. They'd never have thought of going into business here.'

'I thought it was just selling building materials.'

'It was, to start with, but when they got talking to the old man whose yard it was and when he confessed he couldn't lay one brick on top of another, or knew what to do with pipes or electric cables, it made them think. Soon be rolling in dollars the pair of them, I'll bet.'

'Then it was a good move.'

'It's the land of opportunity for some. Sometimes, I wonder . . . '

'What?'

'Oh, nothing really.'

'Out with it!' She jabbed him playfully in the ribs.

'It had crossed my mind to give it a try, emigrate.'

'Oh.'

'Is that all you can say?'

'What would you do? I can't see that there would be much call for your skills in the building trade.'

He laughed. 'No, it was just a passing thought.'

'I know you too well, Edwin Leeson. It was more than that.'

'Well, I've seen what it's like over there, what there is to offer.'

She sighed. 'How could I ever go and leave our Phoebe-Ann? God knows she's got little enough in life, but for me to go three thousand miles away!'

'You see, it was a passing thought. We couldn't do that to her. Southampton will be far enough.'

'I asked her to come for her Christmas dinner but

371

she won't. She said she'll come over for an hour in the afternoon.'

'Fine Christmas she'll have with him.'

They both fell silent, each engrossed in their own thoughts, until the loud hammering on the front door made Emily jump up. 'Who on earth can that be?'

Phoebe-Ann fell into her arms as she opened the door.

'You're half frozen. Where's your coat? What's happened?'

Phoebe-Ann was shaking and her teeth were chattering with cold and fear. 'I . . . he . . .'

'Calm down! Calm down and tell me what's wrong?' Emily had taken the rug from Albert's chair and had wrapped it around her sister's shoulders.

Phoebe-Ann tried again. 'He . . . he's dead.'

Emily's eyes widened with disbelief. 'Are you sure?'

'Yes! Yes! I killed him! I killed him!' Phoebe-Ann lapsed into hysterical sobbing.

'I'd better go and see.' Emily turned towards the door but Edwin stopped her.

'Wait! Wait a minute, Em, until we get to the bottom of this. Phoebe-Ann, what happened? Tell us slowly. Em, get her a drop of brandy. She's frozen and she's obviously had a terrible shock.'

Haltingly, between sips of brandy, Phoebe-Ann told them and when she'd finished Emily looked at Edwin pleadingly, not knowing what to do.

'We've got to think quickly. You're sure he's dead, Phoebe-Ann?'

'Yes.' Her voice was hoarse.

'It could have been an accident.'

'No! No! I hated him so much . . .'

Emily looked down at her sister. Phoebe-Ann was so upset she didn't know what she was saying. It *must*

372

have been an accident, but she still couldn't let Phoebe-Ann go through the experience of having to face a trial and a jury. 'How long had you been in?'

'I don't know.'

'Think! Think, Phoebe-Ann! It's important.'

'A few minutes, that's all. He . . . I saw Vinny Malone on the corner of Dove Street.'

'And he'd given Jake the drink?'

Phoebe-Ann nodded.

'Phoebe-Ann, you've got to be brave now.' A plan was forming in her mind. 'You've got to pull yourself together and go and see Ma Malone.'

'No! No!' Phoebe-Ann cried, while Edwin looked at Emily as though she'd lost her mind.

'What for, Em?'

'She's got to go and tell them that he's . . . he's dead and that it is Vinny's fault. He got him drunk and left him alone. He fell out of the chair and hit his head and you found him like that. You've got to do it, Phoebe-Ann! No-one else can!'

Phoebe-Ann looked at her blankly. She didn't understand what Emily was saying. Didn't she understand that it was she who'd killed him? Why was she saying it was Vinny Malone?

'Don't you see, Edwin, it probably was an accident but if she has to go to court, before a jury . . .'

Suddenly, Phoebe-Ann saw that Emily was trying to protect her. She gave a cry and started to sob.

'Stop it! Stop it, Phoebe-Ann! You've *got* to do this and you've got to do it now, before anyone else finds him!' Emily gripped her sister's shoulders and pulled her to her feet. 'As soon as you've been and told them, come straight back here and we'll all go to the police station.'

'Phoebe-Ann, if we could go with you we would,

but it's got to look as though you've run straight out without even putting on your coat,' Edwin urged.

Phoebe-Ann was feeling a bit calmer. Everything was taking on the semblance of a dream. 'I'll go.'

Emily clung to Edwin as she watched Phoebe-Ann leave the house and break into a run. 'Oh, I hope it works! She couldn't stand going to court, not on top of everything else. She would condemn herself out of hand by saying how much she hated him. It would just break her.'

'Let's hope she doesn't have to go to court. That was quick thinking, Emily.'

She sagged wearily against him. ' "Needs must when the devil drives" Mam always used to say.'

Phoebe-Ann had to stop to get her breath when she reached the corner of Mona Street. She *had* to do this, Emily said so. She had no choice. It was either lie or . . . The alternative was too terrible to think about. She stumbled on and beat on the door with both her fists. A front door opened a little way down the street and as she continued her hammering a few more were opened. Eventually Ma Malone opened the door.

'What do yez want 'ere? Clear off!'

'He's dead! Jake is dead and your Vinny killed him!' she screamed. Oh, it was so easy to scream she thought.

The door was flung open. 'Yer lyin'! Yer lyin'!'

'I'm not! Just you come and see. I'd just got in, I passed Vinny on the street, drunk, and he'd got Jake drunk and he'd fallen out of his chair and banged his head on the range! He's dead! He's dead and you killed him, Vinny Malone!' She was almost hysterical with fear and shock. 'I'm going for the police!' And before either Ma Malone or Vinny or Seamus, who had crowded into the lobby, could say anything she turned and ran.

The minute she turned the corner, Emily shrugged on her coat and Edwin did the same.

'Get that rug, she must be frozen stiff by now.'

Edwin picked up the rug and, as Phoebe-Ann leaned against the doorpost, he put it around her shoulders.

She was in such a state that no-one doubted her story. The desk sergeant looked grim, took some particulars, disappeared and returned with a detective.

He looked closely at Emily. 'Don't I know you?'

Emily stared at him puzzled. 'No.'

'Wait now, I never forget a face, it's part of the job. Princes Avenue? All that betting nonsense with Miss what's 'er name?'

Emily nodded. 'Miss Nesta Barlow,' she supplied, wishing he would stop looking at her and get on with things. He was unnerving her.

'Right. Now, what's all this about? Who's supposed to be dead?'

Phoebe-Ann was crying, her head on Emily's shoulder and it was Edwin and Emily who answered all the questions.

'It's a bit of a mess, isn't it?' he said, not unkindly, when Emily finished speaking. 'Don't worry, we'll get it all sorted. Bit more serious than the last time, miss, however . . .' He didn't finish, for the double doors were thrown open and all the Malones crowded in with Ma in their midst.

There was pandemonium, with Emily shouting that it was all Vinny's fault and look at the state of her poor sister. She clutched the arm of the

375

detective, as if seeking assurance and protection.

Vinny was denying everything, Peader was swearing at him and Ma wailed like a banshee and called on all the saints in heaven to witness her loss and her grief.

'For God's sake, shut up the bloody lot of you!' the desk sergeant bellowed and the shouting died down.

'Right. You lot over there against the wall and the rest of you,' he nodded towards Emily, Edwin and Phoebe-Ann, 'sit there.' He pointed to a long wooden bench. 'Stop that bloody noise, woman!' he yelled at Ma Malone who stopped wailing and glared at Phoebe-Ann who was too distraught to notice.

'Now, I'm going to take Mrs Malone here into the interview room until my lad gets back to inform me whether this Jake Malone is really dead.'

Franny moved towards the door.

'You, stay put or I'll throw the lot of you in the cells, coming in here and turning the place into a circus! I know you lot of old. You'll stay where I can see what you're up to and if he is dead, then we'll be having a few words with you, Vinny Malone.'

Emily helped Phoebe-Ann to her feet and followed the detective through a door on their left. Edwin noticed that Vinny had gone very pale and that Ma's venomous looks had been transferred to him.

They sat in the small room and a policeman came through, bringing three cups of tea.

'Has the other constable come back yet?' Edwin asked.

'Aye, he's just come in. They'll be in to see you in a few minutes. Drink that up, love, you've had a nasty shock,' he added, looking at Phoebe-Ann.

'What about them?' Edwin jerked his head in the direction of the door.

'All looking very sheepish, except the old one. Not even a tear in spite of all that bloody wailin'. Tough as old boots.'

There was no more noise coming from the bridewell waiting room and, after a little while, the detective appeared and sat down.

'Now then, Mrs Malone, tell me what happened, in your own words and in your own good time. There's no need to rush or get even more upset.'

Haltingly and between stifled sobs, Phoebe-Ann told him of her encounter with Vinny Malone, of going in, taking off her coat and then finding Jake.

Emily held her breath, praying that God would forgive herself and her sister for the terrible lies. But she just couldn't have seen Phoebe-Ann broken. She could never have stood an interrogation.

'That's all for now. Get her home and get her to bed and I think I'd get the doctor to give her something to make her sleep. We will probably have to speak to her again, but not tonight.'

'What will happen now?' Emily asked as she helped Phoebe-Ann to her feet.

'We'll see what meladdo has to say for himself but it looks as though it was an accident. There will have to be a post-mortem and an inquest, but I wouldn't worry her with all that now.'

There was no sign of any of the Malones as they left but none of them gave it much thought, they were all too relieved and too drained.

Edwin left them at the top of Lonsdale Street and went for Dr Whelan.

Albert had the kettle boiling and a hot brick was wrapped in flannel. 'I've made up the bed for her.'

'Thank you. What an ordeal.'

'You should have let me come with you.'

Emily smiled at him. 'It was like Fred Karno's circus in there. All the Malones turned up. It's better that you stayed here.'

She eased Phoebe-Ann down in the chair beside the fire.

'Did they . . . ?'

'Believe her? Yes. I keep trying to tell myself that it was the only thing we could do. It *was* an accident but I just didn't want there to be any doubt about it. She couldn't have stood it.'

Albert poured out three cups of very strong tea and added a drop of brandy to each. 'What else did they say?'

'They took a statement and they might have to talk to her again. They were going to talk to Vinny Malone but they said it looked as though it was an accident. There will have to be a post-mortem and an inquest.'

Albert looked relieved. 'I know it's a terrible thing to say, at this moment, but it really is a blessing in disguise, Emily.'

Emily nodded slowly. Yes, it was a blessing. Phoebe-Ann was at last free of him.

When she'd seen Phoebe-Ann's eyelids close and the trembling stop, and Dr Whelan had gone, she went back downstairs and sat at the table, covering her face with her hands.

Edwin put his arm around her. 'It's all over now, Em. You did the right thing, the only thing you could have done. No-one is really to blame. Not Vinny for getting him drunk, not Phoebe-Ann for flying at him like that. She couldn't take much more of him but she never meant to kill him.'

'I know, but I can't say I'm sorry he's dead and maybe it's better for him as well.'

'There won't be many who will mourn him.'

'It's not going to be much of a Christmas, is it, with this hanging over us all?'

'There's nothing to an inquest. They'll just ask a few questions and it will be all over. Accidental death.'

'Like Mam,' Emily said.

'What do you think she will do after it's all over?'

'It will take her a while to get over it.'

'She'd be better to leave here altogether,' Albert said.

Emily smiled wearily. 'I think that's what she will do. Leave Liverpool and go to Rhys. I think she's paid enough for her mistake and she deserves some happiness now.'

'I think we all do, Em. We've waited long enough for it.' Edwin took her hand and squeezed it.

Chapter Twenty-five

On the first of February, Emily and Phoebe-Ann went to Toxteth Park Cemetery. It was a bitterly cold day and, in the weak sunshine, the frost sparkled like silver on the bare branches of the trees. They were both well wrapped up and Emily carried a small bunch of early primroses.

The inquest was over. The verdict was accidental death, and Rhys was due that very afternoon to take both Albert and Phoebe-Ann back to the small Welsh valley. For Albert it would be a poignant homecoming, for Phoebe-Ann a new life, for she'd promised to marry Rhys as soon as they got back. The lines of sorrow and suffering were still etched on her face, but the dark shadows had gone from beneath her eyes and her cheeks were once again tinged with the rosy glow of good health. The coat and hat she wore were of good quality, as were her shoes and bag and gloves. All paid for by Rhys, and in his letter he'd told Emily to stifle all Phoebe-Ann's protests. He wasn't having people talk about his future wife in a derogatory way. She could look forward now to a life of peace and comfort and security. The past was behind her. She wasn't the girl that Rhys had fallen in love with, but she had learned many hard lessons; she would appreciate everything he could give her to a much fuller degree. She wouldn't be sorry to go. Liverpool had nothing to offer her now except memories and most of them were bitter.

Emily placed the flowers on the well-tended grave with the marble headstone and gilt lettering. She'd never come here again but she knew Lily would understand. She'd waited so long for love and marriage. She'd taken Lily's place when they'd all needed her. She'd given Phoebe-Ann every ounce of love, protection and support that it had been in her power to give. Now it would all be bestowed on Edwin. Rhys would take good care of Phoebe-Ann.

She looked back sadly over the years. They had both travelled a long way on the road of life since the days they'd spent in service to the Mercers. She, too, was leaving this city she'd always called home, this great, sprawling metropolis with its elegant, gracious buildings and wide thoroughfares, its slums and its squalor, the mighty river its highway and lifeblood, its ships that plied the sealanes of the world, beckoned home by the winking beam of the Bar Light and watched over by the Liver Birds. Tomorrow, she and Edwin were to be married and then they would travel to Southampton but they wouldn't stay there. They would sail on the *Mauretania* to join Jack and Jimmy. Neither of them had wanted to stay now. It would be a new life in a new world and Edwin had joked that it would seem funny to travel on the *Maury* as a passenger, albeit third class, and not as a member of her crew.

She reached out and laid her hand on the cold marble stone. 'I know you understand. It's time for us to go, Mam. Time for us to leave Liverpool.' She turned towards her sister and took her hand.

Phoebe-Ann smiled at her. 'You've never let me down, Emily, and I love you for it.'

'Then she'll rest happy, Phoebe-Ann. She'll rest in peace now.'

THE END

MIST OVER THE MERSEY
by Lyn Andrews

The Chatterton family was posh, everyone could see that – far too posh for Scotland Road, the Liverpool slum area where they had ended up. Nancy Butterworth and Abbie Kerrigan, lifelong residents of the place, tried to befriend Dee Chatterton, but Dee's snobbish and sick mother wanted her family to have nothing to do with the rough street children. Mr Chatterton, meanwhile, weighed down with the worry and shame of having lost all his money, tried ineffectually to get together a home, and was not too proud to accept help from plump, good-hearted Bridie Butterworth and her neighbours. In the corner shop the Burgess family looked forward with excitement and trepidation to the arrival of their young cousin Sean from Dublin, and Nancy was not the only girl to lose her heart, and much else besides, to the Irish charmer.

But with the arrival of 1914 things were to change dramatically for the inhabitants of this poor but closely-knit community. And the Chattertons, the Butterworths, the Kerrigans and the Burgesses found that money and social position meant little when the horrors of the First World War invaded their lives and took away their sons.

0 552 14058 9

A SELECTED LIST OF FINE NOVELS
AVAILABLE FROM CORGI BOOKS

THE PRICES SHOWN BELOW WERE CORRECT AT THE TIME OF GOING TO PRESS. HOWEVER TRANSWORLD PUBLISHERS RESERVE THE RIGHT TO SHOW NEW RETAIL PRICES ON COVERS WHICH MAY DIFFER FROM THOSE PREVIOUSLY ADVERTISED IN THE TEXT OR ELSEWHERE.

☐	13718 9	LIVERPOOL LOU	*Lyn Andrews*	£5.99
☐	13600 X	THE SISTERS O'DONNELL	*Lyn Andrews*	£5.99
☐	13482 1	THE WHITE EMPRESS	*Lyn Andrews*	£5.99
☐	13855 X	ELLAN VANNIN	*Lyn Andrews*	£5.99
☐	14036 8	MAGGIE MAY	*Lyn Andrews*	£4.99
☐	14058 9	MIST OVER THE MERSEY	*Lyn Andrews*	£4.99
☐	14060 0	MERSEY BLUES	*Lyn Andrews*	£4.99
☐	14096 1	THE WILD SEED	*Iris Gower*	£5.99
☐	14447 9	FIREBIRD	*Iris Gower*	£5.99
☐	14537 8	APPLE BLOSSOM TIME	*Kathryn Haig*	£5.99
☐	14566 1	THE DREAM SELLERS	*Ruth Hamilton*	£5.99
☐	14567 X	THE CORNER HOUSE	*Ruth Hamilton*	£5.99
☐	14553 X	THE BRASS DOLPHIN	*Caroline Harvey*	£5.99
☐	14686 2	CITY OF GEMS	*Caroline Harvey*	£5.99
☐	14535 1	THE HELMINGHAM ROSE	*Joan Hessayon*	£5.99
☐	14692 7	THE PARADISE GARDEN	*Joan Hessayon*	£5.99
☐	14333 2	SOME OLD LOVER'S GHOST	*Judith Lennox*	£5.99
☐	14599 8	FOOTPRINTS ON THE SAND	*Judith Lennox*	£5.99
☐	13910 6	BLUEBIRDS	*Margaret Mayhew*	£5.99
☐	14492 4	THE CREW	*Margaret Mayhew*	£5.99
☐	14499 1	THESE FOOLISH THINGS	*Imogen Parker*	£5.99
☐	14658 7	THE MEN IN HER LIFE	*Imogen Parker*	£5.99
☐	10375 6	CSARDAS	*Diane Pearson*	£5.99
☐	14400 2	THE MOUNTAIN	*Elvi Rhodes*	£5.99
☐	14577 7	PORTRAIT OF CHLOE	*Elvi Rhodes*	£5.99
☐	14549 1	CHOICES	*Susan Sallis*	£5.99
☐	14636 6	COME RAIN OR SHINE	*Susan Sallis*	£5.99
☐	14606 4	FIRE OVER LONDON	*Mary Jane Staples*	£5.99
☐	14657 9	CHURCHILL'S PEOPLE	*Mary Jane Staples*	£5.99
☐	14476 2	CHILDREN OF THE TIDE	*Valerie Wood*	£5.99
☐	14640 4	THE ROMANY GIRL	*Valerie Wood*	£5.99

All Transworld titles are available by post from:

Book Service By Post, P.O. Box 29, Douglas, Isle of Man IM99 1BQ

Credit cards accepted. Please telephone 01624 675137,
fax 01624 670923, Internet http://www.bookpost.co.uk or
e-mail: bookshop@enterprise.net for details.

Free postage and packing in the UK. Overseas customers allow
£1 per book (paperbacks) and £3 per book (hardbacks).